The Road to War

PETER TONKIN

First published in 2019 by Sharpe Books.

For

Cham, Guy & Mark

As always.

TABLE OF CONTENTS

Caesar's Spies Book 4

ITALY

I: The Proscribed

i

Three men were hurrying through the streets of Rome late one afternoon early in *Februarius*. The year was 712 *ab urbe condita,* since the founding of the city. Two years, less a month and some days, since the murder of Gaius Julius Caesar. A few scant weeks since the dead dictator had formally been nominated *Divus Julius*, Julius the God, an official State Deity by the Senate.

The Consuls for this year – confirmed on the *kalends* of *Januarius*, the first day of last month – were Marcus Aemilius Lepidus and Lucius Munatius Plancus and the year would be known by their names, though everyone in the Republic knew the real power lay with the Triumvirs Mark Antony, the murdered god Caesar's friend and colleague, and young Octavianus his adopted son and heir.

Octavianus who called himself Julius Caesar Octavianus, *Divus Fili*, son of a God, these days and, like Antony, would stop at nothing to avenge his divine father's death. On those directly involved, their supporters, associates, family, and friends.

The weather that day was wet and bitter. The afternoon was darkening unnaturally early, filling Rome's streets and alleys with thickening shadows. But the interiors of *tabernae* taverns, shops and public buildings were bright with lamplight, which spilled into the gusty overcast, so it was still possible to make out some details as the little group hurried from one bright doorway to another.

The man in the lead was clearly a slave. His aged body was spare but wiry. His eyes and cheeks sunken. His chin was grey with ill-barbered stubble. His mud-coloured tunic was threadbare and clung to his torso in the same way as his grey hair was plastered to his skull. When the bitter wind blew hard enough to lift the cloth of the short sleeves, it was just possible to see his owner's brand among the gooseflesh on his shoulder. It was easy to count the ribs beneath his skeletal arms. He was bareheaded and wore an old-fashioned slave-ring round his neck. Every now and then he glanced over his shoulder to make sure his two companions were still following close behind.

These men were vastly different. Although it was impossible to tell their age, it was obvious their bodies were strong and bulky. Well-fed and young. They both wore heavy cloaks through which rich tunics could occasionally be glimpsed. Hooded capes of oiled wool designed to keep them warm and dry. The footwear at the ends of their muscular legs was solid if otherwise unremarkable and their feet were further protected by thick woollen socks which reached up to meet their heavy leather *braccae* trousers. It was possible to differentiate them only by noting that one was taller and more massive than the other. Their hoods were pulled forward, but it was obvious to the meanest observer there were no owner's brands on these shoulders; no slave-rings round these necks.

*

There were a number of observers paying attention to the trio as they hurried by. Suspicious eyes followed them along the *Vicus Patricii* down from the Esquiline Hill, as they passed the *Subura* to reach the *Forum Romanum* by way of the *Argelitum,* as swiftly as possible without running fast enough to call attention to themselves, for these were still the early days of the Triumvirs' bloody proscriptions. The lists naming the condemned had not yet been torn off the Senate House door by the wind or the rain, though the writing was nearly impossible to read now. Anyone could find themselves among the proscribed – their name put forward by dissatisfied wives, angry offspring, impatient heirs, ruthless rivals, vindictive or greedy neighbours. Even by slaves who harboured grudges – with or without good reason.

There were some 2,000 names on the original list, and a reward of 25,000 Attic *drachmae* to any citizen bringing the head of a proscribed man to Mark Antony or Caesar Octavianus. A slave was paid 10,000 *drachmae* for his master's head, automatically freed and offered the dead man's right to citizenship. Added to which, all across the Republic, but especially here in Rome, there were execution squads. Soldiers answering directly to the Triumvirs themselves, were out hunting for particular victims who had somehow raised the personal anger of the Republic's rulers. These *carnifices* butchers were well rewarded for their bloody work. The same rewards were given to anyone who gave information about where someone proscribed was hiding. Anyone caught trying to save the proscribed was added to the list. All the belongings of the victims, including their slaves, were to be confiscated and sold at auction.

The Forum was crowded with the severed heads of the men named on those increasingly illegible, illimited lists who had not managed to escape. A few of them, like that of Marcus Tullius Cicero, still quite recognisable, at the apparent whim of the glutted crows which had done little more than peck out his succulent eyeballs. Though the huge iron spike driven through his forehead, securing the great orator's cranium to the front of the rostra, was beginning to rust and a dark red line divided his vacant sockets, ran over his battered nose and his gaping mouth was overflowing with blood. As though the lolling tongue, so famously run through with hairpins and a stylus by Antony's wife the fearsome Fulvia, could still bleed, more than two months after the brutal desecration.

ii

'You're sure about this, Lucius?' called the taller of the two hooded figures, his voice carrying easily to the companion at his shoulder. His accent was Roman and patrician, his tone abrupt; that of a man used to command not only in his household but also on the battlefield.

'Deuterus says so,' answered the other figure breathlessly, gesturing towards the slave, whose Latinised name was Greek for 'second' describing his place amongst the other possessions in his owner's household. His accent was as patrician as his companion's, but his tone more youthful; less decisive.

'Both of them?' demanded the taller man, angrily.

'Both mother and my sister Calpurnia,' young Lucius answered, clearly scarcely able to believe it.

'To see *Octavianus*?' the taller man's voice quivered with simple outrage.

'And beg for our names to be removed from the proscription lists…' The young man's answer dropped almost to a whisper.

'Has your mother no understanding of the price the little *corruptus* pervert Octavianus demands?' wondered the taller of the two, incredulously.

'I have no idea. You know how she is. Not of this world. Cato's daughter. The essence of Stoicism …'

'It's all over the city that Octavianus only grants favours like that in return for sex. Just like Antony, in fact. But word is, Octavianus has been hoping to get a mother and daughter both at once…'

'I know…'

'And that's what your mother is offering him? Herself – *herself* of all people – and her daughter. Your sister Calpurnia. *My wife!* In exchange for our freedom.'

'She's desperate, Messala…'

'*Demens* mad, more like! To even dream that our *gravitas* dignity would allow us to accept such a sacrifice! But Deuterus thinks we can get there in time to stop them? That's what my Calpurnia told him?'

'Yes. She is terrified. Of Mother as much as of Octavianus. But I pray to the gods she is right and there is still time to stop them. Or we have put ourselves in the most deadly danger for no reason at all.' The young man's voice quavered with something more than breathlessness.

'And you trust Deuterus, do you?'

'He has served our family for years. My father bought him long before he married Mother. And he has been with the household ever since. Even after Father died six winters ago, soon after Caesar and Iscauricus became Consuls. Even after the Civil Wars and the turmoil of the proscriptions. Calpurnia could not have chosen her messenger more wisely.'

'Hmm…' growled Messala, clearly unconvinced.

*

This conversation was sufficient to take them into the *Subura Major* at its junction with the *Vicus Collis Viminalis.* To their right, on the north side of the road, there stood the tall *insulae* tenements, their upper reaches packed with apartments that grew smaller and smaller with each floor. Their main doors guarded by bulky *janitors* armed with clubs. At street level, they contained mostly taverns and shops where the crowds of plebeian freedmen and their families who thronged the *Subura* bought their meagre day-to-day requirements.

The plebeian area was by no means exclusive to the hopelessly poor. *Divus Julius* had lived in the *Subura* in his youth. But as well as the upwardly-mobile, the dangerously criminal lurked here. This had been the stamping-grounds of Clodius and Milo, leaders of the most ruthless and dangerous street-gangs, whose power had been so great that they had even sought to rule the city. Both were now dead and had been supplanted by *Galliae* The Gaul and his brutal cohorts. Who, if they did not yet rule Rome, nevertheless ruled these streets and alleys. And who were almost as efficient as the Triumvirs' execution squads at collecting proscribed heads and the riches they could bring.

At least the foul weather kept the streets relatively empty, thought Messala. For he and Lucius were dangerously exposed here. Had been from the moment they came out of hiding. If they lowered their hoods they stood every chance of being recognised and executed; beheaded on the spot. Messala had served in the legions before his name was added to the proscription lists and the city was still full of old soldiers, many of whom would know him at once – most of whom would behead their own mothers for 25,000 Attic *drachmae.* And young Lucius was also well-known – the son of a famous father and of one of the most famous women in the Republic. Though one was long dead and the other notoriously remarried. Both men tempted out of seclusion by the slave Deuterus and the astonishing news he brought from his terrified young mistress.

But anyone with their hood pulled forward – just as theirs were now – automatically stirred suspicion, begged confrontation and demands for identification. Even on a foul day like this one when any sensible person forced outdoors would be doing his utmost to protect himself against the sleet-filled wind, unless he was a slave. But, despite Messala's concerns, the three men hurried on unmolested, turning out of the *Subura* into the *Argelitum* and almost running down into the *Forum Romanum* itself. Like patrician citizens practising for the famous race of the *Lupercalia* festival, due to be held on the Ides of the month in a few days' time.

Octavianus' office, according to the information Deuterus had been given by his young mistress Messala's wife Calpurnia, was currently in the Temple of Juno Moneta. A logical place for the young Triumvir to work, even though it stood high on the Arx, a spur of the Capitoline Hill, joined to the precincts of the Temple of Jupiter Optimus Maximus by a narrow ridge. Even though it also housed a menagerie of geese and chickens used by the city's augurs to see and understand the plans of the gods at the open-air temple of the *auguraculum.* Because beneath the temple of Juno Moneta was the mint which supplied the city and much of the Republic with its coins. And Octavianus, was, after all, accepting fortune after fortune in gold and silver possessions confiscated from the proscribed, turning statues, plates, cups and jewellery into ready money as fast as he could. Into the immense funds urgently needed to finance the campaign he and Antony planned to mount against Brutus and Cassius in the east as soon as the campaigning season started.

But also, so the rumour went, maintaining a private bed-chamber beside his work area where he could discuss with desperate wives, mothers, sisters, and daughters just how far they were willing to go in their attempts to get their fathers, husbands, sons, or brothers removed from the proscription lists. Octavianus, it seemed, had inherited more than his adopted father's ruthless political acumen, fabulous possessions, army of clients and considerable fortune. Like *Divus Julius*, he had the blood of a satyr flowing in his veins.

And Messala's mother-in-law had somehow convinced her daughter, his wife Calpurnia, that together they might seduce the little pervert into taking Lucius and Messala off the list. Unless the two men and the slave could catch up with their women and stop this madness before it went any further.

iii

The *Forum Romanum* was busier than the streets surrounding it; crowded with more than the heads of the proscribed. The business of the Republic carried on whatever the weather. *Divus Julius'* half completed *Basilica Julia,* standing along its southern side, was bright with public and private spaces – courts, businesses, committee rooms, as was the *Basilica Opimia* beside it. Magistrates sat upon the Tribunal, hearing cases that could not wait for better weather. Slaves hurried between the citizens, statues, columns, basilicas, and temples on missions: clutching bills from businessmen and letters from lovers; carrying baskets, shopping lists; heavy purses, heavier litters and flaming torches that guttered and spat beneath the downpour. All of them, noted Messala grimly, better fed, and clothed than Deuterus, who was clearly unfortunate in being owned by an unworldly mistress with preoccupations far removed from the welfare of her household.

He glanced up to his right. The Capitoline Hill loomed there, with the Temple of Jupiter Optimus Maximus at its crest, outlined against the sleety sky. And, nearer, at the end of that ridge, stood the Temple of Juno Moneta, the mint, Octavian's office: their destination. The disguised patrician ex-soldier felt his heart clench at the thought of what might be happening in Octavian's office even now to his beloved Calpurnia and her mad mother.

But Messala's dark thoughts were interrupted before they were properly formed. A tightly organised squad of soldiers in full armour carrying *gladii* swords and *pugiones* daggers at their belts came across the Forum towards him, pushing through the crowds. Like a trireme breasting a stormy sea. Led by a centurion, he noted. Who marched at the point of a triangular boar's head formation, as though attacking an enemy army. The soldiers were clearly about some business too important to be affected by inclement weather or bustling crowds. Which, for a disturbing heartbeat, he supposed might include arresting Lucius and himself.

The slave Deuterus stopped abruptly the moment he too saw the soldiers. Stopped walking and started bellowing in a surprisingly loud voice, 'These men are proscribed! They are Lucius Calpurnius Bibulus and Marcus Valerius Messala Corvinus. Proscribed! Proscribed! I claim my reward and my freedom!'

*

The only heads that did not turn towards the shouting slave were the severed heads on the rostra. A kind of surge went across the Forum like a great wave rolling across the ocean. All other movement seemed to stop. Everyone stood still, staring. The wind died. The rain eased. 'Proscribed!' bellowed Deuterus again. 'These men are proscribed!'

Only the soldiers kept moving. And there was no doubt about their destination now.

Messala swung round, looking for some way to escape. But he saw at once that there was none. The nearest roads, the *Via Sacra,* and the *Vicus Jugularius* were both packed. The hill-slope leading up the Capitoline notoriously steep and covered in wild undergrowth, except for where the statues of the Gods stood watching. There was no hope of turning and fleeing back the way they had come, for that way only led to the *Subura* and the ruthless head-hunters of The Gaul's brutal gang.

Lucius and he were trapped here and the legionaries would arrive in a heartbeat. All of them armed as well as armoured. Like any soldier in his situation, however, Messala did take action. His fist smashed into the slave's shouting mouth. Deuterus staggered back and fell to the ground. Messala aimed a kick at his head that would have rendered reward and freedom pointless by killing him there on the spot.

But a surprisingly gentle voice close behind him said, 'I wouldn't do that if I were you.'

Messala swung round to face the speaker and the squad of legionaries standing at his shoulders. Oddly, it was not the soft-voiced centurion who claimed Messala's immediate attention, even though his face was strikingly handsome. It was the soldiers standing either side of him. On the right stood a hulking brute of a man wearing a gladiator's helmet instead of a standard legionary issue, the sort of helmet usually worn by a Murmillo or a Thracian. Above the projecting rim was the image of Nemesis, Greek goddess of Retribution. Below the rim, two latticed sections closed to protect the soldier's face, especially his eyes. The right eye gleamed ferociously from beneath a thick, beetling brow. The left was painted on an eyepatch that covered what was obviously an eye-socket as empty as

Cicero's. Below the patch, the legionary's cheek was scored as though by a lion's claws.

On the centurion's other side stood a soldier who it took several heartbeats for Messala to recognise as a woman. He had seen female gladiators – *gladiatrices* – before. But it had never even occurred to him that a woman could serve as a soldier – other than the various descriptions of Queen Hippolyta and her Amazon army. She was tall, broad-shouldered, deep-chested. Even in the metal scale armour she was wearing it was clear that, unlike the legendary Amazons, she still had both of her breasts. Her face might have been carved of ebony wood or obsidian, statuesque, even with the drizzle beating against it. Wide brown eyes, almost as dark as pitch, regarded him emotionlessly without a flicker. As he eventually looked back at the quietly-spoken centurion, confronting a long face ending in a square chin, with the faintest gleam of stubble as though it had been brushed with copper. A long Grecian nose above thin lips and icy grey eyes. Weighing him up and deciding how to proceed as though considering a problem by Pythagoras or Euclid.

And Messala knew that his life hung in the balance.

iv

Gaius Julius Caesar Octavianus *Divus Fili* glanced up from his accounts as one of the temple slaves, assistant to the *janitor* doorkeeper priest, came into the room as the commander of Caesar's praetorian bodyguard closed the door behind him. Although Octavianus counted amongst his friends and clients *Divus Julius'* private secretary the fabulously wealthy financier Lucius Cornelius Balbus, who had a cohort of Greek slaves capable of overseeing the Republic's accounts, there were times when Octavianus wished to have a firm grasp of the current financial situation himself. Antony didn't seem to care about any money he wasn't planning to spend on parties, whores, or wine. Poor old Lepidus was busy with his consular duties. And somebody needed to have a firm grasp of realities.

The proscriptions were falling worryingly short of expectations in their most important aspect. For their main objectives had been two-fold. To rid Rome of anyone the Triumvirs could not trust to stay supportively quiet while they carried their war of revenge eastwards – which seemed to be working well enough. Almost all the men who had supported Brutus, Cassius and their gang of murderers were either dead, in hiding, or on the run.

But the second objective, to raise enough funds to mount the campaign of revenge in the east, was much less satisfactory. They were still millions of Attic *drachmae* short by the look of things. He and Antony could not afford to go to war with Brutus and Cassius because they did not have sufficient funds to pay a large enough army; to finance even a short campaign, let alone a lengthy one.

Oh, he knew well enough that they controlled more than 20 legions between them. Or they did in theory. But the legions were not fully manned – except for the IVth, the Vth – the *Alaude* Larks – the VIth *Ferrata* Ironclads, the reconstituted VIIth and the *Martia*. Bringing the rest up to strength would be a lengthy and expensive business. Increasingly, it was becoming clear that the legions were motivated by money above all else. Would not stir – let alone fight – unless glittering promises turned into regular pay. Unless things improved soon, they would be lucky to set out before the autumn.

Octavianus glanced up, frowning, as the slave crept across to the table's edge and hovered distractingly. There were only two circumstances under which the young Triumvir could be disturbed: the arrival of an urgent message from Antony, or the arrival of a female supplicant here to trade her honour for the safety of some relative.

'Well?'

'Two ladies, Caesar. Cloaked and veiled. They say they are mother and daughter. Nothing more.'

'Here to plead for…'

'They did not say, Caesar.'

'And have they been searched? I do not relish the thought of a knife in the back while I am, as Antony would no doubt say, doing some *stabbing* of my own.'

'No, Caesar. It seemed probable you yourself might find the prospect of an intimate search amusing. Your praetorians will be within earshot at all times.'

'Perhaps. Show them into the bedroom. I will join them by and by.'

The slave bowed accommodatingly, crept out of the room, and silently closed the door behind him.

*

Octavianus tried to settle back to work, but his imagination and his twenty-year-old body kept betraying him. At last, he thought. Both mother and daughter at the same time! He found himself praying to Venus that the mother was not too old – the daughter not too young.

Perhaps the goddess would deliver a mother approaching her late thirties with a daughter not quite twenty. That would do nicely. A mature matron following the current fashion for having her body oiled and depilated. A daughter boasting enticing tufts of downy curls at the humid junctions of arms and legs. He could almost feel the contrast with his fingertips – the smooth eggshell of hairless skin over pubic bone; the warm and fragrant peach-down masking trembling folds and clefts. One woman experienced; the other almost virginal still. The mother's body fuller, rounder; the daughter's almost boyish but still nubile. He cupped his hands, one spread wider than the other, imagining the breasts that would fill them, one pair larger and softer than the other.

The mother, perhaps excited – as some have been – by the vision of herself as the heroine of some Greek legend, sacrificing herself for her husband and family. Or made breathless by the sheer wickedness of what she was doing. He chose to remember little of those others who had lain like marble statues hating him more with every thrust and themselves into the bargain, as likely as not. Hating the husbands whose proscription had caused them to experience this disgusting indignity. But the daughter. How would she react? Would she yield shyly to the most powerful man in the world? Would she be terrified? Excited? Would she secretly hope for a child with the blood of divine Caesars in its veins?

He had to discover if the reality lived up to his vividly sensual imaginings. Mother and daughter… How similar would they be in appearance? How different? A conundrum he was bursting to explore in every intimate detail. Once he had assured himself neither mysterious supplicant had brought a knife to a love-match.

He rolled up the papyrus financial sheet he had been studying. Swept an eye over the work table, assuring himself it was all tidy. He rose, easing his suddenly constricting clothing, turned towards the almost invisible door that connected with the bedroom, took one step towards it.

The slave from the outer office came back in again, the commander of his praetorian protection squad close behind.

'I am sorry to disturb you, Caesar,' said the slave, his voice a terrified whisper. 'But there is a message here from Antony and the messenger will not wait.'

'What…' demanded Octavianus, outraged, preparing to hurl a great deal of fatal wrath at the cringing slave.

But the praetorian stepped forward. 'The messenger said to tell you, Caesar, that his name is Septem. He said that might make a difference.'

II: The Centurion

i

The centurion's name was Iacomus Artemidorus. His code name, by which he was familiar to a widening range of powerful and influential people, was *Septem* – Seven. This was because immediately before his secondment to Julius Caesar's nascent secret service, he had been first spear, senior centurion, of the old VIIth legion, which had been disbanded since *Divus Julius'* death and reformed almost as soon as the prospect of war against his murderers drew nearer. The one-eyed man on Septem's right was Ferrata, late of the VIth legion, the Ironclads. And the tall dark-skinned woman on his left was Puella, who had once been body-slave to Marcus Junius Brutus, *Divus Julius'* leading assassin. The legionaries ranked behind them were an equally random lot selected from far and wide for their various – variously lethal – skills. The centurion and his squad were carrying an urgent message from Mark Antony to Octavianus and they did not have a lot of time to waste.

Artemidorus looked at the two men standing in front of him and the slave writhing on the icy cobbles. As he did so, the rest of his command spread out, keeping at bay anyone in the Forum whose interest had been piqued by the slave's announcement, that the two heads currently hidden by oiled-wool hoods were together worth fifty thousand Attic *drachmae*. 'Was the slave telling the truth?' Artemidorus asked, his voice still deceptively gentle. '*Are* you Lucius Calpurnius Bibulus and Marcus Valerius Messala Corvinus?'

The taller of the two pulled his hood back to reveal his face. He had piercing blue eyes beneath dark brows which overhung them like those of an eagle. An almost Roman nose jutting between pronounced cheekbones, and square chin with a dimple at its centre, darkened by the shadow of a black beard. Full lips – as ready to sneer as to smile made him every inch a patrician. 'I am Marcus Valerius Messala Corvinus,' he said steadily. In a calm and reasonable tone that belied the latent arrogance in his physiognomy. And, thought Artemidorus, the extreme danger of his situation. 'My men knew me as the Tribune Messala. When I served with the Martia legion.'

'I've heard of Tribune Messala of the Martia. And you are

proscribed?'

'I am.'

'And your companion is...?'

'My brother-in-law Lucius Calpurnius Bibulus,' admitted Messala as the young man also pulled his hood back to reveal a surprisingly youthful face, scarcely bearded, round-eyed, soft-cheeked, pink-lipped. Septem found himself wondering whether young Lucius had even attained the *toga virilis* of manhood.

'And what madness prompted two men on the proscription list to go running around in the Forum on an afternoon such as this?' he demanded, as though discussing matters of little importance at a party.

Messala opened his mouth to reply but Lucius beat him to it. 'My *mother*'s madness,' he called, his voice trembling with outrage. 'She has taken it into her head that she can talk Octavianus into striking our names off the list…'

'He will if her daughter Calpurnia accompanies her. Calpurnia is not only Lucius' sister but also my wife.' Messala concluded.

Artemidorus' gaze fastened on the outraged boy. If he resembled his sister then her husband's outrage was entirely understandable, he thought. For Lucius was one of the prettiest young men the soldier had ever seen.

Then a simply breathtaking truth struck him. 'But your mother is…'

'Up there!' snarled Messala, his icy control slipping as he gestured towards the temple on top of the Arx. 'She is getting ready to sacrifice herself and my wife in the hope of saving our heads!'

'Right! Then let's take your heads up to Octavianus himself,' decided Septem, his tones suddenly those of the senior centurion of the old VIIth legion ordering his men into battle. 'And we'll do so while they are still attached to your bodies. To see whether mother and daughter have managed to save them or not.'

*

Two of Septem's soldiers picked up the slave and carried him as the boar's head formation of legionaries, with Artemidorus at their head and Lucius and Messala in their midst, quick-marched into the *Via Sacra* and from there went into the twisting *Clivus Capitolinus* pathway past the temple of Young Jupiter and on up onto the Arx, past the *Auguraculum* with its prophetic bird-cages. Then, past the Temple of Venus Erucina, protectress of prostitutes, and beside it, the aptly-placed Temple of Mens – of Proper Thinking and Self

Control.

'What is the slave's name?' demanded Artemidorus, reasoning that he had better get the most accurate details possible if he was going to have to discuss the situation with young Octavianus himself.

'Deuterus,' snapped Messala.

'Deuterus,' Artemidorus turned to the bruised slave. 'Explain what is going on here.'

The old man, terrified by what he had done and by what had resulted from it – fearing at least a near-fatal whipping or even crucifixion – babbled the details as clearly as he could through swollen lips and loosened teeth. 'My lady, the *domina* Calpurnia, and her mother have gone to offer themselves to young Caesar Octavianus. My lady sent me to warn her husband and brother to come out of hiding and rescue her.'

'They just strolled up to the Arx on the off-chance, did they?' persisted Artemidorus.

'No, sir! They went in litters. And heavily veiled. No-one would ever suspect their identity. Not even Caesar Octavianus until they allowed him access to their persons. Intimate access...'

'That's enough!' snapped Artemidorus, both to Deuterus and to Messala who was taking another swing at him. 'If the ladies are so well disguised, then not even Octavianus will know who they are if we can get to him in time. And fortunately, my mission is to get to him as quickly as possible.'

The centurion's terse analysis carried them up onto the holy precinct in front of the Temple of Juno Moneta. Still in a tight phalanx and with a discipline that impressed ex-tribune Messala, they marched up the steps to the main door of the temple. The temple attendants saw – and heard – them coming so they didn't have to hesitate. The doors opened, and they marched into the sacred space as though they were invading it.

'We are here to see Caesar Octavianus,' snapped Artemidorus as they crashed to a halt. 'We bring an important message from Mark Antony.'

'Caesar is occupied,' answered the *janitor* priest in charge of entrances and exits. Fortunately for himself he kept his voice low and respectful. Even so, Messala growled and took a step forward, before Artemidorus' firm hand on his shoulder restrained him.

'Triumvir Mark Antony insisted,' he snapped. 'No matter what Caesar is *preoccupied* with, you will have to interrupt him.'

'But Caesar's direct orders…'

'... will have to be overridden by Antony's direct orders,' snapped Artemidorus, running out of patience. 'Either you do it or I will do it...'

'No!' howled the *janitor* priest. 'I will...' Turning on his heel, he vanished into the shadows.

'You might have had some trouble, though,' said Ferrata quietly. 'Caesar's probably got a wall of praetorians between here and wherever he's got the women.'

No sooner had he spoken than a soldier appeared from the shady depths. 'I command Caesar's praetorians,' he snapped. 'What is this about a message from general Antony?'

'I have been commanded to pass this to Caesar at once,' answered Artemidorus, equally abruptly. He held a papyrus scroll sealed with Antony's seal. 'And I have a verbal message to accompany it. Which is for Caesar's ears alone. If he hesitates to admit me, tell him my code-name is Septem. That might make a difference.'

ii

'Had it been anyone other than you, Septem, I would never have admitted them.' Octavianus was seated behind a desk laden with scrolls and tablets of various sorts. All closed, and tidied. Apparently finished-with, Artemidorus observed. If he was in time, it had been a close-run thing.

'I am flattered, Caesar,' he said. 'But I do not believe I am taking advantage of your indulgence. Antony's messages are of vital importance to both of you. And Antony believes you will see that urgent action will be required as soon as you are made aware of the situation.' As he spoke, conscious that his words were beyond formal, stilted, Artemidorus was searching the room behind the impatient young man. He saw the doorway hidden in the shadows. Closed. Caesar's impatience and strained courtesy both strongly suggested he had not yet gone through to the women. As did the fact that he was behaving normally. Because once he realised exactly who they were, even he was likely to be utterly surprised and deeply shocked.

'Your message?' Caesar's abrupt question interrupted the spy and messenger's thoughts.

As he handed Caesar Octavianus Antony's sealed scroll, Septem began to put together the briefing his exasperated commander had given him less than an hour ago. 'Antony has just received some very disturbing intelligence,' he began. 'He is informed that several weeks ago, Sextus Pompey took the considerable risk of moving his entire fleet out of Massalia. And that includes the Senatorial fleet which Cicero gave him command of when the Senate was getting ready to go to war with Antony and yourself. Using periods of calm weather, which were few enough in all conscience, he has managed to smuggle them south along the west coasts of the chain of islands that includes *Corsis* and *Sardis* until he reached *Sicilia*. Here, with the support of the treacherous governor of Africa Province Quintus Cornificius, he overran the island. Capturing and perhaps killing the governor. He is now established there in complete control. With the largest, best-supplied and best-crewed fleet in *Mare Nostrum*.'

Octavianus looked up at Septem, frowning thoughtfully. 'If this is true, then it's very worrying,' he said.

'But that's only the beginning. Antony has it on good authority that Sextus Pompey is directly attracting men you've proscribed. You offer 25,000 Attic *drachmae* for proof they are dead. He is offering 50,000 to anyone on your list who stays alive long enough to join him.'

'Is he?' Caesar was thunderstruck. 'How in the names of the gods can he afford to do this?' His stunned gaze swept over the piles of accounts on the table in front of him.

'That's the final element Antony wants me to warn you about! For you will need to discuss it with Lepidus, he says, the next time Lepidus comes to you for money to feed the city.'

'Well?'

'Sextus Pompey has managed to take full control of the grain supply routes. Whether the grain comes from the African provinces, Egypt, or through Syria or Judea from Parthia and the East, he controls it. He is offering it to us at fifteen sestertii a measure.'

'Is he by the gods! That's extortionate!'

'And he's apparently willing to sell it to Cassius and Brutus for ten sestertii a measure!'

'He must be stopped! As soon as possible!' Octavianus' hand slammed open-palmed onto the table. Then he caught his breath realising what must inevitably come next.

'Antony agrees, Caesar. But of course *Sicilia* and the Africa Provinces are in that section of the Republic which is now under your personal control. Therefore it is up to you to stop Sextus Pompey. Antony is preparing to invade Macedonia, which is in his sphere of influence of course, to find and destroy Brutus and Cassius. Something he is hesitant to do until his support and supply routes on both land and sea are secure from Sextus Pompey and his fleet.'

'So the war against the *Libertores* Liberators must wait until I have taken action against Sextus Pompey. But I will need to build and man a fleet of my own! It will take months. A fortune! I must get Rufus and Agrippa to work on this!'

'A fleet powerful enough to beat Sextus Pompey, of course, will be powerful enough to counter the *Libertores* fleets commanded by Gnaeus Domitius Ahenobarbus and Lucius Statius Murcius, who are currently anchored off *Rhodos*,' added Artemidorus. 'And if Antony is going to move east with any security, as you observe, he will need your fleet in a position to support him.'

Octavianus sat for a moment, his mind racing. Artemidorus could read his thoughts with almost laughable ease. The main support bolstering the tottering popularity of the Triumvirate in the face of the brutal proscriptions, was the promise Antony, Lepidus and he had made to the legions that they would invade Macedonia and avenge *Divus Julius'* death on Brutus and Cassius, his murderers. But the task was proving more difficult than the Triumvirs had envisaged. The proscriptions were raising less money than they had hoped. Recently disbanded legions, like the VIIth, were being slow to reform.

The problems with Sextus Pompey and the *Libertore* fleets commanded by Ahenobarbus and Murcus were now further compounded by Pompey's invasion of Sicily and his pirating of the grain supplies. Octavianus had the immediate responsibility of stopping him – but would need a fleet to do so. But the cunning Antony could prepare his invasion very publicly. Because, even the best-prepared army could not operate far from home unless its supply and communication routes were secure by land and sea, thus putting the young Triumvir in a trap which might cost him his popularity – and, in the end, his power. Octavianus had to take *immediate* action.

Without thinking, he glanced over his shoulder at the secret door which now contained a dangerous distraction, rather than a powerfully erotic temptation. Then, he turned back to find himself under the disturbingly piercing scrutiny of Septem's eyes.

iii

'There is one other thing which Fortuna has brought to my notice, Caesar,' continued Antony's spy smoothly. 'Though it concerns you as a man as well as a Triumvir.'

Thrown off balance, Octavianus looked at Septem open-mouthed. The number of men who could speak to him like this was small indeed. But Septem had saved his life more than once, so he closed his mouth and listened.

Antony's messenger leaned forward slightly, rocking up on the balls of his feet. The hobnails in the soles of his soldiers' *caligae* boots screeched softly on the marble tiles of the floor. 'As my men and I were crossing the Forum with Antony's message, we came across a situation that I feel I must bring to your personal attention at once,' he said. The formal introduction gave the young man time to clear his mind and focus on the soldier's words.

'A situation…' Octavianus was catching up.

'Two men were being denounced by a slave because their names are on the proscription lists.'

'So you killed them and have their heads outside? Now that I have established how little money there is and how great the demands for more have become, you want fifty thousand Attic *drachmae*, do you?' he demanded bitterly.

'No, Caesar. Under the circumstances it seemed wiser to bring them straight to you. So they are outside but still alive.'

'Circumstances? What circumstances?'

'The men are Lucius Calpurnius Bibulus and Marcus Valerius Messala Corvinus, Caesar.'

'Very well. Antony added their names. There are no special circumstances that I can see…'

'Except, both men have suggested that an attempt is being made to have their names removed from the proscription list.'

'An attempt? What attempt?' Octavianus still had not worked out what was going on.

'Calpurnia, the wife of Marcus Valerius Messala Corvinus has accompanied the mother of Lucius Calpurnius Bibulus; both have apparently come in disguise to throw themselves on your mercy, Caesar. Calpurnia is Lucius' sister of course, which makes the women mother and daughter…'

Artemidorus could see that Octavianus understood the full implication of his words now. But he continued, just to make absolutely sure. 'Of course Lucius' and Calpurnia's father Marcus Calpurnius Bibulus died six winters ago. His widow remarried but clearly would still do anything in her power to help the children from her previous marriage. As their mother, you understand. Not as the wife of her new husband.'

Octavianus was pale, blinking rapidly. Artemidorus had never seen him so shocked. 'Remarried!' He whispered. 'But she still thinks to come to me! Is she *mad*?'

'That is a point currently being debated,' answered Artemidorus. 'But the immediate situation is one you can resolve instantly and easily. Clearing it out of your way and putting a stop to any negative rumours that might begin to circulate as a result. More stories designed to recruit more legions to the *Libertores*' camp.'

This time when Octavianus glanced back at the door, his expression was one of absolute horror.

'What do you suggest?'

'Write two releases, one for each man. Strike their names off the lists. Allow me to take the signed documents to the women and let them go to their men. They will not want to let this situation become any more widely known than it is already. I can arrange for Lucius and Messala to escape from the city in secret, while telling no-one, not even Antony; and ensuring silence from my men as well. You will be able to ensure silence from your praetorians and any temple priests aware of the situation, I'm sure. The women can go back to their lives as though nothing has happened – because nothing *has* happened.'

*

Artemidorus hesitated outside the half-hidden door. He felt almost as tense as if he was on a battlefield, disturbingly aware of Octavianus' gaze on his back, like a dagger between his shoulder blades. There was a breathless, almost hysterical muttering beyond the portal, where Messala's wife and her mother were clearly deep in disagreement. He hoped his hands weren't sweating, because the pardons so grudgingly signed and sealed might all too easily smudge into illegibility. Like the proscription lists the priceless documents were designed to counteract. Hesitating for a heartbeat longer, he decided against knocking and opened the door instead.

The hissed argument was replaced by muted screams. He stepped forward, to find himself confronted by two figures, one behind the other. They were both fully dressed in featureless robes, impenetrably veiled – as mysteriously anonymous as it was possible to be. Except that he knew exactly who they both were, knowledge which in itself could prove fatal. There was a moment of silence. Until the figure in front, frozen with protective arms spread over the slighter figure behind, began to speak, her voice wavering with astonishment and the beginning of relief.

'You're not Octavianus! I know you, though. You're...'

'Septem, *Domina*. You know me as Septem. I came to your house regularly after the death of *Divus Julius*, a messenger between Antony and your husband. Not Marcus Calpurnius Bibulus, of course. Your second husband. I also carried messages after you had left Rome and before your husband travelled east.'

'Septem. Yes. I remember. What are you doing here? Does Octavianus know?'

'Yes, *Domina*, he does. I bring the documents you have come here to collect. And I bring a message from both your son and your son-in-law. Who are outside in the Temple, waiting to accompany you home.' He held up the pardons as the second figure gave a gasp of pure relief. 'As they now may do with absolute safety, for they are no longer proscribed.'

The mother of Calpurnia and Lucius Calpurnius Bibulus raised her veil with an unsteady hand and looked Septem straight in the eye. How pale and sickly she looks, he thought. How fragile and yet how beautiful. How can he bear to be so far away from her?

'This is like some kind of wonderful magic. How in the names of the Gods did you do it, Septem?' asked Porcia Catonis, the widow of Marcus Calpurnius Bibulus, the wife of Marcus Junius Brutus, leader of the men who murdered *Divus Julius*, commander of the army Antony was preparing to attack.

iv

'You can see young Octavianus' point, though,' said Ferrata in an unusually forgiving mood. Probably generated by the vast amount of cheap Alban wine he had consumed. 'I mean look at what he's stuck with: Fulvia for a mother-in-law. How terrifying is that? And the child-bride Claudia for a wife. What age is she? Eleven? He probably has to teach her how to wipe her *culus* arse rather than how to warm his bed.' He looked around the table, mountained with food and forested with cups and amphorae. 'More than that, I hear that after the wedding ceremony, Fulvia took the poor lad aside and said, *You lay one finger on my baby daughter and I'll do to your* mentula *dick what I did to Cicero's tongue*.' He pounded the table, weeping with laughter. Everything on it jumped, slopped and clinked. Some of the food toppled off the plates. All the others laughed as well, even Puella.

Everyone else in the *taberna* looked around at the noisy group –

then most of them looked away quickly for all seven of them were wearing armour, swords and daggers. And the one making the most noise was a one-eyed *monstrum* of a man who looked as though he could bite the heads off babies. Their helmets were sitting on the floor at their feet. Which were shod in legionary *caligae* boots. Even though this was the favourite watering place of The Gaul's murderous gang, Septem's little command gave off such an air of menace that even the most ruthless gave them a wide berth. 'Fulvia and her threats are enough to put anyone off, I'd say,' continued Ferrata, 'let alone a sickly weed of a…'

'*Tace!* Shut up!' hissed Puella. 'Here they come!'

Septem and The Gaul were crossing the *taberna*, deep in conversation. As befitted a soldier whose main work was completed under cover, outside the rules of war and the twelve tables of the law, Septem had a wide range of acquaintance which included murderous gang leaders as well as all three Triumvirs, many of their most deadly enemies, their wives and families.

Septem's narrow eyes swept round the active unit which was the heart of his *contubernium* of soldiers and spies, as The Gaul and he crossed the room. They made a traditional eight-man tent-group as though they were still in the legions – in numbers at least. In every other regard they were more like a Spartan *crypteia* death squad. They had license to kill even outside the proscription lists if the need arose. And it was only a couple of months since they had killed Cicero himself. It was Septem who had nailed the dead orator's head to the Rostra.

Besides Puella and Ferrata, there were five others present. The soldiers who had made up the boar's head formation which crossed the Forum and took Porcia's children and son-in-law to Octavianus. Sitting beside Puella there was Quintus – Gaius Quintus Tarpeius late of the disbanded VIIth Legion and seconded to Septem's command now that the legion was reformed. A sinewy *gallus* fighting cock of a man, he was the oldest, most experienced of the group – a *trierius*, most dangerously battle-hardened and best-equipped of legionaries. He had been the leader of the third rank in battle, the line against which attacking soldiers were doomed to shatter and die. Beyond him sat the gigantic ex-tutor to Lepidus' children so aptly named Hercules, expert in all the military arts from wrestling to horsemanship, who had been a member of the group since soon after *Divus Julius* Caesar's death. Soothsayer and haruspex Spurinna's manumitted slave the golden curled, blue-eyed, quick-thinking Kyros was next. Like Artemidorus he was Greek by birth, and amongst the earliest to join the group. Then, finally, there were two further specialists. Both recruited more recently. Beside him sat his companion and perhaps lover Nonus – codenamed *Notus* Writer – seconded from Lepidus' army, whose forte was secret communication; the creation and breaking of codes. And finally there was the aptly named Furius, the group's *carnifex* interrogator.

There were another half-dozen more loosely associated with them. Spurinna the soothsayer who predicted *Divus Julius'* death and warned him to beware the Ides; Antistius the physician who performed the dead dictator's autopsy; Adonis, the Senate recorder who had witnessed the murder and recalled it in detail; his sister Venus; Crinas, Antony's medical nurse and Glyco, Octavianus' military surgeon. The number of medical men emphasised the danger of their work almost as forcefully as the absence of Mercury, their scout and messenger, killed during their attempt on Cicero's life, Tyro, tortured and crucified for refusing to reveal their secrets and the beautiful but treacherous Cyanea who had done so. Who was still out there somewhere, plotting her revenge after Septem threw her naked to the rioting mob.

*

Septem and The Gaul eased themselves into the last two seats at the crowded table. The Gaul, a huge man in every regard, reached for a roast chicken and a handful of *farcimina* sausages. Then he sat munching, both hands busy as he and Septem completed their negotiations. 'Two men,' he said round a huge mouthful. 'Out of the city and over to Dyrrhachium in secret.'

'Two men to begin with,' confirmed Septem. 'I made a promise to their womenfolk.' He reached for a grilled sausage while there were still some left. 'In secret. No names. As far along the *Via Egnatia* as you can get them.'

'Pity they're not going to Sextus Pompey,' mused The Gaul. 'He'd pay for their transport I hear. One hundred thousand Attic *drachmae* for the pair.'

'They want to go to Brutus. And you know you'd be charging up front no matter where they were going. Or who to.'

'Bloody funny, though, Antony's man smuggling Antony's enemies out to Brutus' camp.'

'Nothing for you to worry about. Or even to remember. If you want to stay healthy. Take the money. Do the job. Forget it ever happened.'

'All right. No need to get nasty…'

'Not me. Octavianus himself has ordered it.'

'*Merda* shit! Now that *is* a threat. All right. Pay the rate and they get the ride. Across the strait from Brundisium to Dyrrhachium and as far on into Macedonia as I can manage. Anonymous. In secret. They may have to wait in Brundisium, though. There might not be a calm sea and a following wind. It's not even the sailing season for a month or so.'

'Tell that to Sextus Pompey. He's smuggled a fleet from Massalia to Sicilia through *Decembris* and *Januarius* by all accounts.'

'Well, I'm no sailor but that sounds like a really risky business. Almost as risky as mine. But nowhere near as risky as the stuff you get up to. What's next?'

'I want you to get ready to take us. We might not be going – but then again we might. It's up in the air at the moment and all down to Antony in the end. Once the first two are clear, there's every chance we'll be heading east as well. Without making too much of a fuss.'

'Hercules' *mentula* club! Are you going over to Brutus as well?'

'You'd better hope not. If we were, none of your men with any knowledge of the fact would walk out of here alive. And neither would you.'

The Gaul hesitated for a moment, wondering whether to call Septem out. But he wryly decided the soldier was probably right. His lethal *crypteia* could almost certainly take every man in here, including himself.

Septem watched, reading his mind, his long, copper-chinned face slowly folding into a smile. 'Now that we've cleared that up,' he said, 'let's talk about the special rate for helping eight of us go east in secret. If and when it comes to that.'

V

Porcia Catonis Brutus considered herself in the polished metal mirror that stood against the wall of the *caldarium*. A slave worked assiduously, keeping the surface clear of the steam rising in wavering clouds from the hot pool behind her. The *caldarium* slaves had just finished oiling, massaging and depilating her. One of her women waited with a robe as she left the private bathhouse to return to her apartments. But she lingered, surveying the prize which that little *blatta* cockroach Octavianus had lost.

Her naked figure was tall, slim, unusually rosy because of the heat and the ministrations of the masseur. Breasts and belly that often brought dear Brutus to tears gleaming softly as the scented oil caught the lamplight. Or so his letters said. What he would do if he ever found out she had been willing to prostitute the body he coveted so constantly, she simply did not dare to guess. And to Brutus' greatest enemy of all men! How could she have been so stupid? She considered the pale column of her right thigh, particularly the shadowed inner slope where she had even thought of strapping a dagger – until she realised that killing Octavianus herself would undo everything she was trying to achieve. And lead to her own death and Calpurnia's death – and a renewed, more effective, search for Lucius and Messala. What utter madness had driven her to risk everything like that? Not even the unexpectedly painless success of her scheme could take away the horror that she now felt.

But the answer was as plain – and painful – as the weeping wound on that same thigh. Where, in another moment of madness, she had driven a dagger deep into her flesh to prove she was as able as any man to bear pain. And to bear therefore the weight of whatever had been troubling her darling Brutus so deeply. The wound had never healed, and still gaped slightly. Disturbingly similar to that other cleft close above it which her ardent husband loved best of all.

But the answer was simple. Her duty as a mother outweighed even her duties as a wife. Would Brutus accept that as an excuse? Or would he refer – as he did almost everything now – to Gaius Cassius Longinus. Cassius' answer to her plea would be simple and immediate: whipping and divorce. Or, like a Vestal whose virginity was lost, living burial. Yes, she could just hear Cassius' cold, unforgiving voice. 'Bury the bitch…'

The thought made her shiver and she realised that the heat which soaked into her while she lay in the scalding water was all gone. The self-indulgent near-agony had been wasted after all. She was as icy inside as the evening was outside. She gestured to the slave and lost herself in the warmth of the robe. But, it only warmed her skin.

*

Together with the body-slave, Porcia hurried through to her chamber. The walls were hung with warmly coloured rugs and tapestries, further heated by the golden light of the lamps and candles all over the room. The bed was piled with coverings. But the floor was a mosaic of marble tiles whose chill seemed to burn through the soles of the soft leather slippers she was wearing. The mosaic itself pictured Amphitrite frolicking with mermaids and dolphins in an icy blue ocean. Two more slaves waited for her there, one she recognised as coming from her daughter Calpurnia Messala Corvinus' household, re-established now the proscription had been lifted, even though Messala, like Lucius, had sneaked away in secret. 'What is it?' she demanded, pulling the soft robe more tightly about herself, in a fruitless attempt to dispel the chill.

'*Domina*, my mistress sends her respects and deepest affection.'

'Yes, yes. Get on with it.' Calpurnia, like the absent Lucius and even Messala, for whom she had a soft spot, was currently an unpleasant reminder of the near disaster of her visit to Octavianus.

'It is the matter of the slave Deuterus, *Domina*. My mistress wondered whether you had finished considering his fate.'

Porcia's eyebrows rose. 'He betrayed my son and my son-in-law to the mob. He would have taken his silver and his freedom when they were slaughtered and beheaded. He dies.'

'Of course, Domina. But you were considering crucifixion…'

Porcia was silent for a moment, then she said, 'Well, he may be a traitor to our household, but he's hardly Spartacus. And he's served us since childhood I understand. Let us be merciful. Strangle him.'

'Strangle him. Yes, Domina.'

'Use the method Cicero used on that pig Antony's stepfather during the Catiline affair. Do it with a bowstring.'

'Yes, Domina.'

'But don't be too quick about it. I want him to have time to reflect on his treachery.'

The slave hurried out to oversee Deuterus' lingering Ciceronian execution.

'I am still cold,' snapped Porcia to the remaining servants. I want more light, a writing desk and a brazier. Stoke it up really high. Maybe I can get some warmth into my body as I write to my *maritus* the *dominus*!'

As the slaves hurried to obey her orders, Porcia changed into a new, more formal robe that was warmer and dryer. Her mind was filled with what she was planning to tell Brutus in her next letter. The treacherous slave Deuterus' fate didn't even enter her mind. After all, what was a slave? – a possession that talked. However, Septem's part in her salvation did linger in her memory; he was a soldier and of little more social account than a plebeian freedman. But he had managed to serve her and Brutus well. And there was something unexpectedly powerful about him. Something, oddly, that reminded her of *Divus Julius* himself.

*

The final item to be brought into the room was the brazier. As soon as it arrived, she dismissed all her slaves and pushed a rolled carpet across the bottom of the door to keep out the icy draught. Then she returned to the little desk beside the brazier and settled to writing her letter. This was something she always did alone, for even under normal circumstances it required her full attention. But the brazier kept distracting her with its brightness and its heat. It was a filigreed metal box on four solid legs, piled with charcoal that had, as she ordered, been well-stoked up. The main body of the burning mass in the metal container was cherry red but the top was a wavering crown of bright blue flames. The heat it gave off was fierce. Even so, Porcia found herself moving closer and closer to it as she settled to writing the letter. As one of the most educated women in the Republic, daughter of a famously eccentric father who educated her almost as though she were a boy, her handwriting was clear and fluent. She prided herself on the fact that she always wrote to Brutus herself – without having to insert an amanuensis between them. He too always wrote back himself – though his handwriting, in the Greek style after his education in Athens, lacked the simple flowing beauty of hers.

Soon she was in the act of communicating with the man she loved so completely. Her shivering eased, but her eyes began to water, and her nose started to run. Thoughtlessly, she wiped it on the sleeve of her robe, wondering whether she was catching a cold. She moved even nearer to the brazier, just in case. By the time she had completed the second lengthy paragraph, she realised she had a headache. She looked up blearily, feeling a little light-headed. She would summon a physician in case she had caught anything serious, she decided. But she would finish the letter first. Then, she settled to work once again. Her concentration on the careful phrasing was such that she hardly noticed her heart was racing and her breath was shortening until she was panting as though she herself had just completed the race around the city at *Lupercalia*.

By the time the letter was complete, she was feeling sick and dizzy. She signed it, blew it dry, rolled it and sealed it. Wrote Marcus' name on the outside as she always did, and stood only to keel over and tumble headlong to the floor. The shock of falling brought her briefly to her senses. She saw the letter rolling across the colourful mosaic which seemed to be brightening and darkening as she watched – heaving, as though it really was the sea. As though Amphitrite, her mermaids and dolphins were beginning to come to life. Her stomach wrenched, and bile burned the back of her throat.

She managed to control herself, though it required an enormous effort of will. She decided the time had come to get up and summon her slaves. But when she tried, she discovered that she could not. Her arms and legs seemed too heavy to move; she could hardly stir at all. She took a deep breath to call for help, but no sooner had she sucked in the air than her heart was pounding painfully, her head was splitting, and she was panting like a dog on a hot day.

She panicked then, writhing helplessly and calling feebly. Twisting and turning as she tried to roll towards the door. But darkness was gathering around her as though the lamps and candles were being snuffed, one by one. She had no idea what was happening to her. It was just a strange draining away of all her energy, as though every laboured breath she took was strangling her – as she had just ordered Deuterus the slave to be strangled.

She thought she saw her beloved Brutus in the shadows by the door and with one last effort she tried to reach him. She kicked the brazier instead and it topped over, vomiting burning coals over the floor towards her. The clots of fire hissed and spat, spreading across the marble mosaic until they were stopped by her drool-slick chin and her gaping mouth. The red-hot coals piling up against the blistering flesh almost as though she had been trying to eat them.

But mercifully by that time she was dead.

III: The Mission

i

'Had you any idea she would do anything so foolish?' mused the tribune Enobarbus as he and Artemidorus and hurried towards Antony's *tablinum* office. His tone was an unusual mixture of shock and concern, eventhough it was now some time after the discovery of Porcia's body.

'So foolish to go to Octavianus with her daughter, hoping for mercy for her son and son in law?' asked Artemidorus, cynically.

'So foolish as die by swallowing burning coals!' The tribune shook his head in sad wonderment.

Artemidorus shrugged. The news of Porcia's death was still the major talking-point in Rome, eclipsing the faintest whisper of her secret appeal to Octavianus' better nature. Which resided in his *subigaculum* underwear these days, he thought. News of her terrible fate was heading eastwards, no doubt, as fast as a galloping horse. Apparently with Porcia's last letter to Brutus.

In the days since the discovery of Porcia's body, her mother-in-law, Brutus' mother Servilia, had taken control of the situation. Safely ensconced in rooms in the great villa belonging to Cicero's friend Atticus, beyond the reach of Antony or Octavianus, she had organised a funeral and a cremation for her dead daughter-in-law. Whose ashes were currently awaiting formal entombment in the Brutus family's great vault. She had also taken Calpurnia under her wing, and put her in a guest suite in Atticus' villa. Servilia was irresistible, thought the spy as he followed his superior into his commander's briefing; a force of nature like an earthquake or a great storm. Like Fulvia.

'No,' the spy answered Enobarbus' question. 'I had no idea she would do anything like eating hot coals.' However, he had wondered more than once, during the intervening days, whether he had said or done anything to push Porcia into her desperate act.

'Only Cato's daughter could have dreamed of such an exit,' said the tribune, still shaking his head.

'Cato, who fell on his sword after the battle of Utica,' said the spy. 'Cut his stomach open. Eviscerated himself but didn't die. Did you know that? Then, when his physician tried putting his guts back into his belly he pulled them out again, handful after handful until he did manage to kill himself. So maybe the way his daughter went wasn't so strange after all.'

'Hmmm,' said Enobarbus, clearly unconvinced. The praetorian, guarding the entrance to the corridor leading out of the massive atrium to Antony's *tablinum,* slammed to attention as they walked past, heading towards the second praetorian guard standing at the newly installed office door itself. 'Even the general is feeling the weight of public disapproval,' said Enobarbus, nodding towards the new security arrangements. 'Though there hasn't been a serious attempt on his life since the incident with Myrtillus. Off the battlefield, that is.'

'It was Minucius Basilus who hired the assassin Myrtillus,' said Artemidorus. 'Though I know Antony is still half-convinced Octavianus had something to do with it. But Basilus was chopped to pieces by his slaves late last year and Myrtillus is long gone. What little was left of him after Antony's interrogation, was thrown off the Tarpean Rock then dragged on a massive hook to the Tiber and chucked in. Nothing to worry about there.'

'I think it was his attempt to tax the women and their reaction that really rattled him. Not to mention his own mother sheltering a boy on the proscription lists then publicly demanding that he execute her too if he took the boy's head…'

'Mothers!' said Artemidorus. 'Sometimes I think they're more trouble than they're worth!'

'That's only because you have no idea who your mother was. Or your father, come to that,' said the tribune, as the praetorian opened the door to Antony's office.

Artemidorus glanced away from Enobarbus with a snort of laughter. Instead he found himself looking at the shining praetorian guard disdainfully, with the professional soldier's contempt for the young man in his special silver-coloured armour, all gleaming. Parade-ground ready – never soiled on a battlefield; someone who clearly spent more time polishing his sword than using it. Typical of the kind, he thought. All show, no substance.

*

There were four people in Antony's *tablinum*, all of them looking down at a diagram spread across a large table, held in place by two *amphorae* and a couple of glasses. It was just possible to see it was a map of the eastern section of the Republic: triumvir Antony's empire. The east coast of Italy was sketched down one side, only the ports of Brundisium and Barium to the north of it drawn in any detail, for Italy was Lepidus' responsibility, just as everywhere west of Italy was Octavianus'. The rest of the map covered Macedonia, Greece, Thrace, Asia Province, Syria, Judea and Egypt in detail, the inland provinces behind them less so. More distant countries like Dacia, Armenia and Parthia were simply names written across blank spaces. Waiting to be invaded and pillaged before being added to the Republic – and the chart.

Fulvia stood beside her husband, her attention focused on the most detailed section, one finger pointing to the middle of Macedonia, just north of the city of Philippi. It was not unusual to find Fulvia attending Antony's briefings. Like *Divus Julius* his friend and mentor, Antony was happy to allow an unusual breadth of opinion in his planning meetings. He had a simple rule – if you were in the room, you were welcome to have your say. So Fulvia was no stranger here. As Cleopatra had been no stranger to *Divus Julius'* briefings in Alexandria. Or, of course, to his bed – something Antony was still immensely jealous about.

Opposite Antony and his wife stood two men that Artemidorus recognised at once. Proper soldiers, he thought, the fancy parade-ground splendour of the praetorians lingering in his memory. These were Gaius Norbanus Flaccus and Lucius Decidius Saxa. Both Norbanus and Saxa were widely experienced commanders as well as powerful politicians and reliably quick-thinking generals. Both had served with distinction under *Divus Julius*. And Saxa had aided Antony at the battle of Mutina.

'Ah,' said Antony glancing up. 'There you are. Tribune. Septem. Welcome. As you can see, we were just discussing my campaign through Macedonia in pursuit of those murderous bastards Brutus and Cassius. Laying down some plans for when the fighting season opens.'

'If we have the legions, of course,' added Fulvia. 'Even my Lord Antony's reputation can only carry them so far.'

'Over the Alps and back, for instance,' he added, beaming with self-satisfaction.

'They need paying as well.' Fulvia snapped.

'Feeding, equipping and paying,' agreed Antony. 'And that's where the problems start. Tribune, have you and Septem had any thoughts on the matter during the week or so since our last meeting?'

The two men glanced at each-other and then at generals Norbanus and Saxa. They had already been mulling over Antony's situation with the rest of the *contubernium* at some length over the last few days in preparation for this meeting.

Spy and spymaster joined the others at the table's edge. Tribune Enobarbus spoke first. 'Any and all preparations you undertake, General, will have to be lengthy and detailed. And, unfortunately, as the lady Fulvia observes, *expensive*. As far as we know, Brutus and Cassius have seventeen legions between them. Brutus is in Sardis with seven. He pointed to a spot just north-east of Ephesus in Asia Province. Cassius is in Syria with ten.' His gesture over Syria was much less precise. 'All seventeen legions are well equipped from the caches of arms that *Divus Julius* left ready for his Parthian campaign, which Brutus, Cassius and their supporters have managed to steal. The legions are also well paid from last year's taxes which were all collected and on their way to Rome, until Brutus and Cassius captured them as well. But they have been scouring the local communities for more. Some cities have apparently been told to pay ten years' taxes in advance at once. Other, poorer, cities have had part, or all of their populations sold into slavery.' He looked around the table. No-one showed much emotion. It was not unusual for cities to sell citizens into slavery to pay their taxes.

'The legions in the east are well led. 'Artemidorus added, taking over the intelligence analysis. 'Brutus is the weaker, less experienced, general but he is largely served by men who followed Pompey the Great and were decommissioned after he lost the battle of Pharsalus – who have no liking for *Divus Julius,* his memory, friends and relatives. On the other hand, Cassius is at the head of an army at least partly made up of men who followed him to safety out of the bloodbath at Carrhae – who would follow him to Hades and back if he asked them to. But an important element of his army – nearly half, in fact – is comprised of the four legions that *Divus Julius* left in Egypt to protect the grain supply and the pro-Roman Ptolemaic dynasty…'

'Cleopatra…' said Antony, almost under his breath. Fulvia shot him a look that would have done credit to a gorgon.

'Those are the legions under the *imperium* of general Aulus Allienus which Cleopatra sent to support Caecilius Bassus in his stand against Cassius,' continued Enobarbus. 'But Bassus' own legions went over to the enemy before Allienus arrived. And when he did, his men changed sides as well and joined Cassius. This leaves Egypt relatively undefended, just as Cassius is massing his armies in Syria.' Enobarbus' finger pointed to the border of Syria south of

Tyre, where only the boundaries of Judea with Galilee to the north and Jerusalem at its heart reached down to the shore of *Mare Nostrum* and stood between Syria and Egypt.

Enobarbus' light, slightly nasal baritone continued as he explained the thinking of Septem and his *contubernium*. 'We believe he would have invaded Egypt already but for two things. First, there is severe drought there. The Nile has not inundated for two years. Consequently, the grain harvest has failed. The stores set aside for the Egyptians – as opposed to those sold on to Rome – are exhausted. The population is starving. On the verge of open riot, in fact, a situation Lepidus will have to be careful to avoid here in Rome if and when the Egyptian corn supplies dry up. Secondly, there is plague all throughout the country from the Delta right down beyond the city of *Waset*, which we call Thebes. Though Alexandria seems relatively untouched so far. The most recent reports suggest more than half the population of Egypt is sick, dying or dead. As you can readily imagine, there are few things Cassius wants *less* than responsibility for a starving nation ready to riot and riddled with a highly contagious sickness for which there is no cure. He hesitates, therefore, within easy reach of Egypt. Tempted by the fabulous wealth it represents, worried by the terrible risks. But nevertheless he remains a potent threat…'

ii

'And that is important,' Artemidorus took over the intelligence briefing once more, his voice more clipped and urgent. 'Because at least one vital element of your proposed campaign must turn on Egypt and Queen Cleopatra. I assume that is at least part of the point of sending such a detailed message about Sextus Pompey to Octavianus…'

'Which is accurate in every point,' inserted Fulvia.

'Indeed, *domina*, which makes it all the more potent. But the real objective was not to inform him of the danger Sextus Pompey represents. It was to distract him from one or two other obvious truths while putting him under some very real pressure. He is clever and insightful, after all. Not to mention well advised. But he and his advisers are young and inexperienced, especially in the arena of political contests. He is, perhaps, over-awed by the weight of his responsibilities, having accepted his portion of the Republic on the mistaken assumption that because it was the smallest and most overlooked it would also be the quietest. Assuming that this would allow him to focus on his real task – which is to outdo you, General, to outdo you at every possible occasion and work towards his long-term goal of ultimate power. Sextus Pompey is an unexpected, unwelcome but unavoidable distraction.'

'Sextus Pompey must be dealt with and be *seen* to have been dealt with,' added Enobarbus. 'No matter what demands of time, money and military commitment which that entails – all at the wrong end of Italy.

'While you, General, focus your attention on the spot the Lady Fulvia was pointing to when we arrived,' Artemidorus continued. 'Macedonia. You need to get your legions over to Dyrrhachium and on down the Via Egnatia as soon as possible. To show the people throughout the Republic that you are taking care of *Divus Julius'* murderers while his son and heir has gone boating in Sicily.'

'An impressive summation,' rumbled Norbanus, who was a great bear of a man. Muscular torso and massive shoulders straining the seams of his tunic. Fists like a pair of hams resting on the map as he stared down at Macedonia.

'Indeed,' agreed Antony.

'Just so,' Saxa nodded. The skin under his thinning hair catching the lamplight. He was the fox to Norbanus' bear.

'But,' inserted Fulvia, 'you mentioned Cleopatra…' She spat the name as though it had an unpleasant taste.

'Indeed, *domina*,' answered Artemidorus. 'While Octavianus is distracted, I assume the General will be sending his legions across to Macedonia as fast as he can and letting everybody know that he is taking action. But, the problem is that by no means all of the legions are ready. He has the Vth *Alaude*, the Larks, together with the IInd and the XXXVth. All of whom followed him over the Alps and back, as he observed. The reconstituted VIIth, the VIIIth and a few more are nearly there. Maybe eight legions in all up to scratch and set to go. That, I assume, is why generals Norbanus and Saxa are here. To go on ahead of the main force with whatever legions are ready, prepare the ground, while clearly demonstrating to everyone in Rome that the general here is taking decisive action directly against the men who murdered *Divus Julius*, head to head. While, as I say, Octavianus is seen to be sailing off in the wrong direction altogether and fighting someone of no apparent importance. Which, combined with other factors, is likely to do Octavianus' standing with the public and the legions no good whatsoever whilst making general Antony the most popular man in the Republic.'

'What a nice change that would be!' Observed Fulvia with a decided edge in her voice. 'But, *Cleopatra…*'

*

Enobarbus took up the narrative once more. 'So,' he continued smoothly, 'after generals Norbanus and Saxa have taken the battle-ready legions east, the *dominus* General Antony will no doubt get the rest of the legions down to Brundisium and up to strength in numbers, equipment and training before shipping them across to Dyrrhachium. Which will take time as well as money, particularly as Octavianus is likely to need his own battle-ready legions – the *Martia*, the IVth and so-on – to man the warships he will eventually send against Sextus Pompey. So they are out of the equation for the time-being at least. It seems unlikely, therefore, that general Antony will be able to start moving the bulk of his legions across to Dyrrhachium before mid-to-late summer, which is the main weak-spot in the plan. Because it will give the navies working for Brutus and Cassius, under the *imperium* of Lucius Murcus and Domitius Ahenobarbus, plenty of time to start blockading the ports of Barium and Brundisium. Stopping the movement of the army across the sea or cutting the lines of communication and pirating the supplies if the army has already reached Macedonia.' He paused. There was a moment of silence.

'But,' said Artemidorus, quietly, 'there is one other navy powerful enough to defeat Murcus and Ahenobarbus. Only one. And that is Cleopatra's. However, Queen Cleopatra is not popular in Rome and she knows it.'

'Nor in this house,' added Fulvia with an icy glance at her husband.

'Which might well motivate her to take as little action as possible,' continued Artemidorus smoothly. 'And wait to see who comes out of the inevitable confrontation victorious – Antony and Octavianus or Brutus and Cassius. But, on the other hand, she must be well aware that the Roman people may be more indulgent if she joins the war of revenge for the murder of *Divus Julius*. By whom, after all, she had a son and heir, Caesarion. However, the situation is further complicated. She has shown her hand by sending Allienus and his legions to help us. But now, as we have already discussed, Cassius is at her borders with ten legions. She is defenceless, her people starving and riddled with plague. She will need careful prompting if she is going to look away from more pressing problems at home to go on a naval adventure across *Mare Nostrum* in support of the general.'

'But it's a gamble she would be willing to take if I know her – *and I do*,' said Antony, carefully avoiding Fulvia's eye. 'The odds against winning are considerable. But the rewards of victory could be incalculable. The thanks of the man who rules the Republic – a special relationship with Rome re-established, even stronger than it was in *Divus Julius*' day. The ability to call on forty legions – not just four – to secure her borders and calm any rebellious subjects. A certain, inviolable future for herself, her children, her dynasty. She would gamble almost everything for a prize like that!'

'Oh!' said Fulvia, at her most theatrical. 'If only we had someone we could send to Alexandria to explain all the fabulous things she could win, simply by lending Antony one little navy…'

iii

Artemidorus took Quintus and Ferrata to the next two meetings. The first was early next day and it was with the tribune Enobarbus. As befitted a man of equestrian standing, on Antony's short-list to become his legate – a citizen of considerable potential on the *cursus honorum* ladder of power, therefore – Enobarbus lived in a villa on the Quirinial hill. He was an only child of long-dead parents and he had yet to marry; still more interested in soldiering than social or political climbing. The villa was far too big for him, but he had a small army of devoted slaves who kept it tidy and welcoming whether he was in residence or – as much more often – away on campaign.

His *tablinum* office was not as large as Antony's. But that was because Antony's office, like the villa that housed it, had been built by Pompey the Great at the height of his power. Unlike Antony's, which had added curtains and doors for privacy and protection, Enobarbus' opened from the atrium in traditional fashion and looked through into the immaculate peristyle garden, and there were no pretty praetorian guards. The stormy weather had passed and the garden was bathed in watery sunshine, whose golden tints gave extra life to the first spring flowers venturing into bloom beneath the still-dripping bushes and trees.

Enobarbus greeted the three men and called for slaves to bring chairs and *jentaculum* breakfast. They sat around the tribune's table. The three put their head-gear on the floor easing the swords and daggers on their belts into a comfortable position. Their host, unarmed and dressed in a simple tunic, leaned back and surveyed his guests as though seeing them for the first time. Taking his leisure as he ordered his thoughts.

Like many in the old VIth legion, the Ironclads, Ferrata was from Hispania and had the olive skin and thick black hair usual among his countrymen. He was built like one of the great bulls common in his country. His nose was not unlike the great animals' muzzles. His one remaining eye was dark brown. The false one painted on the eye-patch matched it, glowering threateningly. A bellicose effect enhanced by the parallel scars on his cheek and the ragged remains of his left ear. Septem had no doubt brought him for his wide practical experience, and for the fact that he was probably the most effective bodyguard in the spy's command.

Breadth of experience was certainly why he had brought Quintus. Although apparently just an old soldier – albeit a *triarius*, cream of the crop in the legions – he was actually of ancient patrician blood, fabulously wealthy and master of a huge villa on the Esquiline hill which Septem's *contubernium* used as their headquarters in Rome. He was apparently ageless, deceptively slight but whip strong, limitlessly energetic, impossible to outrun, outmanoeuvre or out-fight. His hazel eyes sparkled with intelligence and the broad forehead above them spoke of almost limitless knowledge. While the scars on his taut-muscled arms and surprisingly large hands hinted at massive familiarity with battles of all sorts. His on-the-ground experience was unrivalled. In whatever way Septem decided to proceed, Quintus would be deeply involved in the practicalities of planning, arming and supply. Then he would be at the forefront of any action.

Jentaculum arrived and the tribune leaned forward. Not to eat but to demonstrate he was ready to get down to business.

Ferrata's unspoken hope that the food would be as impressive as the setting was dashed at once by the arrival of Caesar's breakfast – *emer* bread and *posca* vinegar water. Quintus, the old soldier and rigid traditionalist grunted his satisfaction and took a mouthful of each, using the vinegar to soften the bread. The tribune spymaster and his centurion secret agent left the food untouched as the briefing began.

'It is precisely as we calculated,' began Enobarbus quietly. 'But the deadlines on the one hand are shorter while being longer on the other.'

Ferrata chewed on a crust of *emer* bread and frowned – this kind of oratory was beyond him. He wrestled with the idea that things were going to get tighter in the short-term while they would loosen further down the line. He suspected that what the tribune meant was that Septem and their group had better move fast – while the tribune, Antony and their men could put their feet up for a while. But the frown made the discomfort in the side of his head flare into agony, so he let his expression relax. As the pain that so often pierced his head eased, he focused on what the tribune was saying.

*

'Antony wants you across in Macedonia as fast as possible. You choose who to take with you and how best to proceed. He will furnish any supplies or funds you need if you submit a detailed list to him. Arms and armour too, though I have to say it's more likely the Quintus here can supply all of your requirements in that area. You go by way of Macedonia for several reasons. First of all it is the quickest and easiest route east – until the sailing season starts in April. Secondly, even when the sailing season does start, any vessel heading east and south across *Mare Nostrum* from Italy will more than likely run into trouble from the fleets of Murcus and Ahenobarbus. Last reported around *Rhodos*, ready to come and blockade Brundisium. Thirdly, you will be an effective scouting party for Norbanus and Saxa. Who will arrange some men to accompany you – then wait for them to catch up so they can pass on whatever intelligence you will have gathered. Such intelligence will, of course, become more and more vital, the closer you get to Brutus and his legions. Because, fourthly, the plan is for you to get as far east as practical before heading south: Thessalonika, say, or Neapolis south of Philippi. That way you will be well behind Murcus and Ahenobarbus who will be coming west and north with their fleets – hopefully safe from their interference. You will take ship at the first convenient port and by mid-to-late March you will be in Alexandria. That's where your real work begins.'

'Convincing Queen Cleopatra to send a fleet to break any blockade, then to guard Antony's supply lines,' nodded Artemidorus.

'As well as gathering any intelligence you can on Cassius, his position and his plans. And, because of Antony's nightmare visits by Cicero's ghost, discovering exactly what there is at Actium in Greece.'

Artemidorus nodded. He was of the Stoic leaning, believing the gods and all the other supernatural beings that peopled Roman superstition were distant and uninterested in human affairs – if they existed at all. But Antony had convinced him that the headless, handless ghost of Cicero had visited on more than one occasion. Saying – despite the lack of head, lips or tongue – he would see Antony at Actium.

Enobarbus continued, ‘Of course, if you are successful, you will be coming back with the Egyptian fleet and with enough intelligence for him to launch his campaign. Antony thinks if all goes well you could be off Brundisium by June or July, able to come straight ashore and report to him.’

‘But he’ll be in Macedonia by then, surely…’ Artemidorus frowned.

‘He thinks not.’ Enobarbus shrugged. ‘He agrees with our assessment that it will take all summer to get all his legions battle-ready. Remember he learned a lot during the Civil War – and even more at the battles of Forum Gallorum and Mutina. Both of which he lost…’

‘If it’s going to be legion against legion,’ said Quintus, ‘he will have to ensure he has the best troops as well as the best supplies and weapons, the best communications and plan.’

Ferrata, chewing the leathery bread, nodded his agreement.

‘And the best navy,’ added Artemidorus. ‘Even if it is Egyptian.’

‘Why isn’t he relying on Octavianus’ fleet after he destroys Sextus Pompey?’ wondered Quintus.

‘Because Octavianus isn’t going to destroy Sextus Pompey,’ answered Enobarbus. ‘You know that as well as I do. All of you. Antony is absolutely certain of it. Octavianus will build his ships – or Agrippa will build them for him. He’ll train his men. He’ll set sail for Sicily. And Sextus Pompey will kick the *excrementum* out of him!’

‘Then he’ll come back to Antony with his tail between his legs,’ concluded Artemidorus. ‘That’s the general’s plan at least. His navy – whatever is left of it – and his legions will come with him, ready to follow the general’s orders. And the war against Brutus and Cassius will begin in earnest in Sextilis or September, with Antony in total charge; nineteen legions – maybe more – against Brutus and Cassius’ seventeen or so.’

iv

‘This is more like it,’ observed Ferrata as he realised the second meeting of the morning was to be held in one of his favourite *tabernae* in the *Subura*. In place of *emer* bread and *posca* he ordered *farcinem* and Alban wine. ‘Not too much water,’ he told the serving girl. 'And I want the sausages crispy. I'll have some olives and cheese while I'm waiting.'

'And a chicken!' boomed The Gaul's great voice as he swaggered across to join them. 'The fattest you've got.'

'Better bring more Alban, then,' concluded Quintus.

'How are the first two packages?' asked Artemidorus as The Gaul sat on the strongest-looking stool there. It creaked beneath his weight.

'Still stuck in Brundisium,' he answered. 'Waiting for a wind. Been there for a couple of days…'

'We may catch up with them then. We leave as soon as possible and travel as fast as we can.'

'You may catch up with them or you may not. Depends on the wind and the weather. It's extra for added sacrifices and libations to Poseidon, Jupiter and Juno, but probably worth it. From what I understand, your two packages are keen to move on.' He paused, then added, 'I don't think they've heard the news…'

'They're safe in the meantime?' Artemidorus asked. Neither man was likely to know about Porcia, her death or her funeral, he thought. *Yet.*

'In a *hospitium* I know with a couple of my best men keeping a discreet eye on them.'

'Good enough. Now, the plan is for my *contubernium* to leave the city without anyone else noticing. We're heading down to Brundisium as well, so that will involve travel along the Via Appia. Maybe the Via Latina if we want to split up. We've debated the way forward and it seems best if we travel in two or three smaller groups. Ideally as parts of larger companies. But speed is as important as anonymity.'

'Riding, then; not walking, marching or travelling by cart or carriage,' emphasised Ferrata with a side glance at Quintus who was almost as helpless on a horse as he was aboard a ship.

'But who apart from messengers and soldiers would ride down to Brundisium?' Quintus demanded with a frown.

'Let me think about that,' said The Gaul, just as the chicken, sausages, cheese, olives and wine all arrived at once. With a pile of fresh-baked rolls.

'There's more,' warned Quintus. 'We also need to take some equipment with us…'

The Gaul leaned forward. His voice dropped. 'I know the sort of equipment you deal in Quintus. And it just so happens that there was a robbery down by Brundisium a while back. Army blacksmiths. Shocking I know! Depriving the legions of state-of-the-art weaponry. But I happen to know where it ended up and I guarantee it's as good as anything you can lay your hands on. Good basic stuff – nothing strange or over-fancy. But state-of-the-art as I say. Cutting edge.'

Quintus grunted. Sat back. Grabbed a sausage before Ferrata and The Gaul ate the lot. Lowered his standards and took a soft, crusty roll as though he was undermining the entire civilisation.

Artemidorus sat forward. 'We could go disguised as messengers or a cavalry unit,' he allowed. 'As long as no-one is likely to recognise us.'

'I was thinking more of a wedding party,' rumbled The Gaul round a mouthful of chicken, sausage and white roll. 'Riding south to a ceremony in Lucera, say. Or a group of priests and priestesses bound for the Temple of Vesta in Tibur. Wrong direction I know – but you get the idea. Once you're out of the city and out of sight you can allow yourselves a little latitude. Or the Temple of Venus in Pompeii come to that. The Temple of Hera at Paestum. The more I think about it…'

The Gaul had just arrived at this point in his thoughts when one of his men pushed into the *taberna* and rushed across the room.

'Message from Brundisium,' he gasped. 'Just arrived by fast messenger. Nearly killed his horse…'

'Yes?' snapped The Gaul who did not relish being presented with crises in front of clients.

'The two items we were moving…' The messenger's gaze flicked over to Artemidorus. Then back to his boss.

'Yes?' snarled The Gaul again.

'The men watching them have been found with their throats cut. The men they were guarding have vanished. Can't find them anywhere, living or dead.'

V

One of the things *Divus Julius* had done in preparation for the Parthian campaign, which he had never undertaken, was to create a fast-communication service between Rome and Brundisium. There were special manned waypoints every ten military *miles* with horses for messengers to exchange as they rode south with vital news or orders. The Italian system had almost fallen into disuse since *Divus Julius'* death, but Antony occasionally used it last year to send orders to the legions that had been massed at Brundisium, called back from Macedonia but not yet put into the field against Decimus Albinus in Mutina. So it was still manned by bored soldiers and stable-hands with little to do but feed and groom the restless horses and stare hopefully into the distance. But once in a while, *commercium* traffic on the Via Appia would be thrust aside by a squad of Antony's praetorians thundering south or north along the road with their distinctive uniforms, mounts and pouches.

Next morning, just after dawn, one such squad left the Porta Capena Gate in the Servian Wall and vanished southwards. There were seven messengers – a larger number than usual but by no means unheard-of. They were led by a tall centurion who rode with a monster at one shoulder – a massive man missing one eye and one ear. And a tall praetorian at the other shoulder of obvious Nubian descent. None of the trio looked particularly happy with their gleaming uniforms or their perfectly-polished weaponry. Behind them came a giant, large enough to dwarf even the one-eyed monster, and a soldier whose face seemed fixed in a permanent furious scowl. Behind the five of them came two more men – ordinary legionaries in the standard uniform and trappings of Legio VII. Unlike the smart and shiny praetorians, their armour was well-used and ill-fitting – too large on one and too small on the other. Probably legionary slaves – though they looked more like gang-members than soldiers.

Except for the one-eyed monster who wore a gladiator's headpiece and facemask, the praetorians wore the distinctive helmets of their cohort and carried the round shields at their saddle-bows with symbols of Venus Victrix, thunderbolts and scorpions. Leather saddle-bags marked with the symbol of Mercury, god of messengers as well as of physicians. They rode fully armed – sword pommels and dagger hilts all glittering brightly, even in the dull daylight. Hardly a head turned as the little squad charged by, cloaks bunched high on shoulders to cover the lower parts of their faces, protecting mouths and noses from the icy wind of their passage. Folded nearly high enough to meet their distinctive headgear; almost as though they were travelling in disguise.

Changing horses every ten military *miles* and following the road at a steady gallop, they had completed more than one-third of their 344-*mile* journey when they reined in that evening, utterly exhausted. Their leader chose a welcoming *hospitium* rather than the next Spartan military shelter *Divus Julius* had set up. He and his companions were not practised messengers, used to riding day in and day out. They were all stiff and sore. A bath, a meal and a good night's sleep were needed now. At that moment, these seemed more important than following Antony's orders. Not that they were in a good mood with the massive gang-leader – half convinced he had chosen the praetorian disguises as a joke at their expense.

But they would have to wait in the port-city in any case. Because, at a more reasonable hour this morning, Senator Quintus Tarpeus with his retinue and slaves had departed the city, also heading south but at a slightly more sedate pace – in a covered chariot pulled by four horses with attendants seated on another, less stylish, wagon full no doubt with the necessities a Senator required on the road. And even the slaves rode astride. All in all, not counting the bodyguards The Gaul had added to their undercover progress, the two groups consisted of Septem's entire ten-person *contubernium* of code-breakers, physicians, guides and weapons experts; men and women who knew the terrain they were about to cross; several others who had been to Alexandria – with *Divus Julius* in 706 and 707 AUC since the founding of the city, a group that included Artemidorus himself. And they were all due to be in Brundisium in five days' time. Though the squad disguised as praetorian messengers might conceivably make it by mid-morning the day after tomorrow. Which would give them a couple of days to find out who had killed The Gaul's men and why. Not to mention to discover what had happened to Lucius and Messala.

*

Artemidorus paused at the *hospitium*'s threshold, looking up at the great winged phallus lamp which hung above the door as the bustle in the stables behind him died. The massive good-luck charm gave off light while warding off evil. Unconsciously, he felt the golden *fascinum* charm hidden in the pouch that hung at his belt. Not because he believed in the efficacy of such things, like Ferrata, Furius and most legionaries. But because Puella had found the thing on the ground immediately after the *crypteia,* hurrying to execute Cicero, had been ambushed. Ferrata seriously wounded and their guide, the messenger codenamed Mercury, had been killed.

Artemidorus himself was certain the charm belonged to the tribune Popilius Laenas, who had finally taken Cicero's head and hands to Antony in Rome, claiming all the glory and the reward until the record had been put straight. A man who had tried to rob and kill them before and who nursed a murderous grudge against Septem and his entire command. But who worked for Octavianus now, albeit under the direct command of the young Caesar's ruthless chief of intelligence Gaius Clinius Maecenas. Enobarbus, however, had told him that Centurion Lucius Flavius Felix had lost one identical to this. Felix, who also worked for Octavian, but under Agrippa's command, a very different kettle of fish to the brutal, murderous Laenas. A man who was approachable – or so it seemed on the surface at least.

Dismissing such thoughts, Artemidorus pushed the door open and, with a nod to the *janitor* and a gesture to the portrait of Janus on the wall beside him, entered the *vestibulum*, passing swiftly into the atrium as the others followed – except for Furius who was making sure the horses were stabled. It was a dull evening towards the latter end of *Februarius*. Unsurprisingly, the place was quiet. The landlord bustled forward to greet such a promising group of guests in person and, within a few minutes, Artemidorus had negotiated bed and board – and discovered that the establishment boasted a proper bathhouse large enough to accommodate them all. And, indeed, the other guests, currently availing themselves of it.

The landlord's daughter guided them to their rooms. She was a plump blonde girl with a dimple at the corner of her smile and a little rash of freckles across the bridge of her turned-up nose. Her wide brown eyes lingered on Artemidorus until she met Puella's icy gaze. Then her interest seemed to settle on Ferrata instead, overlooking the ruin of his face to focus on the virile strength of the rest of him. The weary travellers put their kit in their assigned rooms and trooped down to the bathhouse on stiff legs, as the aroma of a pig roasting on the spit by the fire in the atrium followed them. As the others went into the disrobing room adjacent to the icy *frigidarium*, Artemidorus glanced into the *caldarium* to see how many masseurs there were – for he had a suspicion that all his command would need their ministrations. He looked into the steam-room and froze.

For there on the bench of the nearest masseur lay the familiar figure of his opposite number in Octavianus' spy network; Agrippa's most trusted agent – Centurion Lucius Flavius Felix.

IV: Brundisium

i

'No,' repeated Lucius Flavius Felix, 'it wasn't a coincidence. Or some trick of the Goddess Fortuna. We've been waiting for you. Well, if not you then someone like you. Look. It doesn't take Aristotle or Socrates to work it out. With young Octavianus forced to focus on Sicily, it was obvious Antony was going to try for Macedonia behind his back. Steal his thunder. Win back the affection of the legions that he decimated and who went over to Octavianus in consequence. And if he's planning on making a big show sending his legions across from Brundisium to Dyrrhachium, then he'll want to send a scouting party first. To make sure his grand gesture doesn't turn into a comic accident like a play by Plautus. Agrippa has teams of men waiting at all the likely stopping points between Rome and Brundisium. We've been here for a couple of days. It just took longer for you to show up than we thought it would.'

Artemidorus, his four companions, Felix and his three all sat around a table in the middle of the *hospitium*'s atrium. Their slaves shared a table with the men The Gaul had added to the *cryptaeia*'s number; a hulking brute called Bibulus and a slighter, more intelligent ruffian called Casticus. Both tables were piled with crisp-skinned roast pork, sausages, chicken and bread. There were *amphorae* of wine – but they remained untouched. There was an air of tension and no-one wanted to reduce their focus if negotiations were about to start – or their reaction-times if violence erupted instead. The landlord stood behind his serving table, keeping watch over things. His daughter, who had overseen the slaves bringing the food, hovered behind his shoulder, eyes wide.

Although they had removed their armour, the weary travellers had yet to change out of their travelling clothes or bathe. Felix and his men were relaxed in clean tunics, fragrant with scented oils, seemingly unaware of the tension in the air. But they all had their weapons at their belts. Artemidorus stroked the winged phallus *fascinum* in the pouch beside the sword on his right hip. Even if Felix was playing a double-game, he thought, it was better than being confronted by the brutal tribune Popilius Laenas. A man he had seen torture people to death at Octavianus' prompting. Who had destroyed entire villages in the Alps while scavenging for Decimus Albinus. Spitting babies on *pilae* spears, crucifying priests against the walls of their burning temples and using village elders and their wives for target practice with slings and arrows. Laenas, who harboured more than one grudge against Septem, now for stealing his thunder over the execution of Cicero.

But for the moment, Artemidorus held his peace. The spy was calculating not only how best to discover the truth about the *fascinum* and the ambush but also how much information he might be willing to share with Felix about the current missions. He slid out his dagger, leaned forward and stabbed a piece of pork, signalling to the others that they too could start to eat.

'And you happen to have chosen this particular place because…?' he queried, round a mouthful of melting meat.

'For the same reason as you did!' Felix leaned forward and copied his motions. His men also fell-to with a will. The food was extremely good. 'It's by far the best and most comfortable *hospitium* for miles – and the only one with a bath.'

'Very well.' Artemidorus nodded. 'And your orders are…?'

'If we come across you, to join you – as far as Brundisium at least,' answered Felix, apparently without a second thought. 'Send a man back to inform Agrippa and Octavianus what's going on which I will do when we have finished this delightful meal. Wave a fond farewell from the dockside, then ride back to Rome as fast as I can and report to Agrippa and Octavianus myself.'

'And that's all there is to it?'

'That's all there *was*…' Felix drew the word out. Silence settled once more, broken only by the sounds of meat being torn apart and eaten.

*

'But now?' probed Artemidorus, snapping a piece of crackling as though it was a dry twig.

'But *now*,' answered Felix, 'although I see many familiar faces smiling in such an amicable manner around the table and drooling pork-fat down their chins, there are several others I expected to see who are notable by their absence. Particularly Quintus. You never go anywhere without Quintus.'

Artemidorus said nothing, as he tried to read the truth behind the apparently unguarded assertions.

Felix continued, waving a chicken-drumstick. 'Therefore, I can only assume that Quintus and the others will be coming along later. At a more sedate pace. Also in disguise to cover their activities until they are well clear of Rome at least. Hopefully a disguise they find less embarrassing and more effective than yours. *Praetorians!* A joke, surely!' He chuckled companionably, almost conspiratorially. 'However, they are disguised, they are probably bringing all sorts of interesting equipment, funds and further orders. Even if you've come this far without Quintus, you won't set sail without him, so I can just continue as ordered – but send two men back to Agrippa, perhaps.' He bit off most of the flesh from the drumstick and chewed. 'One to report your whereabouts and the other to look for Quintus and his company along the way. I'd better send one of my more intelligent men in case their cover is more convincing than yours.' He paused. Chewed some more; swallowed. Continued, 'Though it does exercise my mind a little to work out why you are in such a hurry to get to Brundisium when you will only have to wait there until Quintus shows up. Is there something else going on that I haven't quite worked out yet?'

Still Artemidorus said nothing.

Felix proceeded with his speculations as he reached for more chicken. 'The only other element I had not anticipated was the involvement of your interesting-looking legionaries over there. I might be tempted to add these two unexpected elements together and speculate that those awfully disguised soldiers are working for the people who helped with *your* disguises. The Gaul, let us say for argument's sake. Who has, I believe, helped you come and go undercover before. And that there is, in fact, something going on in Brundisium. Something to do with him and his gang which needs looking into as soon as possible – while you are waiting there, perhaps.'

Still Artemidorus stayed silent. He reached for more pork, his gaze never leaving Felix's.

'It is fortunate, then, that my team are not the only unit sent out from Octavianus' camp. For when we arrive in Brundisium, I believe we will find tribune Popilius Laenas and his centurion Herrenius also waiting there.'

ii

'It's not natural,' said Ferrata. 'Eating and then bathing. It's the wrong way around. Like putting your back-plate over your belly as you strap your armour on.'

'Not that you've ever been able to afford anything other than a coat of mail in any case,' observed Furius.

'And you only have that because it's army issue,' added Hercules.

'Mind you, now you're a praetorian and take it up the *culus* like the rest of them, you can get some really pretty plate armour next time you're in Rome with your boyfriends,' added Furius, overlooking the fact that he was also disguised as a praetorian. 'If you can get a plate big enough to go over that great belly…'

'The thing to do,' advised Puella, before things got ugly, 'is to go and grab another meal as soon as you get out of here. Then everything will be in the natural order again.'

'Now that's a good idea!' said all three of them like the chorus in one of Plautus' comedies.

Artemidorus and his *crypteia* were in sole possession of the *caldarium* except for the slaves by the massage benches. He dismissed them with a gesture so the four of them could speak more freely. But, they would still have to be careful. For it was as though these walls had ears, he thought.

They had all worked together in such close proximity for so long that none of them gave Puella a second glance as she eased her naked body into the scalding water. 'You think he's telling the truth?' asked the statuesque Nubian, as she slid down to sit beside Artemidorus.

'Part of it, probably,' he answered.

'The best lies start with a grain of truth,' she nodded.

'True. But the only other element which he and Laenas might be involved in is our attempt to get Lucius and Messala safely out of Italy. And quite frankly if there are people lying around in Brundisium with their throats cut, then it's no great surprise to find that Laenas and Herrenius are there.'

Ferrata, who was also convinced the state of his face was Laenas' fault, joined in the conversation. As with Puella's nudity, they were getting used to him with his eyepatch off. 'So you think Octavianus may have sent his *carnefaces* executioners after Messala and the boy?'

'Porcia's death has changed everything. Her name is on everyone's lips,' shrugged Artemidorus. 'She is the tragic heroine of the great drama resulting from *Divus Julius'* murder. Did she kill herself through guilt at her husband's part in it? Did she hear a rumour that Brutus himself was dead? Brutus and she were closer even than normal husband and wife, remember – they were also first cousins.

Had his mother Servilia got something to do with it? She disapproved of the match most strongly and has a dangerous reputation. The entire city and a growing portion of the Republic is all a-buzz with rumour and speculation.' He readjusted his position in the steaming water, hoping to ease the muscles up the insides of his thighs. But that only made his saddle-sore backside more uncomfortable.

'The last thing Octavianus wants,' he continued, 'is for people to start saying that Porcia ate hot coals out of guilt because she'd gone to him with Calpurnia expecting to get *futabat* screwed to save her children! You know the reputation he's getting for dipping his wick in whatever vessel comes by. Especially as there isn't a lot of evidence to prove that he *didn't* screw her. While the papers removing Lucius and Messala from the proscription lists seeming to be strong evidence that he *did*!'

'Maybe that's it,' rumbled Hercules. 'Maybe he just wants those papers back.'

There was a silence as they considered this, their expressions slowly moving from consideration to disbelief. 'I can't see him stopping at that,' decided Artemidorus at last. 'Not if he's sent Laenas and Herrenius after them. Papers retrieved, *and* throats cut. Much more likely! Make doubly sure.'

'Well, let's hope they are hiding somewhere safe and sound,' concluded Puella.

*

Artemidorus was woken by a scream that choked almost instantly into silence. He sat up and discovered that his dagger was already in his hand. And that Puella was sitting beside him, also armed. The door of the room they were sharing with Furius and Ferrata stood ajar. Enough lamplight came through it to define a figure that could only belong to the Spanish soldier. He glanced over his shoulder, revealing the source of the scream and the reason for it. The landlord's daughter stood in the corridor holding a lamp in one hand while the other, closed to a fist, was pressed against her mouth. She had knocked gently and woken Ferrata who had answered the door at once and without thinking. And without his eye-patch. The ruin of the left side of his face was enough to make anyone scream. 'I thought I'd got lucky there, Septem,' he whispered. 'But Acilia here wants you.'

Artemidorus eased himself away from Puella and stood. Both, like Ferrata, were dressed in underclothes, too stiff and sore for love-play. Even so, he caught up his tunic and shrugged it on as he crept across the room, still with his dagger in his hand.

'What is it, Acilia?' he breathed.

'Come,' she answered. 'Quietly.'

'Where to?'

'You'll see. Come!'

'A woman of few words,' observed a shadow close behind him. He stepped out into the corridor, Puella at his back.

They moved silently through the *hospitium*'s upper floor, their shadows huge and grotesque on the walls and ceilings around them. Artemidorus had assumed without much thought that the inn would share the same basic design as the vast majority of villas, *tabernae* and *hospitiae* that he had stayed in during his life. But after a while he realised that Acilia was leading Puella and him into corridors and levels he had never imagined. Like Theseus and his shadow following Ariadne through the Minotaur's maze, they went deeper into the unknown. Until they came to a ladder. Leading up to yet another level – which must be immediately under the eaves, he thought. He looked up. There was a square hole cut in the ceiling. And where he might have expected it to be utterly dark up there, a faint light glimmered instead.

'Careful,' whispered Acilia. 'It's a bit dangerous.'

With one glance at Puella, Artemidorus took his dagger between his teeth and swarmed up the ladder like a Cilician pirate. He hesitated a few rungs from the top, then thrust his head up through the hole, turning automatically towards the light.

Which revealed, sitting side by side and looking sorry for themselves, Lucius Calpurnius Bibulus and Marcus Valerius Messala Corvinus.

iii

'We were trying to return to Rome in secret, so we could pay our final respects to the Lady Porcia,' whispered Messala. 'We slipped away from the two men guarding us and hired a couple of horses. We hadn't been here long before the soldiers showed up. Trapped us, effectively, because we couldn't figure out a way to get past them and escape. Then Lucius fell off the ladder when Acilia tried to hide us, and we were *really* trapped!'

Acilia and Puella had joined them and the light of two lamps was illuminating the Spartan living space that the two men had clearly been occupying for several days, since the arrival of Felix and his men. Artemidorus nodded. They had been lucky to enlist the help of Acilia and her parents. One glance at the way the young woman looked at Lucius explained how that had been achieved. And, as things had turned out, they had been wise to settle on concealment rather than risk discovery. Especially as the men who slit their bodyguards' throats might have been the men who hunted them down first. If he found himself speculating that the cut-throats might have been Popilius Laenas and Herrenius, at least circumstances seemed to prove it could not have been Felix.

'News of Porcia's death hit poor Lucius here particularly hard,' Messala was whispering urgently. 'He heard it just as gossip down by the port in Brundisium. You know the way bad news travels. And they said she killed herself! And in such a terrible fashion! Under the circumstances, I was worried about my Calpurnia too, of course…'

'Is it true?' choked Lucius, his voice breaking. 'That Mother killed herself by eating hot coals?'

'Looks like it,' answered Puella, while Artemidorus was still seeking some way to honey over the dreadful news.

'I must go to her! Even in death…' The young man moved further into the light and Artemidorus realised that his left leg was bandaged from the foot to the knee.

'No,' he said. 'I don't want either of you to go anywhere near Rome. It looks as though you'll have trouble getting out of this hiding place, let alone covering a hundred miles or more up the Via Appia.' He gestured at the bandaged limb. 'Besides, there's nothing you can do. Either of you. Your mother's funeral rites and cremation are over, Lucius. They were overseen by Servilia.' He glanced away from the stricken boy and met Messala's steady gaze. 'Servilia has also taken Calpurnia under her wing. They are both safely in Atticus' villa. All you can do if you go back is to undo the good work you have done so far. And almost certainly put yourselves at serious risk.'

'But we have the documents Octavianus signed…' said Lucius.

For the time-being you do, he thought grimly. 'Which may turn out to be worthless or worse,' he said. 'Your mother's death has changed the game completely. I don't think you'll be safe until we get you both out of Italy and beyond the Triumvirs' immediate reach.'

Lucius opened his mouth to argue, but a new voice cut his protestations off. 'Septem's right, you know,' it said, not bothering to drop to a whisper. 'The faster you can get to Brundisium and across to Macedonia, the safer you will be.'

They all swung round, and there, with his head and shoulders poking up through the trap-door, was Lucius Flavius Felix.

*

Felix's voice was followed at once by Ferrata's, more distantly, echoing up from below. 'Is this all OK with you, Septem? Furius and I have the three down here surrounded. We followed them as they were following you. Tramping around like a herd of bullocks. They'd better pray they never come across the Ghost Warriors in the Germanian forests! *And* they just brought fists to a knife fight.'

Felix gave a bark of laughter that sounded genuine to Artemidorus. Instead of answering Ferrata, he asked Felix, 'So, where do we go from here?'

'Finding these two doesn't change anything for me. I have no orders concerning them. So if they want to get to Brundisium and you want to get to Brundisium and we are going to Brundisium, I suggest we all travel together.'

Artemidorus paused, deciding whether Felix's words were the open invitation they sounded like – or an order with an unspoken threat to back it up. He strongly suspected Octavianus' squad of soldiers would not let Ferrata and Furius sneak up on them again. He sensed a rivalry beginning to build between the two groups.

'I don't think the young man will be able to ride with his leg like that,' observed Puella softly. 'He needs to see a physician.'

He met her frowning gaze and nodded. Then he turned to Messala. 'We have a physician as part of our *contubernium*. He should be here in a day or two. With Quintus and the rest. Why not leave Lucius here until Crinas can see him? Then he can come on along with Quintus and his group. They have a chariot and a cart. If he can't ride a horse he can sit in one of them. In the meantime you can choose – either come with us or wait with him.'

'You go on, Messala,' said Lucius quietly. 'Acilia will look after me until Septem's second *quadriga* team arrives. Then I can come on with them as he suggests.'

'I can bind his leg in the meantime,' said Puella. 'See whether any bones are broken. Make him more comfortable.' She nodded towards Lucius.

Artemidorus thought for a moment, then called down to Ferrata, 'It's all good here. We'll be down in a heartbeat.'

iv

They arrived in the bustling military port-town of Brundisium a little less than four days later, as the afternoon of the fifth day since their departure from Rome was drawing towards evening.

They could have arrived much earlier had Antony not given Artemidorus more than one set of orders. To be delivered to various recipients along the way. The first set concerned the legions which were stationed in a huge encampment just outside the port. The IIIrd was there as were the reconstituted VIth and VIIth, both manned and officered with legionaries familiar to Artemidorus, Messala, Felix and Ferrata. As they came through the main gate and into the familiar geometric layout of the massive camp, the travel-weary group were welcomed by the officers in charge not only as bearers of orders and news from Rome but also as old friends.

Their arrival prompted a convocation of the legates and tribunes who were currently in camp, and senior centurions as well. Which, although it took some hours to assemble, nevertheless allowed Artemidorus to pass Antony's, Norbanus' and Saxa's orders, both to specific officers and more generally to the men who oversaw the legions all at once. But the price exacted for this was their attendance at one of several informal *cenae* feasts hastily thrown together to welcome them. Felix and his companions dined with the other tribunes of the IIIrd; Furius and Ferrata with the centurions of the VIth; Artemidorus, Messala, Puella, and Hercules with the tribunes and legates of the VIIth. The slaves and gang-members ate with the troops.

'That's about it is it?' asked Flavius Servius Clio the Legate of the VIIth as they sat round a map table piled with steaming piles of roast mutton, amphorae of unwatered wine and field ration bread. Not even attempting to imitate the formal layout of a *triclinium*. Seated on camp-stools and chairs rather than reclining on *klinae* couches. Attended by legionary slaves, however, as though in Antony's own villa. The wind battered against the leather walls of Servius' command tent, making the cooking-fires outside roar and flicker like volcanic eruptions as the slaves rushed in and out with trays of food. 'We wait 'til Generals Saxa and Norbanus show up, and put ourselves under their *imperium*? Then we're off to Macedonia?'

'Exactly the same as this time two years ago,' said Publius, the senior centurion, and Artemidorus' replacement now he had been seconded into Antony's secret service. 'When we were waiting for *Divus Julius* to lead us into Parthia.'

'Except that the VIIth was on Tiber Island if I remember correctly,' said Hercules.

'Even so,' said Servius. 'All we do is wait.'

'Not quite,' answered Artemidorus. 'You need to pick a small command of your best men, led by one of your most trusted centurions. A standard century of eighty should do. They need to be ready to come with me and my group and wait at strategic points to guide you when generals Norbanus and Saxa get over to Macedonia and start to move upcountry from Dyrrhachium. We'll be crossing at the first possible opportunity. Maybe a hundred mounted men and their back-up in all – counting your command and mine. Much easier to move than several legions. All we need is a week or so of calm days, a couple of triremes and a couple of transport ships. You need the best part of a month of good weather to move your legions, ancillaries, horses and equipment.'

'True enough. I'll start sorting out your men tomorrow. A century you say.'

'Maximum. Fifty good men would suffice. Speed is paramount. Keep them here until I send for them. If I take them into Brundisium and have them hanging around in some billet there, there'll only be trouble.'

'True. Now, what's this I hear about Antony being haunted?'

'Oh that story's got around has it? He's dreamed he's seen a ghost once or twice.'

'Cicero's?'

'He can't be certain. It has no head or hands.'

'That narrows the field – well *no hands* does. There must be thousands wandering around with no heads. Being joined by yet more, day after day. And it talks, they say, even though it's got no head?'

'It says *Actium*, apparently.'

'Actium! What in the name of the gods is there at Actium?'

'It's part of my mission to find out!'

'They say *Divus Julius* still visits Brutus,' mused centurion Publius.

'And Brutus' wife Porcia.' Servius asked. 'What's this I hear about her?'

'She's Messala's mother in law – or was,' Artemidorus said quietly. 'Perhaps he should explain…'

*

The guards at Brundisium's main gate were uneasy about letting armed soldiers past with their weapons still at their belts. But both

Artemidorus and Felix carried warrants from their Triumvir masters. And what Octavianus' *imperium* did not cover, Antony's certainly did. For both were well known and popular in Brundisium.

Artemidorus and Felix had also been here before, more than once, on duty. But Messala had visited the town most recently, so they took his advice about accommodation. He guided them down to the harbour where a sizeable *hospitium* stood facing the sea. It was positioned on a hill-slope above the largely empty troop-billets, stables and storehouses that were designed to accommodate entire armies as they moved, legion by legion, between here and Dyrrhachium.

The *hospitium's* setting was excellent. The prospect less so, thought Artemidorus. Looking eastwards towards Macedonia, all he could see was a low grey sky resting like the roof of a granite cave on a restless, leaden sea. The vessels in the port all sat at anchor, oars stowed, sails furled, hulls pitching restlessly even in the comparative shelter of the inner harbour. The merest glance revealed half a dozen transport ships. Wide-bodied and barge-like, with tall masts rigged for square sails, their sides smooth wooden cliffs without holes or boxes for oars. However, secured to the quayside and slightly less restless, were two fully-decked triremes with gang-planks reaching from deck to quay, guarded at each end. Their sides were protected by fenders made out of straw bales. The boxes designed to contain the teams of rowers projecting over the quayside, clearly high enough to accommodate the rising and falling tides. The vessels' hulls were well over 120 *pedes* feet long and looked to be over twenty wide. Probably designed to double as transports as well as warships.

'I'll go in and see if the landlord can accommodate us all,' said Felix, breaking into Artemidorus' thoughts and nodding towards the *hospitium* as he slid off his horse and jumped to the ground, throwing the reins to one of his men.

A few moments later he was back. 'Looks like we're in luck,' he said. 'Food and shelter for all – and a short walk to the local baths.' He turned and strode off.

'Good,' said Artemidorus. He dragged his gaze away from the anchorage and turned. At his gesture, everyone followed Felix towards the inn with its stables and promise of food and rest – except for Artemidorus himself and Messala.

'After we've dumped our kit, Messala, you and I will take The Gaul's men and look for a local magistrate. See what we can discover about your two dead minders. Once we know more we can let Felix in on the situation. But let's not get ahead of ourselves.'

'I still can't believe it,' said Messala, dismounting and leading his horse towards the inn. 'They must have been killed almost immediately after we left…'

'Looks like you had a narrow escape then,' said Artemidorus, walking beside him, their two horses following, steaming in the icy wind. 'Because I doubt that a couple of Roman gang members will have been anyone's prime target.'

Once the stable slaves had taken the horses, Messala joined Artemidorus' *contubernium*, following Artemidorus, Puella, Ferrata and Furius to the rooms assigned to them.

'So,' he said as he returned to the massive, table-filled atrium at Artemidorus' shoulder, much of the travel dirt sluiced from hands and faces. Still strongly redolent of horse, however; still in need of a bath. 'You think whoever killed our guardians was really after us?'

'It must have occurred to you as a possibility,' said Artemidorus. 'Even if you only found out a couple of days ago, you've had plenty of time to mull it over.'

'Do you think they're still here, then?'

'It's a possibility. Not likely enough to call for armour but enough to warrant swords and daggers. Even within the city limits, so we'd better be ready to explain ourselves if we bump into the magistrate's *vigiles* patrols. Maybe Puella, Furius and Ferrata ought to watch our backs; for the time-being at least.'

*

The *capitaneria* harbour master's office was easy to find – and he was able to direct them to the villa belonging to the local *praefectus* magistrate, which was fortunately close to the port and also to the Temple of Hercules, where the bodies were still laid out. The *praefectus* was a tall, thin, balding patrician called Jovinus Caesennius Sospes. His *janitor* was reluctant to admit them, but Artemidorus' orders from Antony on their scroll with his personal seal, were referred to the *atriensis* steward, who brought it to the attention of his master, who agreed to see them, apparently without bothering to open and read them. Sospes had just finished his *cena* when they arrived, but he was in no mood to let their questions interfere with his evening's entertainment. And the odour of horses that they still gave off threatened to upset his delicate digestive processes. So he called for one of his cohort of *vigiles*, whose name was Cessy. He took them to view the corpses and answer their questions.

'We found them down an alley behind the docks,' said Cessy as they followed the backstreets leading to the temple. 'There's been a lot of trouble in that area recently. Above and beyond our usual gang stuff. I guess you get that up in Rome too. Our gangs are nothing much in comparison to what I hear about Roman ones. No. We have a couple of military triremes sitting at the quayside.'

'We saw them,' said Artemidorus. 'They look like handy vessels if they are well-crewed and commanded.'

'They're trapped here by contrary winds. Their crews are bored and restless. They're all out for trouble, both the sailors and the oarsmen when they're allowed ashore but especially the marines. The two sets of marines seem to have taken a dislike to each-other. They fight whenever they meet, which is often, because there are only so many *tabernae* near the waterfront. They're stuck here until the weather moderates or the wind changes. Keeping them fed and watered is a hell of a task. So they're allowed ashore on a regular basis you see, because the weather may not moderate 'til *Maius*. But the bottom of it as far as I can see is that the centurion commanding the troops on one of them, the *Aegeon*, is an arrogant little *nothus* bastard as rich as Croesus and has a habit of slipping my boss Gistin the Head *Vigile* a bag of *sestercii* to get his men out of trouble even if they've started it, which they usually have. But the other one, young Gaius Licinius of the *Galene* hasn't got two *obols* to rub together so his men always end up with the dirty end of the stick which puts them under lock and key in the *praefectus' carcer* prison – until Gaius Licinius can get enough money together to buy their freedom. Still, he does his best for them and they love him.'

The *vigile*'s words gave Artemidorus pause for thought. He had served on galleys in the past and knew the standard structure of crew and auxiliaries. The hull, sails and propulsion were under the command of the captain, the *navarchus*. He consulted with his *gubernator* who doubled as pilot and helmsman. Together they guided the ship, reading signs in the sea and in the sky. Beneath them there were the deck-crew of twenty or so sailors, who controlled the simple square sail. And then there were the oarsmen, volunteers on the legionary payroll rather than the slaves popular with Cilician pirates. They were usually trained to use swords and daggers though they were by no means as handy as marines in battle. There would be one hundred and seventy of them in a trireme like *Galene* or *Aegeon*, arranged in three teams, each team responsible for one bank of oars. To a certain extent, they were led by the *pausarius*, the hammer-man, who beat out the rhythm. The men sang as they rowed. So all the *pausarius* did was to dictate the rhythm of the *celeuma* or rowing song as the *navarchus* captain ordered. Unless the ship was rowing into battle, when the men rowed in silence.

But from Cessy's words it seemed both triremes were fighting vessels, as well as transports. So each also housed a complement of marines – legionaries discriminated from their land-based colleagues by their blue uniforms and standing below even praetorians in the military pecking-order. If Artemidorus ended up moving large numbers of men eastwards with him, the marines could come ashore and wait for the ships' return.

V

'But they don't usually kill each-other.' The *vigile* interrupted Artemidorus' thoughts. 'Even if they did, it would be a broken head or a stab with a dagger. Certainly not cut throats. No-one from either crew recognised them, though, when we paraded them all past. So the *dominus* says to hang onto them for a while in case someone comes to claim them. Save the municipal purse the expense of disposing of them with any luck. Which is OK I guess because it's winter and cold, so they aren't going to ripen like they would in the summer.'

As he spoke, the watchman led them all to the Temple of Hercules and, with a nod to the priest *janitor*, into the cool shadows inside. The bodies were laid out in a small interior room which was so dark that they could make nothing out until the temple slaves brought lamps. The moment they did so, they all stepped forward and stared at the dead men. Their throats had been cut. But that wasn't the half of it. Before the daggers slit their *jugulae* gullets, someone had beaten their faces to pulp. And taken a hammer to their hands, judging from the state of them. 'I suppose that's Otho and Saccus,' said Castus, one of The Gaul's two gang members with a quiet intensity that Artemidorus found worrying. 'They didn't die easy.'

'I'd like to talk to whoever did this,' growled his companion Bibulus. His hands closed into massive fists.

'Messala?' prompted Artemidorus.

'Otho and Saccus,' answered the tribune. 'I never knew their names. But yes. It's them; our guides and guardians.'

'And,' said Artemidorus quietly, 'the only reason I can give for anyone doing this, is that they were looking for Lucius and yourself.

And supposed these poor bastards knew where you were.'

'Well, let them find me,' said Messala. 'That's the quickest way. And we can get it settled before Lucius arrives with your man Quintus. Let them find me. Then we can *all* have a little chat!'

But no sooner had he finished speaking that several more watchkeepers ran into the temple. 'Cessy,' the first of them called. 'There's a battle broken out down on the docks. Those sodding marines again.'

Their guide straightened. 'That's Gistin, the head *vigile*,' he said, nodding in the direction of the rat-faced man who had spoken. 'Coming, Gistin…'

'Well bloody get a move on then. It's like Carrhae all over again down there…' But then Gistin broke off, looking at Messala, frowning. 'It's him!' he said, his voice shaking with shock. 'Him to the life. Just as they described him! And they said they often came back to look over their work!'

'What are you talking about?' Artemidorus demanded.

'*Him*!' The chief watchman pointed at Messala. 'He's the one who did this!' The finger swung towards the battered corpses of Otho and Saccus then back to Messala again. 'We have witnesses who saw everything. Described them in detail. This man and his young accomplice!'

*

Jovinus Caesennius Sospes' villa was unusual, in much the same way that Acilia's parents' *hospitium* was. The standard layout of the villa had been extended to make a residence well suited to the *praefectus* of a busy port and military facility. Added to the usual accommodations, was the large, secure room *vigile* Cessy had already mentioned. A sort of above-ground version of Rome's Tullianum prison. Less than an hour later it was proving large enough to accommodate a dozen battered and disgruntled marines in their blue naval uniforms. And Messala.

'No, Centurion. I'm afraid that will not be possible. Your friend is accused of the most dreadful crime. I cannot release him into your custody even if you do hold authority directly from Mark Antony himself.' A tiny twist of his thin lips showed Artemidorus what the magistrate thought of the Triumvir. 'And as my man Gistin here says, he and his accomplice have been identified – described in great detail – by witnesses who saw them in the act but were unfortunately too late to intervene.'

Sospes exchanged a look with Gistin, who nodded his agreement with a smirk. 'Described them clearly *dominus*. So there can be no mistake.'

Sospes nodded in reply. 'Furthermore, I understand the dead men were free citizens of Rome. So this is a clear case of murder as covered by the twelve tables of the law. He must wait here until I can question him and allow him to face his accusers. Neither of which is likely to happen tonight. You may, if you wish, bring him sustenance and I will have my watchmen, or my house-guards deliver it to him and oversee him as he eats or drinks. As they will while he uses the latrine and so-forth. He will not be comfortable, but he will be well looked-after. That is as far as I can go I'm afraid.'

vi

Still faintly redolent of horses and sweat, Artemidorus had gone with Gistin the chief watchman to report to Sospes himself and demand the immediate release of the young tribune, something that was a mere matter of form, really. Patrician tribunes would not be expected to remain incarcerated, no matter what they stood accused of. As Messala had no villa here, it was almost inevitable that he would be returned to the *hospitium* by the docks and held there, under guard, perhaps, but still in his own room with every facility and amenity. So he followed the watchkeeper to Sospes' office while Puella, Ferrata and Furius kept an eye on things by the locked prison door. Outside the *praefectus*' office door, standing despondently and clearly forbidden entry was a young man Artemidorus had no trouble identifying as the legionary commander of the *Galene*, come to seek his men's release. 'You'll have to wait,' said the watchman. 'As usual.'

Gaius Licinius shrugged. His gaze met Artemidorus', then fell, like that of a defeated gladiator in the circus.

But Artemidorus' demands also fell on deaf ears. He was not used to having his official requests turned down. Or his unofficial ones, come to that. It hadn't even occurred to him to bring Antony's commission back with him. But the magistrate was adamant. His natural reaction to having his *dignitas* undermined in such a manner was simple outrage. And apart from his house-guards, he had at least twenty watchmen within calling distance. All armed with a lot more than buckets, as the brutal manner in which they broke up the fight between the triremes' crews had proven.

But after a moment of reflection, Artemidorus realised that he was more suspicious than angry. Cessy's unguarded words about the willingness of his bosses to be swayed by bribes abruptly brought a thoughtful frown. The ease with which the rich-as-Croesus commander of the *Aegeon*'s complement of soldiers could get his men free – as opposed to the difficulties faced by Gaius Licinius of the *Galene* who didn't even have two *obols* to rub together. Whose men were in the locked room with Messala while he was forced to kick his heels out here, almost as powerless as Artemidorus now found himself to be. Perhaps the willingness to accept bribes went higher than chief *vigile* Gistin.

Artemidorus wondered for an instant whether he should point out to Sospes, whose sympathies clearly lay with *Divus Julius'* murderers, that he was standing in the way of a proscribed patrician trying to escape to Brutus' camp. But no – he was far too close to being convinced that the magistrate's motives were financial rather than political. And that the revelation would only make Messala an item that could be sold to a wider range of bidders for an even higher price.

Glancing round the *tablinum* as Sospes delivered his patronising verdict, Artemidorus was struck by how little there was in the way of books, papyri, busts, statues and adornments. The room already looked as though it had been stripped by a rapacious mob. Like the villas of the proscribed in Rome. Just like the corridors and public spaces he had seen in Sospes' villa so far, he realised. And because, looking at matters from the *praefactus*' point of view, the need for ready money might explain the lack of expensive adornments – might well outweigh all other considerations after all. If Sospes was of the *Libertores*' faction, then it was only a matter of time before he found himself proscribed. And at least one factor famously contributing to the deaths of Cicero, his brother and his nephew was that when they tried running to safety last *Decembre* they found they had too little ready money to pay for their escape. Something a man like Sospes would no doubt try to avoid – no matter where the vital extra *sestertii* came from.

*

Artemidorus followed Gistin out of Sospes' *tablinum* office, still deep in thought. Gaius Licinius had gone. The corridor was as empty of humanity as it was of statuary. Perhaps the *praefectus* had started selling off his slaves as well as his statues. 'Which way back to the locked room?' he demanded.

'Down there, *dominus*.' The *vigile* gestured to a long corridor. 'I can't come with you myself, I'm afraid. But you'll probably bump into a slave. They'll lead you…' The head watchman scurried off in the opposite direction, clearly about some important business. Artemidorus remembered the look Gistin and Sospes had exchanged when talking about the witnesses. He took half a dozen steps down the indicated corridor, making sure the hob-nails on his boots crashed loudly against the floor-tiles. Then he paused, turned and, making sure he was unobserved, tip-toed back. At the far end of the corridor he had taken, Gistin was just letting himself out of the *posticum* side door to the villa. Stepping out into a dark alley and vanishing into the shadows.

Artemidorus began to follow the scampering rodent. He regretted that there was no time to contact the others, all too well aware of the danger of following men he did not trust through sections of cities he did not know well. Heading for clandestine meetings with people he suspected of torturing and killing hulking gang-members; with a cloak over his tunic instead of a suit of mail.

For whatever good that would be against a well-honed *pugio* or the needle-sharp point of a *gladius*.

V: Laenas

i

Although the path they were following was in complete darkness, the scuttling watchman's body was silhouetted against the brightness of a wider *via* at the far end. An avenue running past the front of this villa and many others whose civic-minded owners kept blazing flambeaux outside their doors. Dodging from shadow to shadow, Gistin led Artemidorus back down towards the docks, unaware he was being followed. Retracing the route up which he had brought Gaius Licinius' arrested crewmen. But at the last minute, he turned right into another narrow alleyway. This was also familiar from the break-up of the fight and the arrest of *Galene*'s marines. There was a *taberna* down here. It hadn't looked as big as the *hospitium* on the dockside, but it had been large enough to accommodate nearly fifty men from the two warring triremes' crews. And it clearly had rooms upstairs, from where a line of heavily-shuttered windows overlooked the alley and the more distant quayside. Artemidorus paused on the corner. And was about to follow Gistin, when the hairs on the back of his neck prickled. He was being followed himself. He glanced over his shoulder, raking the shadows with narrow eyes. No sign of life or movement, other than that created by the wind which also generated sufficient noise to cover all but the loudest sounds. He would never hear a quiet footfall close behind him, or the whisper of a blade sliding out of its sheath.

No help for it now, he thought. He plunged into the shadowy side-street with one hand on the pommel of his *gladius* and the other on the grip of his *pugio*. The hesitation, brief though it was, allowed Gistin to pull well ahead. Artemidorus caught a fleeting glimpse of him turning off the narrow alley and apparently into the *taberna* itself. But it was hard to see clearly, for the fight that had erupted there had caused a significant amount of damage. The front of the place was in partial darkness – interior lamps and exterior flambeaux extinguished. So the only light came from the flame of the huge phallic *fascinum* that still hung above the door, creaking and flaring unsteadily.

Artemidorus ran on, trying to catch up with the little *vigile*. His *gladius* slapped distractingly against his right thigh as his *pugio* bumped against his left hip. He was tired, dirty and extremely hungry – by no means in the best condition to face such an adventure. As he discovered a few moments before he planned to turn into the shattered front of the *taberna*. For Gistin had not gone into the building itself, he had vanished into an even smaller alley running up beside it, knocked on the *posticum*, and had been greeted by someone waiting for him at the side door. It stood ajar, allowing just enough light out to gild the outlines of two men standing head to head, deep in conversation. He recognised Gistin at once then caught his breath as his worst fears came true. For the other figure was Octavianus' ruthless *carnifex* torturer, tribune Popilius Laenas. Young Caesar's intelligence chief Maecenas' most murderous secret agent. The man who had taken Cicero's head and hands.

He hesitated again for a heartbeat, then tensed his body ready to run up the alley and challenge the whispering men. But even as he did so, his hood was torn back and the icy blade of a *pugio* rested across his throat.

*

'*Salve* Septem,' growled a familiar voice. 'If you're so interested in the tribune's conversation, why don't we join in?'

'*Salve*, Herrenius,' answered Artemidorus to Laenas' faithful and brutal centurion. 'That's just what I was planning. So let's get on with it.' He took his hands off the grips of both *gladius* and *pugio* and allowed the centurion to hustle him forward.

The wind eased so that the voices in the distance came clearer. 'One of them at least,' Gistin was saying. 'The *dominus* will hold him as long as you want. If the price is right.'

'But only one?'

'My second in command Cessy says he overheard this one saying that the other one will be here in a day or two with someone called Quintus…'

'That's my man Quintus,' Artemidorus broke into the conversation, his voice as cold as the blade of the *pugio* stinging his gullet.

'I thought it would be, Septem,' answered Laenas easily. As though he knew the spy was there all along. 'As soon as Gistin here said *Quintus*, not to mention of course that we saw you out of our bedroom window as you observed *praefactus* Sospes' watchmen breaking up the fight outside our door.'

'So, Tribune,' persisted Gistin, 'do we act now or wait?'

'If we wait we double our money,' growled Herrenius.

'Not quite double it,' answered Laenas easily. 'Because, one way or another, the good *praefectus* will supply so much more and allow us to recover the bribes we have paid him so far but a further element, certainly – an extra two thousand five hundred Attic *drachmae* – enough to make us pause for thought.'

Artemidorus gave a cynical grunt. 'So, you have bribed the *praefectus* to bring you Messala and Lucius, whose heads are worth just as much as Cicero's was. Whose pardons, signed by Octavianus, may be worth still more. *One way or another* as you say. And then you take Sospes' head as well – worth an equal amount when you add his name to the lists in the Forum. But before you take it you make him return the money you used to bribe him in the first place! Money, with all the other money he has accrued, to finance his escape to the East but which he won't need, of course, once you've taken his head..'

The *vigile* stepped back into a shaft of brightness that showed the simple horror on his face. 'You plan to take our *praefectus*' head?' he choked.

Laenas turned towards him, his face catching just enough brightness to illuminate a rueful smile. 'Sorry, Gistin,' he said. 'Septem has seen through us all. And that means you know too much.' The right half of his body moved forward in a short, brutal gesture, as though he was shoulder-barging the watchkeeper. Who staggered back, gasping for breath and looked down to see the handle of a dagger sticking out from his chest.

As the watchkeeper crumpled silently into the gutter, Laenas reached down to jerk his dagger free. He rolled the corpse onto its back with a casual kick. He reached down again, to wipe his dagger clean on Gistin's tunic, and to cut the dead man's purse free of his belt. He straightened, hefting the leather bag in his hand. 'I told you, Herrenius,' he said, oozing satisfaction. 'Every *sestertius* we paid him is still in here. They always do that. Too mean to share it and too scared of losing it. It's always on their belts, which is more or less where the traitor Sospes' bribes will be – with all the money he's amassed from selling his possessions in preparation for his escape. How rich will all that make us?'

'Is it worth waiting for the boy, then?' asked Artemidorus. 'What difference will one more head make?'

'To me and my fortune, not a lot as I said,' answered Laenas. 'Oh but to Maecenas and Octavianus, all the difference in the world. Given what the boy knows about his mother, his sister and the young

Caesar. As, I'm sure, my personal assurance that *your* tongue is forever silenced in the matter will do as well.'

'And who will assure him of *your* silence, Laenas?' asked Artemidorus. 'Yours and Herrenius'? As you both seem to know as much as Messala, Lucius and I do? Who will guard the guards in the end?'

'*Me*, perhaps,' said a new voice as Felix joined the conversation by sliding his dagger across Herrenius' throat.

ii

'Now this is interesting,' purred Laenas. 'Looks like you're in trouble Herrenius – almost as much trouble as Septem. One wrong move, two cut throats and Felix and I will be moving on with our lives.'

'I wouldn't count on that, tribune,' said Puella as she stepped out of the shadows behind Felix, sword in hand. Laenas gave a shout of laughter – which was cut off when Ferrata stepped out of the shadows behind him, sword in one hand dagger in the other. He didn't need to say he still suspected Laenas was responsible for the damage to his face or the death of his friend. The simple hatred seemed to shine out of him like light from a lamp.

'A dramatic moment,' said Felix cheerfully. 'Laenas, you get to choose whether the drama in question is a comedy by Plautus or a tragedy by Sophocles.'

'I'd suggest we go with Plautus,' said Artemidorus, 'and die another day.'

'I agree,' said Laenas, beginning to recover his arrogance. 'Plautus it is. *The Pot of Gold* seems appropriate. Herrenius, let's get rid of this corpse and continue as planned. Our immediate plan, Septem, is to do nothing but await events, primarily the arrival of your man Quintus and young Lucius Calpurnius Bibulus, his head and his pardon; both, perhaps, for the taking.'

Herrenius' blade moved away from Artemidorus' throat – at, he assumed, much the same speed as Felix' moved away from his.

*

'He's working on the assumption that there's nowhere we can go,' said Felix as the four of them walked back to the *hospitium*. 'And, under the circumstances, precious little we can do. He's going to bribe that poor fool Sospes to make sure none of us gets out of the city gates while using his *vigiles* to watch us while we're trapped in the port.'

'Which he's probably done already,' answered Artemidorus.

'True.'

'Just as he did by getting the *vigiles* to look for Messala and Lucius by describing them as the murderers. An intelligent move, especially as he's now recovered some of the bribe money.'

'Now that it's worked – they did catch your young tribune, didn't they? A clever move, which now looks as though it's trapped us here 'til Quintus arrives.'

'I agree,' nodded Artemidorus. 'But unless he's thought a good deal further than that then he's already failed. Because Laenas has only ever been a land-based legionary as far as I know. I would wager that he hasn't realised that, by its very nature, it's impossible to completely seal a port. Unless you have a navy to help you.'

'Meaning?'

'You'll see. Puella, Ferrata, can you do without anything to eat for a while longer?'

'Yes,' answered Puella. 'It's a bath I want, not a feast.'

'Each to his own,' growled Ferrata who ranked sustenance over cleanliness on all occasions.

'Right. You two go back to the *hospitium*. Puella, pick up my saddle bag with Mercury's winged staff on the side and meet me at Sospes' villa. Ferrata, sneak out as best you can. Steal a horse if you have to and ride for Legate Servius or Centurion Publius of the VIIth. Tell them what's going on.'

As the pair of them hurried off to do as ordered, Artemidorus turned to Felix. 'Right, down to the harbour then. There's someone there I want to talk to.'

Artemidorus was fortunate. The man he wanted was just coming ashore, walking wearily down the gang-plank that reached up to the foredeck of his trireme. 'Centurion Gaius Licinius,' he said. 'Going back to try and get them out again?'

'Yes,' answered the young soldier, managing to fill the single syllable with a world of bitterness.

'Mind if we come along with you? I'm personally responsible for the one prisoner who does not belong to you. And one of my men is still waiting at the door.'

'It won't do you much good to come with me,' said Gaius Licinius, 'unless you have a bag of *sestertii* as big as a silver pig.'

'Oh, I have that. And so much more,' Artemidorus assured him.

The three men walked side by side up to the prefect's villa. Once again the *janitor* was hesitant to admit them, but the steward sensed trouble and asked them to wait while he summoned the master. It was growing very late now. But there was little doubt that Sospes had been summoned from his bed. The wait they endured alone hinted at that – for he was dressed in his formal toga when he finally arrived and was wearing all his badges of office. But even that measured insult turned out to be a good thing in more than one way. First, it gave the spy, interest piqued, a chance to examine the stripped room even more closely, mentally cataloguing the missing artefacts as he did so. And secondly, it allowed Puella to arrive with Artemidorus' saddle bag. As she stood watching, he continued his inspection of the empty niches in the office walls until one at last brought him up short. More than a niche or alcove, it was a traditional household shrine. Fully adorned, with the names of dead forbears likely to visit from the Elysian Fields or wherever beyond the Styx they currently resided, all numbered and ranked in generation after generation. But the shrine was empty. Where the statues of Sospes' household gods and *lares* should have stood, there was nothing.

This more than anything told Artemidorus that – for all his airs and arrogance – the prefect was a desperate and terrified man on the verge of fleeing for his life. The spy's first instinct was to warn him about Laenas' murderous plans. And, had Sospes allowed him to take breath he might well have done so.

iii

The prefect launched straight into another patronising diatribe, his nostrils twitching along with his thin, pallid lips. 'I see you have sunk to the depth of the common pauper Gaius Licinius. I suppose I should have expected nothing less. And now you come crawling, reeking like a stable slave, with your pleas for mercy and promises to pay for your friend's freedom as soon as you are able. Disturbing the sleep of officials whose only motivation is to do their job in a manner that will bring credit to their name, advancement to their standing and glory to the Republic! Were my wife still alive, I would call the full weight of the noble house of the *Papirii Masones* on your heads. Even in these degenerate times, I believe their power and influence would have you both condemned to the Circus to fight and die or be consumed by wild beasts! I anticipate your questions and the answer is NO! And now you have left it too late even to bring them drink and sustenance, so the entire rabble can go without anything until I see them myself tomorrow. Or the day after.'

Artemidorus simply held out his hand. Puella passed the saddle bag. The centurion pulled out a document, unrolled it and began to read as though the prefect had said nothing. 'I, Marcus Antonius, Triumvir, through the power of the senate and people of Rome declare my good servant Centurion Iacomus Graecas Artemidorus my ambassador to speak with my voice and act with my will. I call upon any and every citizen of Rome no matter where in the Republic they may be, their dependents, families, servants and slaves to obey him in all things or face impeachment before the Senate or proscription forthwith depending on which the Centurion considers more expedient…'

'Words!' snarled Sospes. 'And empty ones at that. Antony has no power here. And neither do you. I am the power here. I, my watchkeepers under the command of Chief *Vigile* Gistin! And, should I need to call on them, the marine detachment of the trireme *Aegon* under the command of centurion Severus Manlius Torquilatus.' He glared around the room with the expression Marcus Licinius Crassus had worn while looking over the tattered remains of Spartacus' defeated army. Never knowing that in the not-too-distant future his own army would be slaughtered with his son and himself on the Parthian battlefield of Carrhae.

Sospes was drawing breath to continue with his diatribe when there came a thunderous knocking at the door. A moment or two of outraged vituperation, then Ferrata arrived with Centurion Publius of the VIIth legion. Both fully armed. Both crashing to attention the moment they entered. 'My command is drawn up immediately outside, Centurion,' Publius said to Artemidorus. 'One century of legionaries, fully armed and mounted. Awaiting your orders!'

*

An hour later, Artemidorus, Puella, Ferrata, Furius, Hercules, Messala and Publius were seated around the largest table in the *hospitium*'s ample atrium. As they settled down to some serious eating and drinking, Felix joined them. Followed swiftly by Gaius Licinius, the *navarchus* captain of *Galene,* his *pausator* hammer-man and the *gubernator* pilot and helmsman who worked so closely with them. The bustle outside slowly died as Publius' men and their horses were settled to rest in the ample dockside provision for legionaries and cavalry.

'What I want you to do, Publius, is arrange patrols to work with the *vigiles*. Their new leader will be a man called Cessy. He's not the brightest spark in the fire but he seems honest and willing. No more bribes. No fights. No arrests if you can help it. Licinius, can you offer secure accommodation aboard *Galene* if we need it?'

'Of course…' the slightly dazed young officer would have offered anything to the man who was so suddenly sorting his life out for him. It was like the unexpected discovery of a big brother willing to stand against the world with you.

'Right. That circumvents Sospes and puts things back in our hands for the time-being, though we will have to keep a careful eye out for Popilius Laenas, who won't be happy that we have emasculated his puppet law-keeper – and probably ruined several of his most devious get-rich-quick schemes. He's helpless for the moment but he'll think of a way round whatever we do, given time.'

'Perhaps he should be in Sospes' prison,' suggested Gaius Licinius.

'Too dangerous. Too dangerous even to slit his throat and dump him and Herrenius in the harbour,' said Artemidorus. 'He's working for Octavianus – remotely, but even so. We have to handle Laenas very carefully indeed. Cross him when we can and block his murderous schemes. But never give him a genuine complaint to take back to young Caesar – unless there is no alternative.'

'That's like going into the Circus Maximus with one hand tied behind your back,' said Gaius Licinius.

'Even so. That's just the way it is,' Artemidorus answered. 'Publius, could you send two of your fastest and most reliable men to Rome? They need to take a message for me to the tribune Enobarbus. He'll pass it on to Antony. But I suspect that Brundisium is going to need a new *praefectus* any day now. And one who backs the Triumvirate. *Navarchus*, *gubernator*, I need *Galene* ready to sail at a moment's notice the moment the weather moderates. We may get to use the sails but if not, get the oarsmen ready for a long haul towing a fat troop carrier or two if need-be. I know the sea will stay choppy for some time after the wind drops or shifts to a new quarter, but it is of critical importance that I get my men and equipment, Publius' men and their horses to Dyrrhachium at the earliest opportunity. There's only one other thing I need to do before I bathe and get to bed. Licinius, would you care to accompany me aboard *Aegeon*? It would be discourteous not to bring centurion Severus Manlius Torquilatus up to date with the new arrangements. And in any case, I'm on the hunt for a missing household statue.'

iv

As Artemidorus and Gaius Licinius hurried past *Galene*, there was the sound of muted cheering and the guard at the foot of the gangplank leading up to the foredeck slammed smartly to attention, as did the four soldiers also standing guard beneath the flambeau on the deck itself. The guard at the foot of *Aegeon*'s gangplank was asleep on his feet and hardly registered the two figures brushing past him to bound up aboard the ship he was supposed to be guarding. The legionaries at the head of the plank were no more wakeful, but Artemidorus had no intention of exploring the vessel unannounced. Especially as he had a strong impression that Severus Manlius Torquilatus was likely to be every bit as arrogant as Sospes had been. And one way or another, the spy was going to have to rely on his co-operation.

He presented himself formally in a clipped, military tone that rode over the keening of the wind in the rigging. Explaining who he was and what he wanted, as the guards woke up properly, riding the rise and fall, pitch and roll of the deck as though he were a sailor rather than a spy. It was this fact, and that he was accompanied by the familiar figure of Gaius Licinius, that impressed the soldiers with the need to pay close attention. Then, as soon as Artemidorus had finished speaking, one of them turned and marched off to summon the centurion Severus.

Severus did not keep them waiting as long as Sospes had done. But he was not happy at being roused in the middle of the night. As he approached down the deck, led by the returning guard who now carried a smaller version of the flambeau burning above on the foredeck, Artemidorus got an opportunity to compare the two centurions on whom, at least part of, the next stage of his mission relied. Gaius Licinius was slim, muscular and tall. Under most circumstances his movements were economical, decisive. Severus was unexpectedly portly. He puffed along behind his blue-clad marine, his black curls glinting in the light as though oiled. As he neared, Artemidorus saw brown eyes under frowning brows above little walls of fat which sat on top of his rubicund cheeks and ran into the jowls where his cheekbones should have been. Gaius Licinius had intelligent blue eyes, a long, lean nose and a square jaw. Severus' was short, turned up and sat above a mouth that would have graced a Cupid on a wall-painting. There was little evidence of any chin at all. As he arrived, his face moved almost comically between the sneer it was accustomed to wearing when talking to Gaius Licinius and the respectful frown designed to flatter the unknown but clearly powerful man standing beside him. At least, until he noticed that the stranger had not bathed in some time and smelt distinctly of horses. 'Centurion Iacomus Artemidorus,' he said, eventually as he came to a stop but not to attention. 'Do I know you?' The implication being that were this dirty stranger anyone of standing then Severus would most certainly know him.

'*Primus pilum* senior centurion of the old VIIth,' said Artemidorus. 'Seconded to Triumvir Mark Antony's personal staff. I speak with his voice, as I have just finished explaining to *praefectus* Sospes. Soon to be ex-*praefectus* Sospes.'

'Ahhhh…' Much nervous revelation and calculation was contained in that one long syllable. 'And how can I be of service to Triumvir Mark Antony and yourself, Centurion?'

'Can your quarters accommodate the three of us while we talk things over?'

'Certainly. I have a modest *tablinum*…'

*

Because two of the teams of oarsmen sat in boxes built onto the outside of the hull, some of the interior, especially at the lower levels, was available for accommodation and cargo stowage. The marines had their own section below – though the vessel had the facility to erect wooden-walled castles on the weather deck which could also be used as cabins as well as battle fortresses. The marines' sleeping area was entered through a hatchway on the after deck and so Artemidorus got to walk almost the whole length of the ship, looking down into the rowers' boxes with their oars stowed securely along the tops of the benches usually occupied by the *triniti*, top rowers. Out across the deck to the stormy anchorage, counting the number of transport vessels anchored there, by counting the signal lanterns suspended in their rigging. And, finally, up at the crosstrees of the naked mast with the sail tightly furled. Though none of it was quite as ship-shape as *Galene*'s. The rigging sighed and whispered. The fenders screamed as the waves threw the weight of the hull against them. The wind sounded in the open oar-holes, occasionally playing the entire ship as though it was a flute. He found himself humming the old rowers' song, the words running through his head in the rhythm that guided the rowers:

HEIA *VIRI NOSTRUM REBOANS ECHO SONNET* ***HEIA***

'*Hey men! Echo resounding, send back our Hey*!' he sang softly to himself. Balling his fists and easing his shoulders as he sang. As though he was going to heave on his oar at each repetition of *Hey*!

At the foot of the companionway was another legionary out of uniform, holding a terracotta lamp with three fat wicks burning with three tall flames. Severus took this, held it high, and stooping, led the way forward. Back towards the distant foredeck.

In *Aegeon's* aft section, with the main deck low above them supported by beams that made it lower still, rough wooden-walled cabins had been constructed on either side of a narrow corridor. Their entrances were ineffectually sealed by curtains, which swayed with the ship's motion and fluttered in the breeze that somehow managed to sneak in.

'Not far now,' Severus assured them. But Artemidorus was hardly listening. Stooping with the practised ease of someone who had served on ships in the not too distant past, feeling his hair brush the rough wood of the beams. His head full of the old rowers' song while his ears were filled with the familiar sounds of being on shipboard. His gaze moved to where the light of the lamp illuminated. Until, in the last cabin before Severus' modest *tablinum*, he saw what he had been seeking. A shelf in an apparently vacant compartment revealed by a flapping curtain and lit for a moment by that three-flamed light. On which were standing precisely the sorts of family gods and *lares* so obviously missing from *praefectus* Sospes' villa. But then he hesitated for a heartbeat before he followed the others and the light. His satisfaction at having found Sospes' bolt-hole challenged by the suspicion that there was someone hidden in one of the other curtained chambers who was watching him.

*

For an hour or more, the three men sat squashed around Severus' table, discussing Artemidorus' plans and how best to fulfil them. How to accommodate the men with him and those with Quintus, the wagons, Publius' century and their horses for the one-day trip across to Dyrrhachium. It would certainly require both vessels, and Artemidorus was experienced enough to realise that he would also need some of the *oneraria* cargo vessels he had already spied to transport the horses, the wagons and at least some of the troops. Towing them right across to Dyrrhachium was out of the question, however. So the crossing would only be possible for all concerned if the wind shifted into the west and sat there for some days.

But the involvement of *oneraria* – how many and how big – was something they would have to decide upon in more detail when Quintus arrived and the two ships' captains with their helmsmen and the harbourmaster saw what all would be required. The three soldiers made what plans they could then summoned a slave amanuensis to record their basic decisions.

'I'll meet with the two *navarchs* and their *gubernatores* first thing tomorrow. If you could inform them,' said Artemidorus at last. 'I'll be in the harbourmaster's office at the end of *hora duo* the second hour after dawn. They'll know whether any cargo vessels we need are available and where we can find them quickest. In the meantime, I would like you to work with Publius by splitting your men into patrols to back up the legionaries he has out and the *vigiles*. Severus, I suspect you already have an agreement with Prefect Sospes to get him over to Dyrrhachium as soon as possible. I suggest you send a squad to bring him aboard now. Tonight. His life is at risk every moment he is unprotected. And Gaius Licinius, I assume facilities aboard *Galene* are similar to these, so I would like you to prepare two cabins the same way that Severus here has prepared the *praefectus*'. For Sospes is by no means the only man in immediate danger.'

'You would allow me to smuggle a friend of Cassius' out of Italy?' said Severus, stunned. '*You*? Antony's man?'

'I am myself smuggling two men recently named on the proscription list who are on their way to Brutus,' answered the secret agent easily. 'We live in complicated times, Severus Manlius.'

V

Artemidorus was returning from his meeting with the triremes' captains and helmsmen at the harbourmaster's late next morning when the bustle around the *hospitium* warned him that something important was happening. It took him only moments to deduce that Quintus and the rest of the *contubernium* had arrived.

The spy's first thought was that this almost instantly put Messala and Lucius in immediate danger from Laenas and Herrenius. Who had only been holding back as they waited for just this moment. His overriding concern, therefore, was to get the two young patricians into the safety of *Galene*'s marine quarters before the murderous tribune and his vicious centurion could catch up with them.

He was hurrying forward when he heard his name being called, and turned to see Cessy, the new Head *Vigile,* with a couple of his watchkeepers running after him. 'Centurion,' gasped the *vigile*, 'you must come! Quickly!'

Artemidorus stopped, torn. 'Can it wait Cessy?'

'No, Centurion.' The little man shuddered. 'You must come now!'

'Which of these is more reliable, Cessy?'

'Lollius here,' Cessy pointed at a tubby, balding man with quick brown eyes.

'Lollius. This is very important. I want you to go to the trireme *Galene*. Find Centurion Gaius Licinius and tell him I, Centurion Artemidorus, said he must send some men to bring Messala and Lucius aboard at once and double the deck guards. Do you understand?'

Lollius repeated his orders accurately and hurried off to fulfil them.

Artemidorus pursed his lips in mild frustration at being forced to delegate something so important. Then turned. 'What is it, Cessy?'

'Come…' the *vigile* said more but was hurrying away so swiftly that his words were lost. Artemidorus strode after him. His frown deepening and his heart sinking as he saw where they were heading.

Had the villa of *praefectus* Sospes seemed deserted and ravaged on his earlier visits, it was even worse now. The main door stood ajar. There was no sign of the *janitor*. Artemidorus slid his *gladius* out of its sheath and pushed the door wider. Likewise, as Artemidorus followed the two *vigiles* through the atrium, the officious *atriensus* was notable by his absence. Artemidorus slid out his dagger, noting with mild surprise that the hairs on his forearms were all erect as though suddenly swept by an icy breeze. The house was eerily silent, except for the occasional whimper of wind and the echoes of their footsteps. Artemidorus knew what had happened even before he caught the first faint whiff of iron on the unquiet air. Long before Cessy silently pushed open the door to the *tablinum*.

Sospes was seated at his desk. His hands lay on the wooden top amid a jumble of papyrus scrolls, nailed in place by short iron spikes. His fingers were spread, and it was clear that most of them had been broken. Behind his shoulders at head-level was a square vacancy that Artemidorus vaguely recalled as having contained one of the few pieces remaining in the room, a box of some kind. It was gone. And he could see quite clearly that it was gone because the prefect's head, which should have obscured it, was gone too.

Experienced in such matters one way and another, Artemidorus understood that the supercilious patrician – no doubt in considerable discomfort judging from the state of his hands, had been alive when his head was removed. With one expert lateral stroke, delivered side to side rather than back to front, almost certainly with a well-sharpened cavalry *spada* long sword rather than a *gladius* and probably in the instant after he admitted that the fortune he was planning to use for his escape was contained in the missing box. There was surprisingly little blood on the wall or the shelves. But a huge puddle of it soiled the ceiling immediately above the corpse, and was still dripping sluggishly onto the spotted toga, the broken hands and the ruined papyri. And a trail across the floor marked where the severed head had bounced almost as far as the door. 'I shouldn't have trusted young Severus to act as swiftly as I needed,' he said. 'He seems to have let me down.'

'No, Centurion. That's not fair,' said Cessy. 'Centurion Severus came himself. I was here. He told the *praefectus* you suggested he would be safer in the cabin they were preparing for him aboard *Aegeon*. But the prefect refused to go. He said he would take no advice from a mud-covered soldier who stank of horses, even if he did speak with Antony's authority and have a century of cavalry at his command.'

'That was his last mistake, then,' said Artemidorus. 'Have him moved to the Temple of Hercules and put him beside the other two.'

'Then what, Centurion?'

'Then I'll have to work out a way to deal with this. One that does not end up with Octavianus adding my name to his proscription lists.'

*

Artemidorus, Publius, Felix and Cessy climbed the stairs towards the door of Laenas' *hospitium* room in single file. Artemidorus arrived at it first and knocked as the others assembled on the landing behind him. Using his left hand, as his right hand contained a roll of papyrus.

'*Immea*! Enter!'

The curt imperative was still echoing as Artemidorus pushed the door wide. The room was unexpectedly large and well-furnished. There was a sizeable bed, a desk by the window whose shutters stood ajar, giving a good view of the via below. Beside the table were two chairs – both occupied. On the table was the box missing from Sospes' study. Hanging from the back of one chair was a rough sack that contained something the size and weight of a cabbage. The bottom of the sack was sopping with blood which was dripping into a small puddle on the floor. Leaning against it was a long cavalry *spada* with a blood-smeared blade and a wickedly sharp-looking edge.

'You're slowing down, Septem. I expected you some time ago,' sneered Laenas.

'I had some errands to run on my way here,' Artemidorus answered.

'Collecting your little *factio* gang together,' nodded Laenas. 'Associating with The Gaul is having an unfortunate effect on you. Didn't you dare meet me face to face?'

'Doing you a favour, as a matter of fact. Saving you some trouble.'

'How thoughtful. In what way?'

Artemidorus held up the scroll. 'Collecting young Caesar's pardons from Messala Corvinus and Lucius Bibulus,' he said. 'These are clearly no protection now, and will be no use to them when they get out of Italy in any case. So you're welcome to them. The men to whom they are addressed are under guard and out of your reach.' Artemidorus lobbed the pardons at Laenas, who watched as they landed on the box, bounced onto the table and then fell onto the floor, rolling until the puddle of blood snared them like lime on a twig snaring a bird.

'Generous,' said Laenas. 'But unnecessary. I could have got them myself even more easily than I got this,' he gestured at the box.

'Take them and go, Laenas. There's nothing more for you in Brundisium. No more money. No more heads.'

'You hear that, Herrenius?' Laenas pulled himself to his feet and faced Artemidorus – though he continued speaking to his companion. 'This jumped-up Greek nonentity thinks he can order me about. Thinks because he's one of Antony's bum-boys that he outranks Caesar Octavianus' agents. That, because he's a centurion with a *cohor* gaggle of soldiers at his beck and call, he can give orders to a tribune. That just because…' As he spat the last few words he thrust his face even closer to Artemidorus', spraying the rock-like centurion with spittle and outrage.

Artemidorus punched him on the chin, as hard as he could. The blow started below his waist on the right side beside his *gladius*, and rose with incredible speed and with every ounce of the soldier's strength behind it. It connected with a crisp *crunch*! Artemidorus thought for a moment he had broken his knuckles. But even if he had, it was worth it.

Laenas had never been punched before. He had seen men in the arena fighting with *cestii* spiked gloves and knuckle dusters. He had seen legionaries sparring as part of their training but had never taken part himself. As a boy and young man, the closest he had come was an occasional bout of wrestling. Even in battle he had never been punched like that, his helmet's cheek-flaps protecting much of his face.

There was a look of incredulous outrage in his expression for less than a heartbeat. Then his eyes rolled up and he crashed backwards onto the floor. Herrenius leapt up, but Felix kicked his chair so that he stumbled over it and fell. Then Felix kicked him in the head and he too lay still.

'Right,' said Artemidorus. 'That went well. Cessy, take them to Sospes' prison cell and lock them in. Publius, mount a guard on the door. Allow them the usual amenities but watch them closely. Felix, I plan to let them out just before we sail, when everyone else is safely aboard. But I'm relying on you to do that if I don't get the chance. And let's hope that whoever told me the weather might not moderate 'til May was mistaken.'

VI: Cache

i

As soon as Artemidorus stepped out of the *hospitium* after *jentaculum* next morning, he sensed a change. The wind was fitful and slightly warmer. The overcast was showing signs of breaking up and the moderation of weather meant that the sea was a little calmer. The rollers coming in from the strait between Brundisium and Dyrrhachium were smaller and slower. Certainly, the *onerariae* transport vessels anchored in the harbour were less restless and the two triremes tethered to the quayside were no longer heaving against their screaming straw-bail fenders.

Artemidorus pulled his cloak a little tighter, wondering whether he should have strapped on his *gladius* and *pugio*. Even with Laenas and Herrenius locked away, he could not shake off the feeling there was more trouble brewing. He stared at the two triremes, glad he had still insisted Messala and Lucius sleep aboard. Messala was in the luxurious accommodation aboard *Aegeon* that Sospes no longer needed, and Lucius was safely under Gaius Licinius' wing aboard *Galene*.

'Things are looking up,' growled Quintus, arriving at his shoulder. He took a bite from the *emer* bread that formed his breakfast.

Artemidorus nodded. 'Better get ready to move and pray the gods aren't just teasing us,' he said.

Artemidorus had spent a busy afternoon after seeing Laenas and Herrenius locked safely away. He had emptied their room and checked through everything he found there. Which included a lot of money and several documents, the most important of which were commissions from Octavian's spymaster Maecenas, which did not contain any direct orders – merely a general demand, not too dissimilar from the commission he himself held from Antony. He also found Octavianus' pardons to Messala and Lucius – carefully retrieved from the floor and wiped clean of Sospes' blood. He had nowhere safer to store everything, so he left it all where it was, warned the innkeeper and left an armed guard on the door.

Then he reunited Sospes' head with the rest of his body and made arrangements for the dead *praefectus* to be returned to Rome and whatever family he had there. For cremation and interment in the family vault according to custom. He thought of sending for the household gods and any other effects Sospes had been keeping in the accommodations aboard *Aegeon*. But more urgent matters distracted him – and so he sent no-one. A couple of decisions he would come to regret.

The entire *contubernium* then discussed their position and plans all afternoon, evening and far into the night. Felix and his men had been – courteously but firmly – excluded from everything except the meals. The Gaul's men Castus and Bibulus and centurion Publius had been admitted to some of the deliberations as well as to *prandium* and *cena* – but by no means all of them. Not, to be fair, that there was anything much that needed to be kept secret from any of them. The food in the *hospitium* was excellent. So excellent, that Artemidorus almost regretted sending it to Laenas and Herrenius in the late *praefectus*' prison. At least this morning's breakfast – dispatched to the prison with two of Publius' legionaries – was traditional hard bread and watered vinegar wine, for he saw more than enough trouble with Octavianus and Maecenas looming without allowing their murderous agents to starve.

The Gaul's two gang-members joined them. The massive Bibulus and the slighter, more intelligent Castus standing at their shoulders, also looking out across the harbour. 'Boats,' said Castus. 'I fucking hate them.'

'All good Romans do,' agreed Quintus feelingly.

'Lucky you're not coming with us then,' said Artemidorus to the gang-members. Quintus had no choice. Nor did Ferrata, Puella, Furius and Kyros who also joined them. Ferrata and Furius like Quintus still chewing on the remains of their breakfast.

'Right,' said Artemidorus. 'Lead on, Castus.'

*

Some time later, the little group stopped as Castus gestured at the doorway leading into a modest villa conveniently placed to communicate with both the docks and the town. 'This is a funny time to be visiting a *lupinaria*,' said Ferrata, a world of experience underlying the observation.

'A brothel's a funny place to come looking for an *acervus* cache of stolen weapons in any case,' added Puella.

'A clever place to hide them, then,' suggested Kyros. Castus and Bibulus nodded their agreement.

'Well, I for one am happy to check the quality of everything inside,' offered Furius. 'Weapons and she-wolves alike.'

'I'd be happy to help,' added Ferrata.

Kyros, still young enough to be sensitive and half in love with Notus in any case, blushed.

Puella grunted, unamused.

Quintus did not dignify the byplay with any comment. Instead, he stepped forward and hammered on the door.

ii

The brothel's *janitor* was clearly an ex-gladiator. He was huge, liberally scarred and armed with a club that would have flattered Hercules. Castus pushed to the front as Artemidorus and his men took the measure of their potential opponent. 'The Gaul sent us, Gaipor. He told us where to come, who to contact and what to say. He said to tell you *Bellona's guarding them.'*

Gaipor the door-keeper hesitated for a moment, accepting the coded phrase but still checking out the soldiers expecting to pass because of it. A calculating gaze swept over them, measuring the situation; the request; the best way forward. 'No-one told me there'd be a bleeding cohort of you,' he rumbled.

'Let all of us into the atrium,' suggested Castus. 'Then we can decide who goes to look at the cache and who stays. Looking for a little early entertainment, perhaps,' he added as Gaipor still hesitated. 'This lot aren't short of a *sestertius* or two.'

'It's been a long night – the latest of many,' added Furius. 'We're up early in all sorts of ways.' He winked.

'This one'll have to pay extra,' warned Gaipor, gesturing at Ferrata. 'On account of his face and such.'

'Happy to pay extra up front,' answered the Spaniard. 'The lucky girl'll probably pay it back after we've finished. Satisfaction guaranteed.' He winked his one good eye as well. The effect was horrific.

The massive janitor chuckled. 'Can't argue with a confident man,' he decided. 'Come in. I'll send a slave to rouse Suadela the *domina* and we'll see what's what.'

*

The *lupinaria*'s atrium was unusually spacious and well-appointed. Brothels in Artemidorus' experience – which was, admittedly much slighter than Ferrata's – tended to be poky establishments – little more than a couple of rooms with single beds and girls who were more desperate than seductive, whose specialties and qualities were advertised in the graffiti scrawled on the walls outside; one up from sleeping in the *deliquia* gutter. But that was not true of this one, which was clearly in a profitable line of business. Not too surprisingly, with so many legions camped so close inland and a modest navy caught at anchor in the port. But, like the *janitor*, and the strapping slave he sent to fetch the madam – like the madam herself, no doubt, named Suadela after the Goddess of persuasion and seduction – this was an unusual establishment. There was a strikingly graphic mosaic on the floor depicting Europa being ravished by Jupiter in the shape of a particularly well-endowed bull. 'I like that bull,' whispered Ferrata. 'It reminds me of me.'

'In your dreams,' said Puella.

'You wouldn't believe what goes on in my dreams,' answered Ferrata cheerfully. 'This lot for a start.' He gestured at the walls where there were illustrations exemplifying all the possible – and some frankly impossible – sexual positions.

As they were assessing their surroundings, the curtain over an inner doorway parted and a statuesque woman entered. As Artemidorus suspected, given the quality of the house she was running, she was clean, carefully made-up, and fashionably coiffed, even this early in the day. Although she was approaching middle age, her dress was expensively stylish and her demeanour as decisive as that of any Roman matron. The air of command she exuded worthy of Fulvia or Servilia, her eyes almost worthy of Cleopatra. '*Domina*,' said Gaipor. 'These are the ones The Gaul told us to expect.'

'There's quite a few of them,' she said uneasily. 'More than I thought there would be.'

Why would a woman such as this seem to be unnerved by half a dozen men, two of whom must be familiar to her by reputation if by nothing else? wondered Artemidorus. But then he understood. Sospes and at least some of his *vigiles* would have been her guarantors of protection – at a price. But now both Sospes and chief *vigile* Gistin were as dead as The Gaul's first two emissaries, things must look disturbingly uncertain to her. 'We mean you no harm,' he assured her. 'We have come simply to inspect what you have been guarding.' He opened his cloak. 'We're unarmed,'

'Yes, you are,' she agreed. 'But only until you get your hands on what I have hidden in the *cellarium*.'

iii

Artemidorus, Quintus, Puella and Castus followed Suadela through a doorway leading down a staircase into the brothel's cellar. She was flanked by two slaves carrying oil lamps. And that's not all they were carrying. They were both armed to the teeth. Probably with samples of the weaponry they were here to inspect. There were three rooms opening off a short corridor. One on either side at the foot of the stairs. Both behind half-open doors which stood in mute evidence of the honesty of the occupants. Or of their fear of Suadela, Gaipor the *janitor* and the dangerous-looking slaves, he thought. Each room filled with the kinds of stores required by a busy establishment that housed, clothed, tended, and fed a range of occupants. And – on regular occasions at least he supposed – several guests. It was a decidedly elevated *lupinarium* – not quite a *hospitium* – but close enough.

And then there was the third entrance at the end of the corridor. A massive frame with huge hinges supporting a door that looked as though it could withstand a battering ram. Suadela pulled out an iron key and thrust it into a solid, modern-looking lock. Turned it and stood back. The muscular lamp-bearers heaved the heavy door open and followed the swing of it, stepping inwards side by side. Entranced, Quintus pushed forward, elbowing past even Suadela, as he focused on the treasure-trove. Artemidorus followed him, but lingered near the doorway – alert for the slightest movement that threatened to slam the door shut and trap them inside. His gaze raked over the equipment that lay carefully piled there. Armour made of overlapping metal hoops sewn onto stout leather lining. 'The new segmented design,' said Quintus, clearly impressed. 'It's the latest thing. It's heavier but much more protective than chain and scale mail or toughened hide.' He lifted overlapping shoulder-sections. Leather *baltaea* skirts with studded frontpieces to offer protection from the waist to the knees. Greaves to protect shins. 'These are only useful if you come out of line or lose your shield,' he said. 'Still, better safe than sorry.'

He turned to a pile of helmets also of the latest design, their distinctive coloured horsehair crests revealing all this had originally been destined for the legendary Martia legion. Decimated by Antony close by here; one centurion in ten beaten to death by his colleagues as Antony and Fulvia watched. As Enobarbus witnessed and reported. The Martia deserted the General in consequence and were serving with Octavianus now, bound for *Bruttium*, the far south of *Italia* and the waters off *Sicilia*.

'Who in the name of all the gods paid for this?' whispered Puella, awed.

'Octavianus,' answered Artemidorus.

'The boy's not short of a *sestertius* or two,' Quintus observed. 'And I reckon he owes us after setting Felix and that bloody bastard Popilius Laenas on us.'

'Laenas,' echoed Suadela. 'You know Laenas?'

That one question changed things considerably.

That a woman like this should use a tone like that when enquiring about someone who had been in Brundisium for only a few days spoke volumes. 'Yes,' Artemidorus answered. 'We know him as an enemy. He killed the *vigile* Gistin and the *praefectus* Sospes, not to mention two of The Gaul's men.'

'He and that brute that travels with him hurt two of my women badly.'

'We have a physician, Crinas, with us. I can ask him to examine them if you would like.'

'No, thank you. We have a physician we can call on. But all of us are worried the two of them might return, especially now the *praefactus* and the chief *vigile* are dead.'

'Don't worry. We have him locked in the *praefectus*' villa in a room only slightly less secure than this. We plan to release him when we leave. But he will be riding straight back to Rome. And, should you be concerned, we will almost certainly be leaving a squad of marines behind. And some legionaries from the VIIth to keep the peace until the Triumvir Mark Antony sends a new *praefectus*. We can order them to protect you and your establishment.'

'They'll probably take extra care to look after your girls as well,' observed Castus, sounding very much like Ferrata, his voice oozing concern.

'You'll have to deal with Antony's prefect when he arrives,' said Puella. The two women exchanged a glance which told Artemidorus neither of them thought dealing with Antony's man – or, indeed, almost any man – would be much of a problem. Apart from Laenas, apparently.

*

Beside the piles armour, helmets and armoured aprons, there stood rack upon rack of swords, *gladii* and *spathae* – short stabbing swords and long sharp-edged cavalry swords. A third rack of *pugiones* daggers. Their blades all shining like silver; their scabbards piled on the ground beneath them. Quintus took a *gladius* and tested first the point and then the edge. 'If the blade can hold an edge this sharp for any length of time during combat,' he said, 'then it could become almost as effective as the point.' He hefted the sword thoughtfully.

'But that would only be important if the shield wall broke up and you were forced into open combat,' said Puella. 'And that's where the leg armour would be useful too.'

Quintus nodded, grudging agreement with her assessment. But frowning as he did so. Artemidorus smiled. The old-fashioned *triarius* did not like the idea of legionary units breaking up and going into open combat like untrained barbarians. But he was experienced enough to know it sometimes happened – even in the best of legions. And that was where a *gladius* with a cutting edge equal to a cavalry *spatha*'s would come into its own. He tested the edge again. 'You might well be able to inflict a serious wound with this. Lop off an arm, maybe…'

Then there were the *pilae* spears, robust wooden handles capped with thin metal shafts ending in gleaming, sharp points. 'General Marius' design,' confirmed Quintus, happier to be dealing with good old-fashioned weaponry. 'The metal shaft bends on impact so the spear can't be pulled free – of shield, armour or flesh; and can't be used again.' Beside the *pilae*, a mound of square, curved *scutae* shields – the modern design taking over from the old oval ones. Hide over layered wood, with metal bosses and lightning bolts worthy of Jupiter himself. The one designed to sow fear – the other to smash faces. 'Metal bound edges,' Quintus observed approvingly. 'No expense spared.'

'This looks like impressive equipment,' said Artemidorus. 'Though, I note there are no bows or sling-shots. Does it go with what you've brought?'

'Yes. I have bows and slings of all sorts anyway. We should take it all, though,' said Quintus. 'We can use the armour. It's better than the mail and toughened hide you've all been wearing. Almost up with my breast- and back-plates. The rest of the stuff is like some of what I've brought. But the quality is exceptional. What our *contubernium* can't use we can pass onto Publius for his men.'

Artemidorus turned to Suadela. 'I'll make arrangements for my men to come and remove all of this,' he said. 'Is that going to be acceptable?'

'Filling a brothel with soldiers?' she said, her poise recovering now that her initial fears seemed to be put to rest. 'It may go slowly but I think we can handle whatever comes up.'

'I'm sure you can,' said Artemidorus.

He accompanied Suadela back up to the atrium, ordering Kyros to follow – then to go and fetch Publius and a squad of his legionaries to empty the brothel's cellar. But, as the secret agent lingered in the airy chamber with its erotic illustrations, Gaipor the massive *janitor* brought in the new head *vigile* Cessy. 'Centurion,' gasped the watchkeeper. 'Thank the gods I've found you! The prisoners! They've managed to overpower and slaughter the legionaries you sent with their breakfast and the men I had guarding the prison cell. They've escaped!'

iv

Artemidorus' strode to the head of the cellar steps. 'Quintus,' he bellowed. 'I want you and the rest up here. Now.'

As he waited for his legionaries to obey, he swung round to face Suadela. 'Centurion Publius' legionaries will be here soon,' he said. 'Even if Laenas and Herrenius have any intention of disturbing you – which is very unlikely – Publius' men will protect you. In the meantime I have other responsibilities…'

Suadela rested her fingers lightly on his forearm. The hairs became erect at her touch. 'Will you come back?' she said softly. 'Make sure we are all alright?'

'I will,' he promised, matching her tone without conscious thought. And turned to see Puella watching them, from the cellar doorway, her expression unreadable.

The rest of his little command arrived, and he led them out of the house at a dead run as Cessy lingered for a moment, passing on the details of Laenas' escape to the worried woman. Fortunately, the whole of Brundisium overlooked the harbour so it was easy enough even for a stranger to make his way to the quayside without getting lost. The six of them pounded onto the stone jetty side by side. Slowing to a walk as it became clear that the guards at either end of both *Galene*'s and *Aegeon*'s gangplanks were still in place and on watch. Even so, Artemidorus ran aboard *Aegeon*, calling, 'Messala! Messala are you aboard?'

Instead of Messala, the centurion Severus Manlius ran up onto the deck. Immediately behind him came another man. A stranger, but one that Artemidorus vaguely recognised. 'He's not here,' said Severus. 'He's gone to the *hospitium* for *jentaculum*. Is everything alright?'

'No,' answered Artemidorus as he turned. 'Laenas and Herrenius have escaped.' Then he and the others were pounding back to *Galene* calling for Lucius – with precisely the same result.

A few moments later, Artemidorus found the two missing men in the *hospitium*'s *atrium*, eating their breakfast with Publius and some of his senior legionaries, unaware that anything was wrong. In a few terse phrases he informed them of Laenas' escape and warned them to be especially vigilant. While he was doing this, Cessy caught up with him. 'I suppose I'd better look at the cell,' said Artemidorus. 'Publius, send some men to double the guard on Laenas' room in the *taberna*. That's the most likely place they'll head for.'

He paused, mind racing. He had foreseen Laenas' escape as only the most remote possibility. But had he planned well enough for it, unlikely though it had seemed? Leaving so many of his ill-gotten gains in the room he and Herrenius shared was a potent temptation; neither man could be certain of what had been left there – but they must surely come to check.

Only time would tell. And the worst thing he could do in the circumstances was to stand here. Thinking. Planning. Doing nothing.

*

The *praefectus*' cell was a mess. Bread and wine lay scattered, shards of terracotta plate and glass vessels liberally spattered with gouts of blood. The soldier who had brought breakfast lay face-down in the mess, just as the two guards lying outside gave mute testimony to a simple but effective escape, as successful as it was brutal. Artemidorus shook his head and turned as Publius ran in. 'Whoever brought *jentaculum* failed to leave his *pugio* outside with the guards by the look of things,' he said. 'A tiny error, but enough.'

Publius' gaze swept icily over the mess. 'Where will they be?' he grated.

'The most likely is their room in the *tablinum*,' answered Artemidorus. 'I've left enough in there to slow them if they take the time to check it through. Otherwise, they'll be at the stables stealing the fastest horses they can. They know that anyone who catches them in Brundisium after this will kill them without a second thought.'

'Let's go then.' The centurion from the new VIIth turned impulsively.

'You go on,' said Artemidorus. 'Take all the men you need. I'll follow in a moment. There are aspects to this I still have to think through.'

'You seem to have everything pretty well covered to me,' Publius flung over his shoulder as he left.

'No,' answered Artemidorus quietly. 'I'm not sure that I do.'

The next person to enter was Felix, who arrived almost as precipitately as Publius. He and Artemidorus looked silently at each other, then Artemidorus asked, 'Where do you stand on this, Felix? They work for Octavianus the same as you do…'

'Not quite,' answered Felix easily. 'They work for Maecenas and I work for Agrippa.'

'There's a difference?'

'Like the difference between night and day.' Felix took a deep breath. He glanced around the room and out into the corridor, satisfied himself that they were completely alone – that only the dead could hear him. 'It's as though young Caesar is two men in the same body. You must have seen it or suspected it yourself.'

Artemidorus remained silent. He had seen it all too clearly.

'The cold, calculating, ambitious leader who has his eyes fixed firmly on power so that he can raise Rome to the place in the world he knows she deserves,' Felix continued. 'As though he wants to take a city made of mud and turn it into one made of marble. The builder. Agrippa.' He took a deep breath, glancing around once more. 'And then there's the other side. The willful boy who lusts after more than simple political power, who wants to make everyone obey his every whim, gratify his every lust. Who enjoys dominating, hurting, humiliating, debasing those around him – like the women who come to him begging for their menfolks' lives. The *carnifex* torturer. Maecenas.'

'So Laenas as Maecenas' man is the vicious torturer. While you, as Agrippa's man, you are part of the builders, are you?'

'Yes!'

'Playing fair, looking out for friend and foe alike. You stand with Socrates – the measure of your actions is whether they are *justificus* righteous, correct or virtuous?'

'*Yes*!'

'Then how do you explain this?' Artemidorus reached into his pouch and pulled out the golden *fascinum* Puella found at the site of the ambush that had killed Mercury and disfigured Ferrata. He lobbed the golden phallus at Felix who caught it easily, despite its weight. 'Puella found it at the site of the ambush. The tribune Enobarbus told me you lost one like it.'

This was not the way he had planned to deal with the conundrum posed by the golden good-luck charm but there was no turning back now.

V

Felix examined the thing. 'Not one like it,' he said. 'This one.'

'And?' Because he had moved outside anything he had planned or prepared, Artemidorus found that he was slipping dangerously out of control, his rage rising unmanageably.

'I lost it. And I very much wanted to get it back – as I told your tribune Enobarbus. But it's not mine,' said Felix, meeting Artemidorus eye with his most honest and forthright expression.

'Whose is it, then?'

'You know the answer to that! Who loves gold more than anything – except notoriety? And hurting people, of course. Who has had a golden statue made of himself standing wearing a victor's laurels with his foot resting on Cicero's severed head?'

'Laenas. But if it belongs to Laenas and was found where the trap that killed and maimed my men was sprung, how do you fit in?'

'My men and I were there in the woods surrounding Cicero's villa in Formia last *Decembris*. You know that. We saw another group of legionaries moving through the brush towards the Via Appia as you and your people came riding down it, but we made too much noise and disturbed them. As they melted into the shadows, one of them dropped this. I picked it up, hoping to use it later to identify them. But then we heard the attack on your *crypteia* and hurried towards the sound. We arrived in time to see your attackers vanish and you preparing to respond. And respond you did – with a hail of arrows and slingshots. We thought it better to retreat ourselves rather than to try and explain what we were doing there. And as we retreated, I too lost this. My proof…'

'That the man who sprung the ambush was Popilius Laenas,' said Artemidorus.

'*So, it was*,' said a third voice. Cold and supercilious. 'And proof that I can snare the pair of you whenever it takes my fancy!'

Artemidorus and Felix swung round to find Popilius Laenas and Herrenius standing in the doorway. Both armed and drenched with drying blood.

Artemidorus looked at Octavianus' three spies. His passion to know where Felix really stood outweighed his frustration at being caught in one of Laenas' traps. Again. But this time, at least he himself was the only one at risk.

'What's the plan, Laenas?' Felix was demanding as Laenas wrestled the golden phallus out of his fist and slid it into his blood-soaked pouch. The point of his dagger at Felix' throat.

'Simple,' grated Artemidorus, rage beginning to mount still further. 'They can't risk being seen anywhere as they are. Look at them. And yet they have things to do and places to go – let alone laying their hands on some transport to help them run from here to Rome with as many of their ill-gotten gains as they can carry. They need hostages to keep them safe while they collect as much as they can. And get horses – and maybe a wagon. And as hostages go, we're about the best they can hope for.'

'Precisely,' said Laenas. 'I'm surprised you didn't see all this earlier, Septem! Perhaps Antony shouldn't be placing quite as much trust in you as he does, eh?'

*

The four of them walked out of the *praefectus*' villa with Artemidorus and Felix in front, Laenas and Herrenius behind, blades at their throats. 'To the *taberna* first,' ordered Laenas. 'I hope for your sake you left everything there where you found it.'

'Everything except Sospes' head,' answered Artemidorus. 'That's with his body on the way back to Rome.'

'Pity. But with luck we can overtake it and reclaim our property. But our passes signed by Gaius Cilnius Maecenas are there still? Our gold? The pardons for Messala and Lucius signed by young Caesar?'

'Yes. All of it.'

'Excellent! Then all we'll need is for you to carry it to the stables for us, load it onto a couple of fast horses and pray that we leave in a good mood.'

'What?' said Felix. 'No bath? No change of clothing? No quick farewell visit to the brothels?'

No further attempts to take Messala's and Lucius' heads? thought Artemidorus. But he said nothing.

Cessy and a couple of his *vigiles* were the first men to come across the four soldiers. 'Keep back,' warned Laenas, moving his *pugio* just enough to bring a drop of blood to Artemidorus' throat. The new chief *vigile* obeyed, but stayed keeping guard as they all walked slowly down the slope of the *via* towards the dockside and the *taberna*. But at his silent gesture, one of his men scurried away. 'We'll have more company soon,' said Artemidorus.

'Better pray they behave sensibly. For the sake of your throat if nothing else…' sneered Laenas.

'Kill us and you die a heartbeat later,' warned Artemidorus.

'Unless his *crypteia* get really angry,' added Felix. 'In which case you won't die for a good long time, no matter how much you beg for it.'

'Well,' said Laenas, 'let's hope it doesn't come to that. But rest assured, if anyone comes within a sword's-length, We'll cut your throats from ear to ear.'

Publius and a squad of his legionaries arrived then. Publius assessed the situation in an instant and gestured his men to stand back with the *vigiles*.

'Keep them coming, though,' said Laenas. 'We need some strong arms to move our stuff, especially our gold.'

Looking past the soldiers, Artemidorus saw a flicker of movement in the distance. Puella.

vi

They were nearing the harbour and Artemidorus was being distracted by something he could not quite put a finger on – even in this critical situation – when the next group showed up. Messala, Lucius, Severus, and Gaius Licinius with some of their blue-clad marines came crowding up from the dockside. They blocked the road leading down past the cross-roads to the harbour. Everyone stopped moving. Artemidorus refocused on the situation. He could feel Laenas straining to get on – beyond the crossroads, just up from the harbour, perhaps a hundred paces away, was the side-road leading up to the *taberna*, his documents and his gold.

'Move!' snarled Laenas. He pulled his blade harder against Artemidorus' throat. The marines obligingly fell back, led by their centurions and the two fugitive aristocrats. Laenas and Herrenius were able to move forward once again. More slowly, their pace dictated by the men in front of them.

But the stand-off remained. Messala clearly in charge, calling their bluff, Maecenas' deadly agents all too aware that Felix had spoken the truth – if either hostage died, then their bargaining position was destroyed. Laenas and Herrenius would face a fate far worse than anything they had inflicted upon their own victims in the past.

'Take *us*,' said Messala as he walked backwards into the opening of the cross-roads. 'It's us you want. Take us instead.'

Lucius nodded mute agreement, his face folded into a stoical frown, worthy of his maternal grandfather Cato.

'Tempting,' jeered Laenas, his eyes glued to the young patrician. 'And suicidally heroic. Except for one thing. You know very well we'd lose control during the exchange. You'd have us spitted like pigs for roasting.'

'We might do just that in any case,' said a new voice.

At the sound of it, Maecenas and his marines stood aside. Moving in a planned maneuver, like a squad on a battlefield. And there, in the middle of the cross-roads side by side stood Quintus and Furius. Both armed with reticulated bows in the Parthian design. Arrows nocked and bowstrings taut. Behind them stood Kyros and the towering Hercules, both equally well-armed, ready to fire. Four steel points aimed unwaveringly over the captives' shoulders at Laenas' and Herrenius' faces, gleaming wickedly in the watery sunshine. They stopped moving forward, hesitated there at the heart of the cross-roads, automatically ducking behind their hostages, using them as shields against this unexpected threat. Everything froze for an instant.

Then out of the roads on either side, came a whip-crack and a hissing whisper. Laenas' head slammed left just as Herrenius' slammed right to clash together with brutal force and the pair of them fell backwards onto the roadway, their daggers dropping from senseless fingers. Artemidorus and Felix stepped forward, free as Puella and Ferrata walked watchfully out from the side-roads and onto the main thoroughfare, each of them winding a sling around their fingers.

'An excellent stratagem,' said Felix. 'Though a little too reliant on the accuracy of your slingers.' He shivered slightly, looking at one-eyed Ferrata whose slingshot had whispered so close behind his own skull. 'Still, all's well.' He shrugged, turned. 'Have you killed them?' He asked, his tone betraying the fact that he didn't much care either way. He stooped, felt in Laenas' pouch and retrieved the golden *fascinum* as Artemidorus kicked the daggers away.

And as Quintus answered, 'I hope not!' He eased his bow and removed the arrow. 'Killing them wasn't part of the plan.'

*

By noon, Crinas had established that neither man had died, would die in the immediate future – would suffer more than a massive headache when they woke, even though the slingshots had hit them on their temples, where their skulls were thinnest. The unconscious men had been bound and secured in a strong cart together with their papers and personal possessions at Artemidorus' insistence – and in the face of some forceful arguments for their immediate execution. But he agreed that their weapons and the gold they had extorted from Sospes and the rest should remain behind. In Cessy's safe-keeping until Antony's new *praefectus* arrived and decided what should be done with it. Except for the bag Laenas had cut from the dead Gistin's belt. Artemidorus gave that to Castus and Bibulus with orders that they should also get a cart and take the corpses of his murdered colleagues back to The Gaul in Rome. There was enough gold there to ensure a proper burial. Though he suspected that gang members, like gladiators, all paid into a fund that ensured proper burial if anything went fatally wrong. Unsurprisingly, The Gaul's men happily took the gold and vanished in search of a cart.

Publius detailed a squad to take the cart laden with Laenas, Herrenius and their effects as far as the VIIth legion's camp and hand it over there to the tribune, who would make arrangements to return the lethal pair to their masters in Rome. It was up to him whether they went on in the cart and under guard or on horseback with their documents and their freedom. Artemidorus sent a letter strongly advising the former course. Felix warned him most earnestly, that sending them back in a cart would make Maecenas an implacable enemy as well, perhaps even more so than killing them would do. A matter of his *dignitas* – the humiliation of his agents would be bound to rebound on him, not to mention on his master Octavianus.

'Maecenas' enmity is a threat that will find a place low on my list of potential dangers,' said Artemidorus. 'Very low in fact, because by the time Maecenas finds out what happened here, my *contubernium* and I will be somewhere in Macedonia with much more immediate threats to worry about: Brutus and his seven legions, for instance.'

'True enough,' allowed Felix. 'I, however, shall be going back to Rome and reporting to Agrippa later – keeping well clear of any trouble resulting from whatever manner in which Laenas and Herrenius are returned.'

'I'd hang onto the golden *fascinus*, though,' suggested Artemidorus. 'You're going to need all the luck you can get.'

'That's funny,' said Felix. 'I was thinking of giving it to you. For the same reason.'

'For Hades' sake just pass it over to me,' said Ferrata. 'I'll try and keep the good luck going for everybody.'

'Or to me,' suggested Puella, not to be outdone. 'After all I found it in the woods after the ambush.'

'Oh right!' said Ferrata. 'That's just what you need! The dearest dream of every woman I've ever known: a bloody great penis made of gold.'

But Artemidorus straightened to his full height, looking around, understanding what had been nagging at his subconscious during the day so far. 'No,' he said. 'Better give it to poor old Quintus. It looks to me like the weather's broken and we'll be taking him out onto the big rough *Mare Nostrum* in a day or so.'

MACEDONIA

VII: Trireme

i

"HEIA** VIRI NOSTRUM REBOANS ECHO SONNET **HEIA!"

'*Hey men! Echo resounding, send back our Hey*!' sang the oarsmen of the trireme *Galene,* throwing their weight and strength back as their oars bit deep into the water of Brundisium's outer harbour. The song was tuneless, raucous, rhythmic. The oarsmen were chosen for their strength and stamina, not for their beautiful voices.

Artemidorus sang along with them under his breath, not only because he had served his time as an oarsman in a galley, but because, like them, he was happy to be clear of Italy. To be escaping the simple boredom of being trapped in Brundisium by contrary winds for such a long time but also, in his case, to be heading for the next stage of his mission.

He was standing on the stern of *Galene* beside the *trierarchus* captain and his *gubernator* navigator. Alone except for the *gubernator*'s men and some deck-crew. His *contubernium*, Gaius Licinius and his men were all either further along the deck or snugly below, except for Quintus who was right at the bow, trying to make sure that his regular fits of vomiting did not land directly on the rowers in their boxes sticking out of the sleek ship's sides. The *fascinum* was clearly ineffective thought Artemidorus. Perhaps his involuntary gifts to Poseidon would prove more successful.

Neither the captain nor the navigator were paying much attention to the singing centurion nor his seasick companion. The captain was dividing his time between the drumbeat of the *pausarius* time-keeper below. But he was equally concerned about the strain his ship's movement was putting on the great hawser that joined the oar-powered vessel to the wind-driven cargo-ship it was towing out onto the restless sea.

Both ships had their huge square sails deployed and, the navigator assured everyone, they would fill with a steady westerly the instant they came out of the wind-shadow of the land they were leaving. In the mean-time there was the gentlest zephyr of an evening breeze flowing down the hillsides, over the town and out towards the east. Just enough to make the sails flap occasionally; nowhere near the power they needed to make full sail towards Macedonia.

Ironically, thought Artemidorus, they would move out of the wind-shadow at about the same time as the hills' real shadow – thrown by the late-afternoon sun westering sedately astern – would start to sweep over them as though the westerly breeze was the darkness itself. The wind-shadow at least was something that the captain was clearly trying to take account of, for his sail would fill first as they came out of it and if he moved away too forcefully before the cargo vessel was also under way, there was no telling what harm might be done to his stern – or the other ship's bows.

*

At this moment, the navigator's whole being concentrated on ensuring they came out of the harbour entrance safely. He had two burly sailors controlling the great *ansa* handle of the steering oar, which plunged on the right of the incurving sternpost, immediately behind the outward reach of the rear-most rowing box, burying its huge blade into the foam at the beginning of the vessel's wake. The navigator was lending a hand himself. Literally, varying the angle of the steering blade with a series of gentle pushes as he squinted along their course, calling warnings to the captain whenever he wanted one bank of oars or the other to vary their rhythm and help adjust the long hull's heading. For, although the harbour mouth was wide, the sea beyond it inviting, it was guarded by an island that stabbed down from the north, like a dagger aimed at their left side: a dagger of land that continued invisibly beneath the surface in a reef of sharp-fanged rocks.

Artemidorus turned, resting his hands on the warm wood of the ship's rail, looking north. Beside them further to the left, approaching the wide harbour mouth in convoy, *Aegeon* was also using her oar-power to tug a second transport out into the wind. Her *trierarchus* and *gubernator* doubtless even more acutely aware of the island and the reef as she took the northward course, smashing through the modest swell, pitching just sufficiently to lift her streaming metal-sheathed ram out of the water, surging smoothly onward, none of her motions wild enough to disturb the steady rise and fall of her three banks of oars.

Artemidorus filled his lungs to bursting with the fresh salt air. He fought to contain his excitement which had been building almost uncontrollably today during the ritual libations and sacrifices that preceded any venture out onto the deep and dangerous sea. Both Severus and Gaius Licinius had left some of their marines behind to make room for those legionaries who could not be fitted into the cargo vessels under tow behind them with their mounts, tack, equipment, legionary slaves, their carts and mules. But both centurions had insisted on coming, with as many marines as they could find room for. There might well be work for them to do in Dyrrhachium if Brutus had left any of his *Libertore* troops there to guard against an invasion – even such a modest one as this.

ii

Artemidorus found the opportunity to talk to Messala and Lucius while they were waiting to embark on *Aegeon* with Severus. Discussing how they proposed to get along the Via Egnatia and then to Brutus' camp. Slowly, it seemed, for they had no papers or travel documents. But they were by no means the first proscribed men to escape eastwards. Others had made it through. So would they.

What did they propose to tell Brutus about their escape from Rome, he asked, about their journey eastwards and their companions at the outset of their journey when they eventually reached Brutus' camp? Their answers were evasive, as though the prospect of a safe escape from Italy had changed their attitude to Artemidorus and his *contubernium*. The patricians no longer relied on their equestrian and plebeian protectors. Who, they now recognised all too clearly, would be their enemies as soon as they landed in Macedonia. They had yet to decide the details, they explained. There was nothing more to say. But Artemidorus feared the worst. The spy was still in two minds about how Brutus was likely to react to the information that legionaries under Antony's command were able to cross to Dyrrhachium this early in the season.

As he said to Quintus after the meeting – which seemed to have settled less than he'd hoped and simply added to his concerns, 'The best outcome for us is that Brutus sends his fleet to blockade Brundisium immediately on hearing their news. Their presence alone will confirm that the sea-lanes are open. But Antony will still be preparing his legions to cross much later in the summer, so a blockade won't inconvenience him too much, especially if Octavianus can defeat Sextus Pompey and bring his fleet round behind them. But if they do move the *Libertore* fleets, it will allow us to sail safely through waters the *Libertores* have left to come west. However, if Messala and Lucius put too much emphasis on our mission to Alexandria when they report, it might well mean that the *Libertores* will leave sea-patrols off Greece and Rhodes with orders to stop us getting through. They've clammed up and I know there are things they're keeping from me – in spite of all that they owe us.'

'You could always release Furius to do his worst with them,' suggested Quintus. 'Or just kill them outright if you're worried they'll damage our mission and if there's nothing further to be got from them.'

'No,' decided Artemidorus. 'Not after all we've been through together. We'll just have to trust Fortuna smiles on us and try and find a captain in Thessaloniki or Neapolis who knows the waters of the Levant well enough to smuggle us through to Alexandria no matter what.'

'In other words, a pirate,' said Quintus. 'I can see *that* going well...'

*

These discussions took place amid the embarkation and the rituals associated with it, a process which had taken all yesterday and most of today. Which, as the captain and navigator explained, was much to their advantage: primarily it meant that they were setting off late-afternoon just at the top of a full tide, whose steady fall would hasten their exit, while still leaving sufficient water beneath them to keep them safe from rocks and shoals. Years of experience supported by the notes in their *periploi* sailing manuals suggested that the crossing would take between sixteen and twenty hours, depending on tides, currents, water, wind and weather. It was all very well leaving Brundisium in gathering darkness, but trying to get into Dyrrhachium in anything less than broad daylight – and ideally on a tide swelling up towards full – would be a dangerous undertaking indeed. For, although the Macedonian port city sat at the top of a wide and welcoming bay, the harbour entrance was narrow – guarded by a breakwater and a lengthy jetty which almost met at their tips like the claws of a gigantic crab. So they proposed to complete most of the crossing in the dark, hopefully guided by the stars, reaching their destination tomorrow morning. If the night was overcast and the stars invisible, they would be able to complete their final approach guided by the landmarks along the Macedonian coast.

Artemidorus was hopeful that the break in the weather would last. The clouds were high, and blowing away to the east. The darkening sea ahead a silvery mirror scored with shadows and white dashes where the moderating waves broke into diminishing puddles of foam. All was set fair for a clear, cold night with crystal skies and stars like pearls.

On that thought, Artemidorus felt the first firm puff of wind against his left cheek. A thunder of stirring sailcloth drowned the muttering of the soldiers further down the deck. He turned to his right, looking upwards, to see the great belly of the sail fill as the lusty song from below was for a moment overcome by the creaking of mast and yards, the squeal and hum of sheets and halyards – and the bellows of the deck-crew fighting to adjust them as the trireme came fully under way. The tow rope tautened and screamed, spraying drops of salt water like Niobe's tears as she wept for the slaughter of her children. For an instant *Galene*'s majestic progress slowed. Everyone aboard, it seemed, looked either at the screaming tow-rope or the groaning mast. Then the drag on her eased and she gathered way again. He turned, looking back past the incurving sternpost, just in time to see the huge sail of the *oneraria* cargo ship behind them fill as well. The tow-rope slackened, and the crewmen ran to pull it in as the sailhandlers tied their line off. A glance to northward showed *Aegeon* and her cargo-vessel going through the same. Tow-rope slackening as great sails bellied out.

And as it did so, all of Artemidorus' concerns about the past and worries about the future seemed to slide into the background.

They were fully under way at last.

iii

Cena was cold rations that evening. *Galene* had facilities to cook hot food, but she was so crowded that the captain decided a fire large enough to serve them all would be too much of a danger. Fire used for anything less important than signalling was forbidden. So the braziers remained unlit while the lanterns and flambeaux which lit vital areas and warned other shipping of *Galene*'s approach were ignited and swung aloft. They were all in position soon after sunset and the light on the *pharos* at Brundisium shone out low on the shadowy horizon behind them.

Everyone except the oarsmen gathered as the evening slid rapidly toward full night, sharing tough *emer* bread baked in Brundisium that morning, olives and cheese, cold chicken and pickled fish. Washing it with water – for the captain and the centurion wisely forbade wine on board. The rowers were fed and watered at their places after they had stowed their oars and settled. Then, everyone aboard turned to their plans for the night voyage – without baths or much in the way of entertainment.

Most of the passengers would be sleeping in the marines' accommodation below – but a few remained on the deck, protected from the wintery chill by their *sagae* soldiers' cloaks. The oarsmen prepared to sleep on their benches, wrapping their arms around each-other for warmth, until their efforts would be required in the morning as they approached the harbour.

The sailors, captain and navigator ate and drank while standing at their posts and did not sleep at all. While the ship was under way, they needed to attend the sail and rigging constantly – check their position and course against the stars, ensuring that their heading was that dictated by the sailing notes. There was a brief discussion as to whether they should send watchkeepers to the bow. But as the captain observed, only someone as mad as they were would be out on a night this early in the season. And no-one he could think of was anywhere near as mad as that.

Artemidorus chose to stay awake with the navigators, too excited to contemplate sleeping in any case. The rest of his command were housed in the makeshift cabins below, though by no means all of them used the facility – Gaius Licinius' senior marines double-bunking to make room.

Quintus ate nothing at *cena*. Instead he took his modest ration of food and drink then threw it directly over the side as an offering to Poseidon. 'That's where it was going in any case,' he said. 'This way I just save time and effort.' Like Artemidorus, he remained on deck, close to the side-rail. But he moved to the stern where the men controlling the vessel stood under a blazing torch and a lantern hanging from the inward curve of the sternpost, except when the captain sent men forward to adjust the rigging or the *gubernator* walked into the darkness to clear his vision and consult the stars. Puella also came up to stand with Artemidorus. They settled silently side by side and the centurion began to wonder if he was imagining the air of tension that had been lying between them since he had shown that unexpectedly powerful reaction to the beautiful brothel-keeper Suadela's touch. He reached out to slide an arm around her, but she moved away, glancing meaningfully at the group of men standing under the light at the ship's stern.

*

Artemidorus nodded, turned and walked purposefully down the deck, past the sleeping bodies there, noting Quintus and Hercules amongst them, and on down to the deserted bow with its incurving stempost from which hung another lantern large enough to throw a puddle of golden light amid the shadows of the deck and the vastness of the darkness beyond.

He arrived at the point of the bow and stood, hands on the rail, simply awed by the enormity of the night. He had forgotten how the low flat line of the horizon on a calm sea out of sight of land could make the sky seem so immense. The numberless stars seemed to crackle as they burned, and a full moon was rising above invisible Macedonia dead ahead. As he watched, entranced, it laid a silvery track across the sea – a phantom path for the trireme to follow as it surged onward, pushed by that steady westerly wind. Out here, the night gathered round him, threatening to overwhelm his senses. The wind blowing at his back was warm and occasionally carried the scent of the oil from the lantern hanging above his head. It sang in the rigging and seemed to enhance the rumble of the waves. His body swayed to the dictates of *Galene*'s long hull as she rode the waves, pitching slightly, rolling occasionally, creaking and groaning as she did so.

There came a stirring in the shadows and Puella materialised at his side as though she was the very spirit of the night. Her body slid hard against him and his own body reacted forcefully. He took her in his arms, as she crushed his body to hers. Her skin seemed to burn against his even through the clothing they both were wearing. He glanced over her shoulder in search of a comfortable place for them to make love. But, apart from the bare boards of the deck, there were only the coils of rope lying ready to be attached to the anchor, a harbour buoy or the jetty. He felt a surge of frustration as she moved against him, breathless with longing. He knew she preferred to make love lying down, but circumstances and desire dictated that they would probably have to do it standing. Controlled by forces as irresistible as those governing the vessel they were riding.

'Shall we go below?' he whispered.

'No,' she answered. 'Here. Now!'

Moving together, they eased away from the puddle of light beneath the lantern into the darkest shadows available, becoming two shapes of utter blackness beneath the gleam of the moon and the stars. Invisible, even to the legionaries lying on the deck midship – had any of them still been awake – they leaned back against the bow-rail, their hands busy with underwear as they both sought to raise their tunics and remove any hindrances to their desire. With the rail across her lower back, Puella arched her body, thrusting her hips forward, to meet his answering movement. The whole of their world shrunk to the feelings that their desire unleashed.

Which was why neither of them saw or heard the approach of the second vessel running without lights or warning of any sort straight across the trireme's path.

Until, with a thunderous explosion of sound and an earthquake shudder of impact, the two vessels came together, *Galene*'s ram smashing through the other ship's side. The blade of her high prow smashing mast, sail and rigging away as the unfortunate craft was ripped open, rolled over and ridden down.

iv

Galene hesitated, her mast groaning and rigging humming with the strain, then thrust onwards through the wreckage, unstoppable under the steady power of the wind in her huge square sail. The couple on the foredeck staggered, almost fell in a tangle of limbs and clothing. Tore themselves apart even as the first legionaries sprang awake, and the captain came rushing forward calling, 'What was that?'

The rumbling scraping of wreckage against his ship's sides continued; joined by shouts, screams, faint and helpless calls for aid that also swept down the ship's length, then rapidly began to fade astern into silence. Sailors traditionally never learned to swim, thought Artemidorus grimly. To swim was to tempt the gods. To swim was to prolong the agony and put off the inevitable. To risk a death far worse than drowning – between the jaws of a shark, or any other of the monsters that peopled the terrible deep.

Straightening his tunic as he ran, Artemidorus made it to the bow with Puella close behind. The impact set the lantern swinging and the beam of brightness enhanced the light of the moon. The last splinters and tatters whirled away down the trireme's side. But neither of them noticed this, nor the shouting figures helplessly entangled in the rigging that bound much of the mess of mast and spars together.

Because there was a man directly below them, clinging to the ram itself.

By some little joke of Poseidon, he had managed to scramble onto the metal-bound out-trust which was ten *pedes* feet in length and three wide. But *Galene* was not a youthful vessel and, although her long hull had been well-enough maintained, the ram was covered in weed and barnacles, making its surface treacherously slippery. On the other hand, the impact had scraped some areas clear of everything down to the bare metal. So the sailor's condition remained teasingly in the hands of the Sea God, as the waves through which the trireme was driving hit the helpless survivor like the blows of a *pugil* armed with spiked boxing gloves.

The captain arrived and noted that there was no obvious damage to his own vessel with one glance. Then turned and ran back through the stirring crowd of legionaries, calling to the helmsmen, 'All's well up here but don't get the steering oar tangled in whatever floats past! Send the sailhandlers to check the mast and rigging. And send a party below to check the bow from the inside just in case,' all apparently without even registering the existence of the survivor or his perilous position.

Meanwhile, Artemidorus grabbed the nearest coil of rope and began to wind the end round his waist. Seeing what he was planning, Puella said, 'No. I have much of your strength but only half your weight. I will go down to him and you can pull us both up. There should be men to help by the time I have him safely.'

Artemidorus nodded and looped the rope raound her slim waist, cinching it tight. She clambered nimbly over the rail by the stempost, the light of the swinging lantern revealing for an instant that she had not replaced her underwear. He passed the rope round the small of his back, walked the few steps to the rail she had just climbed over and braced himself against it as her weight came onto the line.

'Lower me,' she called. 'Do it quickly!'

*

The trireme's prow was by no means a simple piece of marine design. It was adorned with a range of decoration meant to win the help of the goddess of calm waters after whom the ship *Galene* was named and the creature most closely associated with her. Above the huge main ram, there was a second, smaller ram, the head of a dolphin, cast in the same metal as that covering the main ram itself, which projected for six feet including its beak. Above that there were wreaths cast in metal and others carved in wood as offerings to the goddess, whose divine head was carved on the incurving stempost looking straight ahead – just like the eyes painted on the vessel's sides immediately behind the prow.

Artemidorus was able to watch Puella as she scrambled down the forecastle using these as a makeshift ladder. Hands on the rails, feet on the uppermost wooden wreath as she paused before stepping onto the metal wreath below then reaching down to feel for the out-thrust of the dolphin's head. Then she hesitated for a moment as the spray, exploding upwards from the brutal wave-wash, started to soak her, moulding her tunic to her body as though the cloth were a layer of paint.

The lone survivor realised she was there at this point as she was less than ten feet above him. He could hear her over the smash and wash of the waves around him as she called to Artemidorus, 'More rope!' Her figure lit by the beams of the low moon. The shadows cast in contrast to the moonlight – hoped Artemidorus as he obeyed her curt instruction – preserving her modesty from the stranger staring in wonder straight up her clinging tunic. Then her weight came fully on the rope as she steadied herself on the dolphin's head and swung down to come within the stranger's reach – if he dared to stand erect on the unsteady, slippery, wave-washed little platform.

As Puella began to scramble down the last few feet, he pulled himself to his knees and reached up with one hand – the other still gripping the decorated metal of the cutwater. Then, once his hand had closed round her ankle he let go of the cutwater, heaved himself erect and clasped her round the waist, burying his face in the small of her back, immediately above the swell of her buttocks.

Artemidorus staggered as the weight on the line wrapped round him more than doubled, pressing him against the rail as though threatening to cut him in half at the waist. But then Quintus' hand closed on the rope followed by Hercules' a heartbeat later. The three men shared the burden and slowly began to pull the stranger and his rescuer up out of danger.

iv

'My name is User,' he said, later, when they had all got their breath back.

'User,' said the captain – to whom they had taken him.

'User,' confirmed the shipwrecked sailor. His voice a deep rumble, as though his massive chest were a hollow cavern.

His name told Artemidorus several things. First, he was most likely to be Egyptian in spite of the way he looked. A supposition supported by the heavily accented Greek and sketchy Latin he had employed to thank Puella, and by the manner in which he was dressed. Secondly, that whoever named him – parents, sponsors, priests – had been disturbingly prescient. *User* was Egyptian for 'Strong'. And so he was. He stood almost as tall as Hercules. His shoulders were broad, his chest deep. If his belly was flat and his hips narrow, then the muscles of his torso and thighs gave the lie to any thought that he might be starved or scrawny, as did the muscles of his arms, which ended in huge, powerful hands.

Even his face was muscular. His forehead was furrowed with lively wrinkles that deepened whenever he thought or spoke. His thick black eyebrows overhung his deep-set dark brown eyes, moving with the same muscularity as his forehead. His nose was long and straight but spread into powerful, bullish nostrils. His lips were thick and strongly formed. His chin was square and stubbled with black beard shot through with silver that matched the close-cropped curls on the great dome of his skull.

He wore a linen skirt that reached his knees beneath a loose fitting linen robe the colour of sand. He wore no jewellery – no necklet, bangles or armbands, cuffs or rings. Also he wore a simple leather belt and no weapons. However, this strange survivor was clearly no mere deck-hand or oarsman. He was almost certainly the captain or the pilot at least. Not, he thought, a centurion like Gaius Licinius, though there was no denying his almost military air of command. So, more likely, a merchant owner sailing with one of his trading vessels looking for business. Or, of course, a pirate out seeking prey. But he must be the owner and commander of an Egyptian vessel of some kind, sailing secretly and without lights this far north for some probably nefarious reason. A man worth watching. His whole presence seemed to pulse with power which became unashamedly sexual when he looked at his beautiful rescuer, who was in turn regarding him with little less than wonder. For, unlike almost everyone she had met in her life so far, User's skin was even darker than hers.

'I thank you for saving me,' User continued. 'Even though it was you who ran me down, destroyed my ship and killed my crew.' His gaze rested on Puella for the first part of the statement as he bowed to her and kissed his fingertips – and on the rest of them for the second part as he came erect and looked down at them. Artemidorus noted that there was little sign on that statuesque ebony face of any sorrow for the dead men left bobbing in – or sinking beneath – the trireme's wake.

*

There was no hope of letting the wind out of the sail, running out the oars, turning the ship around and going to search for survivors. User did not ask it and neither the captain nor his pilot offered to try. So *Galene* ploughed on along the track left by the rising moon until it faded. And then, guided by the stars, sailed on as everyone aboard returned to what they had been doing before the collision. Except for

Artemidorus and Puella; all passion quenched, they sat under the lantern hanging from the stempost with the man they had rescued and talked quietly – as the suspicious spy watched for the slightest sign of duplicity or evasion in the Egyptian's story. While observing the expression in those dark eyes whenever they rested on Puella. And the beautiful woman simply looked at the man she had saved like a mother watching her first-born child.

'I am a merchant,' User explained with apparent honesty. 'My vessels trade all across the eastern section of what the Romans arrogantly call *Mare Nostrum* – their sea. I trade in many goods: olives, oil, papyrus, cloth, grain, marble, spices, slaves, silver, gold. With warehouses in Carthago Nova, Narbo, Massalia, Carralis, Syracuse, all along the coast of Greece, Thessaloniki, Neapolis south of Philippi, Ephesus, Xanthus – where I have a family – and Tyre.' His expression softened as he mentioned his family.

'And is Xanthus your home port?' asked Artemidorus. And was pleased to receive the answer he expected and, indeed, hoped for. '

'No. My home port is Alexandria.' User's expression softened further. 'My greatest warehouses are in the ancient city and suburb of Ra-Kedet, which you Romans call Rakotis,' he continued. 'Near the Moon Gate, on the Eunostos Harbour looking across to the Temple of Poseidon. I have a house in Ra-Kedet which was home to my family until I moved them to Xanthus. My brother and his family have it until I move my own family back.'

'We are going to Alexandria,' said Puella simply. Before Artemidorus could ask the obvious question – if his largest warehouses were in Alexandria, why was his family in Xanthus?

User glanced around the trireme, then out at the lights of the other vessels in the little convoy before telling Puella, 'It would be a brave man or woman to make so long a voyage at this time of year. I myself, aboard the vessel I have just lost, have been creeping along the coast from port to port, bay to bay, rarely out of sight of land. It has taken many weeks to get this far. We sailed from Xanthus at the end of the season, wintered at Heraklion in Kriti which you Romans call Crete. Then we set out northward at the earliest opportunity. To the first and the bravest go the greatest prizes, is it not so?' His dark gaze brooded on Puella for a moment, then he continued. 'But our *trierarchus* and *gubernator* proved to be less adventurous than I. So our brave voyage degenerated into island hopping. From Heraklion to Antikithera and Kithera, across to Kalamatha, then Kefalonia to Ithaca, to Lefkada, then across to safe haven in Aktio bay where we were storm-bound for a while...'

'Actium,' said Artemidorus, giving the Greek bay its Roman name. 'What is there at Actium?'

User shrugged. 'A big inlet with a narrow entrance that is safe in most weathers. Other than that, nothing. No town. Not even a village. An ancient temple, deserted and so ruined it is almost impossible to guess which of the gods it was dedicated to. Apollo, perhaps.'

'Nothing,' echoed Artemidorus. He glanced at Puella, who returned his gaze. It had been part of Artemidorus' mission to discover what there was at Actium and send word to Antony at the earliest opportunity. And now by fortunate coincidence it seemed that he had.

But User appeared to notice nothing. His list of landfalls rumbled on. 'We also called at Igoumenitsa, protected by the island of Kerkyra which the Romans call Corfu, then Sarande, Borsch, Vlore. Then out to sea on the last of the easterly wind – which was no doubt keeping you bottled up in Brundisium. My captain being certain that the wind would shift westerly and we would be able to ride along with it and into Dyrrhachium. He was correct. Fatally so, for that is precisely what he was doing when we had the misfortune to cross your path. But tell me of your plans. You cannot be hoping to sail the little fleet whose marker lanterns I see astern back out of Dyrrhachium then south to Alexandria.'

'We are not planning to sail directly to Alexandria, no,' answered Artemidorus, matching User's apparent openness. 'Nor do we propose to follow your path back southward along the Greek coast and from island to island. We will go ashore at Dyrrhachium instead and take the Via Egnatia east from Dyrrhachium to Thessaloniki or Neapolis then get a ship from there. We plan to move swiftly and hire a vessel at the first suitable port. We hope to be in Alexandria by the end of *Maius*.'

User gazed at Artemidorus for a moment, then at Puella for a heartbeat more. 'It is a good plan,' he said, making no mention of the obvious fact that it would only work if Artemidorus and his associates were planning to take with them passports of almost magical power – and enough gold to bribe a fleet-full of cowardly captains. 'It will ensure you get to Egypt the quickest way possible. I will come with you.'

V

'Do you think he's telling the truth?' asked Quintus. 'Can we trust him?'

As *Galene* came within sight of land next morning, Artemidorus and Puella briefed the others, Quintus and Publius, on User's story and suggestion over a scant *jentaculum* that consisted largely of leftovers from last night's *cena*.

'What he has said seems to be true enough,' Artemidorus answered. 'And he gave convincing details about Actium for us to send back to Antony. But, as for trusting him, it's what he didn't say that makes me a little uncertain.'

'What do you mean?' asked Ferrata.

'Our intelligence, such as it is, suggests the waters he says he has been sailing through are effectively controlled by the navies belonging to Brutus and Cassius. Their admirals Ahenobarbus and Murcus have their ships quartered in Rhodes, but they must have patrols out. Scout ships, *liburnae*. Not to mention the smaller fleets commanded by Parmensis, Spinther and Tillius Cimber. Did User not see them? Never come across them? It makes me wonder.'

'Whatever the truth,' added Quintus, 'even if the *Libertore* navies missed him, there are still plenty of Cilician pirates, even after Pompey Magnus' campaigns against them. They would only let one of their own pass safely. Yes. He may be a spy, or he may be a pirate. Each one seems equally likely. And, on balance I'd guess, rather *more* likely than that he's merely an innocent merchant who just wants to be our friend.'

'But what does that mean for us?' asked Publius uneasily. 'Will you take him with you or leave him in Dyrrhachium?'

'Oh there was never any doubt about that,' answered Artemidorus. 'Whatever he really is, whatever he's up to, User comes with us. If he's an enemy I want him close-by, so I can keep an eye on him. If he's a friend, he could prove to be invaluable – on the road, in whichever port we decide to leave from, and most of all in Alexandria itself when we get there.'

*

The atmosphere in Dyrrhachium was very different from Brundisium. And Artemidorus could see why. Dyrrhachium was an outpost in a hostile land. Cut off from Rome and her legions unless Aeolus and Poseidon, gods of wind and wave, were in a kindly mood; and even if they were, as long as generals Ahenobarbus and Murcus with their rebel fleets did not set up a blockade.

Everything and everyone that disembarked from the four vessels through that long day, received a carefully cautious welcome. The leaders, Artemidorus – with Quintus and Puella – Publius, Severus and Gaius Licinius were welcomed and entertained to a formal *cena*. Before being billeted in the houses of the city's leading families. For one night only. Those less recognised – Messala, Lucius, the mysterious stranger Artemidorus had seen aboard *Aegeon* and of course the shipwrecked User – were given a much less formal welcome, along with the rest of Artemidorus' *contubernium* and were recommended to the better *hospitiae*. The marines and legionaries were left to their own devices – and probably had the warmest welcome of all in the *tabernae* and *lupanarae* of the dockside. But they and their slaves were officially housed in the legionary accommodation on the outskirts of the town while their animals were stabled nearby.

Unusually late, because of the routines of unloading, the formalities of welcome and the assignment to their welcoming accommodation, Artemidorus and Puella went to the baths. And as they relaxed in the steaming *caldarium*, they discovered they were not the only members of their group with this idea. The imposing ebony statue that was a naked User, fresh from *cena* and gossip at the *hospitium* he shared with the other commanders, stepped out of the shadows and into the water beside them.

'So,' he said to Artemidorus without any preamble. 'You, Antony's man, have been smuggling his proscribed enemies safely out of Italy. Most impressive. I am trying to assess whether such an action is immensely brave or incredibly foolhardy.'

'Tell me when you've made your mind up,' said Artemidorus. 'I'm not too sure which one it is myself.'

The Egyptian gave a shout of laughter. 'I can see we shall be firm friends,' he said. 'As long as we do not fall out over this beautiful woman.'

'Time will tell,' said Artemidorus. 'She will make up...'

'I will make up my own mind as to that,' said Puella.

'Will you! More impressive still! If ever you wish to make a direct comparison between us...' He lifted his hips just enough to bring his *mutinium* member into submarine view.

As if she hadn't observed it as he stepped languidly into the steaming bath, thought Artemidorus wryly.

'If I do, you will be the second one to know,' she said, apparently unimpressed. 'But who told you about Messala and Lucius?'

'They told me themselves as they prepared to leave.'

‘To *leave*?’ demanded Artemidorus, surprised.

‘They will have gone already. They and the friend they made aboard *Aegeon*. All riding eastward as though Ammit the Devourer of the Dead was after them.’

‘A friend?’ asked Artemidorus, remembering the glimpse he had caught of the man aboard Severus’ vessel.

‘A friend to them and to Marcus Junius Brutus, apparently,’ rumbled User. ‘A courier, held up for some time by contrary winds in Brundisium but riding eastwards now as fast as he can with the lady Porcia’s last letter and, so they tell me, the sad news of her death. And, of course,’ he continued, unconsciously expressing Artemidorus’ own thoughts, ‘with intelligence that the sea lanes are open and that Antony’s legionaries – if not yet his legions – are crossing into Macedonia.’

VIII: Via

i

The Via Egnatia started and ended at the *pharos* in Dyrrhachium. That tall stone and concrete tower, whose light shone westwards in the darkness out over the harbour towards its opposite number 80-*miles* distant in Brundisium.

Just as the town itself was different from Brundisium, the *via* was very different to the Via Appia, which Artemidorus and his *contubernium* had followed from Rome to the coast. Italy was calm for the moment and quietening as the proscriptions ran their course. The Appian Way travelled over vine-covered mountains, through groves of olive bushes, orange and lemon trees, beside rich farmland, past prosperous cities where the twelve tables of the law governed a largely quiescent population. And, ultimately, past legionary camps where entire armies waited peacefully for their orders.

Macedonia was still border country and the nature of the Via Egnatia reflected that. There were tribes to the north of it in Illyria and Thrace who were always restless – sometimes bellicose. And there were the *Libertores* in the south and east, plotting the downfall of the Triumvirate, their friends and associates. The Thracians, and the barbarians to the east of them, had never really settled and the death of *Divus Julius* had made matters worse. The Scordisi were threatening to invade the rich domains the Romans held with a suddenly weakened grip. Tempted by the fruitful *latifundi* estates and the wealthy cities that clung to the sides of the *via* – like the fertile acreages, prosperous villages and bustling townships that had grown up along the banks of the Nile before the drought and the plague decimated them.

Divus Julius had planned to conquer the Dacians who had crossed the Danube and were threatening to come south. Any one of these disparate groups could – and did – send raiding parties south to gather plunder, slaves and information in preparation for a proper invasion. Or, on the other hand, to scout the ground for the inevitable day when the Romans came at them in full battle-order once they had stopped slaughtering each other. Antony had recalled the legions – in spite of the Dacian threat – but he had done nothing to disturb the arrangements along the *via*. Knowing he, too, would need to bring his armies east one day.

The military nature of the road was further reflected in the army terms for the facilities that the soldiers staffed in anticipation of government messengers, military couriers, patrols, legions, cohorts or armies coming past. In place of *hospitiae* were *stationes*. Not to mention proper *castra* defensible army camps, way points and *castra oppida* security posts where passers-by had to produce the proper paperwork before being allowed to proceed. No doubt, thought Artemidorus, Messala and Lucius would stick very close indeed to the messenger hurrying towards Brutus. Who would have all the passes required to hasten his progress – and theirs into the bargain. One of the details they had suspiciously failed to mention during his interview with them the day before yesterday.

Brutus and Cassius had also done nothing so far to close the road coming east from Dyrrhachium, for they and their legions were concentrating on Asia, Syria and perhaps even Egypt. But, just like Antony – and, indeed, the Scordisi and the Dacians – they would have sent out spies to assess the situation in case they did need to come westward. Spies who would have to gauge conditions and preparations along the one and only route Antony and young Caesar would have to follow when they brought their armies to the final, inevitable, battle.

*

After breakfast next morning, Artemidorus assembled the *contubernium* on the dockside in the space between the four unladen ships and the start of the *via*, where the soldiers and slaves of Publius' command, guarded by the marines from *Aegeon* and *Galene*, filled the warehouses with horses, carts, mules and bustle. The clouds above the towering *pharos* were darkening. The wind was threatening to swing back into the east. The captains of all four vessels were looking nervous – keen to get back to Brundisium as soon as Aeolus and Poseidon permitted. It certainly looked like a better option than being stuck in Dyrrhachium.

As usual, Artemidorus stood flanked by Quintus and Ferrata, but Puella stood by User, who had joined them for the planning briefing as he proposed to do for the journey to Alexandria. Artemidorus looked thoughtfully at the assembled faces: towering Hercules and quick-thinking Kyros: his friend and, perhaps lover, Nonus their scribe, and Furius their *carnifex* executioner – though they were all adept enough at killing. All of them except for Crinas, the physician. The only ones who seemed out of place to him under the new circumstances were the Senate secretary Adonis, with his fantastic memory, and his almost identical twin sister Venus, slaves of *Divus Julius'* murderer Trebonius – who had been himself been tortured to death by Dolabella in Smyrna late last year and was the first of *Divus Julius'* killers to die.

Venus and Adonis were incalculably useful in Rome. It was Adonis, after all, who had recorded, remembered and explained Cicero's fatal joke about Octavianus – that he should be '*congratulated, elevated, exterminated*'; that throwaway line in the midst of a speech to the Senate which alienated the young Caesar and proved to be the start of the old man's downfall. Artemidorus recognised he had made an error in bringing them here. However it was one which he could turn to his advantage. 'Adonis, Venus,' he said. 'While the rest of us prepare to leave, I want you to go with User. He will describe to you, in the greatest detail, everything of note about Actium. I want you to record every scrap of information he gives you and then take that information back to General Antony as speedily as you can. I will dictate to Notus a pass that should get you along the Appian Way swiftly and safely – with an escort from *Legio* VII if necessary – and confirmations that you have been formally manumitted and are now free Roman citizens. After briefing General Antony, I want you to report to Consul and Triumvir Marcus Aemilius Lepidus. Adonis, he will no doubt put you back to work keeping Senate records. And Venus, he will also find a place for you in his household. But remember, you still both work for me. That is your prime responsibility. There will be all sorts of information that, with a little intelligence, you can gather, either in the Consul's household or on the Senate floor. We will talk when I return.'

The brother and sister looked at each-other, frankly relieved to be taken out of the adventure at this early stage and return to the safety of Rome. They went to User, who cheerfully accompanied them to the villa they had slept in the night before, where they would record all the details he could remember about Actium.

As the three of them vanished towards the town itself, Artemidorus said, 'Right. Now it's time for the rest of us to get organised.'

ii

By mid-morning the *contubernium* was almost ready to depart. They were dressed for travelling through potentially hostile country and probably inclement weather. Their wagons were laden, mules in line between the traces. Ferrata and Furius, acting as quartermasters, had returned from Dyrrhachium's markets with the last of the provisions they had purchased. The escort Publius had detailed to accompany them for the first part of the journey was mounted and ready, while the rest of the centurion's command was still sorting themselves out – too well aware they would inevitably be travelling more slowly than Artemidorus and his people. Not least because that number of mounted soldiers would need to forage for food while the spy's unit could carry most of their necessities with them. And in any case was a small enough group to make full use of the way-stations, towns and villages along the road.

Artemidorus had dictated Venus' and Adonis' paperwork to Notus, talked to Publius, the two centurion marine commanders and the two captains, saying his goodbyes and making certain he was leaving everything in good order. Venus and Adonis had gone aboard *Galene*, under the wing of Gaius Licinius, ready for the return journey. Only Quintus and Puella were missing. The former because Artemidorus had detailed him to find User the kind of kit he would need to ride east with them. Puella because she thought a woman's eye would make the process of dressing the mysterious merchant more effective. The three of them were therefore the last to appear. And, thought Artemidorus, whoever had made the final decisions had done a good job. The big Egyptian was now clad in a red legionary tunic, with a blood-red *sagum* cloak to match. His massive torso was covered in the overlapping hoops of armour laced down the front that Quintus had been so impressed to discover in the cellar of Suadela's brothel. More overlapping bands sat on his shoulders, making them appear even larger. A red scarf stopped his neck from chafing. His forearms were protected by *manicae* metal arm guards and his shins by iron greaves. He wore a long, sharp cavalry *spada* on his left hip and a *pugio* on his right. They had even found some *caligae* big enough to accommodate feet that were almost as big as Hercules'. Only the white cotton headdress with its square top and wings falling to his armoured shoulders betrayed his origin as Egyptian. He carried, slung over one shoulder, a waterproof, hooded cloak of oiled wool – the only non-military part of his new wardrobe.

'Transformed from a sailor to a soldier, as you see,' he rumbled, approaching Artemidorus with a grin.

'And from a legionary to a cavalryman,' answered Artemidorus. 'Do you ride?' He nodded and Kyros led a tall stallion forward whose coat was as black as User's skin.

'As though I was born to it. Like a Greek Centaur.' User crossed to the horse and stroked his nose, breathing gently into his nostrils, befriending the animal. 'Shall I play the tutor centaur Cheiron to your Hercules – by which I mean *you*, not your huge friend?' he asked mockingly.

'As long as we don't end up like the centaur Nessos and Hercules – killing each other because of a beautiful woman,' said Artemidorus.

User gave a laugh and vaulted into the saddle. Artemidorus did the same and at his signal they were off.

*

They rode three-abreast south out of Dyrrhachium on the road that led down towards Apollonia. This first section was the Via Egnatia, swinging eastwards after 35-*miles* or so, leaving a smaller road running down the last stretch to the city of Apollo itself. As soon as they were clear of the town, the road rose slightly, its 20-foot width sitting on a man-made causeway between the sand-dunes, the beach and the sea on their right and low, swampy ground on their left. Artemidorus rode in the middle with User on his right and Quintus on his left. Puella rode behind User and it seemed to Artemidorus he could feel her eagerness to come level with them once the via was wide enough. Ferrata as ever had his back and Furius followed in Quintus' wake, while the others formed as tight a group as possible behind them. With the slaves and the supply carts behind them and Publius' patrol bringing up the rear.

Even though it was the end of *Februarius*, the ice on the swamps to the inland side of the via was beginning to melt and the driving rain brought by the easterlies over the last few days had made pools of swamp-water grow into lakes. 'This is bad country,' observed User. 'In Egypt we have found pools of stagnant water like that breed miasmas which spread disease. There is one particular illness many fear. Once contracted, it never seems to go away. If you suffer from it, you have bouts of faintness, almost like the falling sickness. They come upon you without warning. Even the strongest constitution is hard-put to resist them.'

Artemidorus nodded, frowning. 'We have such an ailment in Rome,' he said. 'Though I hear there is a new ailment decimating Egypt. We're getting word of a kind of *plaga* sweeping down the Nile…'

But the merchant's attention had wandered. Away to his right, the triremes were pulling the supply ships out to sea. Setting sail in the afternoon, for fear the wind would change.

'With this wind they could be at Brundisium in sixteen hours and arrive in the dark. But if they take their time, the voyage might last twenty hours, arriving after sunrise. They're wise to move, I think.'

'And you have ships that can, do you?' challenged Quintus.

'Sail across the wind? Yes. Have you never been to Egypt and seen the boats that navigate the Nile? I will take you aboard one of my own fleet and you will see.'

iii

They stopped for their first night at the village of Kavaje 20-*miles* south of Dyrrhachium. The via, having followed the sea-shore, moved east a little while still running southwards so that there was swampy ground on either hand, but even in the gloom of the wintery afternoon they could see hillsides away on their left gathering into mountains further inland. There was nothing much to Kavaje beyond a tiny, ill-supplied way-station and a corral containing half a dozen horses. Artemidorus talked to the local commander, and established that three men had ridden through earlier in the day without stopping, changing their horses or showing their papers. The state of the place and the lackadaisical attitude of the soldiers staffing it did not bode well for Antony's arrival later. But, thought Artemidorus, Publius would be along soon. It was fortunate the *contubernium* and their escort had brought their own provisions, equipment and leather-walled tents. They set up camp as the day darkened and the sky began to fill with low, black clouds.

They were glad to leave in the morning. But the weather had turned again, and it was slow-going through the relentless, driving rain which arrived, as User predicted, on the wings of a cold north wind. By the second night they had passed the swamps and reached the *Mutatio Claudiana* less than 15-*miles* further along the via. Here the great road turned abruptly away from the highway on down to Apollonia and swung left into a wide, flat river valley guarded on each side by forested hill-slopes. And there, on the soggy riverine plain between the steep valley sides was the transit camp. With military efficiency it was bright with lamps and flaming torches against the gathering darkness. And could afford to be so for it was walled – if not quite fully fortified – like a legionary overnight *castrum*. It covered much of the valley right up to the bank of the river which supplied, no doubt, plentiful fish as well as unending fresh water. Too much fresh water, for it was threatening to flood.

As Artemidorus led the first section of his tightly-packed command through the *porta praetorim* main gate, guards, slaves, and stablehands scurried about. By the time he reached the end of the Via Praetoria and was dismounting outside the solid-looking commander's accommodation, the rest of his weary travellers were crowding into the facility behind him. The door opened, and a tall man came down the steps. 'Welcome,' he called. 'We've been expecting you. Tribune Messala, Centurion Lucius and the courier accompanying them said last night that you would be here today!'

'They have gone on, I expect,' answered Artemidorus as he dismounted.

'First thing this morning. As though the Friendly Ones were chasing after them!'

*

The commander of *Mutatio Claudiana* way station was a centurion called Ventidius Rufus. Which was not surprising as his hair was flaming red. In Artemidorus' experience, such men were short tempered and given to violence. But this Rufus could not have been more patient and friendly. 'Fortuna is smiling on me,' he said as he welcomed eight guests to a traditional nine-person *cena* after they had seen to their men, horses and wagons – and he had checked their passes and documentation, then showed them not only to their accommodation but also to the *mutatio*'s modest bathhouse.

'No news from Rome or civilised company for months – and now two sets of dinner guests one after another! I have to tell you, though, that your friends did not fare as well as you, for they arrived unannounced. And you have them to thank for your more generous welcome – it was prepared because of their warning!'

Artemidorus smiled gratefully and made courteous noises, though he noted an undercurrent almost of threat in Rufus' words. He suspected Messala had set Rufus to entertain them so richly that they would be slow to depart in the morning. It was fortunate the three men in front of them would soon have drawn so far ahead that this sort of thing would no longer be possible, he thought. Though, as he lay on his dining couch with Puella at his back and User at her back, he wondered what other little tricks and traps the devious Tribune would leave in his wake to slow them further. No matter how well they had got along together in Italy, here in Macedonia Messala was Brutus' man and therefore a bitter enemy.

But it was impossible to resist Rufus' good-natured enthusiasm. He and his two senior officers lay on the *lectus immus*, host's couch;

Artemidorus, Puella and User on the *lectus medius*, first guest couch, and Quintus, Ferrata and Crinas were surprised to find themselves on the *lectus summus*, second guest couch. 'You will not be surprised to know that our simple country fare consists mainly of fish,' said their host. 'But obviously we keep our own hens and herd both goats and sheep. And, to be fair, the river can supply more than eels, carp, pike, trout and tench. And we are fortunate the coast is not too far, so we have Poseidon's offerings as well as delicacies both to eat and drink shipped in from all over the *Levante*; our area here where to Roman eyes the sun appears to *levare* rise.'

Rufus' introduction hardly prepared them for the feast. There were olives, cheese – both goats' and sheep's, salt and sweet. Hard-boiled and roasted eggs. Huge river pike stuffed with eels. Storks stuffed with sparrows and blackbirds. A roast dolphin served whole. The most delicious honey from local bees, which was hardly sweeter than the wild figs and pomegranates that completed the feast. And a dizzying array of wines from Greece, Macedonia, Syria and Egypt accompanied the food.

The conversation followed traditional lines to begin with. Rufus told his guests about himself, his command, his men and their duties, as was the host's social duty. The legionaries behind him on his couch elaborated with some soldier's stories that were almost as salty as the goats' cheese. Then the enquiries turned to the guests, and in due course to Rome and the situation there. The five newcomers and the man they rescued were asked to elaborate on what Messala and Lucius had revealed the night before. Then, more delicately – guardedly – the conversation turned to politics. Like the city fathers in Dyrrhachium, Rufus and his men seemed to be walking a fine line between Antony, Octavianus, Brutus and Cassius – trying to ensure their future no matter who won the inevitable battle for final control of the Republic.

In spite of his attempts to be careful what he ate and drank, Artemidorus felt over-stuffed and light-headed when at last he went to the bed-chamber assigned to him. One of three side-by-side which housed Puella and User as well as himself. They left together, which was unfortunate – he would have liked to have discussed their red-headed host with the ever-insightful Puella but not with User. Was Rufus just too friendly? Was his open-handed generosity more than it seemed? Or was he just, as the spy suspected earlier, being careful to protect his future no matter which way the wind blew.

Mulling these thoughts over, Artemidorus lay on his pallet,

thankfully keeping his tunic on. For it seemed he had hardly closed his eyes when a commotion in the corridor jerked him awake. He leapt off his bed and ran to the door. Tore it open and froze. There was just enough light in the corridor for him to see Puella wrestling with User. Both of them gasping and grunting. Instantly aflame with rage at the sight of this attempted rape, Artemidorus stepped forward, fist raised, when, providentially, he heard what Puella was whispering so urgently. 'Latrine...'

And, as though the word had magic powers, he felt his bowels clench.

iv

Crinas was there before them. 'It was probably the figs,' he said, as they rushed to join him. 'Overripe figs are notorious.'

'At least it's not poison,' said User, raising his voice above a certain amount of background noise.

'I wish it had been,' said Puella. 'Death would be better than this.'

'The point is,' said Artemidorus. 'The point is – did Rufus do this on purpose? Is it a trick to slow us down?'

A question that seemed to be answered almost immediately when their host joined them, and silence fell.

The night was long and taxing. Whether he had done it on purpose or not, the effect of Rufus' generosity was that they were unfit to proceed next morning. Many of the others had eaten the honey-sweet figs, so the fact that their commanders were not fit to travel did not result in any negative comment from the men. And the cooks did not have a busy time next day.

But Artemidorus and his followers did move on early in the morning of the fourth day – for, quite apart from any other consideration, Publius and his sizeable command would certainly be arriving soon and *Mutato Claudiana* could only accommodate so many.

The weather showed no sign of easing as *Februarius* slipped over into *Mars* so that the fourth day was a bitter slog to the next *statione* 20-*miles* along the via with the weather, which had been at their backs now blowing in over their left shoulders. The next *statione* was the *castrum* of Ad Quintum – little more than a command post and a set of unexpectedly palatial baths heated by the hot springs nearby. The centurion in command was happily explained that his men had built the baths because there was nothing else to do except perform drills and prepare for visitors who never seemed to come.

Three travellers had passed through more than two days ago, but had not stopped – merely changed horses. And they had been the first strangers since the messenger bringing news of *Divus Julius'* death.

Basic though it was, the *statione* could accommodate the majority of the travellers, though some had to pitch their tents. But at least the food was plentiful – for those whose stomachs had settled. And there were no figs. A lengthy soak in the scalding *caldarium* did much to revive Artemidorus, Puella and User. Ferrata and Quintus had not succumbed to Rufus' figs and so needed little in the way of restoratives. 'I swear,' said Puella, 'Ferrata's insides must be as strong as his armour.'

'Iron by name, iron by nature,' agreed Artemidorus. 'And there is nothing in nature that can stop Quintus.'

'Except of course the sea,' concluded User.

'As he will point out to you,' said Artemidorus, 'going to sea is unnatural. If the gods had meant us to go to sea, they would have given us fins and gills.'

*

The via sloped gently downhill between Ad Quintum and their next stopping point of Trajectus on the banks of the River Skumbi twenty *miles* further on. The way station's name simply meant 'Crossing' and there was a bridge over the river there which they did not use, for it carried a road that led away southwards into the wilderness and the mountains beyond; mountains which in turn led to Greece. There were mountains close to the north as well, clad with black forests which set Quintus to reminiscing about Germanian Ghost Warriors who came and went silent, deadly, black-painted and naked through just such terrain. Soldiers' stories that came back to haunt him; to haunt all of them, in fact, but not until a few more days had passed and they arrived, weary and travel-sick, at Heraclea Lyncestis more than 100 wild and mountainous *miles* further along their route. At the end of a day which had blessedly been dry and, for the time of year, surprisingly warm.

The city of Heraclea Lyncestis had been founded by Alexander's father Philip II of Macedon, and named in honour of Hercules. It had once been an important element of Macedonian rule, guarding the kingdom's northern border; but under Rome it had fallen into poor shape. The only thing keeping it alive was the via which passed through the middle of it. It had been walled, as most cities, towns and *castra* along the via were, especially out here in the wilderness. But along with the outskirts of the city, the defensive walls had fallen into serious disrepair. The garrison that *Divus Julius* stationed there occupied the centre of the place, billeted in buildings on a hill overlooking the main area that was still populated, which gathered round a basilica market and – providentially – a decent public bathhouse. The centurion in charge of them was called Gaius Omerus and he seemed to have a permanent chip on his shoulder. Although he never said so, everything about him made Artemidorus suspect that he felt it was far beneath his dignity to be stuck out here in the back of beyond. His name was unfamiliar, but he behaved like a patrician with forebears as ancient as Brutus'. But he was still just a centurion – and a surprisingly elderly one.

Centurion Gaius Omerus went through a formal welcome. Mentioned that three other strangers had visited several days earlier, and left them to their own devices with no further information. A couple of ill-dressed, grubby legionaries showed them to the capacious, ill-tended billets then they, too, left them to their own devices. Publius' men had to find the stables and see to their own horses – taking care of the *contubernium*'s mounts and mules as well.

As they soaked in the *caldarium*, Omerus grudgingly directed them to, Quintus observed, 'I don't like this place.'

'Why ever not?' wondered User, his tone dripping with irony.

The *triarius* looked over at Artemidorus, who nodded, giving him mute permission to voice concerns which the spy suspected they both shared. And Quintus sought the permission because he didn't trust User either. But then, Quintus' trust was a hard thing to earn.

'It's out on the edge of nowhere,' explained the old soldier, taking User's question at face value. 'The Dacians are far too close for comfort. The garrison is under strength, apathetic, badly led by that sad bastard Gaius Omerus and stuck in a *castrum* that really needs proper work. The only reason I can think of that the whole place hasn't been ransacked and put to the torch is that the citizens running the interesting market down there have come to some sort of agreement with the local brigands and the Dacians behind them. Probably Omerus and his garrison as well, now I come to think of it.'

'One,' emphasised Artemidorus, 'that may well involve them mentioning to their murderous friends, any suspicions they might have about travellers along the via passing through. What they might be carrying, what it might be worth so forth.'

'Information, now I come to think of it,' said Puella, 'that Messala and Lucius might have let fall on *their* way through. They've given themselves enough of a lead to make sure that any message they leave here will get out into the mountains well before we show up. They slowed us at *Mutatio Claudiana* with the figs. Maybe they'll want to stop us here.'

'That's certainly a possibility,' agreed Artemidorus, 'The figs would be about as far as Ventidius Rufus would have the guts to go – because he daren't identify himself with Antony's enemies too early in the game. He has to realise the general will be bringing an army though eventually. And the whole Republic now knows what happens to people Antony and Octavian don't think they can trust. But this far east, there are other forces at play. Military forces who don't care about Antony and his armies. If Messala can set the Dacians on us, for instance, then that would certainly be to Brutus' benefit and everyone here could wash their hands of us and claim innocence. Messala is more than capable of working that out!'

'Always assuming Brutus and Cassius haven't showed up with their seventeen legions in the mean-time,' added Ferrata.

'All it would take is a lead long enough to be sure any information they let slip can get to the nearest Dacian camp – three or four days, as Puella says,' mused Quintus. 'And there's certainly enough in our wagons to tempt a raiding party. Arms, supplies, gold...'

'Furthermore,' nodded Artemidorus, 'it seems to me the further east we come, the more the locals – citizens and garrisons – lean towards Brutus and Cassius, which compounds the problems of our stay here. We can't go on until the morning. And there may well be more than one faction trying to relieve us of *vita* and *impedimenta*, life and luggage, tonight.'

V

As they made their way through a surprisingly balmy evening from the baths to their billets – and the promise of dinner – Artemidorus and Quintus assessed the buildings they were passing. Not as ancient architectural gems, traditional Hellenic edifices or beautiful antique temples but as potential defensive positions.

'Though of course,' observed User, 'if the Dacians do hit us tonight, then that's only the start of our troubles. We'd still have to fight our way from here to Thessaloniki.'

'Over a hundred *miles*: three days' journey at least,' nodded Artemidorus, 'through Florina, Edessa and Pella. Once we make Florina, though, we're in Greece and should be safe enough. I don't know what there is at Edessa beyond a way station and whatever's left of an ancient Greek city. But Pella is the capital of Macedonia, where Philip II had his palace, where Alexander himself was born.' He paused, thinking of the manner in which the gods amused themselves. Artemidorus and his *contubernium* were passing through Alexander's birthplace, on their way to the city in which he died, for whom it was named. And where he was preserved, mummified and wrapped in beaten gold, within a crystal coffin open for all to see. 'If we make a run for Florina we can be there within a day.' he said. 'And I suspect only a desperate Dacian would come after us in daylight. Like most *praedatores* raiders they prefer to work in the dark.'

'But,' added Quintus darkly, 'this is where we're supposed to be leaving the escort Publius sent east with us. So we'll be cutting our forces by more than half.'

'So,' mused Artemidorus, 'if the Dacians do hit us tonight, we'll have to give them such a bloody nose that they think twice about doing it again. Give us a chance to make it into Greece.'

'Easier said than done,' concluded Ferrata. 'But I'll bet it will be fun to try...'

The *contubernium*, their soldiers, slaves and their escort were billeted in a range of municipal buildings at the top of the hill. Beside the better-preserved structures that had been requisitioned by the permanent troops. They were positioned above the open market place and, on either hand, the increasingly derelict dwellings of the once-prosperous conurbation. The billets, like the walls defending the city, had fallen into disrepair but they were largely dry, even if their walls were beginning to crumble between the columns that supported the roofs.

The only building that was not falling into ruin was the Temple of Hercules, the demigod who protected the city. This was much larger than the Temple of Hercules Victor in Rome and square rather than round. Like the temple of Jupiter Optimus Maximus on the top of the Capitoline, it had an open precinct around it. The edifice itself stood on a raised section at the top of a flight of steps rising through half a dozen stairs to the front, the back and on either hand. The columns that supported its roof were not bound together by bricks. Instead there was an inner structure, a solid, square brick-built building with a flat roof standing several cubits below that supported by the outer columns. The moment Artemidorus saw it, he nodded with grim satisfaction. 'I think I'll just make a sacrifice in there before I retire,' he said. 'No matter what happens – or doesn't happen – tonight, I'd feel happier if Hercules joined my personal demigod Achilleus, holding his hands over me – over all of us, in fact.'

*

Whereas the sleeping arrangement was clearly just a matter of chance, it seemed to Artemidorus as he returned, his hands still stained with the blood of the lamb lying dead on Hercules' altar, that Fortuna as well as Hercules was smiling on them. For if things went wrong tonight, it would be possible for everyone to fall back out of their half-ruined accommodation into the temple which, with a little planning would make a very effective citadel. This was a fact given extra weight by the lack of any priests or acolytes actually occupying the solid building or its open environs. People who would only get in the way when circumstances became challenging. Especially if their holy precincts were threatened with sacrilege. All of which he had been able to calculate while looking carefully around as he went through the rituals of sacrifice.

After a modest and largely tasteless *cena*, and before allowing anyone to finally bed down for the night, Artemidorus used the last of the early-spring light to make a number of defensive arrangements. Firstly, and most importantly, he made sure the wagons containing their gold and armaments could be moved swiftly into the temple precincts where they could easily be defended. He had the wheels greased so that they moved not only easily but silently. Then he set two squads to the simple enough task of collecting dry wood from the nearest ruins and piling it at the four corners of the precinct. The plans for the defence of the temple itself he left to Quintus, whose experience in this sort of thing rivalled that of *Divus Julius* himself. And he left him fashioning simple ladders out of the longest, soundest pieces of timber retrieved from the ruins.

There was a certain amount of grumbling from the troops, because they were doing things the wrong way around – it was usual to create the *castrum* and then eat *cena*. But most of it was good-natured. And by the time dark arrived, everything was prepared. All of Artemidorus' *contubernium*, their auxiliaries and their escorts knew the plan and their place within it, something that had been achieved almost miraculously, without alerting their lackadaisical hosts – or, it seemed, any of the townsfolk so keen to stay friends with their warlike neighbours at almost any price. Despite the fact that for the first time in some years, there were torches burning in the Temple of Hercules, left there by the Centurion who had sacrificed the lamb earlier.

*

Artemidorus sprang awake from a shallow, restless slumber when a hand closed on his left shoulder. His room was brightened by the flickering flame of an oil lamp held in User's fist. He looked up to see Puella's face immediately above his own. 'They're here,' she breathed. 'Quintus sent us to wake you.'

He sat up, reaching for his belt and *gladius*. His *pugio* was under the folded cloak he was using as his pillow. He rolled out of bed and came erect. User and Puella were in their tunics. Recently roused. Not yet wearing their armour or weapons. 'We need to arm,' he said.

'Quintus says there's time,' nodded User. 'He posted lookouts down along the wall, just as you ordered. They've reported movement. Spotted the Dacians' scouts.'

'Right,' said Artemidorus. 'Get ready for battle. You know the plan.'

Moments later, the three of them were with Quintus in the Temple of Hercules. Artemidorus watched approvingly as his plan swung smoothly into action. The rest of the *contubernium* gathered silently around him, their faces chiselled by shadows beneath the steady torch-flames. The first of the wagons drew up outside the front of the temple, at the foot of the steps leading up to its columned portico. At once, Ferrata, Furius and the rest were in action, pulling out their weapons and heading towards their designated positions. The wagons with the gold and the precious documents arrived. Together with the weapons cache, they made an effective blockade along the front of the temple. One that could be opened and closed as the slaves rolled them one way or another. Most of the *contubernium* slaves fell into position behind them. Publius' legionaries and their well-armed legionary slaves all reported to their posts along the sides and across the backs of the temple.

Silence fell.

They were ready.

vi

The Dacians' tactics were simple and predictable. This was a raiding party, not an army; a sizeable group by the look of things – maybe a hundred in all, or so the watchkeepers reported. But it was composed and led by robbers. Not well-trained warriors marshalled by experienced generals.

They relied at first on silence and surprise. Coming through and over the city's ruined walls like shadows and vanishing into the dark streets between the derelict buildings of the outskirts. Led by local citizens and traitors from the military garrison, they assembled briefly in the darkness beside the billets. Then ran in on silent feet with daggers ready to stab sleeping hearts and slit sleeping throats.

But there were none to be had.

After some confusion, which reached the ears of Artemidorus' command as a stirring and a muttering out in the darkness near their empty sleeping-quarters, they reformed and began to calculate the strength of the enemy who were awake and prepared. The citizens and the treacherous legionaries no doubt assured them that they faced fifty or so men: a cavalry unit without their horses, a *contubernium* of little more than a dozen, including slaves. None of them particularly well- armed. They wore strange armour – if they had had time to put it on – but no had obvious weaponry other than swords and daggers. The strangers certainly had gold with them, for gold had been seen in the market where the soldiers had gone shopping. Fifty men defending a fortune, therefore, against a hundred raiders or more – what could possibly go wrong?

Their second and last approach was the one they used on the battlefield – under somebody else's orders. Somebody more experienced than they were, who could probably recognise a trap when they saw one. They came charging out of the darkness in a solid mass ten men wide and a little more than ten men deep. Waving their swords and axes and howling at the top of their voices. Halfway across the shadowy precinct, still almost invisible in the darkness, they were met by a volley of fire-arrows, which missed them altogether, soaring over their heads to fall behind them. For a moment longer, the shadows persisted and the attacking Dacians were little more than gleaming eyes, glittering teeth and flashing blades. Then, with a sound like the arrival of a gale of wind, two piles of firewood stacked earlier on the outer corners of the precinct burst into flames, flooding the whole place with light.

'*Impetus*!' shouted Artemidorus. 'Attack!' As he spoke, he stepped forward with Quintus, Puella and Ferrata, all of them releasing a volley of slingshots into the oncoming hoard. As Furius, Kyros, Notus and the rest of the archers, given access to the temple's inner roof by Quintus' makeshift ladders, let fly their second volley of fire-arrows. The front row hesitated, more than half of them wounded, dying or burning. Unable to stop, the second row ran over them, only to be met by the same withering fire. There was the better part of twenty men down when the third row arrived, their impetus slowed further as they tried to pick their way over their fallen comrades without tripping up. A task made harder by the onward pressure of two further rows behind them.

Artemidorus slid his sling into his belt and pulled out his *gladius*. Like the others, he had had time to put on his armour and his helmet. Grabbing the shield leaning against the side of the wagon immediately in front of him, he bellowed, 'INCURSUS!' and led the charge himself.

With Quintus, Puella and Ferrata beside him, he ran through an opening between the wagons, made wider by slaves rolling them aside. Immediately behind them came Hercules and User. The Egyptian had replaced his headdress with one of the new helmets. A centurion's matching Artemidorus', with the red horsehair lateral crest and the solid metal peak reaching out to protect the eyes as the larger cheek-flaps were designed to protect the face. If Ferrata had been wearing a helmet like these when Laenas sprang his ambush, he would still have had both his eyes, thought Artemidorus.

As they charged into the Dacians, followed by another dozen legionaries and legionary slaves, all armoured and shielded, so two more columns of legionaries came snaking out of the shadowed porticoes to right and left, catching the Dacians in a pincer movement and relying on shock – for each column consisted of only fifteen men. As they attacked, the bowmen on the temple roof continued to pour fire-arrows into the flame-bright killing ground.

*

Artemidorus' world shrank to a tiny, unimaginably intense fraction of space and time, as it always did in battle. The comrades beside him slammed their shields against his, putting him at the centre of a small but solid shield-wall but leaving just enough space for him to stab forward with his needle-pointed *gladius*. The metal of the new swords might be strong enough to take and hold a keen edge, but the *gladius* was still primarily a stabbing weapon. Two feet of slim, sharp-pointed blade that thrust outward and upward into the bellies of his opponents. Especially of the wild ones who tried to strike at him over the rim of his shield. Raising their arms, expanding their rib-cages, separating their ribs and leaving their torsos open to the upward thrust, even if they wore armour.

Faces appeared over the metal-clad shield-rim, screaming, gaping, eyes rolling, beards slick with spittle or blood. Faces hardly associated with the invisible bodies he stabbed and stabbed and stabbed. Hot blood running over his fist. The weight of dead men standing, toppling forward onto his shield as the life drained out of them together with blood and all the other bodily fluids. The stench of terror, rancid breath, sweat, filth, blood and excrement. The odour of battle. The pressure of his massive companions Hercules and User at his back supporting him as he moved forward. Both men tall enough to be striking over his shoulders at the barbarians beside and behind the ones he was slaughtering. Another face reared. Before he could strike with his *gladius,* the shaft of a *pilum* came over his shoulder its iron point piercing the Dacian bandit's eye, smashing through the socket into his skull, jerking free as he fell back screaming. Hercules using the long spear cannily – pulling it back before the iron shaft began to bend, stabbing forward once again. The flagstones beneath their *caligae* becoming slippery. Another element to be assimilated, thought Artemidorus. Made allowance for.

Another snarling face thrust towards him as he was momentarily distracted by his untrustworthy footing. A battle-axe swung up. He made the automatic riposte of the *gladius* stab without thinking. The blade turned aside almost twisting the handle out of his grip – a longer mail shirt than usual. Jerking his shield up so the rim slammed into the gaping jaw, across the howling throat, he managed to knock the Dacian's helmet back. Immediately, he nodded his head forward with all the force his neck could supply. The extended brow-ridge slammed into the barbaric features, its blunt edge destroying nose, shattering cheekbones. But still the wild man came on. As Artemidorus was distracted further. His abrupt movements had unsettled the shield to his left. His companion there was fighting to maintain footing on the marble slabs of the temple precinct. Slipping, falling...

Artemidorus slammed his *gladius* forward again. This time it pierced the armour, sinking into the Dacian's belly. Boiling blood flooded over his fist. As he did so, Hercules' *pilum* stabbed forward again almost tearing the top of the shattered skull off. Blood and brain-matter cascaded out of the ruined gargoyle, filling his face. He turned away as Hercules retrieved his spear-point. He was just too late. He jerked his sword back. The handle slipped out of his blood-slick grip. It was wedged in the dead man's body. Another great gout of blood sprayed into his face. Blinding him. Even as he let go of his sword and turned, reaching down in the darkness to catch Puella and try to pull her erect once more.

But then he was rudely shouldered aside and someone else was standing over the fallen woman. He dashed the hot blood and slimy brain-matter out of his eyes and reached for his *pugio*. Still turning from the dead Dacian as he tottered there, faceless – almost headless – held erect by the shields in front and his close-packed companions behind. Artemidorus' blood-filled eyes cleared to see User towering over Puella disdaining to use a shield, swinging his *spada* cavalry sword double-handed, forcing the last of the defeated robbers back. Until, side by side, they could both reach down and pull Puella safely erect once more.

As Centurion Gaius Omerus in charge of Heraclea Lyncestis' legionary detachment led his men onto the battleground too late to do anything other than to arrest the survivors and dispose of the dead.

vii

Zeuta, nephew to Deceneus high king of the Daci, sat secured on a chair in the centurion Omerus' *tablinum* briefing room. His battle-rage was still boiling, and it had taken several legionaries to restrain him. Most of the men he had led over the ruined walls were dead and were being piled ready for burning. Crinas and Omerus' legionary physician were tending the wounded – many of whom would soon be joining the dead pile; a few of whom might eventually join their young leader and live on. Zeuta was wounded too, but Crinas had not tended him. His wounds were not serious, despite the fact that he had led the charge from the front. But his rage was such that the gentle Greek could not come close to him – let alone touch him or tend him. Any more than he would have been able to tend a lion or a tiger wounded in the Circus.

Artemidorus, his *contubernium* and the officers from their escort had no idea who the raging Dacian was. They had no way of understanding the bitter words he spat at them. Gaius Omerus and his men might well have recognised him. Or have understood what he was saying. But to admit to either would surely make them look like traitors at the very least. Artemidorus understood this so he asked the two obvious questions, one after the other.

'Crinas, is there a wounded Dacian who seems to understand Latin or Greek, who might be well enough to translate for us?'

'Sadly, not at this moment, Centurion. It is too early to tell...'

'I understand.' Artemidorus shrugged. Then he continued. 'Gaius Omerus, is there anyone in the city who might understand Dacian and who might be willing to act as our *interpres* interpreter?'

'I don't know off-hand. I can send men down into the town to ask...' Omerus tried to look reliable, open and honest. He failed on all three counts – his pale face slick with sweat and shifty with guilt.

'Do so, please.' Artemidorus seemed not to notice the looks Omerus was sharing with his senior officers. 'In the mean-time, Furius, see if you can find a way to communicate with him.'

As Omerus gestured to a couple of his men who vanished through the *tablinum* door, Furius stepped forward to confront the young Dacian. 'Qui es?' *Who are you*, he asked.

The prisoner spat at him.

Furius knocked him unconscious.

'That's a good way to make him talk to us,' said User mockingly.

'It works,' said Furius, unperturbed. 'In the long run.'

The Dacian stirred.

'Qui es?' asked Furius.

The Dacian spat blood at him.

Furius knocked him out.

*

The interpreter Omerus' men brought back was a plump merchant. His clothes were reassuringly in the Dacian style rather than the Roman. He gave off an air of matter-of-fact competence which chimed perfectly with the way in which he went about his business. He said that his name was Brassus.

'That's a Dacian name,' said Quintus equably.

'My father was Dacian. But my mother raised me in his absence. Taught me both her tongue and his.'

'Ravaged?' asked Quintus.

'Romanced,' answered Brassus. 'But my father was a wandering man. A trader. When I was old enough I followed in his footsteps as far as the *flumen* Danuvius and set up a trading route.'

No sooner was he standing in front of the unconscious prisoner than he said, 'This is Zeuta, nephew to Deceneus high king of the Daci. He is the old man's favourite. I would suggest you do not damage him too severely unless you want an all-out war.'

Omerus and his men stirred nervously. Artemidorus had little doubt that they too knew the identity of the prisoner. But possibly not the danger his capture might have put them in.

'Can you talk to him?' asked Artemidorus.

'When he wakes up. But I cannot guarantee that he will talk to me.'

Brassus' fears were well-founded. Zeuta spat blood and teeth at him as soon as the merchant tried to communicate. Furius stepped forward, fist raised. But Artemidorus gestured him to stand back. To his wise eyes it seemed the warrior in the grip of blood-lust had been replaced by the sulky youth too proud to give an *uncia* inch for fear of losing face.

'Crinas, will he die of his wounds if they remain untreated?'

'Of course, in time.'

'Within the next day or two?'

'No. They have stopped bleeding. They will only become dangerous if they are infected. And infection takes time.'

'Very well. Quintus. I want you to take the men who made your ladders and get them to make a cross, a good strong one stout enough to take Zeuta here.'

Gaius Omerus choked. His senior men paled. 'You're going to *crucify* him?' croaked the centurion. 'Didn't you hear what Brassus said? You will bring death and destruction down on us all!'

'I think not. I think I will bring life and liberty to my little *contubernium*. At least until we reach the safety of Florina and the border of Greece! Crinas, Furius, I want the boy stripped and his wounds bound. Brassus, I want you or one of your men to carry a message to Deceneus, King if the Daci...'

And so, at dawn the *contubernium* set out for Florina, riding as fast as the wagons allowed. Accompanied by the escort Publius had assigned them as far as Heraclea Lycensis, who would be returning there the next day. With orders from Artemidorus to give Gaius Omerus and his command a thorough shaking up.

All along the via between their left shoulders and the mountains, bands of mounted Dacian warriors kept watch but did not approach too closely. For, bound naked to a cross stepped securely in the last wagon, hung Zeuta, favourite nephew to Deceneus high king of the Daci, due to be released and returned with Publius' cavalry command once Artemidorus and his *contubernium* were safely in Florina and Greece.

ALEXANDRIA

IX: Liburnian

i

The docks along the back of the port of Thessaloniki were a dizzying bustle. The massive anchorage was packed with vessels of all shapes and sizes. The largest were the warships from the *Libertore* fleets, clearly visiting here for one reason or another: to pick up information, men or supplies not available in their current home-port of Rhodos, for example. Artemidorus saw military *quadriremes, quinqueremes* with four and five banks of oarsmen – but usually with three banks of oars, and one or two even larger *polyremes* with four or even five. These were the vessels he needed to steer well clear of – though he hoped that Messala, Lucius and the messenger would have departed on one of their kind more than a week ago.

After a moment, he redirected his gaze away from the military monsters towards the smaller commercial vessels. The *triremes, biremes* and liburnians that sailed these waters with men like User aboard. Out for profit rather than conquest; seeking cargoes and markets rather than battles and glory. These were the vessels he was interested in. Potential transports for his group of secret messengers between here and the Western Harbour behind the Pharos Island.

'You have no warehouses here?' he asked User, who was sitting beside him on the latest replacement for the black stallion he had befriended in Dyrrhachium. He was speaking in Greek, as he had been since crossing the border at Florina, happy to be back in the land of his birth and much of his youth. Though not precisely in Sparta, on whose barren hillsides he had been discovered as a baby. But, if he had not returned to Sparta, at least he was back in that half of the Roman Sea east of a line from Athens to Alexandria which remained solidly Greek. There was a sense of coming home, whose strength had surprised him. As did the ease with which he slipped back into his native tongue and the mindset that went with it. He detected a similar look in the eyes of the ex-slave Kyros stolen from Kos by Cilician pirates as a boy, the massive Achaean tutor Hercules, and the Athenian physician Crinas.

Ferrata was Hibernian, swept into the Ironclad Legion by Pompey in Spain. Despite her colouring, Puella had been born on Brutus' step-father's estate in Tuscany – the result of a breeding experiment between two Nubian slaves. Furius and Notus had been born in the Subura and so were truly Roman but less so than Quintus who came from ancient Patrician stock who owned a massive antique villa high on the Palatine. User, born in Alexandria was in some ways the most Greek of all of them. Artemidorus' *contubernium* all spoke Greek with varying levels of fluency. Only Puella, the ex-slave who had not been educated in the language, found it hard. But User spoke it even more fluently than he spoke Latin and he promised to help her learn.

It was important that they all spoke Greek. For only User spoke any Egyptian. And Greek was the language of Cleopatra's court. The queen herself came from the Greek and Macedonian stock of the first Ptolemy, Alexander's general Ptolemy Soter, descended in as direct a line as that claimed by Brutus with his forefather who drove King Tarquin out of Rome and founded the Republic. The Queen and Pharaoh spoke Ptolemy Soter's language, therefore, two hundred and forty years after his death. Even though, as Artemidorus knew, she was fluent in more than half a dozen languages. Including Egyptian – the first Pharaoh ever able to talk to her subjects in their native tongue.

'Not here, no,' said User in answer to his question. 'I've never even dreamed of owning anything here in Thessaloniki. Look how busy it is. The rates are ruinous. Property prices a joke – even your famous Marcus Licinius Crassus would have been hard-put to buy much. There's no commercial real estate to be had at any price. You bloody Greeks owned it all long before Alexander was born. As I said, my main warehouses this end of the middle sea are in Xanthus.'

'With your wife and children,' said Puella in her careful Greek.

'In a villa which makes even the family home in Alexandria look like a goatherd's cottage,' nodded User. 'Property prices in Xanthus are much more reasonable.' He turned to the rest of them, explaining, 'The city of Xanthus itself, like Rome, is set a little back from the sea but, as with Ostia, there are good docks all along a sandy, open bay within easy reach. There's a navigable river almost as big as the Tiber joining the docks to the city itself. And the port is excellent for sailing in and out unless there are fearsome easterlies, in which case Rhodos is just across the channel. Closer than Dyrrhachium is to Brundisium.'

'Very well,' said Artemidorus. 'You have no warehousing here, but do you have a reputation? Are you known?'

'There will be captains who know me or know of me, certainly, though none of my own vessels should be in port. But there will be men with local businesses who will know my name and reputation too. I assume you are keen that I organise passage to Alexandria – as well as a good deal – for you, your *contubernium* and all the supplies you are carrying.'

'We can leave the wagons and the horses – sell them if we need to,' nodded Artemidorus. 'But yes: the *contubernium* and what we are carrying. And a swift departure is preferable to a good deal.'

*

Artemidorus' plan to guarantee them safe passage out of the Dacians' country had worked perfectly. The naked, intensely embarrassed Zeuta, bound rather than nailed to Quintus' cross, wedged upright in the last wagon, had guaranteed that his doting uncle kept his raiders in check. And the fact that Publius' cavalrymen then took Zeuta back with them guaranteed their safe passage to their new billets in Heraclea Lyncestis as well. Artemidorus had left orders that the boy and any other survivors be released; and the dead be respectfully returned for burial according to Dacian custom. But it would have to be up to centurion Omerus to make the ultimate decisions.

The *contubernium* stayed in Florina for two nights and a day while Artemidorus organised the final details as well as he could. They were able to reach Edessa by the third night, Pella by the fourth and Thessaloniki in the early evening of the fifth. Coming unchallenged through the city's main gate and heading straight for the docks.

'It's getting late,' said User. 'I suggest we find a *hospitium* and the local baths. After a bit of a soak and a bite to eat, we can go out and do some business. Test the waters anyway. See what's going on this end of the middle sea, who's sailing south, when, and what they think the wind is going to do during the next few days. I know Thessaloniki almost as well as I know Alexandria. Let me be your guide.'

ii

The *hospitium* User took them to was up the hill, well back from the docks but close to the baths. 'I recommend it for several reasons,' he explained. 'It is comfortable, the food is good and the people who run it are welcoming and honest. You may leave horses, wagons, and their contents here without worrying. It is convenient to the best bathhouse in town. Also, for some reason it does not attract many soldiers, sailors, or oarsmen. So, it is largely peaceful.'

They dropped off their kit. They bathed. They ate. Then, dressed in their tunics, armed but without their armour, they went out to less salubrious establishments that were patronised by soldiers, oarsmen and sailors. Especially *trierarchi*, *naucleri* and *gubernators*: captains, skippers, and pilots. User led the way. Artemidorus and Puella followed. Quintus and Ferrata brought up the rear, as ever hopeful that even if the mission failed at least there would be lots to drink. There was hopefully going to be no work for Crinas to do. Hercules, Furius, Notus and Kyros were overseeing the slaves and – despite User's assurances – mounting guards to watch the wagons and their precious contents.

The first dockside *taberna* they entered was huge and packed. One or two heads turned as they entered, but User's face was familiar enough to put everyone at ease. Or, if not his face, then his distinctively Egyptian headwear. After a glance, the men sitting crowded round the tables went back to business. Everyone seemed to accept User as one of their own, but no-one greeted him. No-one called him over to their tables. They walked to the bar, eyes busy as they looked over the blank, unwelcoming faces, bought drinks, took them to a table, drank and left.

The next *taberna* was smaller, less busy. Once again, User's presence raised no eyebrows. It didn't generate any greetings either. But the wine was an improvement on the first's. The third one they visited yielded nothing but better wine still. 'I like this,' said Ferrata, swilling back the contents of his goblet. 'If we keep it up long enough, we'll end up drinking the nectar of the gods.'

'True,' answered Artemidorus, with an edge of impatience in his voice. 'But by the time we find anyone to talk to we'll be too drunk to make much sense.'

'Patience!' said User. 'Remember you are a stoic at heart. You can't control the future – so don't worry about it!'

'Spoken like Zeno himself,' said Quintus. 'But even Zeno would want to get on with things as fast as possible. Before the tide turns or the wind changes.'

'For someone who spends so much time throwing up over the side, you seem to have picked up the basics of ship-handling pretty well,' said User.

'I'm seasick,' said Quintus. 'Not blind, deaf or stupid.'

'User?' came a bellow of surprise echoing across the room.

'USER!'

They swung round at the same time to see a great bearded barrel of a man come rolling through the door. He wore green leggings, a blue tunic and a gold-coloured cap.

'Cilician,' muttered Ferrata.

'Aren't they all pirates?' wondered Puella.

'Those that weren't wiped out by Pompey the Great,' nodded Quintus knowledgeably.

But User stopped the whispered speculation by bellowing back as he rose, 'Halys you old pirate, how are you?'

A moment later the two men were embracing, beating each-other on the back with a cheerful exuberance that must have put their ribs at risk. Artemidorus, who had risen to his feet at the same time as User, grabbed an empty chair from a nearby table so that when they disentangled themselves, there was somewhere for the Cilician to sit. One glance at the man had also prompted him to catch the eye of a waitress. 'More wine,' he ordered. 'Two flagons. No water.'

*

It was inevitable that User and Halys should dominate the early part of the conversation as they all worked their way through the first flagon of excellent Cretan. It immediately emerged that they were old friends, though neither had ever worked for the other. That Halys, having risen from the lowly position of oarsman through *horator* and *pausarius*, to sail-handler and *gubernator*, was now the *nauclerus* skipper of a neat little full-decked *libernian* called *Glaros* Seagull; a bireme with fifty oars a side in two sets of twenty-five, one hundred feet in length and twenty wide counting the rowing boxes but with a draft of only a few feet. 'She can go where I can wade,' boasted the besotted captain, 'in water that only comes up to my belt!'

'So, she's a river boat as well as a seagoing vessel?' queried User, his eyes narrow and the muscles of his forehead clenched in a frown.

'When she needs to be,' answered Halys enthusiastically. 'But she'd be wasted on a river any smaller than the Nile or the Cydnus. She's as fast as the birds she's named after. She can outrun anything else out there in the harbour under sail or oars. She can reach fifteen knots with a following wind and the better part of ten knots in a dead calm. And I have a crack team of oarsmen who can keep up that speed for one of the Roman God *Divus Julius*' new weeks! They're expensive but worth every drachma!'

'But where is she actually going now?' asked Artemidorus.

'Where is your next port of call?'

'And how many passengers could she accommodate?' wondered Quintus, 'without adding too much to her draft or slowing her down in a pinch.'

'Passenger accommodation largely depends on the voyage,' answered Halys cheerfully answering the second question first. 'She's not a passenger vessel, though, she's a trader…'

'*Pirata*,' said Quintus not quite under his breath.

'I speak Latin as well as Greek and a little Egyptian, my Roman friend,' Halys warned Quintus, who did not look in the slightest abashed, especially as the too-cheerful, multilingual captain had not denied that he was, amongst other things, a pirate.

iii

'I am here looking for trade,' admitted Halys as he broached the second flagon of Cretan. 'And where I'm bound depends partly on what I get and partly on the wind. The best outcome is that I find something quickly that I can sell in Ephesus, Tyre or Alexandria. The winds are northerly at this time of year – though not as steady as they are in the summer – and it has taken far too long to get here in the first place, so my preferred course is to the south with the wind behind me. Also, the harbour fees here are ruinous. Not to mention what it costs to get a decent meal, some drinkable wine and a *lupa* whore that doesn't actually *look* like a she-wolf.'

'Spices?' suggested User sympathetically. 'Perfumes? They go through myrrh at an amazing rate in almost every country south of here and the trade routes from the Land of Punt are getting difficult I hear.'

'No myrrh to be had,' said Halys sadly. 'Or Frankincense come to that. Not to mention bears. They're popular in Egypt for some reason – but getting bears or Frankish incense down from Germania is impossible. The Dacians have closed all the roads to the north. I was thinking of turning around and heading for Lebanon. Pick up some cedar wood also for Egypt. But the market for building materials is almost dead there at the moment, together with about half the population. At least that's what I was told in Alexandria last month. Luckily, the plague doesn't seem to have come past Tiperses well upriver; what you Romans call Giza. Though it seems to have left the Holy City of Memphis alone, they say. I'd hoped for a cargo of corn, but they had none of that to spare either.' He shook his head sadly.

'Shocking!' User shook his head in sympathy and shot a glance at Artemidorus. Halys might be an old friend, but that didn't stop the Egyptian setting up the Cilician for Artemidorus' proposal.

'Actually,' he said, picking up on User's cue, 'my *contubernium* and I are looking for passage to Alexandria if we can find a vessel to take all twenty or so of us and our *impedimenta* luggage. And if the price is right.'

'Well, *Glaros* isn't really a passenger vessel as I said. It'd be basic fare if I agreed to take you even if I could load twenty of you aboard. Where have you come from?'

'Rome,' answered Artemidorus. 'We left around the Ides of Februarius, before the Lupercalia.'

'You've come from *Rome*? That *fast*?' Halys expression and tone were sceptical.

'I can vouch for them,' said User. 'I joined them just before they reached Dyrrhachium and I've been with them ever since. We came along the Via Egnatia almost as fast as military couriers. Stopped off to sort out a little trouble with the Dacians and here we are. I have to tell you, old friend, that roughing it on a liburnian will be as nothing to this lot. Except for Quintus there, who'll spend the entirety of any voyage trying to hurl his guts out of his mouth and over the side.'

*

Warehousing at Thessaloniki was every bit as expensive as User warned it would be. But Ferrata and Furius sold the horses in the market next day for so much that Artemidorus had to add surprisingly little of Antony's gold to get accommodation for the wagons and the camping equipment that they contained – which would be of no use at Cleopatra's court or on the *Glaros* which was taking them there. Everything they left behind would be housed safely at the *hospitium* they had stayed in last night. And if they weren't back to collect them before the sailing season ended in October, then the innkeeper could sell them and keep the profits. He was so enthusiastic about this idea that he lent them his own ox-drawn supply wagon and a couple of his stable-slaves to carry everything they did want to take with them down to the dockside where the liburnian called *Glaros* – *Seagull* – awaited them.

Getting twenty or so travellers and their baggage aboard took surprisingly little time. The oarsmen, free men on a salary, were willing to help. There was less space than on the *triremes* that brought them from Brundisium to Dyrrhachium, but also fewer oarsmen, and no marines at all. So there was ample room as it turned out for the *contubernium* and their slaves. Who were in any case legionary slaves, solid, reliable, well-trained soldiers only one small step down from their legionary masters. Planning, like gladiators, to earn their freedom through bravery and battle.

Below-decks smelt of sweat and bilge, though there was good ventilation. Most of all, however, it smelt of the liburnian's most recent cargo.

'Sandalwood,' said Artemidorus approvingly, his tone betraying some surprise.

'African sandalwood,' agreed Halys, 'brought across the Great Sand Sea by camel caravan together with some pretty exotic looking slaves. I loaded it aboard in Alexandria because I couldn't find any other cargo as I said. But I sold it all in Ephesus before coming to Thessaloniki. It was a pretty profitable voyage in the end.'

'Which is about to get more profitable,' said User. 'With what the centurion here is willing to pay for the return journey.'

Halys looked around himself. His passengers filled up little more than half of the space available.

'I might make it more profitable still,' he said, 'If I can pick up a bit more cargo.'

'I'm not sure about that,' warned Artemidorus.

'Well, we'll see,' said Halys cheerfully. 'It's too early in the season for reliable etesian summer northerlies, but we still should get some decent winds. In the meantime we'll be using the oars and going from bay to bay, anchorage to anchorage, port to port, to begin with at least. And if one bay, anchorage or port presents an opportunity to turn a little more profit, then we'll discuss the best way forward.'

User, Puella and Artemidorus followed Halys on deck where the vessel's *gubernator* was waiting, ready to get under way.

'Bay to bay to begin with,' repeated Artemidorus. 'What does that actually mean?'

'Worried about bumping into one of Admiral Ahenobarbus' warships?' asked Halys knowingly.

'Perhaps. But I wouldn't be surprised if you were a little wary of them yourself – Pompey the Great reborn, so to speak.'

The Cilician captain winked and nodded; another tacit admission of occasional piracy. Then he looked across at the pilot. 'It means we get to the coast of Asia Province as quickly as we can,' he said. 'Stopping off at Amphipolis or Neapolis south of Philippi if we need to, then we make for Ephesus, hugging the coast and keeping to shallow water if we spot anything like a quinquereme or a polyreme coming after us. Sneak past Rhodos and into Xanthus. Then we wait – not too long I hope – for a steady northerly which will take us due south from Xanthus to Alexandria. Satisfied?'

'Sounds like a plan,' said Artemidorus.

'No plan ever survives first contact with the enemy,' Quintus pointed out as he went to the side rail and started vomiting.

iv

It took three days to reach Neapolis. On the first, they went ashore, built a fire, ate and slept on the beach of a small cove on the Kassandra peninsula on the first night, instantly regretting having left their tents in Thessaloniki. Fortunately, *Glaros* had enough shelter to accommodate everyone. And Artemidorus had brought food which supplemented the fish that Halys' sailhandlers had caught during the voyage. The second day took them, again without benefit of wind or sail, to the end of the Acte peninsula where they camped almost within the shadow of Mount Athos. The third day brought them to the burgeoning port city of Neapolis. Where everyone in the *contubernium* went ashore to bathe, sleep in *tabernae*, eat and replenish their supplies.

But the market was all-but empty. At this season, there was nothing worth harvesting in the swampy fields between the port and the towns further inland. So, while *Glaros*' oarsmen took a well-earned rest, Artemidorus and User hired a wagon and a couple of horses. Then, accompanied by Puella and Quintus, they ventured along the locally built roadway that ran northwards across the low-lying inland fields. After a couple of *miles*, they came across the east-running Via Egnatia standing almost as high as a wall above them. Luckily, the road they were following was an important one, so there were ramps on either side of the via solid enough and wide enough to allow them to get the cart safely up and down. As they hesitated on the crest of the via itself, Artemidorus looked around. There was swampy ground surrounding them. Swamps almost leading down to the coast on his right and up to the foothills of a range of low hills on his left; low hills with a spur reaching southward which was large enough and solid enough to form the foundations of a sizeable walled town.

It was this town, Philippi, to which they were heading in the hope of purchasing some spring lambs in the market there. The hills behind the old fortified settlement offered good grazing for both sheep and goats. And although early *Mars* was not a good time for most crops, it was the lambing season. So, they were able to return with a couple of mature lambs and a couple of big kids – which would feed *Glaros*' crew and their passengers during the next few stints of the voyage.

The next night, they found safe haven in the port of Aenus, founded by the demigod Aeneus. The lambs and kids remained inviolate as there was food and drink in the *tabernae* ashore. The landlord was happy to share his woes with some itinerant strangers. 'Those bloody Romans,' he said, 'taxing the life blood out of everybody. Threatening to put them to the sword or sell them into slavery if they're too slow to pay. It's just as bad for us up here in Aenus as it is for the poor bastards further south. Ephesus can afford to pay up of course but what about the others? Bloody great fleets sailing up and down the coast threatening blood and fire, legions marching hither and yon not only taking our money – wives, sons and daughters too if they feel the urge – but starving us out of hearth and home with their never-ending foraging. You just watch, masters. If you're sailing south, you'll be lucky to avoid being boarded and robbed blind by their so-called *adlectores* tax collectors.'

*

But they saw none of this during their voyage south next day and the next night they overnighted in a bay on the west shore of a long isthmus. The night was not too cold. They went ashore, killed and skinned one of the lambs and roasted it on a fire near the water's edge. As they sat on the sand watching the spitted carcase cooking, Halys revealed his unexpected poetic side. 'If you look inland,' he said, gesturing eastwards, beyond a mountainous interior, to where a waning moon struggled to shine through the overcast above, 'do you know what you will find?'

There was a brief silence broken only by the crackling of the fire as lamb-fat dripped into it. 'Across another stretch of water to be fair, but level with where we are and little more than ten *miles* distant as birds fly...'

'What?' asked User, his interest piqued.

'Troy,' answered Halys dreamily. 'It makes you think, does it not? Ten *miles* from where we are sitting now, the towers of Ilium stood. Priam the king fought to protect his son Paris and his stolen bride Helen. The sons of the house of Atreus – Meneleus, husband to the stolen Helen, and Agamemnon his brother – sailed with a thousand ships to retrieve her. Ajax was there, and Hector, tamer of horses...'

'And Achilleus,' said Artemidorus, also dreamily, 'the demigod who holds his hands over me. Achilleus fought and died there. And gained immortality, though he always said he never sought it through heroic death.'

'But then,' concluded User brutally, 'almost all of them died. Even the ones that made it home came to sorry ends like Agamemnon himself. Only Ulysses walked away. And the whole place was reduced to ashes.'

V

The next port they overnighted in was Ephesus and that was by far the busiest. It was a tourist destination; one of the most popular in the world. People from all over the Republic and beyond flocked there to see one of the legendary Seven Wonders. And restless politicians from Egypt and her dominions – most notoriously Cyprus – sent representatives to talk treason and revolution with Queen Cleopatra's half-sister Arsinoe who lived under the protection of the Temple of Artemis. But not, Artemidorus noted, Ahenobarbus' ships or Brutus' legions. He wasn't sure whether he found this reassuring or not.

'Have you seen the Temple of Artemis?' asked User, distracting him from his darker thoughts. 'It is one of the Seven Wonders.'

'Yes,' answered Artemidorus shortly, suspecting the question was the opening move in a campaign to take Puella inland and show her some of User's personal wonders, unless he, too, wished to contact the princess Arsinoe. 'And what's left of the Colossus at Rhodos. And the Pharos – which we'll see again soon as we approach Alexandria. And the Great Pyramid which I'll see again if we get a chance to go up the Nile once more. I saw the statue of Zeus at Olympus when I was very much younger. That's about it, though. I haven't been to Halicarnassus to wonder at the Mausoleum...'

'We could probably get Halys to call in there if you're keen. It's about halfway between here and Xanthus. Though, like the Colossus, it was destroyed by an earthquake.'

'At least the gods did it, then. The Temple of Artemis seems to have mostly been destroyed by men. Like Troy.'

'True. But unlike Troy it has always been rebuilt, each time bigger and more magnificent than the last.'

'By city fathers who understand how to gather in the tourist dinars and sestertii – they can't just rely on their Library – even if Alexandria can.'

'Cynic!'

'Well, remember Stoicism started as an offshoot of Cynicism. And no, before you ask, I have not been to Babylon, if that's where the Hanging Gardens ever actually were.'

They had this conversation as Halys and his *gubernator* were sliding *Glaros* into a convenient berth. 'If you're going ashore, take care,' called the captain as he prepared to go to the harbourmaster's office and settle up his docking fees. 'It's a cutpurse's paradise. If you go to a *hospitia* or *taberna* be sure you've agreed the price before you start eating, drinking, sleeping or whoring. They'll skin you alive if they have half a chance. And if you do go ashore make sure you're back before dawn. I want to leave with the first tide. I've a feeling the wind will soon swing northward and I want to be off Xanthus when it does. I suspect User will want to go ashore there to see his family.'

'That's true, when we get to Xanthus I will,' said User. 'Perhaps we'd better give the Temple of Artemis and the Library of Celsus a miss.'

In spite of Halys' warning, Artemidorus, Ferrata, and Quintus did go ashore – leaving Puella to enjoy another Greek lesson with User and a meal of kid. Artemidorus' main motivation was concern for Quintus, who was beginning to look like a shadow of his usual self. Eating aboard ship was a waste of his time, whatever he swallowed just came straight back up again. But as soon as his *caligae* hit *terra firma* he was back on the road to recovery.

*

So they ended up in a local *capuona* where, with a little help from his friends, the *triarius* demolished a thick-crusted pie filled with pork, a plate of *farcinem* sausages and a bowl of fish stew. They didn't talk much because Quintus had more important work for his mouth to do. And so Artemidorus began to pick up on some of the conversations going on nearby.

'... refused to pay, so I heard...'

'... an absolute NO! You may be Marcus Junius Brutus, but you get no taxes from us, no matter how many legions you have...'

'... grasping bastard! Maybe we should have done the same...'

'... you must be joking. The City Fathers would sell us all into slavery first. Just to protect their precious temple and their library...'

'... the temple anyway – it's been burned down often enough, and it costs a fortune to rebuild. And Zeus knows how much princess Arsinoe is paying them to protect her – and the temple. Egyptians are so rich they make Croesus look like a beggar. Less worried about the library though. The one in Alexandria seems to have survived being burned by Julius Caesar. Another grasping Roman bastard if you ask me.'

'... but this was when?'

'What?'

'When did they say this to Brutus? That they refused to pay his taxes? How long ago? Did you hear?'

'Well, I heard about it yesterday and I guess the news was a couple of days old then.'

'So. The better part of a week? That's what you think?'

'I don't know. Not as long as a week. I mean, how long does it take to get here from there anyway?'

'By land? It must be a hundred Roman *miles*. But the roads along the coast are good. A week in a cart, I suppose.'

'And he was in a cart, was he, the *mankas* bloke who told you this?'

'What? No! He was on a horse. Nearly dead it was too. He must have galloped all the way as though the Friendly Ones were after him.

'So, what, two days? Three?'

'I guess so...'

'Well only the gods know what's going on there now.'

'I sure as Hades wouldn't like to be there anyway. How many legions has Brutus got? Seven? *Gamo* Fuck they must all be mad! He'll bloody kill them all is what he'll do. Slaughter every man, woman and child. Just to make sure no one else stands up to him.'

Artemidorus pushed aside his bowl of stew, stood and crossed to the table where the conversation was going on. His heart sinking already, he asked quietly, 'Excuse me citizens but I couldn't help but overhear. What is the name of the city that has refused to pay Brutus' taxes?'

The man who had been telling the story looked up at him. Shook his head sadly as though reporting the death of a close friend.

'Xanthus,' he said.

X: Xanthus

i

Glaros' cutwater slid silently onto the sand, as the oarsmen eased back. She wedged, just enough to hold her still, settling solidly but easily because she did not have a ram on her prow. It would be simple enough to slide off the beach's gentle slope and back out into the deeper water again if things got dangerous.

The bay was empty. Even the dock facilities beyond the river mouth were deserted. There were signs many men and heavy machinery had passed this way, but they were gone now and there were no other vessels nearby. That was why Halys had chosen this landfall, though User and Artemidorus might have preferred something closer to their objective. But the river offered a good way in. All they would have to worry about at the outset were midges and mosquitoes – though it was too cold for most of them – and leeches. The moon was a thin silver bow hanging low behind them, seemingly somewhere above distant Rhodos away to the west. It was easy enough to see, even though dawn was still a long way off.

And a couple of *miles* inland, a city was burning brightly. Just like Troy.

The blazing city did not only generate light. The air was heavy with the stench of smoke. Iron. Roasting flesh. It gave birth to a deep, continuous rumble. The ground, the water flowing over it and even the air above it, shook. Every now and then, depending on the vagaries of the sluggish, burdened breeze, there were crashes, roars, bellows. And a moment or two of heat as though a furnace door had opened.

Artemidorus swung down from *Glaros*' prow, controlling his movement by hanging onto a rope looped round the stempost. Landing, fully armed and ready for battle, like Achilleus on the Trojan beach, leaving his black-sailed ship and leading his Myrmidons to war and immortality: a notion driven deeper into Artemidorus' vivid imagination by one simple fact. The river he was proposing to follow to the flaming city had the same name as the river that flowed past Troy – Scamander in some descriptions; Xanthos in Greek. He turned, holding the rope steady as User, also fully armed, swung over the bow-rail. Behind him came Quintus then Ferrata.

Their heated discussion on the way here from Ephesus had generated a kind of plan. The decision that only four of them would go ashore, fully armed and armoured – but without any legionary identification, so that if they needed to mingle with elements of Brutus' army besieging the city of Xanthus, they would not stand out. In terms of any damage, filth and blood that might reasonably be expected to be soiling them. Given User's current state of mind, getting covered in blood at least should be no trouble at all – legionary blood; *libertore* blood.

Four men, on the other hand, would be sufficient to pose as a unit or patrol and bring User's family out apparently in custody, if the opportunity arose; if, in spite of what Artemidorus had overheard in Ephesus, any of them were still alive. Ultimately, if things went wrong, four was not too large a number to lose. But Artemidorus was well aware the loss of this particular quartet would do untold damage to the mission. As ever, it was a leadership problem that could only be resolved through leadership. And Artemidorus had always been the kind of man who led from the front. Just like *Divus Julius*. Like the demigod Achilleus.

'Remember,' he said in the heartbeats before they set off, 'speak Latin.'

*

The broad river Xanthus led towards the burning city. Its banks forested with tall reeds and rushes, their entangled roots holding the slick mud together so that the four men could lope, as sure-footed as wolves, through the cover of the riverbank vegetation beneath the shadows of the tamarisks. Heads lowered, helmets keeping the rushes and the midges away from eyes and faces, they ran towards the city, shoulders hunched, feet steady, swords ready. The red light gathered around them as the time and the *stadions* passed. Eight Greek *stadions* made a Roman *mile*. Sixteen brought them to the point where the river curved westward, forming a sizeable lake before turning north again to flow beneath the river gate into Xanthus itself.

Here they hesitated as Artemidorus parted the rushes with his left hand and his sword-blade in his right fist and looked across the open space between themselves and the city walls. On one side there were the charred remains of riverside buildings, still sluggishly smoking, the ruins of jetties, quays and piers, the half-submerged wrecks of several boats. Bodies – too many to count – floating face down.

Their blood no doubt attracting the leeches.

They were at least one *stadion* back from the main wall itself. Away to the right and left lay the city's residential outskirts. Smoking ruins that had obviously and easily been overwhelmed and destroyed by Brutus' army. The buildings not only burned but were broken down to make way for Brutus' siege engines, which now stood idle. The state of the wall and the city behind it bearing testimony to their effectiveness. Here too there were bodies, mostly local Lycian dead, easily identifiable because they wore little or no armour. Some wounded, mostly well-armed Romans and some fully-armoured legionaries simply comatose with exhaustion. All covered in blood and soot.

Between here and the city's citadel wall, with the siege ropes dangling down it, stood the ladders, rams, and siege equipment the Romans had clearly used to broach the Xanthian defenses. They were mostly unmanned, for it was obvious most of the soldiers had gone in through the breached ramparts and the broken gates to loot what was left of the city centre with its depositories, coin-mints, and temples, all well-stocked with silver and gold. Not to mention the villas of rich merchants and leading citizens with their collections of art, artifacts, votary regalia and statues. The only ones left on watch were too tired, weak, or wounded to join in the sack of the city.

'Which is closer?' asked Artemidorus, raising his voice above the thunder of the blazing city, 'your warehouse or your villa?'

'My warehouse,' hissed User. 'And that is it!' He gestured with his sword at a charred heap of rubble, still smoldering, with constellations of red-hot charcoal dotted through its massive blackness. In front of it, the ruin of a pier led down to the wrecks of several river boats. Between which bobbed yet more corpses.

'Your villa, then,' said Artemidorus.

'This way!'

Well beyond any thought of concealment now, User pushed out of the rushes onto the flagstones of the quayside and led the way towards the city itself. None of the half-dead combatants paid any attention to the tight four-man squad as they jogged towards the gap-toothed ruin of the city's main entrance with its smashed gates hanging off broken hinges, the splintered wood smoldering like the rest.

ii

Inside the city walls was a kind of blazing Tartarus, the deepest reach of Hades' kingdom, thought Artemidorus. Everything seemed to be on fire. The towering flames ahead seemed to suck in a strong breeze to blow on their backs. They removed their helmets, undid their scarves, and wrapped them round their mouths and noses before putting their headgear back in place and tying the cheek-pieces firmly down. They were by no means the only people to do so. Only the dead had uncovered faces, as the crows had already discovered.

Walls of flame clothed the brick and marble buildings all around. Crowds of legionaries ran hither and thither, all armed, all made anonymous by their masks; none of them carrying ravished victims, enslaved children, or bundles of booty. Simply running for the sake of it, scarcely able to believe there was nothing left here for them to steal. Smoke billowed in choking clouds that seemed to grow thicker as they went ahead. Soon enough the spies were covered in soot. Masked faces black with it – only the pale runnels beneath their streaming eyes breaking the pattern on all their cheeks except User's. Only blood was needed to complete their disguise.

Even User was disorientated by the massiveness of the destruction all around. 'I don't recognise anything,' he yelled to Artemidorus, his voice a whisper in the face of the deafening roar, cloaked further by his mask. He dashed the tears from his eyes and looked around wildly. All there was to see were the walls of flame the clouds of smoke, the other squads of soldiers running in and out of side-streets and, everywhere, the bodies of men and women, young and old – bare-faced, gaping, wide-eyed; blood-boltered, broken, burning.

'Find the forum,' Artemidorus advised. 'It should be at the end of this road. You can get your bearings there.'

User nodded, and the tight four-man squad ran onwards, up a slight incline, along a mercifully wide cobbled street lined with yet more corpses on either side. After a hundred steps or more, dead ahead stood a sizeable temple, so fiercely ablaze that even the marble columns supporting the outer structure, and the divine statues in between them, seemed to be on the point of melting as the wooden beams above cracked like thunder with the heat. Everything that could burn was wildly ablaze. Only the soldiers of Brutus' army were alive. And even they looked as though they had somehow crossed the Styx and entered Hell itself.

*

There was relative quiet in the centre of the forum. The air was less smoke-filled. The noise seemed to have abated, calmed by the scale of the place. The broken bodies littering the marble flags were mostly those of toppled statues. Local dignitaries whose legacies were all aflame, local gods proving powerless in the face of a ruthless Roman war machine seven legions strong.

At the centre of the forum, where the air was coolest and calmest stood a dozen or so men so deep in conversation that they hardly seemed conscious of the destruction all around them, let alone of yet another little group that had just run out of the main street and hesitated, looking around. Artemidorus blinked and wiped his left hand down his face, sweeping the tears towards his damp kerchief, looked more closely with clearer eyes. The group of men was surrounded by guards, standards, and eagles. Every one of them was in full battle armour. But they were not shy about badges of identification, standing or honours. He glanced at his companions. User was still searching wildly for a familiar street. But Quintus and Ferrata had their three eyes fixed where Artemidorus' were – on the group of men in the centre of the Forum. Before any of them could speak, User shouted, 'There!' and began to run across the open space. His route was going to take him close to the men beneath the eagles, so Artemidorus and the others followed him willingly enough. They did not fear recognition. Their armour was dirty, and their masks were held solidly in place by their cheek-flaps.

But, he observed, the situation did not hold true the other way around. For the men engaged in the earnest discussion did not wear masks. They seemed to have managed to remain untouched by the smoke. Several had removed their helmets altogether, in the face of the fearsome heat. So, as he ran past them, going as close as he dared, Artemidorus was able to see their faces clearly. And, with a lurch that nearly caused him to stumble, he recognised some half-dozen of them. General Brutus himself, the Casca brothers, his Legates: Publius Casca who stabbed *Divus Julius* first on the Ides and Gaius Casca who tried so hard for the second strike. Beside them, a young Athenian student Artemidorus vaguely recognised as Quintus Horatius Flaccus who published poetry under the name of Horace, wearing the badges of a *Tribune Mulitum*. And, beside Horace, another grim-faced Tribune: Marcus Valerius Messala Corvinus.

Artemidorus' stumble attracted Messala's attention. He looked up. Their eyes met. A kind of recognition crackled between them. And Artemidorus remembered more vividly still, as he turned away and ran, that Troy was where Achilleus died.

iii

Oblivious to the identities of the men he was running past, or the glance that passed between Artemidorus and Messala, User led them across the forum and into the mouth of yet another burning via. This one sloped gently down-hill, running back towards the broken city walls. The scalding wind now blew into their faces, bringing yet more smoke, burning motes and splinters. Their eyes were at risk of more than tears. Ferrata was particularly quick to sheathe his sword and raise his right hand to shield his one remaining eye. The others followed suit even though it limited their vision. They all ran in a tight phalanx down the road, as User looked increasingly wildly right and left, seeking something familiar amongst the raging hellhole that Brutus had made of the city.

At last User stopped so abruptly that they all crashed into him. They staggered on a few steps before they could all stand together. 'Here!' bellowed User. 'This is my villa. Where my wife and family live…'

They don't live there any longer, thought Artemidorus brutally. But he said nothing. The building was just as ablaze as the others. At least there were no half-roasted corpses piled in the gutter outside it.

'What we need to do,' he suggested after a moment, 'is find someone to tell us exactly what went on. I can't believe even Brutus would put every citizen to the sword. Quite apart from anything else, he's too greedy for that. Too desperate for funds to pay and feed his legions. He must have taken prisoners to sell as slaves, women, and children particularly. And if they're on their way to the slave markets we can find them. Buy them back…'

'But we're bound for Alexandria…' said User. 'Your mission, whatever it is…'

'Can wait while we find out about your family. Find *them* if need-be. And get them back to you, if it can be done.'

'Good idea,' said Quintus. 'But we won't find anyone to talk to here.'

'We need to get out of the city,' Ferrata continued the thought. 'Question one of the legionaries we saw slumped beside the ballistae outside.'

User hesitated. He looked at the burning building. The muscles of his forehead clenched. The sweat-slick skin folded into wrinkles as his mind raced, trying to come to terms with the enormity of what was happening to him. Then he nodded. Once, decisively.

'Good,' said Artemidorus. 'Quintus, did you recognise any of the legionary standards or identification marks? Are we likely to bump into any old friends?'

'Apart from Messala, you mean?' asked Ferrata.

'Yes. Apart from him,' snapped Artemidorus.

'No,' said Quintus shortly. 'Most of these boys were with Pompey when you and I were with *Divus Julius*. We didn't mix much except on the battlefield when we were trying to kill one another. And we didn't socialise at all.'

'Right,' nodded Artemidorus. 'Still, it shouldn't be too hard to find someone who knows what went on and is willing to tell us about it…'

'And is too fucking knackered to ask us too many questions in return,' added Ferrata.

*

The soldier they found was a young artillery centurion sitting against the side of his ballista catapult. Pale and faint with agony. The massive siege engine had run over his foot as it was being jockeyed into position and although he had managed to command it effectively, he had remained here, too crippled to follow his men in their search for rapine and riches. 'Not that there was ever going to be anything much,' he said wearily as Ferrata did his best to bandage the crushed foot and Artemidorus keenly regretted leaving Puella and Crinas behind. They knelt on one knee in a semicircle around him, as he explained the terrible siege.

'They refused to pay the taxes. It was as simple as that. General Brutus gave them a clear demand, worked out in terms of what the city earned and what he thought it owed. He didn't even ask for ten years' taxes up front like he did with some of the others. But the city fathers refused. No negotiation. That was that. The general explained the consequences. They said they didn't care – they wouldn't pay. He brought up his legions. They closed the gates. We went to war.'

'A war that didn't last long,' prompted Artemidorus.

'No,' said the artilleryman. 'Only a couple of days. Seemingly, they or another city like Xanthus has done this before. But the city fathers made a simple decision. They fell on their sword. When it became clear they were never going to stand against us the entire city fell on its sword.'

'Meaning?' demanded User, his voice trembling.

'Meaning that fathers and mothers killed their children then husbands killed their wives. Then friends and brothers killed each-other until there were only a few left alive. Then those few set fire to the city so that General Brutus and his tax collectors would get nothing. Then they all killed themselves as well. When the legions got through the gates and breaches or up the ropes and ladders and over the walls there was no-one left alive, nothing of worth remaining and everything they found was on fire.' He gestured towards the inferno on the hilltop.

iv

'Don't give up hope,' said Puella softly. 'They might still be alive somewhere.'

'Nebet would never harm the boys,' User said hopefully. But there was still a world of doubt in his voice.

'Is that her name? Nebet?' she asked.

'Yes. And the boys are User, named for me, and Rasa. She worshipped them. Too much – to my way of thinking. She could never harm them.' User looked around the faces of the *contubernium* searching for the reassurance he could not give himself. His eyes were still streaming, but they were aboard now and the smoke from the city far behind them.

'Then they are still out there somewhere. We will find them,' promised Artemidorus. 'When our mission is completed.'

User nodded, his face folding into an intrepid frown. He dragged a shaking hand down his features, wiping away the tears. He was clear about things and agreed with Artemidorus' decision. Had there been a realistic chance of finding and rescuing his family then that's what they would have done. As there was no immediate chance at all, their mission had to take priority. Every person aboard had lived through a time of war stretching back decades. Civil war for the most part; brother against brother, father against son. They all knew the costs, brutally hard though they might be to bear.

It was dawn. *Glaros* was heading southwards, her sail filling occasionally with a fitful wind, her oarsmen helping her along, their rhythmic song echoing across the sea. The sun was rising over Beroea, Aleppo, far to the east on their left as the last of the night fled westward towards the ruins Carthage away on their right. Alexandria was four hundred *miles* ahead. But Halys and the pilot were confident the wind would freshen and remain northerly. In which case they might make it in a little over a day.

Later that morning, with the wind still skittish and uncertain, they took the smallest of the lambs bought in Philippi and went through the rituals of sacrificing it, primarily to Aeolus God of the wind but also to his son Boreas, God of the North wind. They collected the blood of the sacrifice most carefully and mixed it with the best wine they had aboard. Although no-one was allowed to drink it at sea, they had a good supply of Egyptian wine aboard for Halys traded wine amongst anything else he could load aboard. They poured the rich, iron-smelling liquid over the side as an offering to Poseidon where it was soon joined by the thin and bitter contents of Quintus' stomach.

When a northerly sprang up, showing the satisfaction of all the gods concerned, the sacrificial lamb was skinned and butchered. A goat was also killed and skinned. The two butchered animals cooked over the fire-pot on the deck below the straining sail and were served to all. The oarsmen stowed their oars and the simple fare took on the aspect of a celebratory feast.

The only men who did not join in with the air of mild celebration were Quintus and User. Quintus shook his head, even when offered the lamb's succulent liver. 'It'll just come straight up again,' he said. 'If I send many more offerings over the side, Poseidon himself will need to visit the *vomitorium*.' He gave a weak grin.

User looked at the steaming offal. 'If it was Brutus' liver,' he growled, 'I'd eat it raw!'

'Well,' said Artemidorus, 'one day it might be. Then you can eat his liver – and his heart into the bargain. In the mean-time, we'll keep Nebet and your boys in our minds and try to find them when we get the chance.'

*

User nodded but turned away and walked to the stern of the ship where he stood leaning against the sternpost looking back into the steady pressure of the northerly wind like Orpheus looking back for his lost Eurydice. He knew the truth behind Artemidorus' kindly words. Brutus' legions had slaughtered his family. He would never see them again. Beside which the loss of his wealth and employees, vessels and warehouses in Xanthus was as nothing. What he had discovered in the blazing city last night had turned him from a bystander into a committed soldier.

After a few moments he called to Artemidorus. 'Two things occur to me at once,' he said as the secret agent joined him. 'The first is this –your mission to Alexandria must in some way damage Brutus, who is Antony's enemy, and you are Antony's man. Secondly, that the more swiftly you complete your mission, whatever it is, the quicker we might see the murderous bastard defeated and start looking for my family.'

'So?' asked Artemidorus.

'So. I wish to be more than your travelling companion. I wish to help you achieve whatever Antony has tasked you with. I, my brothers, our vessels and what is left of our fortune are at your service. All I ask is one favour.'

'Name it.'

'That you tell me what your mission is; as much as you safely can. The more I know, the more I can help.'

Half an hour later, User was still standing at the stern rail. Thinking through what Artemidorus had revealed to him. Assessing how the mission, if successful might bring about the death and destruction of Brutus, his plans, hopes and dreams.

But even in the middle of his murderously vengeful thoughts, the seafarer in User was keeping a weather eye out. The vista astern of *Glaros* was not without its beauty. On his right, the shore line they had rowed away from last night still sat low on the horizon. A column of smoke like the result of a volcanic eruption rose above the smoldering city, beginning to blow southward as though pursuing them. Immediately behind them, Homer's wine-dark sea, with the surface reflecting the high azure sky but beginning to stir and seethe under the influence of the following breeze. Away to the left hulked the hilly backbone of southern Rhodos, the length of the island stretching as the land became lower and leaner until only a beach – invisible from here – joined an islet to the main bulk. An isthmus at low tide, he remembered, a true island only at high tide.

His memories distracted him, and he turned a little, shading his eyes against the wind and the glare as he looked at that little island away on the far horizon. He had taken Nebet and the boys there once for no real reason, just for pleasure. So unlike him, the stern, almost Roman *paterfamilias* he had become more recently. If only…

But then he frowned. The shape of the distant island was wrong. His eyes must be playing tricks he thought. He blinked and discovered that his eyes were streaming once more.

Artemidorus and Puella joined him, concerned that he was brooding here alone. The insightful Greek spy saw the look of surprise fleeting over the Egyptian's face at once. 'What is it?' he asked.

It was as though the question made User's vision clear at last and his understanding return.

'Ships,' he said. 'Two Roman battle *quinqueremes* have just rounded the island at the southern point of Rhodos and it looks like they're coming after us.'

V

'After *us*?' demanded Halys. 'How can they be after us?'

Artemidorus took a deep breath. It was a long story. He just needed to give the highlights. 'When we brought two men from the lists of proscribed enemies of the state out of Rome and across to Macedonia with us, we knew there was a risk,' he said, 'even though we were ordered to do so by Caesar Octavianus. They were both planning to join Brutus and his armies in the east. We separated from them in Dyrrhachium and they managed to come on ahead of us, travelling with a messenger sent to Brutus with news of his wife's death. A messenger sent by his mother Servilia, I would guess.'

'But they got ahead of us by ten days, maybe more,' added Quintus. 'One way and another.'

'We know they joined Brutus because we saw one of them in Xanthus last night,' Artemidorus continued.

'They know what our plans are,' added Ferrata. 'No details, just in general. Plans and destination. So, no doubt they've passed that information on.'

'In spite of the fact that we saved their lives,' persisted Artemidorus, 'they will not think twice. They know how crucial our mission is. Any message going from Antony to Cleopatra is likely to result in damage to their cause. So, they have obviously taken steps to stop us getting to Alexandria.'

'But how?' demanded Halys. 'How have they had time to warn the ships in Rhodos to come looking for us?'

'Looking for any vessel bound for Alexandria, perhaps,' said User. 'There don't seem to be all that many.' He glanced around the empty sea.

'But even so, how would they have passed the message on so fast?' Halys shook his head. 'It seems hardly possible. Still, a couple of fat tubs like those quinqueremes have no chance of catching my *Glaros*. Not with a wind like this under her tail.'

Artemidorus turned away, unconvinced by Halys' confidence. He looked back at the two distant quinqueremes. Just in time to see, right at the mast-head of the eastern vessel, a shape that could only be a man standing high in the rigging. And no sooner had he recognised what he was seeing than a bright flash of light seemed to beam out from the distant figure's chest. 'They're using mirrors,' he said. 'Mirrors to signal.'

And sure enough, there on the eastern horizon well south of them, he saw an answering flash of light.

'Watch!' he shouted. 'Watch the western ship. She is bound to be signaling too!'

'There,' shouted Furius at once.

'And an answer,' chimed in Kyros. 'From the west and south of us.

'Two ships chasing from behind; two more waiting ahead. If the first pair can't catch us, maybe the second pair can cut us off.'

'They're trying to box us in,' agreed Halys, stroking his beard. 'But they won't manage it. They haven't counted on my *Glaros*' speed.'

'Right,' agreed Artemidorus. But even as he spoke, he frowned, because it wasn't right. There was something else going on. 'Halys,' he said, 'how long would it take the pair of ships ahead of us to close with us?'

'Until after dark tonight,' he answered with a shrug. 'Those two back at Rhodos will never do more than sit in our wake. But the two on either side of us will probably get close after sunset.'

'And in the mean-time?'

The captain shrugged again. 'In the mean-time we keep sailing straight for Alexandria. Douse our lights in the darkness, slip through the gap between them and sail home free.'

*

By sunset, the two quinqueremes that had been following them from Rhodos were still there. Further behind and hull-down, little more than masts and fat-bellied sails standing above the horizon, driven south by the same steady northerly that was helping *Glaros* stay ahead of them. But their busy signals continued to flash. And to be answered by the two quinqueremes closing relentlessly on the left and right fore quarters, being rowed steadily across the wind, and coming together like a pair of jaws.

'They must know we will slip between them in the dark,' observed Halys, over-confidently. 'They are simply wasting their time.'

'Perhaps…' Artemidorus and User went aside with his *contubernium* to discuss the situation.

'It has to be a trap,' said Artemidorus.

'I agree. But how will it be sprung?' wondered User.

'Too early to say. But I agree with Halys. It will be sprung after dark.'

'Let's kill and cook the last of the lambs and goats except for the milkers. Give everyone a solid meal. In case things get strenuous later.' User suggested.

'Just slaughter? Not sacrifice?' asked Kyros.

Artemidorus looked down at him. The boy was gifted, intelligent; a warrior of enormous potential – especially as Puella was training him in the use of both hands to wield weapons so that he would become ambidextrous like her and almost as deadly – while Notus was gently helping him become an excellent forger. But he was still both young and superstitious.

The secret agent looked around his *contubernium* and understood at once that Kyros was not the only one nervous about the impending darkness, especially as it would be the first night of the week or so when the moon was dark. 'A lamb to Erebus and a goat to Nyx,' he said. 'That way we've covered both darkness and night.'

Halys agreed that feeding the oarsmen and the crew was an excellent idea. The lamb and the goat were sacrificed. Their smoke as they roasted darkened the sky above and ahead of the liburnian – a suitable offering to the god of darkness and the goddess of night. Then the blood went over the side to keep Poseidon happy.

As Artemidorus and User took the roasted meat round, they took the opportunity to talk to the oarsmen. 'There's a chance you will be rowing tonight. Be ready. And bear in mind that if you do row it will be in battle order. No singing.'

'Furthermore,' added User, 'when you have eaten, smear the lamb fat and the kid fat along your oars. Oil the leather of your row-holes. There is no point having you working in silence if your oars are squealing like pigs at slaughter.

vi

By the time everyone reassembled by the steering oar where Halys and his *gubernator* stood, it was almost dark. 'Now we'll see,' said the captain. And see they did – but not what he expected. First the quinquereme ahead on their left and then the one on their right lit all their lamps at the stempost – with extra light for the captain and navigator. They ran lanterns up to the outer ends of the spars against which their great square sails were furled. They even ran lanterns up to the mast-heads where the soldiers with their signal mirrors no longer had enough light for their work. And, away on the horizon behind *Glaros*, the pursuing vessels also hung lanterns on the masts and rigging still visible.

'They're trying to frighten us,' huffed Halys. 'Well, we'll show them! Light the lanterns, men. And see if you can't squeeze a little more speed out of the sail. It shouldn't be too hard; the wind has picked up again. Boreas is on our side, as well as Erebus and Nyx. All sacrifices well invested.' He laughed. 'Even yours, Quintus!' he called to the seasick soldier's back as it strained over the nearest rail.

But User and Artemidorus were not as convinced as the ebullient captain that the gods were holding protective hands over them and all was well. The pair of them stood at the foot of the mast, listening as the great sail strained to contain the wind and the spars and rigging strained to control the straining sail. After a few moments, Puella, Kyros, Notus, Furius, Ferrata and Hercules joined them. Crinas remained below almost as seasick as Quintus.

'I would wager,' said User, 'that you are thinking of your personal demigod Achilleus.'

'Yes. As it happens, I am,' nodded the spy.

'Nothing unusual there,' observed Ferrata drily. 'Sometimes I think we have all stepped out of Homer. Achilleus,' he nodded at Artemidorus. 'Ajax the greater,' he nodded at Hercules. 'Briseis,' he looked at Puella. 'You get your choice, User – Agamemnon or Patroclus.'

'Let the boy be Patroclus,' said User, nodding at Kyros. 'If he can stay alive long enough. Notus can play Meriones. I am content with Agamemnon.'

There was a short silence. They all knew that it was the beautiful Briseis who caused the terrible rift between Achilleus and Agamemnon when the warrior wanted her, and the monarch stole her from him. Puella shifted uneasily, feeling the sudden tension there.

'And who would I be?' wondered Furius.

'Ajax the lesser,' answered Ferrata. 'Diomedes if you were better looking; you're certainly a good enough warrior. But as things are.... With that face…' he shrugged apologetically.

'And you, Ferrata,' wondered User. 'Who are you? Odysseus?'

'No,' laughed the Iberian. 'Quintus is Odysseus, widely travelled, cunning and secretive, never reaching home. And I? I am from The Odyssey. I am Polyphemus of course. I am the one-eyed Cyclops!'

As their laughter died, User grew serious. 'But tell us why you were thinking of Achilleus,' he said.

'Not so much Achilleus,' answered Artemidorus. 'As of his Myrmidons and their black ships.'

There was another brief silence as they all thought this over.

'Black ships,' said Ferrata softly.

'You mean ships with black sails and no lights,' said Kyros.

'A pair of them, I'd say, sitting dead ahead between us and Alexandria, with a great rope or net strung out between them, waiting for us to rush through the narrow gap between the two well-lit quinqueremes closing in ahead, charging south at full speed just like we are doing now, straight into their clutches.

vii

'The obvious thing to do is wait until they are just about to close their trap on us and then somehow slip away,' mused Halys.

'That would be easier said than done,' warned his *gubernator*.

'Perhaps not, if we prepared...' Halys stroked his beard thoughtfully.

'*Continued* to prepare,' interrupted User. And he told Halys what he and Artemidorus had already told the oarsmen to do in preparation for silent running.

'Think about it,' said Artemidorus. 'They seem to be relying on several things. First, that we have not worked out their plan yet. Secondly, that even if we do, there will be precious little we can do about it. We can douse the lanterns easily enough, but to make any meaningful change in speed and heading we would have to do some serious sail-handling, difficult enough in daylight – almost impossible in the dark. Thirdly, deploying the oars while the vessel is under way and running at full-speed would be dangerous to put it mildly. It would more than likely cripple us. Damage the oars themselves possibly even snap the rigging and break the mast. Do their work for them.'

'I agree,' nodded Halys. 'It all seems to turn on how fast we can get the sail down and slow enough to get the oars working safely, because only the oars will take us across the wind east or west.'

'We've been thinking about that,' said Artemidorus. 'And we think we have an idea that might work.'

For the next hour, as *Glaros* continued southward at full-speed, with all her lanterns aglow, the oarsmen continued with the preparations User and Artemidorus had asked them to do. Halys and his sail-handling team made subtle changes to the rigging, then sent men to stand – or hang – immediately beneath the lanterns. As close to the brightness as they could come while still concealed by the shadows that seemed to be growing ever deeper. As though Erebus and Nyx themselves were close above the racing vessel, hoping to see what Artemidorus and User were planning.

Halys produced a whistle and agreed a series of signals. Artemidorus' *contubernium* went around the ship from stem to stern ensuring that everyone knew what action to take when they heard each signal. Quintus, faint but intrepid, went below and rifled through the weapons that they had brought with them from Rome – as augmented in Brundisium. When his mission was satisfactorily completed, the rowers got ready to deploy their oars, laying them across the width of the slim hull, with their handles in the laps of the opposite teams, their blades just inside the leather-bound oarlocks. When everything was in position, the lamps down here were doused until there was just enough light to see by – one above the *pausarius* with his drum on the low stage at the stern, one at the bow a hundred feet away and one either side of the mast which stood midships like the trunk of a tree.

So, at last everything was ready. All they had to do was wait.

Which was, of course, by far the hardest part.

*

The quinqueremes were so close now that it was possible to hear the song of their oarsmen keeping the oar-blades digging into the water in unison. It was possible to see the watchkeepers high on the prows which towered above the sleek liburnian even at this distance, lit as they were by lanterns hanging from their incurving stemposts. To see the way the water creamed palely along the length of their massive rams.

Artemidorus stood at his post waiting, trying to calculate Halys' own calculations. How much sea-room remained between those massive rams? Eight *stades*? Ten? More than a Roman military *mile* at any rate. And how far ahead were they? Four *stades*? Less? Three? And how far beyond the two oncoming vessels, drawing ever nearer like the Clashing Rocks trying to crush the Argo, were the black ships waiting, lights doused, nets out, ready to close the trap? It was like a problem set by Pythagoras or Euclid. But it was alive, in motion, ever changing…

He was so distracted by his calculations that Halys' first piercing signal made him jump. The lamps all went out as though by magic. As far as the watchers on the quinqueremes were concerned, *Glaros* must simply have disappeared. At the second signal, which followed almost immediately, Artemidorus and User were in action. Quintus had armed them both with big battle-axes. And in unison they brought the blades down, cutting into the deck rails where the rigging ran through the blocks, severing the lines holding the foot of the sail in place, despite the risk their action posed to the mast itself. With a sound like a thunderclap, the sail flew upward, releasing the wind that had driven the ship southwards. The mast groaned, and the rigging howled even though it had been carefully strengthened for just this moment. Immediately the way began to come off her. Artemidorus stood in the darkness, feeling the ship begin to hesitate, surging, heaving and pitching uneasily, like a galloping horse confused by a sudden change in pace. Slowing. Slowing…

Halys' whistle pierced the night once more. The oarsmen on the right side of the vessel slid their oars out in unison. The *pausarius* beat once on his drum. Fifty oar-blades bit into the sea's surface. The forward impulse on that side stopped. But it continued on the other, swinging the hull in a tight arc. The oars strained. Artemidorus fancied he could feel them flexing, bending. *Glaros* shuddered. The deck sloped. Artemidorus staggered against the rail. The hull uttered a sound somewhere between a howl and a roar. Then it settled. The sail flapped once and fell back against the mast as the wind that had blown from astern now blew from the right instead. The *pausarius* struck his drum again. Then set up a rhythm for six strokes before falling silent.

By which time *Glaros* had completed her turn and was racing noiselessly and invisibly westwards.

XI: Egypt

i

The next day dawned fearsomely hot, despite the season. By the Roman calendar, rewritten by *Divus Julius*, they were just approaching the dog-days of *Mars*, soon to celebrate the calends of *Aprilis*, having been on their mission for well over a month already. But here, still some way north of the Egyptian coast, let alone of their final destination, it seemed that high summer had arrived. The north wind was still at their backs, because they had only run far enough west to be fairly certain that they had evaded the quinqueremes' trap. Then, they turned south once more. Repairing the rigging had taken much of the night but it was done now, and the oarsmen were taking a well-earned rest while the deck crew oversaw their progress south.

Jentaculum of porridge and milk passed. A light, quick *prandium* of bread and warm water followed at noon, while the oarsmen dozed below decks and everyone above sought what little shade there was. But, just as Halys promised, as the afternoon waned towards dinner time, the horizon ahead took on a strange yellow hue, wavering as though they were approaching a sea of molten gold.

Which was apt enough, thought Artemidorus, standing beside the stempost looking earnestly ahead as he went over in his mind what he had revealed to User – and whether he had parted with too much information or too little, for that was the coast of Egypt: a land worth more gold than Rome and Athens combined. Ruled from Alexandria – which boasted more scholars, philosophers, and books than both of the northern cities put together.

Egypt, ruled not merely by a queen, co-regent with her brother as *Divus Julius* had planned all those years ago, but by the Goddess Isis who had inhabited the infant form of Cleopatra at the moment of her birth. Perhaps that was it, thought Artemidorus. Perhaps it wasn't the beauty, wit, or learning; perhaps it wasn't the limitless riches on offer, displayed at every turn with vistas of gigantic opulence; perhaps it was the thought of bedding a goddess that had tempted *Divus Julius* into near-madness and stolen Antony's heart. And to be honest, he could sympathise with both of them. For, as Antony knew too well, Artemidorus himself was half in love with her. An emotion the queen recognised in him, indulged in him, and returned with as much friendship as was proper between a deity and a mortal.

The fact that he had known Cleopatra personally, since *Divus Julius*' Egyptian adventure, and had visited her as *Divus Julius'* emissary and Antony's occasional messenger while she had lived in Rome in 709 and 710 – until the Ides of March that year – was one of the details he had not shared with User. Nor had he revealed the precise details of Antony's messages. Nor the sum of the gold he still carried to smooth the way from the docks to her audience chamber. Nor the priceless gifts he carried – in place of the pomp and ceremony that might be expected in an emissary of Rome. A trust that could only be earned in time – not through promises and threats of revenge.

*

The coastline west of Alexandria was notoriously flat and featureless. But that didn't seem to worry Halys. 'The procedure is quite simple,' User explained. 'We turn left in the last deep water before the tide line and row eastwards parallel to the beach until we see the Pharos. At night it is brighter than any star and during the day it is so tall you can see it for twenty Roman *miles*, especially as it is white.'

'450-feet high, including the statue of Poseidon right at the top of it, yes I know,' said Artemidorus, his tone robbing the words of any possible offence in case the widely travelled Egyptian should feel his new Roman friend was talking down to him and, perhaps, to cover his slight unease at still keeping secrets from the man. 'And on a still day, the smoke from the fire rises straight up and may even be visible for one hundred *miles*. eight hundred *stades*. Yes. I can see how it will guide us to the harbour. And that all we have to do is sail eastwards until we spot it.'

'But?' said User, catching the hesitation in Artemidorus' tone.

'The captains of the quinqueremes will know this as well. They missed us last night. But they still know where we are heading, advised by Messala or Lucius, or both. All they have to do is sail a little west of the Pharos and wait for us.'

'True. I will discuss this matter with my old friend Halys and see if he can come up with a Cilician trick or two.'

'By Cilician trick, he means pirate trick,' said Ferrata, joining Artemidorus on the bow as User went astern.

'Any trick that gets us into Alexandria will suit me fine,' said Artemidorus.

User heard Ferrata's comment and Artemidorus' answer, for neither had lowered their voice. He turned with a bark of laughter. 'No. friend Polyphemus,' he said. 'I rather think what we may need is not a pirate but a wine merchant!'

ii

No sooner had they spotted the Pharos with its golden crown of light, its column of smoke carried inland by the north wind, and its great tower painted blood red in the sunset than they saw the quinqueremes sitting apparently right at its foot, blocking the entrances to both the Great Harbour and the Eunostos Harbour to the west of it. And it seemed that the sharp-eyed watchkeepers high on the Roman vessels saw and identified them at once. As soon as Halys' watchman called out the warning that they were there, it became obvious they were in motion. Four quinqueremes, line abreast. So close together that their oar-tips nearly touched. A huge wall of wood, covered with beaten metal, footed with massive rams, propelled by three hundred oars each, powering straight at them.

Halys watched them approach with a disdainful laugh. 'You see how far out they are? How far from the shoreline? Their draft is the better part of twelve feet where ours is three. Your huge friend Hercules standing on another Hercules' shoulders would hardly be as deep whereas our draft, as I say, might come somewhere between my belt and my armpit. *Glaros* can sail inside them if we want her to, skimming the surf-line like the seagull she's named for. And, remember, they are like Hannibal's elephants compared to our fleet-footed floating gazelle.'

'Is that what you're proposing?' asked Artemidorus uneasily. 'Just to skip along the beach inside them; sail straight past them and into the Western Harbour. Because your draught is shallower than theirs and your speed is so much greater?'

'No, lad,' answered Halys. 'That would be too risky. There are no sailing manuals that tell us about these shores with any accuracy. We could hit a rock or a reef that no-one knew about. In any case, the shoreline all along here is constantly shifting. Only the direct intervention of the gods would get us safely past.'

'And into the grip of a couple of military triremes – or even biremes with a draft as shallow as your own and speed to match,' added Artemidorus, 'just sitting waiting, like the black ships last night.'

He glanced at the shifting, unrecorded shore, prompted by Halys' words. Beyond the narrow surf line, a thin beach gathered up into low dunes and these were soon clothed with reeds and rushes similar to the bank of the River Xanthos, and, behind them, more reeds, standing tall in the gathering evening, nodding their puff-ball heads in the breeze. Then, away in the distance, apparently removed from the reeds by a valley of some kind, low hill slopes which looked as though they were clothed with, of all things, grape vines, the existence of which tugged at something buried in Artemidorus' memory – a distraction that he instantly dismissed.

'Then what's the alternative?' asked Ferrata, interrupting his thoughts. 'Turn and run. Don't come back until they've got bored and gone home? Or died of old age? I don't think poor old Quintus would survive that!'

'No,' answered Halys. User and I have come up with another plan entirely. An Egyptian plan which is so far beyond the imagination of your stupid Romans that it's almost a kind of joke!'

*

'There!' called User from his position in the prow, ten minutes later. The Egyptian was right up at the furthest reach of the bow. He was just visible, one hand on the stempost leaning out over the cutwater almost like Quintus being seasick.

'Thank the gods for that!' answered Halys. 'I was beginning to think we were going to lose the light. Or be run down after all by those Roman elephants!'

'Not something I would recommend,' called User. 'That's how I met my current travelling companions.'

'And lucky to survive the encounter I dare say!' Halys turned to the *gubernator* and his team at the steering paddle. 'We turn here. The wind will help us. I will tell you when to ship the oars.'

Glaros turned right and headed south with the wind beginning to fill her sail once again, driving her onwards while her oars continued to push her through the water, growing shallower and shallower as they ran towards the beach. Artemidorus watched. For it seemed that there was nothing ahead of them but that dangerous, constantly shifting shore.

'He's going to beach us!' called Ferrata, his voice wavering with shock. 'At least Quintus will be happy!'

'Ship oars!' ordered Halys. And, with a rumble, the oars came aboard, just leaving the great sail to push them relentlessly through the low surf onto the pale swathe of sand.

'Steady as she goes,' came User's distant voice.

'Steady!' Halys called to the navigator and his team.

And, with a shudder, *Glaros* came onto the land. Except that she didn't. The land yielded to the south-running impulse of her bow. And Artemidorus realised that what had looked like solid ground was a floating reed-bed. What they were crossing was not a beach but a river-mouth, scarcely wider than the ship itself, the outflow issuing into the sea moving gently, invisibly. Almost stagnant, speaking of thick vegetation, shallow water.

Pushed relentlessly onward by the wind, the liburnian shouldered the reed-beds aside. There was a faint rumble and a slight shudder as her bottom brushed over the river-bed, but the imperative of that steady wind helped push her on. And in a few more moments she was free as the river widened and deepened while the vegetation fell back.

'Through!' called User.

Artemidorus looked over his shoulder – over *Glaros*' stern. Immediately in their wake, the reed-beds had closed, hiding the river mouth once again. His gaze shifted northwards and eastwards to where their pursuers were still powering pointlessly along the sea-shore. Parallel to the beach, several *stadia* out in the deeper water of the *Mare Nostrum,* which the locals called The Roman Sea; and not as a compliment. The quinqueremes, as they had last night, were lighting their signal lamps, which made them easier to see as they approached the narrow mouth of the hidden river. They became a constellation of brightness moving relentlessly westward beyond a wall of beach-backed sand dunes topped by reeds and rushes. The Roman galleys might just as well have been cruising off Brundisium or Britannia for their chance of catching *Glaros* now.

As night fell around them, the dark liburnian sailed invisibly southwards until, abruptly, in the last of the light, she came out of the south-facing river-mouth and into open water. Artemidorus looked about in simple wonder. To his right, the low hill-slopes he had seen earlier, claimed the final red rays of the setting sun, turning the vine-leaves a fiery-red, making the whole hillside seem to flame as the leaves moved in the wind. He began to see, amongst the shadows along the shoreline, low warehouses, and what could only be wine-presses fronted by piles and piles of amphorae. Then, even as he stared, Halys ordered the oars run out and *Glaros* swung left, powering silently forward.

In front of the dazzled spy was a vast expanse of calm, clear water that reached forward, eastwards, in the darkness to a blaze of light almost equal to that of burning Xanthus. But this was no city being torched, sacked and destroyed. This was the legendary marvel; the wonder of the world which was his final destination.

'Alexandria,' he breathed.

iii

Just like Rome, Alexandria never slept, thought Artemidorus. But there the similarities ended. Rome stayed awake all night because its twisting rabbit warren of streets was so congested during the day that wagons were forbidden. Deliveries, therefore, had to take place after dark by traders with special dispensation to come and go through the guarded gates. Rolling and groaning along the stinking streets, wheels screaming like souls in Tartarus. Lamps and flambeaux grudgingly – and dangerously – kept the shadows at bay while ox-carts and mule-drawn wagons delivered everything from casks of fish and nets of molluscs to bushels of grain and amphora of wine. In contrast, Alexandria's streets were wide, straight, laid out in the open grid favoured by Alexander the Great himself. For Alexander had designed the place. Deliveries were welcome at any time. The *vias* and boulevards were clean, fragrant, well-maintained. But still the city blazed and bustled through the hours of darkness. Alexandrians seemed to think that life was too short and too full of wondrous possibilities to waste half of it asleep.

Most of the buildings were stone or brick faced with limestone and marble, like the towering Pharos itself. The lights coming from great blazing sconces were all maintained by the city fathers, or rather, by the city's mother: their goddess, pharaoh and queen, Isis Cleopatra.

And what was true of the city behind its tall, well maintained wall, was also true down here at the Royal Docks on the south side. Docks which formed part of the Lake Harbour that opened out onto the great freshwater Lake Mareotis, across which they had just come. The lake was fed by the Canopic branch of the river, which joined the Nile proper some twenty Roman *miles* north of Memphis. The westernmost branch named for the attendant city of Canopus that stood to the east of Alexandria. But a wide canal ran more directly from the city to the main stream, via the two cities of Elusisda and Canopus which existed to supply entertainments of every sort to the Golden City itself – as Artemidorus knew from personal experience. But, as the reed-blocked channel along which *Glaros* had only just managed to squeeze made clear, the great river was running low.

Even the lake was shallow – though there was still enough water to fill the Lake Harbour.

As he followed Halys and User up onto the brightly-lit dockside, Artemidorus looked around. *Glaros* was by no means the only trading vessel here, for, as User had implied, and he had seen for himself, there was a bustling wine industry all along the lake's southern shore. Mareotic wine, he remembered. Famous the world over, he remembered now as the whole place closed around him with the familiarity of an old lover rekindling the flame, the wine more important than ever now in the face of the Nile's failure to flood for two successive years, robbing Egypt and her people of four successive grain harvests.

But the vessels riding beneath the massive sconces, flambeaus and municipal oil lamps were by no means all trading vessels. Away to the right, in the lakeside version of the Royal Harbour at the salt-water north side of the city, there was Cleopatra's river fleet, at the heart of which sat her enormous golden barge. More than three hundred Roman feet long, it was nearly three times the length of *Glaros*; bigger than the quinqueremes that had hunted them – and twice as long as most of the *polyreme* battleships he had seen. It was fashioned of cedar wood, painted and gilded, forested with tall sandalwood pavilions, scented and silk-walled. He remembered visiting the main decks between the pavilions – the gardens with their fountains and enormous statues. The menagerie with its exotic animals and birds – the most beautiful with their wings clipped to stop them flying away. The palatial living quarters, above-deck and below, accommodation for tens – hundreds – of honoured guests and the slaves required to tend them. The barge was only able to be so enormous, so opulent, because it was never designed to withstand the open sea.

'Septem!' Quintus interrupted his thoughts. 'The Egyptian and the pirate are signalling to you.

*

Antony would no doubt have approved, thought Artemidorus cheerfully, that some of his gold went towards port charges and docking fees – and therefore straight into the coffers of the woman he most truly and deeply loved. Some of it also went towards transport costs – for the gold itself, the precious documents, the arms and armour that the legionary slaves and the oarsmen unloaded from *Glaros*' hold. And a good deal of it went to Halys in payment for the passage. As it had turned out to be more adventurous than expected,

Artemidorus was content that it turned out more expensive than initially agreed.

Then, as the unloading continued, Artemidorus showed his credentials to the dockside officials whose job it was to record the arrivals and departures of men and women, in groups or as individuals, working for the office of the *dioketes* Chief Steward who oversaw such matters. And, once his documents had been checked, thought the spy, word of the arrival of a Roman courier from Antony would be carried to whichever of the palaces Cleopatra and her court were currently occupying. Eventually, in all probability, to Cleopatra herself; even such a modest embassy as this. Especially as he had appeared at the Lake Harbour almost in secret instead of arriving at the Royal Harbour on the Mediterranean side, with the self-important pomp and ceremony that might be expected. Even so, he reckoned, there would be a summons. And he was fully prepared to spend the next days climbing the ladder of influence, seniority and power as one official after another handed him onwards and upwards through the court hierarchy.

Certainly, amongst the details taken so carefully and punctiliously was the address at which he proposed to be staying during his visit – an address which User was happy to supply because he was putting himself in charge of finding them bed and board. Though, thought Artemidorus, he need hardly have bothered to confirm where he lived for it was obvious from the outset that both Halys and User were both well-known in the Port of the Lake.

iv

‘It must be the end of the second night watch,’ said Ferrata, as Artemidorus returned and they watched the bullock-carts fill up. ‘And yet you can hire a cart as easily as if it was the middle of the day!’

‘Not so strange,’ said Quintus. ‘Alexandria never sleeps. Besides, this is precisely the time that *Divus Julius* set off to invade Britannia.’

‘Even so... Not that I’m saying Septem isn’t an excellent substitute for *Divus Julius* in terms of getting things done!’

‘Well,’ said Quintus. ‘Let’s hope this invasion goes better than that one.’

‘From what I remember,’ Artemidorus joined in the conversation, ‘The natives here are a damnsight more welcoming. Or they were when we settled things after the battle in the streets and Royal

Harbour.'

'And the weather's a good deal better too.' Quintus concluded cheerily, more relieved than he could say to have his feet back on solid ground once more.

'Right,' said User. 'That's everything loaded on the carts. It's time to move it all to my warehouses. And get you all some decent accommodation.'

'Decent accommodation,' said Furius. 'That sounds expensive.'

'We'll see,' answered User.

They could have hired horses easily enough and ridden but instead they said goodbye to Halys, his crew and *Glaros*. Then they walked. User sat in the leading cart, so he could direct the driver and Puella chose to sit beside him, but other than them they were all content to go on foot, which allowed Artemidorus and Quintus at least to relive some powerful memories. To bring them back into sharper focus, indeed, for the intervening years had somehow dulled their recollections. For, the place was absolutely overwhelming – especially to anyone on foot. The first thing they walked over almost immediately outside the Port Gates was the bridge that spanned the *Fluvius Novus* Alexandrian canal. 'I had forgotten,' said Quintus, 'that it's so wide as well as so long. And so full of activity even at this hour! Look at the River Harbour! How many boats are in there?'

At his word they paused on the great bridge which allowed the road up from the Lake Port to step over great canal onto the environs of the city itself.

'Is this the Sun Gate?' asked Notus, who was as usual close beside Kyros as they walked up to the city walls from the Canal and the River Harbour.

'I think so,' answered Artemidorus. 'But that's certainly the *Leoforos Argeus* beyond it.'

'If this is the Sun Gate,' called Puella from User's side in the lead wagon, 'Is there a Moon Gate to match it?'

'Yes,' answered User, catching the final part of the conversation. 'There are four of them – Sun Gate, Moon Gate, Canopic Gate and Western Gate, the four great gates standing North, South, East and West.' And on that he passed through the great gate himself and they all followed him onto the *Leoforos Argeus,* Argeus' Boulevard, the second most important thoroughfare in the city

*

It was the scale of the place that Artemidorus remembered most clearly. And yet he was struck by it all over again, almost as though this was his first visit. The gigantic statues, the towering colonnades, as though the place had been designed for gods to inhabit, which, in a way, it was and yet beyond the massive magnificence of the bright-lit porticoes, lived mortal men and women.

'That's the Jewish quarter down there,' observed Quintus, looking right.

'They've been here even longer than in Rome,' nodded Artemidorus. 'Mercenaries mostly, brilliant soldiers; they're dangerously adaptable, as good with bows as Parthians, as good with slings as Thracians, as accurate as Greeks with their *pilae* spears and as effective as Gaulish Auxiliaries on horseback. I hear they even built and manned a fleet when they were stationed on Elephantine Island near Aswan. They're supposed to be up with our Roman legionaries in the use of sword and shield, ruthless, disciplined and damn-near unbeatable under most conditions.'

'And, best of all,' added Quintus thoughtfully, 'it was an army of Judean soldiers who rescued *Divus Julius,* Queen Cleopatra and us during the Battle of Alexandria back in 706. I'll never forget them; brilliant warriors.'

'They're keen businessmen too,' called User. 'Bankers rather than traders I suppose, but none the worse for that. Accurate, honest, their word is their bond. No wonder the Ptolemies have worked so hard to keep them here.'

'Like *Divus Julius* in Rome,' nodded Artemidorus.

'I heard they went into formal mourning for him after he died,' said User. 'What do they call it? Shiva?'

'I believe that lasts seven days,' answered Artemidorus. 'There's a longer period called Sloshim, lasting thirty. I think they held that for him as well, but I was in and out of Rome quite a lot at the time and can't be certain.'

'Still, the point is well made,' said User. 'They are a people who respect anyone who treats them with fairness and consideration. *Divus Julius* did. The Ptolemies do.'

This conversation took them past the first few blocks with cross-roads geometrically positioned to right and left. Then they fell silent and simply looked, wide-eyed at the massive magnificence all around until they came to the greatest cross-roads of all. Artemidorus and Quintus saw it coming, memories stirring once again. The promise of even greater brightness. The nearing bustle of hundreds of feet. Of hooves. The creaking of wheels. Coughing, bellowing, neighing and grunting of dozens of beasts of burden. The chatter of crowds of people talking in so many different languages, thought Artemidorus, finding it hard to contain his excitement at being back, that you would have thought there was no room for so many different countries in the whole world – let alone the Roman Republic.

And then they were there.

'This is *Meson Pedion*, Canopic Street,' said User. 'The greatest thoroughfare in the world.'

The wide road reached right through the heart of the city. So broad, Artemidorus remembered, that *Divus Julius* could march his legions down it in full battle order, twenty abreast even allowing for the square decorative pools and fountains that stood down the centre of it. Now, even in the middle of a balmy, star-filled night, it was bustling. Men and women of all races, costumes and cultures strolled – or hurried – by. There were more wagons; chariots with two or four wheels. Silken-walled litters – wheeled or carried by litter-bearers. Laden pack-horses, mules, oxen and camels. The scent of spices mixing with the odour of the animals and the rich pungency of their droppings. Macedonian and Jewish soldiers in scale armour with pointed helmets sprouting long, thin horsehair crests. 'Those are the city watch if I remember right,' said Quintus. 'Hard bastards every one.' Familiar figures in Greek and Roman clothing, Egyptian men and women wearing much less. Strangers from the Great Sand Sea wrapped in black and white robes and head-dresses with only their eyes showing – and the massive curved swords that they wore at their belts, mostly riding camels – with one hump or two. But some, like kings and conquerors themselves, astride the most beautiful stallions Artemidorus had ever seen, leading long strings of ebony-skinned, exotic looking slaves.

As they turned into this massive thoroughfare, so Artemidorus' view broadened. The enormous star-filled sky seemed to settle like a dark silk cover on the red rooftops, dimmed by the earthly brightness all around. To their left, the Alexandrian Acropolis containing the tomb of Alexander himself, the gilded corpse in a crystal coffin that all the world could look upon. And the Serapium, the famous Temple of Serapis with its gigantic statue of the God. Both stood on the crest of Mount Copron, whose lower slopes were clad in yet more buildings in Greek and Roman design, columned and colonnaded in marble, tiled in terracotta. Illuminated by sconces, torches and lamps – flames flickering in the warm north wind. Alexandria was said to be fire-proof because its buildings were all made of brick, limestone and marble. But both Artemidorus and Quintus knew that was not true, for they had seen Alexandria ablaze.

The one thing that seemed to be missing as far as Artemidorus could remember, were the enormous statues of past pharaohs, lines of sphinxes with the faces of women and the bodies of seated lions and carvings of strange, animal-headed gods and goddesses. Or were they to be found in the great temples around Memphis? He shook his head. He would check with Quintus later. In the mean-time there was far too much of immediate interest clamouring for his attention, to their right, the Gymnasium, with the Public Gardens beyond. The tops of the palm-trees black against the stars. Then the Macedonian Camp where the City's legions were housed, ready to protect the palaces which stood tall and bright beyond them on the sickle-shaped isthmus of the Lochrias and on the island of Antirrhodos close by. Cleopatra herself was up there somewhere, thought Artemidorus, and was surprised at how the notion tugged at his heart.

V

User was shouting over the bustle that seemed to have intensified all around them despite the midnight hour and the unrivalled width of the street. 'On your right, after Temple of Isis is the Broucheiron, the Royal quarter, where the main Library is situated.' Artemidorus smiled at the sudden pride in the usually taciturn Egyptian's voice. 'The smaller Sister Library is there too. Too close to the Royal Docks, as *Divus Julius* discovered when he set fire to some of it as he burned Ptolemy's fleet.'

Artemidorus remembered that. He and Quintus had been there when it happened. Then stationed out on Pharos Island.

But User was continuing, 'Beyond that, though you cannot see it, is the Caesarium, the temple to *Divus Julius* that the divine Queen Cleopatra is having built. She plans to erect two tall *stylae* obelisks or needles in front of it as it overlooks the sea. And there beyond it are the Agora marketplace – though it is also used as a school for philosophers – and our Tychaeum where we worship the Tyche, Goddess of Fortune, who brings the city its luck! And there, beyond that, as I'm sure you can all see, the Pharos stands upon its island. But on the left is the real heart of the city. The Museon which the Greeks call the Musaeum, the Temple Of The Muses, where all knowledge is stored, is discussed, is explored and expanded.' A fluke in the breeze brought a cacophony of snarls, roars and howls together with a feral animal stench. 'And that is where the

Menageries is,' added User. 'Just as we try to collect a copy of every book and at least one representative of every philosophical, astrological and mathematical discipline, so we try to collect a member of every family of animals. We keep them in the Menagerie.'

'If I remember correctly,' said Quintus, his voice low, 'they'd do better to put some of their philosophers in the cages and let the animals go free.'

But User didn't hear. He turned to the driver and whispered an order. They swung left. 'And so we enter my domain,' he announced. 'The ancient city of Rhakotis. Keep looking to your right, though, and you will see how the city's temples, public buildings and villas are little by little replaced by warehouses, docks and shipping. The two halves of the sea-port divided by the great Heptastadion, a man-made roadway seven *stades*, nearly a Roman *mile*, in length, reaching from the shore to the Pharos Island itself. With a fort at either end – usually manned either by Macedonian or Judean troops. It stands tall enough never to be threatened by the highest tide and the arches beneath it allow the water to flow freely from one side to the other

'To the east of the Heptastadion is the Great Harbour which contains the Royal Harbour, islands and island palaces, temples and so-forth. To the west, the Eunostos harbour where my ships are docked at my quays in front of my warehouses. And here, overlooking it all, is the villa that my father's father built and which I now share with my brother. And, as you can see, like everything else in Alexandria, it is large enough to accommodate us all, either in the main house or in the out-houses and servants' quarters that surround it. Though on a night as warm as this, you can sleep out in the gardens if you like.'

*

Artemidorus was put in mind of *Divus Julius'* dead assassin Minucius Basilus and his magnificent villa in Pompeii as he followed User and the wagons up the paved roadway through User's gardens towards the enormous dwelling erected by his father's father. It seemed to him more like a village than a family villa, with its stables, store-houses, out-houses, slave quarters and guest quarters. Even so, the central villa easily dominated. Designed after the style of the Greeks and Romans rather than the Egyptians, it sat perfectly in the Graeco-Roman extravagance of the Golden City – in the Greek style, but not on the Greek scale. User's villa was huge.

Columns towered, holding the roof so high that there must be room for three stories within. The monumental statuary in the gardens, with their decorative temples and grottoes, was also represented standing tall between the columns not to mention the carved marble crowns, coronets and coverings almost on the same level as the columns' capitals which were carved in the Egyptian fashion as lotus or papyrus flowers. All brightly painted and gilded.

The doorkeeper saw them coming and by the time the wagons drew up at the foot of a flight of steps leading to the main door, the entire household was awake. Wiping sleep from their eyes, a squad of slaves rushed out to unload the carts, followed immediately by a man who could only be User's brother and a woman no doubt his wife. And so it proved. Introductions were made as the wagons were unloaded and the legionary slaves helped the house slaves put everything away. The Artemidorus and his *contubernium* were welcomed and assigned rooms. They were given a light, late *cena* under the eye of User's sister in law as User and his brother disappeared into the capacious *tablinum* study to discuss their financial losses in the destruction of Xanthus. And the tragic loss of family to judge by the howls of distress that came echoing from the distant room. But at last the bustle died, the rooms were prepared, the *contubernium* conducted to their chambers and their beds.

A kind of peace settled on the huge villa, and Artemidorus at last fell into an exhausted, if uneasy sleep. Alone.

Until, mere heartbeats later, so it seemed, User was shaking him awake, his muscular forehead folded into a frown. 'There are soldiers at the door waiting for you,' he said. 'You'd better hurry up.'

'Soldiers! What soldiers?' Artemidorus was fully awake and sitting up at once. He glanced out of the lightly curtained window to see that it was full day outside. 'What soldiers, User?' he repeated.

'Queen Cleopatra's guard.'

XII: Isis

i

'Tell them they'll have to wait,' said Artemidorus as he swung his legs out of the bed. 'And send someone to wake Quintus. He'll be coming with me. Ask him to select some of the legionary slaves who packed our stuff away last night to bring our full uniforms, our documents and the gifts Antony sent for us to deliver.'

User was more at ease with giving orders than receiving them. But it wasn't every day that a squad of the Queen's guard came hammering at his door, so he hurried to obey. He had no sooner departed than a house slave arrived with a bowl of warm water and the household's *tonsor*. Artemidorus was more used to shaving himself – but he made an exception today. 'Do your worst,' he said. The *tonsor* smiled and bowed, stropping his razor.

By the time Quintus arrived with several laden legionary slaves in tow, Artemidorus was washed, shaved, trimmed and glistening with aromatic oils. They put the boxes on the bed and began to open them. The first contained dress uniforms. The second, armour from the brothel in Brundisium. The third contained a range of weapons but Artemidorus contented himself with *gladius* and *pugio* as though he was going on parade. Something further emphasised when he pulled out his badges of rank and the *phalera* battle honours that would be attached to the front of his uniform. The fourth contained the documents Antony wanted him to hand to the queen. Personally. And last were two identical boxes made of cedar-wood, bound in gold and richly inlaid, each measuring more than two cubits, three *pedes* feet, square and heavy enough to bring beads of sweat to the face of the legionary slaves carrying them.

At last, both Artemidorus and Quintus were ready. Fully armed in new red tunics, armour in place, steel hoops laced up the front; *sagae* cloaks swinging from their steel-banded shoulders and helmets resting on their hips. With their legionary slaves behind them carrying the document cases and gold-bound gift boxes, they marched into the atrium of User's villa. The rest of the contubernium were there, together with User, his brother and sister-in-law, their children, servants, and slaves. A muted gasp went through the crowd – exactly the reaction that Artemidorus was hoping for. After all, someone had sent Cleopatra's guards. So, it was conceivable that they were being summoned to see a living goddess. He wanted to make the best impression possible because, of course, he was standing in for the most powerful man in the Republic; perhaps in the world.

A unit of Macedonian Guards was waiting patiently at the door. Fully armed, but with their arms and armour practical workaday – very much less impressive than Artemidorus' and Quintus' parade kit. But the looks the shining legionaries received reminded Artemidorus of those he tended to give Antony's pretty Praetorians.

'We have brought you litters, if you wish to ride,' said the Macedonian commander. 'And a tumbrel for anything that might prove heavy.'

'Thank you. We will march with you. But we have boxes that might well go in your tumbrel.

'As you wish.' The Macedonians formed up and set off at a fast march. Artemidorus and Quintus had no trouble keeping up, but Artemidorus and the legionary slaves, no doubt, was relieved the heavy boxes were in the little horse-drawn cart.

*

Canopic Street was even busier than it had been last night but the path in front of the Queen's guard and the impressively turned-out legionaries cleared almost magically. Artemidorus was bursting with questions but the Macedonian commander seemed more focused on getting where they were going as quickly as possible than in conducting conversations. Artemidorus didn't mind, he was content to look at the buildings they were passing and to plan precisely what he was going to say to Cleopatra.

The Macedonians stopped at the steps of the Royal Harbour. Artemidorus found himself looking down at a royal barge. Nothing so huge or magnificent as the one in the Lake Harbour, for this barge was not designed to go up and down the Nile. Rather, it was designed to cross the salt-water harbour to the various islands within it. He stood back to allow the contents of the tumbrel to be carried down the steps and aboard. As he did so, his narrow eyes raked the harbour, cataloguing the range of deep-water vessels moored or anchored there. And there, amid them, was the largest of the Roman *Libertore* quinqueremes that had been trying to stop or capture *Glaros* and her passengers.

ii

Artemidorus and Quintus ran down the marble stairs together and stepped aboard the barge. Quintus gritted his teeth, compressed his lips and no doubt, thought Artemidorus, sent up a quick prayer to Poseidon. It seemed to work. The legionary stood firm and was not sick. The Macedonian Guards followed them, and the oarsmen pulled away. There was ample seating but Artemidorus walked up to the bow so that he could see precisely where they were headed. Keeping close to the land, with Cape Locrias behind them crowned by the Temple of Isis and the Macedonian Acropolis, the barge swung south of Antirrhodos Island. It seemed for a moment that the oars must strike against the Island's rocky southern point, as the current rushed them westwards, but in a moment they were through the narrows. Ahead of them, the isthmus with the temple of the Timoinium on its tip reached out into the bay with the arches of the Heptastadion further beyond. But then the barge swung round to face north and Artemidorus' view changed as the boat moved onto its new course, apparently heading straight for the Pharos itself. The barge swung eastwards into the bay formed by the curve of Antirrhodos Island. The island stretched away on either hand for several *stadions*. Right ahead, dominating the high, curving sliver of land and the bay itself was the palace.

If User's villa had seemed gigantic and ornate when they first saw it last night, it was less than nothing compared with the palace on Antirrhodos Island. Marble steps led up from the royal dock, continuing to rise long after the rocky surface of the island itself leveled off, leading up to the gigantic white-columned frontage, as though the Acropolis in Athens had an older, bigger brother – taller, wider, more exotic, and infinitely more overpowering. The palace behind this overwhelming frontage seemed to reach away forever – though of course it could not have done so for it was constrained by the island's width.

The oarsmen guided the barge to the bottom of the steps with ease. They were met by *stipare* dockers who took the thrown ropes and held the vessel steady as the passengers climbed ashore. The largest Macedonians each took one of the boxes Artemidorus had brought. Their leader gestured that the legionary slaves should wait. Then they all ran up the steps together. To be met at the top by the next level up in palace guards. These ones wore armour made of gold.

'That would be bloody useless in battle,' growled Quintus. 'It's not much stronger than toughened hide.'

'It is impressive, though,' observed Artemidorus.

'That is its purpose,' observed the Macedonian commander. 'To be impressive rather than functional.' His dark eyes lingered on Artemidorus' gleaming kit as he spoke.

'We have guards like that in Rome,' said Artemidorus. 'Praetorians. We eat them for breakfast. It was men like that we slaughtered all around this very bay six years ago when we were fighting alongside your divine queen and our general Julius Caesar, who is also now divine.'

The Macedonian grunted, clearly reassessing the legionaries. 'You find pretty parade-ground soldiers everywhere,' he observed more cordially. 'Mostly the sons of aristocrats who need to do some armed service but don't want to swap the marble halls of power for the filthy fields of battle.'

They came to the top step – which reached pack into a marble-floored precinct before the next flight of steps up to the palace itself began. The Macedonians came to attention. The gilded Egyptians took over. The boxes were handed on with a mixture of relief and amusement as the gold-plated recipients staggered helplessly beneath their weight. But the grim amusement only lasted until the leader of the Egyptian unit called for burly slaves to relieve his men of the burdens. Then they marched across the precinct in a glittering phalanx with the Roman legionaries at its heart.

*

The doors into the palace dwarfed the gates to many cities Artemidorus had seen. There were squads of slaves whose job was simply to open and close them. As the doors swung wide, the golden guards marched in. Artemidorus looked around in awe. He had never visited this palace and could hardly believe the sight. It was square, colonnaded. Columns, almost as tall as those outside, soared upwards, until he had to squint to make out their decorated capitals. It was as though the builders thought only of scale – not accommodation. And, above them, the brightly painted ceiling was so far away as to be almost celestial. This was after all the home of the Goddess Isis. There was a pool in the middle, surrounded by a huge mosaic very much in the Tuscan style still so popular in Rome. But this pool would have floated a quinquereme and in its centre stood a statue of Poseidon from whose cupped hands water cascaded nearly thirty cubits into the small lake at his feet. Whereas the Romans kept golden carp in theirs, there were huge black-backed crocodiles in this one – a gesture to Sobek, crocodile-headed god of the river Nile.

You could have paraded a legion on the mosaic, which showed Poseidon frolicking with Aphrodite and Demeter. Once again Artemidorus was struck by how Greek this city was – and how the Egyptian gods were at home further south in Memphis.

The massive space was full of people in a variety of costumes matching the throng on Canopus Street, but the golden escort marched Artemidorus and Quintus through without hesitating. At the rear of the atrium was a huge square entrance that led into another enormous room. This one was a kind of reception chamber, for at the far side of it another enormous portal consisting of two towering columns and a gigantic carved and painted lintel, opened into the audience chamber. Where it was just possible to see in the distance, Cleopatra, the Pharonic Queen Goddess herself, enthroned on the top of a great marble dais with her co-ruler young Ptolemy Caesarion seated at her side. The young co-ruler was the receptacle of two gods – Osiris and *Divus Julius*, whose offspring he was – not to mention being the son of Isis herself.

The guards stopped. Artemidorus looked around at the bustling scene, wondering whether he might know any of the men assembled here waiting their turn for an audience. And he found at once that he did. For standing on the far side of the enormous chamber was Lucius Calpurnius Bibulus. Also, fully armed and parade-ground smart. His aristocratic lips curled in arrogant, thoroughly Roman disdain at all this entirely suspect foreign opulence.

iii

'Bring the Romans forward!'

Artemidorus never saw who called the order, but the men escorting him were in motion at once, so he and Quintus moved as well. On the far side of the vast chamber, Lucius was also marching forward, escorted by his own golden guards. But, whereas everything that Artemidorus had brought was contained in the chests and boxes being carried behind him, Lucius seemed to have brought only a single scroll in a leather scroll-case. The weight of the boxes slowed the men escorting Artemidorus and Quintus, so Lucius and his men went through the huge portal first and ended up at the foot of the dais ahead of himself and Quintus.

There was a moment of stasis. Artemidorus looked up into the face of the woman he had last seen in Caesar's villa on the top of the Janiculum Hill across the Tiber from Rome. She had been anything but regal then. Shaken to her very foundations by the news that her lover had just been slaughtered by some of the men he trusted most. How different she looked now. Not merely regal but truly divine. On her head the golden *pschent*, the snake-fronted double crown announcing her sovereignty over the Two Kingdoms of Upper and Lower Egypt. Her mask-like face made up in the Egyptian style. Her eyes lined with kohl, brows defined with gold. Her lips rouged. Her cheeks sprinkled with gold-dust. Her robes cloth-of-gold. The *Hequa* crook'd scepter and the ritual flail, both gilded and enameled, crossed on her breast, held by steady fingers laden with golden, bejeweled rings. Artemidorus knew that her form was slight but strong, athletic. And yet with her robes and regalia she filled the massive throne and looked down at her Roman guests from an almost Olympian height.

She and Caesarion were by no means alone on the huge dais. They were surrounded by advisors, secretaries, generals, admirals, all in uniforms and robes that rivaled those of the gilded escort surrounding Artemidorus and Quintus. To either side of the group stood slaves with sensors from which scented smoke drifted onto the sultry air – which was in turn stirred by yet more slaves waving great fans that seemed to be made of the tail-feathers of peacocks and ostriches.

Even though nothing was said, and no signal given, one of the secretaries stepped forward, came down the steps and held out his hand. Lucius gave him the scroll he was carrying. The secretary bowed and climbed back to stand by his queen, still sitting in silence.

The secretary broke the security seal on the case, pulled out the scroll, checked Brutus' personal seal that hung from the ivory-coloured tube, and unrolled the papyrus sheet. He scanned its contents, frowning. 'It is from the Roman General, Marcus Junius Brutus, my Queen,' he said in accented Greek. 'Do you wish me to read it all?'

'What does General Brutus say?' Her voice was low, musical, penetrating, and yet the lips in that divine mask hardly seemed to move.

'The General says that he has many legions and that his friend and fellow Liberator Gaius Cassius Longinus has many more. As well as their legions, they have two large fleets of well-prepared, fully armed warships under the *imperium* of Generals Ahenobarbus and Murcus, which completely control the waters between Egypt, Greece, and Italy. Furthermore, General Cassius' troops are still stationed at the border of your country.' The secretary hesitated.

'We know all of this,' said Cleopatra, her voice dangerously calm. 'What else does General Brutus say?'

*

'General Brutus informs you that he has become aware of an embassy from his enemy Triumvir and Tyrant Mark Antony. He is certain that General Antony is begging for aid in the form of a fleet of warships powerful enough to counter the fleets of Ahenobarbus and Murcus. For only this will give him the freedom of movement he needs to transport his army from Italy into Macedonia.'

'I see…'

The two words prompted the increasingly nervous secretary to proceed. 'General Brutus wishes to inform you that should you even consider doing anything so foolish as acceding to Antony's demands, he will instantly advise General Cassius to invade Egypt with a view to arresting you as an enemy of the Senate and People of Rome and replacing you upon the throne with your sister Arsinoe, who is currently and conveniently resident in the city of Ephesus, which he controls.'

'He says that, does he?'

'His very words, Majesty.'

'And you, messenger. Were you aware of General Brutus' thoughts?' The statuesque mask tilted towards Lucius as though the Queen were one of the mechanical figures Alexandria was famous for.

Lucius remained unimpressed. His whole demeanor was arrogant. He addressed the Queen as though speaking to the lowliest of his clients. 'I was the one who brought him the information about Antony's message, yes,' he sneered. 'And I advised him how best to use that information.'

'I see.' The jeweled fingers trembled slightly, closing to fists on the flail and scepter. The voice remained low, but it too shook.

You stupid boy, thought Artemidorus. You're about to regret your arrogance, and Brutus' into the bargain.

But Cleopatra was speaking. 'Lucius Calpurnius Bibulus, were your general Marcus Junius Brutus here I would have him whipped for such insolence and arrogance. But as he is not here, I will have you served with the same well-merited fate in his place. Take him away.'

'What!' Roared Lucius, outraged. 'I am a messenger! You cannot have me whipped! I claim the privileges and protections of my position!'

'And I am not only a queen but a goddess. You may thank whatever deities you worship that I am content to let you live. Away with you!'

The measured softness of her tone only made the words more chilling. Silence fell on the room – on the entire palace – that reminded Artemidorus of the last moment of quiet before a battle.

Lucius Calpurnius Balbus was dragged away, still shouting about diplomatic immunity until he was silenced – either with a gag or a swift right-hander to his arrogant young jaw.

iv

Cleopatra rose. Caesarion echoed his mother's actions. The councilors stood to attention. She swept down the steps onto the floor of the audience chamber with the boy immediately behind her. Everyone fell back, bowing, awed, including Artemidorus and Quintus. 'You,' she said as she sailed past the secret agent and his gilded escort, 'Wait here until you are summoned. I will consult with you in private. Though apparently I already know what Antony's message will be.'

'If she has that arrogant little *nothus* bastard whipped then she'll probably find herself at war whether she wants to be or not,' said Quintus, watching Cleopatra and her entourage as they vanished through a smaller doorway at the rear of the audience chamber. 'Brutus won't take kindly to that at all.'

'Maybe, maybe not,' said Artemidorus, raising his voice above the bustle as the audience chamber also began to empty. They all stepped back as the court officials and dignitaries followed the Queen down off the dais, talking earnestly but quietly amongst themselves. Hardly surprisingly, thought Artemidorus. Brutus might just as well have declared war immediately. Because Quintus was right. As soon as he heard that his emissary had been whipped, then war was almost inevitable. Wars had been started for less. And yet…

'Brutus' threat depends on Cassius' reaction, though, doesn't it?' he continued as the last of the muttering councilors vanished behind the crowd of suppliants. 'And Cassius isn't going to invade an entire country just because Brutus feels he's been insulted. They may be brothers-in-law but they do not like each other. Cassius still blames Brutus for this whole mess. If he hadn't refused to have Antony killed at the same time as *Divus Julius* and sent a couple of *carnifexes* executioners to Apollonia to take care of Octavianus when the will was read out, things would have turned out very differently…'

'Or if either one of them had had any sort of a plan for what to do once *Divus Julius* was dead…' Quintus shook his head.

'If anyone had thought to get that ruthless bastard Cicero involved at the outset instead of afterwards when it was far too late…' Artemidorus shrugged.

'How different the entire world would be!'

'Just a couple of bad decisions at the crisis point and each of them blaming the other for the way it's all turned out.'

'The Fates must have laughed so hard their ribs began to break…' Quintus fell silent, thinking. 'Besides,' he added suddenly. 'In spite of what we saw at Xanthus, Brutus isn't much of a general, Septem. Not like Cassius. And if Cassius is waiting at the border because he sees more problems than advantages to invading, then a message from Brutus isn't going to make him change his mind. Good general though Cassius is, his reputation rests on the fact that he managed to lead his men safely out of the blood-bath at Carrhae where General Crassus lost his own head. I guess they'd have rather had a good clean death on the battlefield than starve to death in the desert or rot alive with plague. I know I would!'

*

At last Charmian, the senior of Cleopatra's handmaidens, came across the deserted chamber. 'The Queen will see you now,' she said. 'You may go,' she said to the gilded escourt. 'But the slaves may bring the boxes with the Romans into the royal presence.'

Artemidorus, Quintus and the sweating slaves followed Charmian through the smaller doorway and into the private sections of the palace which were smaller but still breathtakingly luxurious, however. Sumptuously furnished and decorated. The sheer extravagance of it all went against everything Artemidorus' Spartan soul and Stoic beliefs held dear. But he did not equate profligacy with immorality. Indeed, if Cleopatra was the embodiment of her country – and Antony sometimes called her *Egypt* as though it was her name – then Egypt was immeasurably learned, clever, quick-thinking, witty, charming and irresistible. As well as being mysterious, unfathomable, incalculably ancient in spirit and belief.

These thoughts took Artemidorus in Charmian's footsteps along corridors lined with exquisite hangings and perfumed carpets, up flights of marble stairs, along scented galleries made of cedar and sandalwood at last to the Queen's private audience chamber, a room which seemed too small to contain a goddess. There were workaday tables and chairs, maps instead of silken hangings on the walls, a window overlooking a courtyard a story or so below. The table was piled with scrolls and letters. Brutus' most recent one lay on top by the look of things. But a sizeable space had been cleared.

'Put the boxes on the table, then go,' said Charmian to the slaves. 'Please wait just a moment,' she added to Artemidorus and Quintus. Then she vanished into the next room.

V

Artemidorus was looking out of the window at the lower courtyard when the queen arrived on silent, sandaled feet. They were erecting a tall wooden post down there. The secret agent suspected he knew exactly what it was and precisely who it was for.

'*Hireh*, Hello, Septem,' said Cleopatra, her voice low and musical.

Artemidorus turned and bowed, finding it unexpectedly difficult to breathe. She had been twenty-five years old when he last saw her and was nearing twenty-seven now. The intervening years had put more lines of strain and worry on her face. Her braided black hair was bound in a simple white Greek headband. Her face was devoid of make-up, her forehead broad, her dark eyes deep and her nose pronounced. Her generous mouth was caught in a half- smile, a dimple at each corner. 'What has Antony sent?' she asked, 'apart from one of his most trusted agents and the redoubtable Quintus?'

'His love. He said to tell your majesty that if he could have discovered which part of him contained his love for you, he would have sent that too.'

Cleopatra chuckled. 'Well I think we all know which part of Antony contains his love. And if he sent *that*, the lady Fulvia might be less than happy – and many Roman matrons simply heartbroken.'

Quintus choked. He had never been this intimate with Cleopatra and knew nothing of her ready – occasionally ribald – wit.

The Queen gathered the gauzy robe she was wearing over her simple linen dress around her slim waist, crossed to a chair and sat. 'So, in place of his *love* he sends letters.' An imperious hand was held out.

Artemidorus handed over the first of Antony's scrolls. 'This is the personal letter,' he explained. 'As your majesty will see at once, it contains his statements of affection, assurances of perpetual regard, both personal and political.'

He picked up a second scroll and placed it on the table where she could easily reach it. 'This contains reports of what he has done since his return from beyond the Alps, so you have a clear understanding of the background to *this*.' He held up a third scroll. 'Which contains his assessment of his – and your – current situation and how he plans to proceed, with your help. As well as details of what he would like that help to consist of, if you are willing and able to provide it.' He put the third scroll beside the second.

'Is there anything in this third scroll that has not been basically covered by the arrogant boy that Brutus sent with his threats?'

'I would guess nothing, Majesty. You can see the situation from here as clearly as Antony can see it from Rome. He cannot allow Brutus and Cassius to continue ravishing the east – especially as it is now his personal province as Triumvir. It costs him revenue and reputation. And of course, his legions are restless. They wish Caesar's murderers caught and punished.'

'As do I. But I have little room for maneuver. Nor does Antony. He cannot move against them until he has some kind of control of the sea,' she nodded. 'Which at present belongs to the fleets commanded by Brutus' and Cassius' admirals Murcus and Ahenobarbus, currently stationed at Rhodos. And by Sextus Pompey in Sicily – who may not be Brutus' friend but is certainly not Antony's ally either.'

'Nor yours,' added Artemidorus, slipping unconsciously into the easy intimacy they had achieved in happier times. 'Given that it was your brother who had his father killed when he came here for help after the battle of Pharsalus.'

'Ptolemy XIII. That stupid little rat listened to the power-mad slug of an advisor Pothinus too often. You know, I showed Caesar where to push the knife in when we executed him.' Her mood darkened suddenly. 'Probably about the same place Brutus stabbed his knife when he killed Caesar.'

'I doubt it,' said Artemidorus without thinking. 'Brutus stabbed him in the groin. Waste of time stabbing a eunuch there.'

Cleopatra blinked with shock at what was clearly a revelation. Recovered. 'No. Indeed. Right in the middle of his neck, just above his shoulders. Slowly. Squealed like a pig at slaughter. Might just as well have beheaded him. And stupid little Ptolemy drowned in the Nile running away from the battle where Caesar, Mithradates and the Judeans under Antipater trounced General Achillas', Ptolemy's and Arsinoe's armies. He wouldn't take off his golden armour so they tell me, so he went down like a stone. Pity the crocodiles didn't get him first.' There was a moment of silence then she continued, 'We are well rid of both of them. If only we were as well rid of that conniving little bitch Arsinoe.'

*

Charmian returned then, with the child Ptolemy Caesarion. Without his formal costume he looked much younger than he had beside his mother Isis on the dais. A serious-eyed little boy of rising five – but a little boy still. 'Charmian says that Septem has brought presents from Antony,' he said. 'Is there one for me?'

'There certainly is, Your Majesty.' Artemidorus' tone softened. He liked the boy – as he had liked and served his father *Divus Julius*. 'Quintus, would you show young Caesarion what we brought for him?'

The boy hurried to Quintus' side as the old soldier opened the first of the two inlaid boxes. And lifted out a toy boat. The model of a *felucca* such as might be seen at any time flitting up and down the Nile. Its hull was made of solid cedarwood, its upper works, mast and rigging of gold. Its high gull-wing sail of linen almost as fine as that his mother wore.

Caesarion looked at it, entranced. 'Does it float?' he asked breathlessly.

'Of course, it floats,' said Quintus. 'Want to try it out? Is there a bath or a pond nearby? Preferably not the one full of crocodiles.'

Cleopatra smiled at her wide-eyed, excited son. 'Use your own bath,' she said. 'Mine is larger I know but they're getting ready to fill it with heated wine.

'For my skin,' she added to Artemidorus after the pair had vanished with the boat. 'To keep it soft and youthful. And, of course, divine. Now, what toy has Antony sent to me? Another boat?'

'I believe so, Majesty.' Artemidorus opened the second box and, with some effort, lifted out its contents and set the present on the table. It was a quinquereme made of gold. Nearly two cubits long and over four high when he erected the golden mast and settled the golden spar. 'But not for your bath, I fear.' He unloosened two tiny silk strings and the sail – with the figure of Isis at its centre – fell into place. He pressed a lever and three banks of oars appeared from holes in the sides and began to move as though rowing the boat forward.'

'Ingenious,' she said, her voice a little breathless, as her son's had been.

'I believe Antony employed an Alexandrian artificer to make it,' he said. 'They are the most cunning workmen in the world.'

'And it is in miniature precisely what he wants from me, full-sized. And just one, whereas he would like at least a fleet and preferably a navy.'

'Yes, Your Majesty.'

He had hardly finished speaking when the sound of a scuffle came in through the window overlooking the courtyard. Semi-articulate threats and curses in Roman-accented Greek. Larded every now and then with cries of '*Civis Romanus sum*!'

'Ah,' Cleopatra's expression hardened. 'Another stupid little rat with inflated ideas of his own importance. Lucius Calpurnius Bibulus, come to his just deserts.'

That was the expression she must have worn, thought Artemidorus, as she showed Caesar where to stick the knife in the back of Pothinus' neck.

vi

Cleopatra rose and crossed to the window, frowning at the little drama unfolding down there. Artemidorus went to stand at her side – as close as he deemed proper under the circumstances.

Young Lucius, still in his shining armour was being half-carried towards the whipping post by several palace guards as a crowd of the advisors from the top of the dais followed to witness the arrogant Roman's punishment.

Cleopatra sighed. 'I may have made an error, Septem. This will give Brutus all the more reason to work towards my overthrow – even if he cannot convince Cassius to invade at once. As I understand it, the boy is the son of his late wife by a previous marriage. Still, too close in blood for comfort. And, as he has correctly informed me, if Brutus has Ephesus then he has little sister Arsinoe. But still, Isis has spoken. He must be scourged.'

'But, Majesty, I heard Isis speak with all the rest who were there. And nothing was said about *how* he should be scourged.'

'What does that mean, Septem?'

'Consider this, My Queen. Isis has spoken. He must be whipped for his pompous arrogance and that of his commander. But he is a mere boy about a man's work. Severe injury might spur Brutus to intemperate action. He sent his late wife's beloved son on a dangerous errand and knows it. His conscience may well be pricked if the boy is hurt too badly. Furthermore, such a thing would cause outrage in the Senate too. Even with Cicero dead, there would be Senatorial voices loudly raised against you. This is, after all Cato's grandson. Shedding his patrician blood would be a considerable risk.

'Perhaps,' he continued, 'Isis would be satisfied were the scourging carried out as demanded. But, while the boy remains dressed in his armour. If Isis was satisfied with *that*, the boy could be returned essentially unharmed. With nothing wounded but his pride, his arrogance – and that of his master – made into a kind of joke. So any attempt to reply would simply make the arrogance seem more ridiculous and cause the joke to get better. Even Cassius would be sniggering in secret.'

Cleopatra clapped her hands. Charmian appeared. 'Go at once and tell the guards there is no need to remove the Roman's armour. But he must still be given fifty lashes.'

'Yes, Majesty.' The woman disappeared. Moments later she reappeared in the courtyard and went to the men still wrestling with the young Roman. Everything stopped as she spoke. The Egyptians all looked up at the window, their faces frowning with surprise. Cleopatra nodded.

Lucius stopped struggling, seemingly giving into the inevitable. Artemidorus had no way of knowing whether he understood the orders Cleopatra had given. But he stood listlessly as his *sagum* cloak was removed, then his belt, sword and dagger. His wrists were attached to the top of the whipping post. He looked up at the window then, his face a mask of confusion as he realised his armoured vest was still in place. Artemidorus stepped back. Things were likely to get complicated enough without the young aristocrat knowing how deeply Antony's secret agent was involved.

The beating began. Lucius was wearing scale armour, hundreds of overlapping pieces of metal that shone like gold, but were probably bronze, thought Artemidorus. Lighter by far than the segmented armour he had on. But by the same token, thinner and less robust. Lucius wouldn't lose any blood, but he would feel the weight of the blows, diminished but still painful; doing much more damage to his pride than to his back.

*

'What are you doing?' he roared as the executioner laid on with a will, bringing his whip hard across the armoured shoulders. 'Is this some kind of Egyptian joke? You are trying to insult me! Cato's grandson! Do you suppose a Roman cannot withstand the pain of a scourging? How dare you! Stop! Stop at once! I demand you remove my armour and go about it properly! Stop! Stop I say.'

But Cleopatra's *carnifex* did not stop. He laid on with a will, counting out the strokes in heavily accented Greek. Almost loudly enough to drown out Lucius' demands that he be stripped and whipped like in the proper fashion, so he could show these effete Egyptians how a true Roman patrician dealt with pain. And the witnesses, one after the other began to laugh at the young man's outrage.

vi

'The boy will go crying back to Brutus,' said Cleopatra. 'Who may be angry or amused. But it is Cassius I fear most.'

'He is the closest to your borders and controls the largest army,' Artemidorus nodded.

'Nearly half of which is made up of the Egyptian legions who deserted to him,' said Cleopatra walking back to the table laden with her paperwork and the golden quinquereme. As she sat she glanced up at the map of her country on the wall. 'They know the country – its strengths and weaknesses too well. If he invades, things will go badly for me.'

'They also know that if he comes into Egypt they will have to march across the Sinai unless he's going to ship them to Perusium, where Antony first won fame. And part of the point of my mission is to distract Cassius' navy away if I can. Allowing Your Majesty freedom of movement here – and giving you an opportunity to put a navy together – will more than compensate for a blockade of Brundisium. That is why I made no secret of the fact that troops were moving across from Italy when I brought Messala and Lucius. They have passed the warning on – but it seems neither Brutus nor Cassius has acted on it yet.'

The queen gestured. The secret agent sat opposite her.

'A good plan, which might still work – if Ahenobarbus and Murcus are sent to patrol the waters off Italy,' she mused. 'Particularly if Cassius can't use their transport vessels, he might find it hard to come as far as the Delta – let alone get across it to Alexandria.'

'If he does not invade, things might still go badly for you in the long run, Majesty. That is why you must support Antony. Antony is your only hope.' Artemidorus leaned forward urgently. 'If Cassius turns back and marches north to join Brutus you may have breathing-space large enough for you to build the ships Antony so desperately needs. But you must go all out to support him to victory. He is your only friend in this. If Cassius and Brutus join forces and prove strong enough to defeat Antony and Octavianus, do you think they will hesitate to come after you and, if not you then Caesarion? Everything that has happened during the last few years has been about destroying *Divus Julius*, his friends and associates. The Triumvirs have the upper hand in Italy because of the proscriptions – but those have only sharpened the hatred of the men who have survived or escaped proscription, their clients, friends and families.

'And of all the rulers in the kingdoms of the east, you are the most closely associated with *Divus Julius*. Even if Cassius achieves a total victory over Antony, he dare not let you or *Divus Julius'* child live. And he is utterly ruthless remember. If he had had his way, Antony, you and Caesarion would all have died on the Ides. Only Brutus' scruples stopped him then. They will not do so again. No. Your only hope is Antony and Antony alone. I like young Octavianus. He is quick-minded, cunning and ruthless. But he too would destroy you if he alone gained victory over Cassius and Brutus. If Antony died in battle, for instance...'

'As I hear the Consuls Hirtius and Pansa did at the Battle of Mutina, mused the queen. 'One, perhaps stabbed in the back by Octavianus and the other poisoned by Octavianus' physician...'

'I do not believe such rumours because I was there. But the fact that they remain current tells you much about how young Caesar is viewed. And there is a side to him I never saw in *Divus Julius.* Sometimes he seems to enjoy watching others suffer. *Making* others suffer. Things would go badly if you or Caesarion ever fell into Octavianus' hands...

*

'But these are only my external troubles,' said Cleopatra some time later after more discussion. 'I have more problems at home. Because there has been no inundation for the last two years, all along the Nile the crops have failed. I have opened the storehouses of the Ptolemies – as Queen – and of the temples – as Isis. But even there, stocks are running low. And the vermin whose natural homes are in the fields have run into the cities and villages seeking food. And they have brought a plague with them that no prayers or powers can stop. I have talked to my priests in Memphis as I have talked with my physicians in Alexandria and no-one has any idea how to help. My Egyptian subjects are starving, dying and restless.' Cleopatra hesitated then added. 'But your very presence gives me some relief, Septem. There is no-one in Alexandria or in Egypt that I can open my heart to as I can to you. And, through you, to Antony. It is as though I have *Divus Julius* here with me again for a little while.'

'Majesty, you have never needed the advice of any man to see your way clearly – or the help of any man to achieve your ends. Even *Divus Julius* danced to a tune you played from the moment Apollodorus laid you at his feet wrapped in a carpet and bag of hemp. And all Antony wants is to dance to the same tune.' He had never been given such a compliment in all his life. He fought to keep the tears from his eyes and knew that he would serve this woman to the end of his abilities. To the end of his life if need-be. Then he asked, 'And no-one nearby has any grain? You have enough gold to buy all the grain you could ever want.'

'Parthia has grain. And although Mithradates' successor King Orontes is loudly supporting Brutus and Cassius – because they are at his borders too – he is willing to sell to the highest bidder. Cassius and Brutus are more interested in using their money to pay their legions and in any case can rely on Sextus Pompey for grain. But then, even if I can buy what I need, there is the problem of getting it here. With Cassius and his army in Judea, hard up against my Eastern border, and his navy patrolling the seas, I have no way of getting the corn from Parthia into Egypt.'

'So it seems that your troubles at home and abroad would be alleviated if Cassius would move back north.'

'And if the Nile would inundate. Yes.'

'Well, the motions of the Nile are out of my control. But as for the matter of Cassius...'

XIII: Hunefer

i

Notus had played little part in the mission so far, indeed at times, Artemidorus thought he had made an error in not sending him back from Dyrrhachium with Adonis and Venus. The only thing that had stopped him was the fact that had he done so, he would have left Kyros heartbroken. But now, he thanked his guardian demigod Achilleus that he had kept the young man with the rest of the *contubernium*.

Notus and Kyros were seated at a table in Cleopatra's island palace, surrounded by her most trusted secretaries and seemingly every piece of writing equipment the palace possessed as well as oil lamps, candles, wax, sand, salt water and a range of scroll-cases. While Artemidorus watched, they were slowly but perfectly recreating the scroll and seal that Brutus had sent. Under Artemidorus' wondering eyes the two young men were flawlessly recreating the papyrus, the ageing, the ribbon, the seal, the greeting, except for Cleopatra's name, at the top; and Brutus' signature at the bottom. Everything except the recipient's name and the message. Those were blank. On another sheet of papyrus beside it, Notus was perfecting his forgery of the handwriting used by Brutus' amanuensis in the original scroll.

The plan had evolved slowly during hours of discussion with Cleopatra and then with two or three of her most trusted advisors. Its central essence was simple, its ramifications and execution less so. Which introduced a potent time element that was beyond their immediate control. Cassius had hesitated for months, but he was a covetous man easily moved to anger. He would surely not hesitate for much longer.

More immediately, however, they were certain that someone from the Roman quinquereme sitting out in the Royal Harbour would be arriving at the palace soon to enquire after Lucius. And the first part of the plan would start with his arrival. But as to precisely when that would be, there was no way of knowing.

After an extremely busy afternoon the queen was relaxing in her bath of heated Mareotic wine, restoring her skin's natural divinity, energy to both her mind and body and preparing for yet another busy evening of formal dining, negotiation, and domestic politics. Far beyond anything the spy or his associates need become involved with, though Artemidorus found the mental image of Cleopatra in her bath disturbingly distracting. Quintus was still boating with Caesarion. The rest of the *contubernium* had been assigned rooms in the palace which was to be – briefly – their headquarters. User had somehow got himself mixed up in their move from his palatial villa to Cleopatra's actual palace. And he remained vaguely attached to them, as he had been since Puella pulled him aboard *Galene*. A bemused *oikonomos* steward had assigned him guest quarters with all the rest; on one side of Puella's, while Artemidorus was on the other. A position the Roman spy was willing to countenance, because the Egyptian merchant might well prove a useful advisor – a vital ally – as the plan proceeded. Everyone had been fed, Artemidorus eating as he talked with Cleopatra and Quintus as he put Caesarion's boat to one side and began to teach him the basic points of swordplay.

*

Artemidorus looked around the room now, smiling at Notus as he sat back, satisfied at last that he had prepared a scroll that looked exactly like the one Brutus had sent and had mastered the handwriting of the man who wrote it at Brutus' dictation. He could now write any message his spymaster in turn dictated, and it would look exactly as though it had come from Brutus himself. The only problem – which they had discussed at length – was the matter of a cypher. Brutus had written to Cleopatra in plain Greek and it was fair to assume that he would write to Cassius in the same language. But what if he usually wrote to Cassius in code?

Artemidorus was trying to think of some way to cover that eventuality and thanking Achilleus once again that he had brought Kyros, a potent code-breaker, as well as his forger Notus, when one of the palace servants came hurrying across the room to him. 'A detachment of Romans from the quinquereme in the harbour is about to come ashore *arkontas* lord,' he whispered in accented Greek.

'Excellent. Lead me to somewhere in the palace where I might meet their leader apparently by chance.'

As he followed the servant, Artemidorus schooled his face into an expression of shock and concern. The plan was under way now.

'Are you from the quinquereme in the Royal Harbour?' he asked the blue-uniformed centurion, without pausing to apologise for the near-collision.

'The quinquereme *Bellona*, yes,' answered the centurion, slowing his pace. 'Why?'

'Is that the vessel which brought young Lucius Calpurnius Bibulus to Alexandria?'

'Yes. With a message to Queen Cleopatra from General Brutus. I am here to collect him when I find him. Find out if the Queen has replied. I have an escort waiting outside…'

'So you haven't heard?'

'Heard what?' The marine came to a stop, frowning.

Artemidorus looked around as though fearful of being overheard. 'Either he or General Brutus' message offended the queen. Apparently, she has had young Lucius whipped for arrogance and locked in one of the dungeons.'

'What! A Roman citizen. A Tribune! A patrician and Cato's grandson… She wouldn't dare!'

'She is merely a woman after all, she seems to have acted without calculating the consequences as a man would do. And, of course, she's an Egyptian…' Artemidorus said the final words as though he had been saying *a prostitute* and saw a thoroughly satisfactory amount of prejudice curl the centurion's finely chiseled Roman lips.

ii

'I was there,' persisted Artemidorus earnestly, frowning into the shocked countenance of the bigoted marine. 'I saw her reaction. I heard her give the order. I heard the message too. General Brutus needs to be informed. He threatened to ask General Cassius to invade. I think he'll definitely want to consider doing that now.'

'Thundering Jupiter! But, with all due respect, Centurion, I don't know you. I can't just take your word…'

The two men strode forward, shoulder to shoulder and arrived in the reception chamber together. Where one of Cleopatra's senior secretaries was waiting, in the full regalia of his office, as beautifully dressed as the richest governor, satrap or prince. Artemidorus could almost hear the marine grinding his teeth.

'You are from the quinquereme *Bellona*?' the official demanded in heavily accented Greek with an arrogance even Lucius had not managed to achieve.

'I am. I have come for Tribune Lucius…'

'The Tribune has insulted the Divine Pharaoh Queen Cleopatra Isis,' interrupted the secretary. 'He has been beaten and is currently imprisoned at her majesty's divine pleasure. Here is a message in answer to the peremptory communication from your haughty General Brutus. If he replies in a more suitably humble manner, then Queen Cleopatra may consider returning the Tribune. Until that time he will remain here. That is all. You may go.'

'But…' the centurion drew himself up, thoroughly Roman, and quivering with outrage.

The secretary clapped his hands and a dozen golden palace guards appeared. Suddenly their arms and armour did not look as though they were merely for show. 'These guards will guide you back to your men and see you off the island,' said the secretary. 'And I would suggest you take your vessel and leave the Royal Harbour before you and everyone else aboard join the arrogant puppy in the dungeons.'

The marine seemed ready to burst with indignation. Artemidorus laid a restraining hand on his shoulder and after a moment, he calmed. The two centurions, one in blue and the other in red, turned, shoulder to shoulder and, surrounded by the guards marched back towards the exit.

'Don't worry,' whispered Artemidorus in Latin. 'I am known here in the palace. I'll see if I can contact the boy. Make sure he's alright. In the mean-time, you'd better deliver Cleopatra's letter to General Brutus together with the news that his messenger is under arrest.'

They reached the front of the palace and Artemidorus stopped while the guards carried on towards the dock and the centurion's marines followed to his waiting harbour barge. At the last moment, the centurion turned and asked one final question. 'Who are you, Centurion? What is your name in case General Brutus asks?'

Artemidorus' mind raced. He plucked a name out of the air and said it without a second thought. Unaware of the effect his action would have in the not-too distant future, deaf to the laughter of the Fates. 'My name is Dellius,' lied Artemidorus smoothly. 'Quintus Dellius.'

*

Artemidorus, User, Puella and Ferrata stood at a window in the palace's tallest tower overlooking the Royal Harbour and the grey waters to the north of it. The quinquereme *Bellona* was moving out of the anchorage, powered by her three banks of oars. By the look of things the *pausator* was beating *battle speed*. The cutwater and the oars themselves were kicking up walls of white foam in the choppy water, the waves running counter to the ship's course as she powered away upwind, straight into the teeth of the northerly.

'So,' said Artemidorus, 'how long do we reckon it will take for the message to get to Brutus?'

'Four days,' answered User. 'I know we made it here more quickly, but we had a following wind and *Glaros* is fast – under sail or under oars. And if *Bellona*'s captain tries to keep up that speed he'll have a couple of hundred dead oarsmen long before he gets anywhere near Rhodos, let alone Xanthus.'

'But then again,' said Puella, 'however long it takes the messenger with Queen Cleopatra's message to find him, surely Brutus will be using his fastest ship to take his own message back to Cassius. Especially if he is demanding an invasion such as he threatened. Maybe not as fast as *Glaros*, but faster than *Bellona* or any of the other quinqueremes.'

'That's true enough,' said User, 'But if Cassius is still where the Queen's spies last reported him – and he must be or Brutus' threat comes to nothing – then the nearest port to him is Ashkelon, which is further away from Rhodos and Xanthus than Alexandria is. And further east into the bargain. We had a straight run south with a northerly behind us. They will have to sail south-east across it to get from Rhodos or Xanthos to Ashkelon. That could slow them. Will do, unless the wind changes. Or unless they are outstanding sail-handlers.'

'So, taking all that into account,' said Artemidorus, 'how long will it be before Brutus' message gets anywhere near Cassius?'

'One of *Divus Julius'* new seven day weeks if all goes well for them; maybe an old-fashioned eight day week if not. If the weather worsens, say ten days all in all.'

'Seven days,' said Artemidorus. 'That's not much time. And there's a lot we need to get done. We'd better get busy.'

iii

'We'll need *Glaros* and one other vessel,' said Artemidorus. 'Something that could easily be mistaken for a Roman *liburnian* or trireme.'

Halys looked across the laden table at User, 'Roman,' he said. 'Why Roman?'

'It's all part of the plan,' said User. 'No expense spared. He gestured at the food and drink supplied by the *taberna* for this meeting. There was easily enough to feed *Glaros*' entire crew. None of whom were here, except for their skipper. But we need a *yes* or a *no* pretty quickly. Time is short.'

'*Glaros* and a Roman-looking *liburnian* to be off Ashkelon within six days.' Halys stroked his beard. Eyed the roast Nile perch, clearly calculating whether he could fit it in his belly on top of everything else he had consumed so far.

'Expense no object,' repeated User. Artemidorus nodded silent affirmation.

'Me and my crew disguised as pirates…' The Cilician captain's eyes narrowed. He reached for a cup of Mareotic wine almost large enough to bathe Cleopatra.

'That should be the easy part,' said Quintus, 'making you lot look like pirates.'

Halys looked at him, his face blank, his mind clearly racing as he gulped the wine. 'I think I'll need to know a little more before I can proceed,' he said at last, putting the cup back down. User reached for the amphora and re-filled it. 'This is starting to sound dangerous,' Halys continued. '*Expense no object* is all too often another way of saying *you're all going to die…*'

User looked at Artemidorus, replacing the amphora carefully. The Roman spy knew that Halys was their best hope of getting everything in place in time. If push came to shove, User would supply the second vessel himself – but his ships were all too obviously traders and they needed something that looked military.

Artemidorus leaned forward. 'I want to take a small unit ashore at Ashkelon as soon as possible to check the disposition of Cassius' army. Talk to Queen Cleopatra's spies on the ground if I can. Her servants will supply contact details. Then I need to get safely back aboard before a Roman vessel coming south-east from Rhodos or one of the coastal ports near to it comes into view. She'll be a fast messenger, carrying a courier from Brutus heading for Cassius. She's not likely to be escorted because she'll be like *Glaros* – too fast for anything else to keep up with. I want *Glaros* to attack her – or threaten to do so depending on the Roman ship's size, speed and complement. Scare the life out of them at least. Then the seemingly Roman ship with me and my *contubernium* aboard will come to the rescue. Either send a complement aboard the other Roman or welcome some of them aboard us. Escort them into Ashkelon at any rate. It's the courier I'm after. And Brutus' letter to Cassius.'

'That's what all this is about? Stealing a *letter*?'

Artemidorus looked around the room. There was no-one near enough to overhear. Especially as the full *contubernium*, all armed to the teeth were seated in a solid steel ring around them. 'Not stealing, no. Replacing Brutus' communication with ours. Ideally without anyone being any the wiser. And then seeing our dispatch delivered to Cassius in place of Brutus' original.'

'You're mad. All of you. Mad as the Meneads tearing Orpheus to pieces! Mad! I've never heard the like…' Halys reached for the brimming goblet.

'Will you do it, yes or no?' demanded Artemidorus, beginning to run out of patience.

'Do it? Of course I'll bloody do it! I wouldn't miss it for the world!'

*

Artemidorus stood with User, Halys, Puella, Quintus and Ferrata in the Royal Dockyards. Even though the day was drawing to a close, everything around them was a bustle of industry. Cleopatra had given a series of orders which were being obeyed as fully and swiftly as possible. New quinqueremes were being built from the keel upwards. Vessels from the Egyptian fleet were being recalled. Commercial shipping was being purchased – forcibly if necessary – and refitted for war. Halys belched, releasing fumes of Mareotic liberally mixed with Nile perch. They had come straight here from the *taberna*.

'There,' he said. 'I told you I remembered.' He pointed at a slightly battered looking trireme currently swarming with shipwrights and their men. She was *Glaros*' big sister in many ways. Her long hull was slim and trim – clearly built for speed as well as battle. But she was different in several vital regards. Between her stempost and main mast stood a second, stubby mast which was currently rigged to take a foresail but Artemidorus saw at a glance that it was also strong enough to support an old-fashioned *corvus* boarding platform, still popular with some hidebound Roman admirals who hadn't really progressed since the naval battles of the Punic War. Secondly, whereas *Glaros*' main deck was a flat expanse, this vessel had a fighting tower erected just in front of the incurving stern-post.

'Perfect,' said Artemidorus. 'Can we crew her?'

'If expense is no object you could crew her and a fleet like her,' said Halys as User nodded his agreement. 'Work is hard to find at the moment; food even harder. And prices just keep going up and up.'

The Roman secret agent squinted. The bow above the ram and the faded eye painted there seemed blank. 'Has she got a name?' he asked. 'I don't see a face carved on her stempost or on her bows.'

'No face,' said Halys. 'But that carving which looks like a closed fist is supposed to be a conch shell, I think. And that would make her…'

'*Triton*,' said Artemidorus. 'She's perfect.'

iv

'You're placing a hell of a lot of trust in a man you hardly know,' said Quintus quietly. The pair were standing on the top of *Triton*'s fighting tower as the team of oarsmen User had found were rowing her round the Royal Harbour, heading for the exit, shaking down the vessel and the crew before they took her out on the actual mission. It was mid-morning next day. They were due in Ashkelon in five days' time.

'Two men, actually,' agreed Artemidorus, holding onto the edge of the tower, watching the harbour speed past. Miraculously, Quintus seemed to be getting control of his chronic sea sickness at last. Though standing so high above the pitching deck was making the secret agent feel a little queasy.

'You know User's after Puella.' Quintus observed.

'She will make up her own mind, just as she did with Mercury.' Artemidorus answered.

'She slept with Mercury to get him to be a double agent working for us as a spy in Octavianus' camp before the battle of Mutina. She made the *contubernium* stronger and more effective but if she goes with User that will weaken us.' Quintus frowned. 'Even if it's just a sympathy *simosia* screw.

'I know.'

'And you're not jealous?'

'Would it make any difference if I was?'

'Fair point; not the slightest. But bear in mind that if User hasn't worked out how independent she actually is, he could see you as a dangerous rival for her affections. There might be a bit of motivation there to move you out of the picture.' He drew his finger across his throat as though the digit were a knife-blade.

'I doubt he'd go that far. Anyway, if we're going to give Cleopatra room to build a fleet large enough to help Antony, then we have to trust User and Halys.'

'They're both pirates.' Quintus persisted.

'Maybe,' allowed Artemidorus. 'But pirates are what we need just now. Don't worry, I'll keep a close eye on both of them.'

'Fat lot of use a close eye will be with *Triton* crewed by User's men under User's command and powered by more than a hundred oarsmen that are also working for him. If he wants your throat cut they'll all be asking where, when and how deep?'

'Two things. One, Brutus slaughtered his wife and children. Fair enough there hasn't been much weeping and wailing over them, but his grief and anger seem real. So does his desire for revenge. If he wants to hurt Brutus and Cassius, helping us is his best way. Secondly, Halys, User and I have one more visit to make before we get under way. And, since you're so worried, you can come along too.'

At User's bellowed command, *Triton* span to the left, sweeping round the end of Pharos Island and into the Western harbour. Even with the *corvus* fitted in place of the redundant foresail, she sat steadily in the water and kept her head high.

There were shouts of exhilaration from the deck below as the *contubernium* voiced their excitement at the neat maneuver. Puella's loudest of all.

*

Artemidorus, Quintus, User and Halys were shown into the royal presence that afternoon by the same secretary who had given Cleopatra's answer to the centurion from *Bellona* for onward passage to Brutus. Cleopatra sat at the pinnacle of the stepped dais where she had been sitting when Artemidorus first saw her. She was dressed and made-up precisely as she had been then. This time, however, she was alone up there, and her hands were empty, resting in her lap. Still, she was every inch the Pharaoh Queen Goddess Cleopatra Isis.

On the marble floor in front of her, hard up against the bottom step, a man was kneeling with his forehead pressed to the ground, his hands spread on either side of it. He was still and silent. User and Halys looked at the prostrate figure and up at the divine ruler. Halys' knees buckled. Down he went, then hesitated, clearly wondering whether to prostrate himself as well. User looked at his beautiful infinitely powerful monarch, clearly at a loss, then tore his gaze away from her gilded face to glance at Artemidorus.

'*Kapetanioi* User and Halys may remain standing in my presence,' said Cleopatra in her liquid, seductively accented Greek.

Halys pulled himself to his feet, gaping at User, half-shocked and half-terrified that Cleopatra knew who he was. User was also taken aback. He glanced at Artemidorus, his muscular forehead frowning with suspicion.

'And you may stand, too,' she said to the man kneeling at her feet. She spoke in Egyptian but the meaning of her words was clear in his actions.

The prostrate man came slowly to his feet. Suddenly, Cleopatra was not the only wonderful creature in the room. He stood well over four cubits tall and he was built to scale. His head, seeming small in comparison to his neck and torso was clothed in the sort of headdress User favoured, held in place by a golden headband with a rearing cobra at the front to match his queen's. His skin was tanned golden and seemed almost metallic. He wore a short white kirtle to match his headdress and a belt of scaled gold, from which hung a *khopesh* Egyptian sickle sword that looked big enough to behead an elephant.

'This is my servant Hunefer son of Sep,' said Cleopatra. 'He is the captain of my guard and the most feared warrior in my army. He has lost count of the men he has killed in combat and as you see, he has yet to be scarred himself. He is also a great hunter and can read the desert as though it were the Book of Ptah. He says little but understands much, including both Latin and Greek. He has recently been in contact with the men I have watching Cassius and his army. He will be coming with you and his mission is threefold. He will guide Septem when you reach Ashkelon and help him spy on Cassius. He will be my eyes and ears, watch how your plan works and report to me when it is done. And he will also watch over Septem to see no harm comes to him.' She paused. Her face grew stern. 'And should Hunefer not return to me for any reason – any reason at all – I will hunt everyone who went with Septem, Quintus and Hunefer and destroy them and their families. Utterly. As though they and their forefathers had never existed.

V

'Hunefer Son of Sep. That's another one I don't trust,' said Quintus as they oversaw the last of their kit being shipped out to *Triton*.

'I trust Cleopatra. So, do you and you know it. He is her eyes and ears so I suppose we can trust him too,' answered Artemidorus. He saw the questioning look on Quintus' face and added, 'Is there anyone you *do* trust?'

'I trust you, lad. I trusted Puella until User came along. I trust Ferrata because he's too dim to be duplicitous. I trust the rest of the *contubernium* to varying degrees. Except for the more recent additions – Notus the forger and Crinas the physician. They haven't faced any particular danger with us. Men are like metal. They need to be put through the fire to be hardened and tested to see if they are true.'

'Well, Hunefer will be tested tonight; the rest in the next few days.'

They spent the day coming and going from the palace on Antirrhodos Island, to the Royal Docks, over to the markets beside the Agora, back and forth to User's villa, out to *Glaros* and *Triton*, preparing for the mission; getting everything aboard that they would need, including blue marine uniforms – created specially by a team of Cleopatra's seamstresses. Then, settling everyone into their onboard accommodation – though Hunefer's needed to be specially adapted. There was no time to waste. It would take four days of hard rowing to get to Ashkelon unless the gods sent a reliable westerly. They needed to leave tonight.

But Septem, Quintus and Hunefer had one final task to complete before *Glaros* and *Triton* could clear the harbour and turn eastwards. They met at sunset outside the doors to the palace. Hunefer had spent the last hour or so gathering the last of his kit together and he stood there now in a mail shirt of scaled bronze, gold belt, armoured skirt, bronze greaves and *manicae* arm guards. The *kopesh* scythe-sword at his belt had been augmented by a dagger and a nasty-looking mace. Both Artemidorus and Quintus were armed as well but not quite so lethally.

'Come,' Hunefer growled in Greek, and led the two Romans into the palace. Cleopatra had said he was a taciturn man, but he was by no means silent now. 'Divine Cleopatra has ordered that this be made to look as real as possible,' he said. 'So no-one has been warned. If there is trouble, we will simply have to fight our way out. Do not hesitate to attack if we are discovered. Anyone who dies will do so under the protection of Isis and Osiris and find everlasting bliss.'

'Does that include us?' wondered Quintus under his breath.

'Let's hope we don't find out,' answered Artemidorus equally quietly. They both loosened their swords and daggers in their sheaths and were glad that they had come in their segmented iron armour.

*

Deep beneath the palace, the dungeons were in a maze of corridors leading off a central guard room. From the depths of the shadows nearest the ill-lit chamber, the three men watched the guards as they sat at a table, talking quietly. On the board in front of them lay a hoop with metal keys attached, an Egyptian invention currently being copied and improved in Rome. A water clock similar to the ones used by the timekeepers in the Roman Senate stood beside it. Guards only needed to measure time if they had a schedule of patrols to keep. And sure enough, after a few moments, one of the guards reached over and reset the device while the other stood and lifted the keys. They exchanged a word or two, then the man with the keys came out of the guardroom. Artemidorus and his companions drew back into the shadows, holding their breath. The guard walked away, unaware of their presence and as they followed him along the dim corridor, Artemidorus noted that he was armed only with a dagger. There might well be a way to overcome him without bloodshed, he thought.

But the instant the guard stopped at the first door, Hunefer ran forward on silent feet, pulling his mace free from his belt. There was a sound somewhere between a *crack* and a *crunch* as he brought it down on the back of the guard's head. The man dropped to the ground. The only other sound was that of the keys hitting the flagstones. Hunefer stooped, picked them up and unlocked the cell door. It was absolutely dark inside, but as Hunefer stepped through the portal, Lucius Calpurnius Bibulus came hurling out, clearly making a break for freedom.

Hunefer moved in front of the would-be escapee. Lucius threw his arms around the giant's waist as though he had any hope of moving him. Hunefer raised his mace so the killing head was pointing upwards then brought the butt of the handle down on the young Roman's skull. Lucius went sprawling beside the dead guard. He was still wearing his armour and the noise he made was considerable. Hunefer reached down and took hold of the unconscious Tribune's mail shirt at the back of his neck, lifting him effortlessly to his feet. The second guard came rushing down the corridor, obviously alerted by the noise. But Quintus had already calculated that and the luckless Egyptian ran straight onto the point of his *gladius*.

Lucius woke up almost immediately to find himself being held erect by an Egyptian giant while two familiar, friendly faces watched him anxiously. And two dead guards lay sprawled at his feet.

'*Gratia*,' croaked the young Tribune hoarsely. 'Thanks…'

'Let's go,' said Hunefer.

'Before we have to kill anyone else,' nodded Artemidorus.

vi

No such luck, he thought a couple of minutes later as Hunefer led them out of the tunnels and up into the main palace, because they immediately bumped into a four-man unit of palace guards. The men in their golden armour hesitated. Hunefer must be familiar to them after all. But before either the Egyptian or Artemidorus could think of anything to say, Lucius had ripped the dagger from Hunefer's belt and threw himself forward with a snarl of rage, clearly keen to make up for the humiliation he had suffered at the hands of Cleopatra's whip master. There was no choice after that. Hunefer pulled out his *kopesh* and leapt forward at the young man's side. The massive curved blade flashed down, opening the first guard's chest from the point where his head joined his shoulder down as far as his belt. The sundered gold breastplate folded back. Blood burst out, flooding the floor. Lucius slipped on it and fell on his face. Hunefer's dagger skittered away from his clutching fingers. The huge Egyptian straddled the fallen Tribune and lunged at the next opponent, sending the blade of his massive sword straight through the centre of the guard's gaudy breastplate as though it was papyrus rather than metal.

Quintus didn't even have time to say *I told you so* before he and Artemidorus were on the next two guards. Their *gladii* went under the golden armour with practiced ease, reaching straight up to their hearts as their boiling life-blood cascaded down their thighs, splashing their executioners. Within a few heartbeats the four-man patrol were all dead. The only noise of any account was – once again – the sound of Lucius crashing to the floor.

Hunefer picked him up. 'We will have to hurry now,' he rumbled. 'We are too easy to spot, covered in blood as we are. Especially the boy.'

But their gruesome appearance proved to be a piece of luck after all. The only other people they met as they rushed towards the main entrance were palace servants and minor courtiers. Unarmed, they all shrank back from the blood-boltered group, with some running away screaming. The crew of the barge who had brought Artemidorus and Quintus in from *Triton* were waiting to return them, and they formed a kind of escort as the three Romans and their Egyptian guardian ran down the steps to the dockside. Then it was just a matter of rowing them out to where their two ships sat ready to depart, *Triton* with a rope ladder hanging from her stern.

Lucius went up first, slowly – still a little groggy. Then Quintus, his face set and his jaw squared at the thought of four more days afloat. Artemidorus and Hunefer hesitated, each wanting the other to go first. Artemidorus turned to the oarsmen in the now blood-smeared boat. 'When the palace guards ask,' he said, praying they understood Greek, 'tell them we held you at sword-point. Made you bring us out here.'

The oarsmen looked at him, faces blank and uncomprehending, until Hunefer repeated the instructions in Egyptian.

No sooner had he done so than a line of torches came streaming out of the front of the palace, heading down for the dockside. 'That looks like trouble,' said Artemidorus.

'Queen Cleopatra wants it all to look as real as possible,' said Hunefer. 'They will pursue us. And kill us if they catch us.'

'Or try to…' said Artemidorus as he grasped the nearest rung, heaving himself onto the ladder.

'Or try to,' agreed Hunefer. And Artemidorus was almost certain the huge Egyptian chuckled.

*

Glaros was already in motion and the moment Hunefer swung clear of the harbour boat, *Triton* began to move as well. Both captains – Halys and User – ordered battle speed until they were clear of the harbour. Artemidorus had a chance to look around the lamp-lit deck as he crossed to the fighting tower and he was pleased to see that almost everyone else aboard was already wearing their blue tunics. Only User was still dressed in native clothing, while the *contubernium* were dressed in their usual outfits. The time they spent liberating Lucius had clearly given them the opportunity to make this very much a Roman military vessel; enough to fool Lucius at any rate. Or so he hoped.

It was clear to Artemidorus that *Glaros* was still the faster of the two. The ram and the *corvus* shaved speed off *Triton*'s slim hull, but User had chosen his oarsmen carefully so they were a mightily effective unit.

As the two ships raced almost side-by side through the narrow harbour entrance with the Pharos towering on their left and the hook of Cape Lochios on their right, the lights from the Palace came streaming up the cape – too late. While others spread out across the water as pursuers clambered aboard some of the sea-ready ships in the Egyptian fleet.

Lucius appeared at Artemidorus' side. 'They'll never catch us,' he said. 'These two must be the fastest ships in the world! And this one's Roman!'

'She was on loan to Queen Cleopatra,' said Artemidorus. 'We were lucky to get hold of her and put our man captain User in command when her *treirarchus* fell ill. Doubly lucky now that we've liberated you, though Hunefer went further than planned and spilt a lot more blood than we'd hoped. All in all, we'll probably have a good few of Cleopatra's warships after us.'

'I had no idea there was anything as quick as this in any part of the Roman fleet! Surely no-one will ever catch us now!'

'I wouldn't wager on it,' answered Artemidorus, guardedly. 'After all, the Roman quinqueremes nearly caught *Glaros* on the way here. You were aboard one of them I would guess.'

'Yes…' Lucius sounded less certain now.

'We obviously can't get anywhere by land. But still, we're at risk as long as we're at sea,' said Artemidorus. 'If we happen upon another Roman ship like *Triton* we should be safe. But Egyptians won't be so friendly, especially if word gets out. You're an escaped fugitive and possibly a spy. Hunefer is a wanted murderer and traitor. I wish I'd bribed someone smaller and easier to control to help with your escape. Still, it's too late to worry now. And there are Cilician pirates, taking advantage of the fact that our navies are fighting each-other instead of chasing after them. I have my suspicions about Halys, *Galene*'s skipper. He seemed friendly enough at first when he offered to help protect us, but he's a shifty sort. I'm afraid breaking you out of prison has made us rely on some disturbingly untrustworthy people.'

'Jupiter! What shall we do, then?'

'Under the circumstances, I think it would be too risky to get right up to Rhodos and go searching on the mainland for General Brutus so we can pass you back to him,' explained Artemidorus slowly. 'The Judean port of Ashkelon is much closer. General Cassius and his legions are close beside there. So, at the moment the plan is this: we'll run along the coast for four or so days, going ashore at night wherever we can. We're running across the outwash of the Nile delta and even though the river is low, it keeps making the shore shift. It throws out sandbanks that are there one day and gone the next. We have to be very careful – especially in the dark. But, we hope to come to port in Ashkelon within a few days' time and pass you into the safe keeping of Cassius.'

XIV: Naramsin

i

It seemed to Artemidorus that Fortuna smiled on him, while Achilleus held his semi-divine hands over him, during the next four days and nights. *Triton* and *Glaros* made good time on their voyage east, moving along the coastline between dawn and dusk, staying as close to the delta as they dared, with a man in the bow taking soundings and keeping a look-out for sandbanks. After a disastrous first night ashore, plagued by mosquitoes, snakes and scorpions, they elected to sleep aboard. The north wind blew the air-borne pests back inland. Scorpions cannot swim. And although they discovered that snakes could, none of the poisonous creatures was able to climb aboard. They set up the fire trays on deck, therefore, sacrificed, butchered and roasted the sheep and goats they had bought in the Agora market, supplemented with the fish they caught wherever they anchored. The Alexandrian bread lasted well enough, as did the fruit and vegetables, after all it was only four days. And at noon on the second day, the wind turned westerly and the sails were set.

Although accommodation aboard was inevitably intimate, from the second night onwards, Puella returned to his bed, so fierce in her love-making that it was almost impossible to maintain a decent level of noise. The first he knew of her return was one hand placed over his mouth and another over his groin. She slid in beside him as he sprang awake, the familiarity of her skin and perfume stopping him reaching for the dagger he always kept under his pillow while he slept. Then her lower hand was replaced by the burning flesh of her inner thigh as her upper hand was replaced by her lips. Her breath smelt of roast lamb and rosemary. She slid right over him and came astride; both of them so immediately aroused that he was able to ease into her with one twist of his hips. *Triton* was at anchor, riding a low sea, and the gentle rocking of the ship dictated the movements of their passion while the creaking of the hull covered the sound of the overladen bunk. But, as he enjoyed the renewing of their intimacy, it never occurred to him that these nights of stifled passion were a kind of farewell.

Lucius also proved naively trusting. He accepted without question the half-truth that *Triton* was a Roman vessel lent to Cleopatra. A left-over from *Divus Julius'* visit in 706. As were the oarsmen in their blue tunics, most of whom spoke Greek and a little Latin – not that Lucius ever talked to them – though this was a good deal less true. They were falsely presented as marines from Pompey's old XXXVIIth *Ponticus* legion, who famously relieved *Divus Julius* and Cleopatra at the siege of Alexandria that year. Most of them were said to be from *Triton*'s original crew, happy to continue rowing – an easy, well-paid duty in the most fascinating and sensual city on earth. Not that Lucius ever asked.

The young Tribune already knew User was an Alexandrian merchant and assumed he would have been a captain at some stage in any case, so he did not raise an eyebrow now. And best of all, he had not seen Artemidorus at Cleopatra's window during his humiliating whipping, so he accepted without question that the man who had saved his life in Rome and smuggled him to safety in Dyrrhachium would arrange to rescue him once again. Even though he knew Artemidorus was Antony's courier, he was happy to accept that now that the Triumvir's message had been delivered, Artemidorus would be willing to help someone from the opposing camp again, because, in the face of Egyptian cunning, barbarism and duplicity, Romans would always stick together.

Although Artemidorus had been shocked by the brutality with which Hunefer chopped their way to freedom, he had to admit that this above all convinced Lucius that they were all on his side rather than Cleopatra's. Finally, he hardly needed to strain his credulity over Artemidorus' decision to take him to Cassius rather than Brutus – the logic of it was undeniable.

It no more occurred to Lucius with regard to his rescue than it did to Artemidorus with regard to Puella, that there was more going on here than he understood.

*

By evening of the fourth day, Ashkelon was in sight. The rays of the westering sun seemed to pick out the square white buildings of the port as they rose up the gentle hillside above the docks. The brightness made it easy to count the masts and spars of the ships crowding the little harbour – bringing supplies and finances to Cassius and his army, no doubt. But not yet Brutus' message, prayed Artemidorus.

Artemidorus, User and Hunefer stood beside *Triton*'s stempost. 'It's time to make a decision,' said User. 'Do we go in and let you take it from there or do I take *Triton* nearer the beach and drop you off first? You and whoever you're taking with you to spy out the land.'

'Fooling Lucius seems to have been easy enough,' said Artemidorus. 'But it might not be so easy to fool the port authorities, especially as they are likely to be working for Cassius.'

'But having the boy aboard is our excuse for being here,' Hunefer reminded him. 'If anyone asks any questions that's what we tell them.'

'True enough. That explains us. But Halys will have to stay out at sea. That's where we need him in any case – keeping a look-out for Brutus' messenger.'

'So,' persisted Hunefer. 'What's the decision?'

'Stick to the plan. *Glaros* stays out here on patrol. We take a small team ashore and spy out the land. User, you wait here until we return then we'll decide about going right into port. I was going to leave Quintus to keep an eye on Lucius – I don't want him going anywhere yet. But he seems to have taken a shine to Puella. I'll leave her in charge of him. We'll be back by dawn...' He glanced at Hunefer who nodded. 'And then we'll have a conference. We'll know the lie of the land by then and can plan our next step accordingly.'

'Bearing in mind,' said User, 'the westerly that helped us get here will also help Brutus' messenger to arrive more quickly. We might not have much time.'

'On the other hand,' said Artemidorus,' a westerly turns Ashkelon into a lee shore. It will keep the ships in harbour bottled up unless they want to row themselves out – and will give you a good excuse for staying out of the harbour for a while longer if Lucius thinks to ask.'

ii

Triton sat in the shallows as close to the beach as possible, her upper works painted blood red by the light of the setting sun. The rope ladder hung off the right side of her stern, its bottom rungs dipping under the glass-green water as the waves passed and the hull heaved. Hunefer climbed down first, stepping off the lowest rung into water that came up to his shoulders. Artemidorus came next well aware that the water would come up to his chin. Then he let go of the ladder and plunged downwards into the chilly sea. Quintus was next, then Ferrata. None of them were wearing armour but all of them had a dagger at their waists.

Artemidorus waded unsteadily ashore, swimming the first part then half-floating until his feet found purchase on the firmer sand. The water might be cold but there was still heat lingering from the sunshine which had been unbroken all day, and the westerly wind was warm. Hunefer was waiting on the sand, looking like one of the massive statues south of Memphis. The spy turned and watched Quintus and Ferrata, neither of whom could swim, floundering ashore. Noting with surprise that one last figure was swarming down the ladder, clearly preparing to follow them. The fact that it seemed to be composed entirely of shadows told him it was User.

Artemidorus Quintus and Ferrata met User at the tide line. 'What are you doing?' asked Artemidorus, very much in character as Septem, the ruthless secret agent. 'You weren't part of this plan.'

'I thought I could help,' explained User blandly. 'I know the country and the people almost as well as your giant warrior. And I've brought extra inducements in case we need to negotiate.' He shook a pouch at his belt which jingled.

'We thought of that and brought our own,' said Quintus belligerently.

'You never know when you might need extra though,' said User. 'Extra inducements of one sort or another…' He rested a hand on the handle of his sword. The spies only had daggers – even Hunefer only had a dagger, though it was almost as long as User's sword.

'As long as *Triton*'s safe,' said Artemidorus, capitulating.

'Safe in the hands of my *gubernator*. She isn't going anywhere anyway. And I get bored easily. No telling what mischief I might get up to if you left me aboard…'

Artemidorus had already considered the danger of leaving Puella to User's tender mercies. The recently-made widower was beginning to look at her with longing. His first thought had been to take User along rather than be distracted by worries about what he might be up to. But the beautiful young warrior was more than capable of taking care of herself. When she rode with the Gaulish cavalry auxiliaries they called her *Bellatrix*, war-goddess because she could be more lethal than any man. In any case, her duties tonight focused on Lucius, so Artemidorus had set his concerns aside. Now, however, it seemed that his original plan had been put in place in any case.

'Let's go then,' he said.

*

There was almost no light by the time the five of them were ready, but the massive Egyptian assured them there was a village nearby. The village, Rafa, was the last township in Syria Province rather than the first in Egypt but Queen Cleopatra had been careful to seed it with her spies. And in any case the Syrian villagers were not well-disposed to Cassius and his rapacious Roman legionaries who were consuming what little food the locals had in storage, and were stealing their stores, livestock and youngsters, boys and girls.

As night continued to gather, Hunefer led the little group over the dunes inland of the beach and along a dry river bed. Full darkness came as they moved quietly, following the riverine twists and turns, their feet careful and quiet on the pebbles of the watercourse, heads just high enough to see over the reed-loud, bush-lined banks on either side. But the darkness was ameliorated at once by the massive number of stars, and by the appearance of a new moon that had grown nearly a quarter full within the last week. Then the heavenly illumination became irrelevant as they spied the lights of a village in the distance.

As soon as they were close to the village, Hunefer led them onto the river-bank, which had been flattened by villagers coming fetch water or wash clothing or with their livestock to drink. There was a pathway also beaten hard across the ground, leading between the desiccated scrub of parched bushes to the village itself.

It was a sad-looking place, especially after Alexandria. A collection of mud-walled huts mostly roofed with palm fronds. Some had doors, most did not. The steady light of the lamps that had helped guide them here shone out of these. The embers of a communal cooking fire still smoldered in the middle of the place. Hunefer strode past it, gesturing for the others to stay still. He ducked into one of the huts. He could not have straightened up, thought Artemidorus, or his head would have come through the roof. A moment or two later, Hunefer returned, with a wiry figure following in his wake. The newcomer was wrapped in black robes, blending with the shadows and making the man – if it was a man – almost impossible to see.

He whispered a word in a language Artemidorus did not understand. 'Come,' translated Hunefer. 'Then he added, 'Naramsin will guide us to the Roman army.'

In spite of his heavy robes, Naramsin set off at a fast lope, like a wolf from the Germanian forests. Hunefer ran at his shoulder. The others fell in behind. The village soon vanished. After a while, the ground began to slope upwards and it became obvious they were running up the back of something shaped like a huge sand dune. Looking up beyond the two almost invisible figures ahead he could see the curving line of a hillcrest etched across the midnight-blue sky. But then, as he looked past the crest itself, he realised that the lower sky was somehow stained as though the blue-black silk of the heavens was being dirtied by grey clouds and dull yellow brightness. He smelled smoke. He heard a distant, muted thunder.

Naramsin and Hunefer slowed as they approached the crest, and Artemidorus realised immediately that this must overlook Cassius' camp.

iii

Moments later, the six of them were belly-down, peering over the hill-crest. And there below them, spread out like a map, the camp of Cassius' legions reached as far as the eye could see. It was a grid of pathways, as geometric as Alexandria's streets. It was lit by flambeaux and patrolled by groups of tiny figures whose helmets and armour gleamed in the flickering light.

Or, thought the spy, that should be *camps*. Each legion seemed to have its own site, though Cassius appeared to have been content with one vast perimeter. Each one a perfect marching encampment with cooking fires, command posts, latrines. Through the middle of it all flowed the one thing that explained why it was sited where it was. The one thing that Naramsin's parched village lacked – a river. Though from here it looked low and sluggish.

Although there were twelve legionary camps down there, each square cantonment was separated from its neighbours by a dark space rather than by a ditch and a wall. But the ditch and wall surrounding the entire gigantic *castrum* was almost titanic. No mere two-*cubit* ditch with wall to match and palisade on top. The ditches as far as Artemidorus could make out were deeper than Hunefer was tall. The earthen walls correspondingly high. The palisade punctuated by watch-towers.

'Where's Cassius?' growled Quintus, jerking Artemidorus back to the present.

Artemidorus turned to Hunefer. 'Does Naramsin know which is the *praetorium*, the General's tent?' he whispered.

The Egyptian and the Syrian conducted a brief conversation. 'Right in the centre of the entire camp,' said Hunefer, 'closest to the river. From here it is just visible. It is the one immediately beside the largest tent, the general's command tent. It is surrounded by *vexillia* flags and has a smaller secure tent beside it, Naramsin says, for the legionary standards and eagles.'

Artemidorus found it, and traced the pattern of roadways leading to it. One wide main road that led from the tent to the perimeter, passed through a gate in the wall and stockade, stepped over the ditch on a wide wooden bridge. The gates and the bridge were guarded. The watch-towers each contained a four-man team. And pairs of legionaries patrolled the palisade just as squads of soldiers patrolled the *vias* of the camp itself. He re-focused his attention on the bridge, which stood nearly two military *miles* distant, he calculated.

'Have you sent anyone in there?' asked Artemidorus.

'Yes,' came the answer. 'We've sent many in but only a few have made it back out. That's why Naramsin is able to describe the placing of most things. But the knowledge has been gathered at a high price.'

'The men they sent in probably didn't have a good enough cover story,' said User. 'Are you planning to go in – and come out again?'

'Yes,' said Artemidorus. 'Ideally, we'll go in with Brutus' messenger. But *yes* in any case. That's why we brought Lucius after all. But I suspect we'll have to be very fast indeed, because that looks like a camp on a war-footing to me. I think Cassius is fed up with waiting. I think he's preparing to invade.'

*

'Is there any way we can be sure of that?' demanded Hunefer.

'We'll have to get closer. Try and pick up some soldiers' gossip. The legions will know the General's mind. And what the legions know, the legionaries discuss, particularly during long night-watches and especially if it promises gold or death.'

'So,' said User. 'We go in now? Like Naramsin's missing spies?'

'We certainly get closer,' answered Artemidorus. 'Hunefer. Can Naramsin get us closer? Preferably down to the ditch.'

A moment or two later, Naramsin's terse answer '*Nem*,' was relayed. 'Yes.'

The Syrian spy led them round the southern end of the hillock overlooking the camp. The ground was rocky and uneven – not suitable for a legionary parade ground or practice area. The men squirmed silently forward, all of them alert for snakes and scorpions. Luckily, the local mosquitoes were congregated close to the river, low though it was, with an entire army of legionaries to feed off. The restless westerly blew in behind them, stirring the dry branches, covering any sounds they made as they snaked towards Cassius' *castrum* and the defensive works surrounding it.

They reached the ditch unobserved. It was impossible to see right into its depths, so Artemidorus took a pebble and dropped it. He was half-expecting to hear a splash – the river would make a convenient moat – but there was a rattle and a click instead, which in itself made sense. If the river was low, the water it contained would be too precious to waste, even on strengthening the already considerable perimeter. It made their next move easier, though. He went first, swinging over the edge. He held his arms out to Hunefer. 'Lower me slowly,' he ordered. Hunefer obliged and the spy found his footing just as the edge of the ditch rose past his face. Four cubits deep, he thought. But dry – floored with some pebbles but mostly just dry earth. The light from the blazing torches in the watch-towers and dotted along the palisade did not reach down here. His companions were black shapes, with occasional dots of silvery brightness where the moonshine glinted off metal dagger-sheaths and sword-handles. His mind raced. Getting in here was easy enough. But getting out again would be more difficult. They would have to lift one after the other up over the edge, then turn back and reach for the last man. Or they could leave someone here to lift them out and guide them back. Logic suggested Hunefer and Naramsin. But would Hunefer be willing to wait and help? Would Naramsin?

'Hunefer,' he said. 'I want you to lower the others. Then wait with Naramsin for our return so you can pull us up again. I will tell you anything we discover, on my oath.'

The Egyptian was silent for a moment. Then he said, 'The divine queen, Cleopatra, says you are a man of honour and a friend to Egypt. If she trusts you then so do I. I do not trust *Triton*'s captain, however. Do you wish him to come with you or to stay with Naramsin and me? Or is this a good moment to cut his throat?'

iv

'I don't like that big bastard,' said User, his voice just audible to Artemidorus who was in the lead.

'That's hardly surprising,' said Quintus.

'Because he doesn't seem to like you much,' added Ferrata.

'Or trust you at all,' concluded Quintus.

'Well, he'd better watch his back when he comes back aboard *Triton*. That's all I can say!'

'How close are you to your brother and his family, User?' whispered Artemidorus, looking back over his shoulder.

'Close enough. Especially now…'

'Better leave Hunefer well alone then. Remember what Cleopatra said if anything happened to Hunefer. "As though you and your family had never even existed." And if by some miracle your wife and children survived what Brutus did to Xanthus, she'll hunt them down and wipe them off the face of the earth as well.'

A brooding silence fell. The little four-man squad jogged along the bottom of the ditch, heading for the right-turn that would take them to the bridge and the main gate behind it. The air down here was cooler and damper. There was an overpowering smell of earth, as though they were already in their graves.

Artemidorus was concentrating on counting his steps. It was the only way he could think of that would give them some idea of whether they had reached the rendezvous on the way back. He was up into the thousands before they reached the corner but he stopped counting as soon as he turned. The distance from the corner back to Hunefer was crucial, the distance from the corner to the bridge irrelevant. They paused to catch their breath, then ran on silently. In the sky above them the moon rose higher and higher. It had reached it's apogee by the time the bridge came into sight and was beginning to set by the time they reached it.

'This had better be worth it,' hissed User.

'You didn't have to come,' Quintus pointed out. 'You volunteered.'

'That shows you're not a soldier at any rate,' added Ferrata.

'Quiet!' commanded Artemidorus. He was sweating with tension, half-convinced that Hunefer was right and that he had made a fatal error in bringing User. One false move or noise would ruin the mission and likely get them all executed – Cassius like Crassus had a predilection for crucifixion; one of the worst ways to go – and the closer they got to the bridge, the more exposed he felt. There were great flaming torches at its outer end. Sconces on the wall beside the gate and also up in the watch towers on either side of the entrance. It was disturbingly bright down here. The brightness somehow made worse by the measured tread of the sentries as they patrolled the length of the bridge between the gate and the outer torches. Above the sound of their footsteps and the creaking of the boards, a rumble of indistinct conversation came and went on the wind. If anything made them stop and look down then Artemidorus and his companions would be hanging from crosses by dawn.

*

Looking around in the flickering light, Artemidorus made a rapid calculation. If they waited far enough back to be sure they wouldn't be visible in the unsteady brightness, then they could hardly make out what the guards were saying, which would make the whole adventure utterly pointless. They would have to take the risk, therefore, and move forward into the safety of the shadows immediately beneath the bridge itself. He sent Quintus first. The legionary, widely experienced in this sort of thing, vanished like a puff of smoke. User went next, Ferrata watching him fiercely with his one good eye. Artemidorus found himself wishing he had thought to bring his sling. But if the merchant made enough noise to require silencing with a slingshot, they were all as good as dead in any case. When User had vanished into the curtain of shadow hanging beneath the bridge, Artemidorus struck Ferrata on the shoulder and the second legionary moved as silently as the first. A few heartbeats later, Artemidorus joined them.

It was not as dark here as it first appeared. The boards comprising the bridge's surface were not all butted hard against one-another. Blades of torchlight sliced between some of them, striping the four silent spies like tigers. And, disturbingly, the shadows of the guards came down as well, as their patrol took them back and forth. Accompanying the slow passage of those shadows, came regular, measured footfalls from above. And, mercifully, a conversation, low but clear.

The first thing that happened, however, was that a long steam of golden urine came arcing down to spatter at User's feet. He started back with an exclamation of disgust – rapidly stifled by Quintus' hand over his mouth and Ferrata's dagger at his throat. They stood in silence as the steaming waterfall continued apparently endlessly.

'By Cloacina,' came a gruff voice from above. 'Don't you ever stop?'

'You know the latrines are all but useless now the river's drying up. We need to sacrifice to Crepitus as well as Cloacina in the hope that either the Goddess of Sewers or the God of Shit will help us out.'

'No need. Word is that General Cassius is getting ready to move. We can't stay here with the river drying and food running low. He'll have to make the choice soon. Back north to join General Brutus or west to invade and pillage Egypt.'

'It'll be Egypt pretty soon.' The cascade eased and then stopped. 'I mean Syria's all very well, but Egypt…' The legionary's tone became dreamy.

'You ever been there?'

'To Egypt? No. But I hear it's like the country of King Midas in the stories – gold everywhere. And the women wear hardly anything. Was it you who told me about the carvings? Someone who was there with *Divus Julius* in 706 brought carvings back and you wouldn't believe…'

'That's it is it? Girls and gold?'

'Is there anything else?'

'Not for the likes of us.'

'Not for the likes of General Cassius either. Gold is power to a man like that: the more gold you have the more legions you can buy so the more power you get.'

'Didn't work to well for General Crassus at Carrhae, they say the Parthians finally killed him by pouring molten gold down his throat.'

'That's my point! General Cassius walked away from that. He's so much better than Crassus was. Give him as much gold as Crassus had and he'll steal the Republic from under the noses of Mark Antony and Caesar Octavianus. And he knows it. No it's clear as day to me. He's got to move – can't wait any longer with the river as it is. And if he has to move anyway, he'll go for Egypt, all that gold and all that power. I'd bet my life…'

'*Cave*! Watch out! That bastard centurion's coming! Back on patrol before he beats you half to death with that vinestock club of his…'

V

Hunefer hoisted them out as though they weighed nothing and they hurried back to Naramsin's village in the pink light of dawn. Artemidorus ran beside Hunefer and briefed him as they went. 'Cassius has to move whether he likes it or not. And chances are he's going to move west into Egypt. I'd say he knows he might well be jumping from the cooking-pot into the fire, but it's such a fine balance. On the one hand there's famine and plague – especially if he goes to the Upper Kingdom south of Memphis. But on the other hand, he gets Alexandria, control of the eastern half of *Mare Nostrum* and more gold than even he could wish for.'

'An interesting commentary, have you discussed these ideas with her divine majesty?' asked Hunefer.

'As a matter of fact, I have. All except for the possibility that Cassius is about to invade, ravage and plunder her country.'

Hunefer glanced at him with, of all things a chuckle. 'No he's not

Septem.'

'Oh! And what makes you say that?'

'We are going to stop him.'

Artemidorus was still turning Hunefer's calm words over in his head as he pulled himself, dripping, aboard *Triton*. He had established to his own satisfaction what Cassius' next move was likely to be. He was not too worried about placing so much faith in the gossip between two legionaries. In his experience, the men knew what their officers and commanders planned pretty accurately. What had they sung at *Divus Julius*' last Triumph?

Here comes old baldy, randy as hell.

Lock up your daughters and your wives as well!

Or had it been '*and your sons as well*?'

Either way, the nameless guards' assessment of Cassius, his immediate position, long-term goals and relationship with Brutus rang true. True enough to inform his own plans at any rate. He was tempted to go below and start dictating to Notus and Kyros the message he wanted them to put into the scroll which had apparently been sent by Brutus. But he knew he simply dare not do so. He had to have sight of Brutus' original first. There might be something vital to include to make the forgery more realistic. And the matter of a code needed to be addressed into the bargain.

As *Triton* eased out into deeper water and dawn became morning, Artemidorus went below, stripped, dried himself and dressed. Then he wandered the ship like an animal caged at the Menagerie in Alexandria. Lucius and Puella were deep in conversation. Quintus and Ferrata were changing – as were Hunefer and User, though the latter had stopped, still dripping, to give his orders to the helmsman. The rest of the *contubernium* were sunning themselves at ease on the deck, along with the oarsmen in their blue tunics. Even the sailhandlers were idle. The sail was furled, the anchor out. Everything ready and waiting.

Ready to burst with tension and impatience, Artemidorus crossed to the mast, looking up at the rigging. Then, without a word to anyone he swung himself up off the deck and began to climb. When he reached the point where the horizontal yards joined the vertical mast, with the sail furled along their length, he stepped up onto them and stood with his left arm wrapped round the top of the mast as though round Puella in his fiercest embrace. Once he was safely there, his body and grasp making due allowance for the movement of the ship – magnified a hundredfold up here. He shaded his eyes with his right hand and began to scan the western and northern horizons.

He saw at once that the seas all around were quiet. Empty and unusually so, given the gentle wind and the clement weather. He felt as though he should be able to see all the way to Rhodos, all the way to Cyprus, and the southern coasts of Cilicia, Asia Province and perhaps even Macedonia beyond. But he knew he was fooling himself.

Instead of continuing to scan the horizon, therefore, he began to look at things nearby beginning with *Glaros*. Halys and his crew seemed just as idle as the men aboard *Triton*. But, just as with *Triton*, there was a look-out standing on the yards keeping tight hold of the mast. Artemidorus waved to him, but there was no reaction. Halys' lookout was scanning the horizons to the north and west. Artemidorus turned and looked at Ashkelon instead, dropping his right hand as he did so, no longer needing to shade his eyes. From this viewpoint it was easy to see half a dozen vessels of various sizes crowded in the modest harbour. They and their crews seemed equally idle. Indeed, the town behind them seemed to be asleep. Frozen, like a mosaic or a picture.

Enjoy the peace and quiet, he thought. It isn't going to last long.

'*Hey*!' The inarticulate hail was so distant that he only heard it because a northerly fluke in the westerly wind carried it to him. 'Hey!'

Bemused, frowning, Artemidorus turned, moving his head like a hunting wolf trying to locate the source of the sound. The watchkeeper on *Glaros*' mast was waving to him. No. Not just waving – gesturing. He shaded his eyes, straining to look past Halys' watchkeeper in the direction he was pointing.

And there, on the blue-green line of the horizon where the sky and the sea came together, was a tiny white speck.

The sail of a fast-approaching ship.

XV: Arke

i

'That woman is amazing as well as beautiful!' exclaimed Lucius, aglow with youthful enthusiasm. 'How she knows all the facts that seem to lie at her fingertips, Jupiter alone knows. Or, Minerva – she is the goddess of wisdom after all. She has explained why we are waiting here outside the harbour and how we plan to go into General Cassius' camp at the earliest opportunity! Whose slave is she? Can I buy her?'

Artemidorus, User, Hunefer, Quintus and Ferrata were locked in conference, discussing how the next part of the plan would play out, assuming that the distant sail belonged to the ship bringing Brutus' courier. The young Tribune's interruption stopped them. They all swung round to look at him.

'She's no-one's slave,' snapped User. 'You can't buy her! She's a free woman and you'll never be worthy of her!'

Lucius gaped at him, then drew himself up, transforming into the arrogant patrician he was at heart. Even though his family's fortunes lay ruined in Rome.

Before he could utter a word, Artemidorus stepped forward. 'User is right, Lucius. Puella is not a slave. You've travelled with us on and off for months now. Have you ever seen any of us treat her like a slave?'

'No… But I just assumed…'

'Well your assumption was mistaken. Puella is a free woman. And if you wish to have anything at all to do with her, you must ask.'

'Or she'll chop off your *verpa* before you can say *spread your legs*,' added Ferrata helpfully.

Outraged and humiliated, the young man stormed off. As the others got back to business, Artemidorus observed. 'Good. Fortuna smiles on us. We want him rattled. We need him jumping to conclusions.'

'But preferably only the conclusions we want him to jump to,' added User.

'Right. So let's go over everything one more time. We have to assume that the ship coming towards us is carrying Brutus' messenger. It's coming from the right direction. The timing is correct. Alternative vessels are few and far-between. So, as soon as it gets anywhere close to us, Halys goes into action…'

'He's the one weak point,' said Quintus. 'I don't trust Halys. Never have. He's Cilician. He really *is* a pirate.'

'Keep saying that in front of Lucius,' advised Ferrata. 'That's what we need him to think.'

'I'll say it in front of everybody,' snapped Quintus, 'because it's bloody well true!'

*

'Look!' cried Lucius, bouncing back along the deck, his outrage overcome by excitement. 'There's a sail! A ship! How did she get so close without us noticing?'

'Because you were trying your luck with Puella again, lad,' said Quintus. 'She'd taken up all of your attention.'

'Do you think it's Brutus' messenger?' asked the young man. 'Coming with news for Cassius?'

'Possibly,' said Artemidorus. 'She's a fast ship.'

'Almost as fast as *Glaros* I'd say,' calculated User.

'Can you see her name?' asked Artemidorus.

'It looks like *Arke* to me.' Triton's captain squinted. 'That would be logical – the messenger of the Titans, even if Zeus did condemn her to Tartarus when the Titans lost their war against the Gods.'

'They gave her wings to Achilleus,' said Artemidorus. 'They were the source of his speed.'

'*Arke*. I should probably go aboard her,' said Lucius. 'But not at sea, obviously; when she's docked. We can follow her in – even allowing for what Puella said about the shores and getting trapped by contrary winds like we were in Brundisium. I could go into Cassius' camp with the messenger. Then you'll all be rid of me.'

'That's a good idea,' said Artemidorus. 'It's more or less what we were planning to do. But we'll wait out here and hail her as she goes past, just to make sure Brutus' courier actually is aboard. We don't want to follow the wrong ship in and get trapped.'

'I don't see what difference it would make,' said Lucius. 'I could still wait for the courier in Ashkelon. There has to be a *taberna* or something.'

'You could. If you had the money – which I don't believe you have. But even if you could find accommodation, Halys and User here are traders. Merchants. They need to be out and about. User has lost a lot of money as well as his home and family in the destruction of Xanthus. He can't afford to get stuck in port. And I haven't paid him and Halys enough to let them sit at the dockside, running up port charges and food-bills. Not to mention the fact that Hunefer is due back in Alexandria as soon as possible. His cover story is all prepared. Our bargain was for him to help get you free, not spend the rest of his life on the run. And I have to get home to Rome. So it's not really all about you.'

'Oh. Right. I hadn't thought of it like that!'

'Well, that's the way it is. Now…' Artemidorus drew breath.

But, before he could continue, Lucius interrupted once more. 'What's he doing?'

'Who?' Artemidorus asked, turning to follow the young man's gaze.

'Halys,' answered Lucius. 'He's turning *Glaros*! He's heading straight for the other ship!' Lucius pointed over *Triton*'s left rail.

'*Stercore*! Shit!' said Artemidorus. 'User! What is Halys up to?'

'I don't know…' User's face was blank. He appeared to be as surprised as the rest of them.

The group of them watched in astonishment as *Glaros*' oars were run out and she wheeled onto a collision course with the incoming vessel. After a moment, Artemidorus turned and ran into the fighting tower on the after deck, climbed up the internal ladder and ran out onto the platform at the top. Moments later, he was joined by the others, Lucius pushing to the front to stand beside him.

'Has he gone mad?' demanded Artemidorus. 'User. He's your friend. What's going on?'

'He must be pretty certain it's the messenger,' said User grimly.

'So?' demanded Artemidorus.

'Ships like that don't only carry couriers,' shrugged the merchant, 'as often as not they carry gold.' He swung round to confront Artemidorus, his face folded into a thunderous frown. 'Don't you see? Cassius has been sitting in the desert for weeks, maybe longer. His legions are all in that massive camp. We saw them last night and that's what I came with you to check. They were on a war-footing. They will have spent the last few weeks readying for battle. On the other hand, Brutus has been collecting taxes, sacking cities, selling slaves. Halys must be betting that Brutus is sending Cassius the one thing every Roman commander needs before he commits his troops to battle – their pay!'

'If he's sending enough gold to pay all those legions,' Quintus breathed, 'it would be a fortune!'

'A fortune for each legion!' added Ferrata. 'He can't have sent *that* much. *Arke* would hardly be able to float if she was carrying all that gold aboard.'

'Well, chances are that she's carrying as much as Brutus can spare. And she's not going to float for much longer in any case by the look of things!' snapped Artemidorus. '*Glaros* doesn't have a ram but her cutwater will shear off any oars *Arke* deploys. And Halys has got grappling hooks and rope. All he has to do is get along side…'

'Which he'll do in short order by the look of things!' snapped User.

'Unless we can stop him,' grated Artemidorus. 'User! Let's go!'

ii

The incoming ship was moving under sail power. She had no oars deployed. *Glaros* surged towards her, the rhythm of her oars moving at *battle speed.* At this distance, they should have been able to hear the rowing song. The fact that there was silence instead told the sea-wise members of the *contubernium* that *Glaros* was ready for battle. She continued to pick up speed, heading straight for *Arke*. *Arke* was close enough for them to see the foredeck crowded with figures staring at *Glaros* – no doubt with utter disbelief. Then, it seemed, they realised what was going on, all at once. Even as *Triton* span, oars out, her own *pausator* pounding out *battle speed*, also rowing in silence. And with *ramming speed* available.

But Artemidorus soon realised that he would not need to do so. *Arke*'s captain did the logical thing. He ordered his *gubernator* to change course away from the oncoming Cilician in order to avoid a collision. But that proved to be a dangerous error. As *Arke*'s head swung northward the westerly wind spilled out of her sail. The great taut belly of the thing flattened; flapped like the wing of a broken bird. The way came off the ship at once. Her head dipped, rose, wavered. *Glaros* bore down on her like a sea-eagle on a fish out of water.

But *Triton* was by no means lagging behind. User's fine crew and the oarsmen were really putting their backs into their work. So, *Triton* soon came onto a converging course with *Glaros* and the helpless *Arke*. Artemidorus shaded his eyes as the three ships came closer together. *Arke*'s oars came out, but went in again almost at once. Obviously, the captain realised that she could never outrun *Glaros* under oar power, certainly not from a standing start. And all that would happen if he tried to do so was that the Cilician pirate would break off the oars on the side she was approaching and cripple the vessel entirely. In any case, he had no alternative but to make a fight of it and a hundred or so sword-trained legionary oarsmen would make a useful force with which to fight the Cilician pirates bearing down on them.

'If I was *Arke*'s captain, I'd be praying that we're as Roman as we look,' said Quintus.

'So we are!' snapped Artemidorus. 'And we'll be alongside in short order. Time to get our armour on and prepare to lower the *corvus*.'

All of them, including Lucius, raced down the ladder, out of the fighting tower and along to the hatch leading to the accommodation and the weapons. The rest of the *contubernium* were getting ready. In a moment, they were all prepared for battle. Except for Crinas, who was preparing to tend the wounded.

Men from the sail-handling crew came past, laden with swords to be distributed to the oarsmen as soon as the *corvus* came down and the need for propulsion was replaced by the need to charge across the old-fashioned boarding platform onto whichever of the vessels User put them alongside.

*

By the time Artemidorus was back on deck, *Glaros* was almost alongside *Arke*. Her speed was easing as her oars were retracted. No doubt the Cilician oarsmen, like *Triton*'s complement, were getting armed and ready to fight. Grappling hooks flew across the rapidly-closing gap between the two vessels. *Glaros*' crew heaved on the ropes attached to them as Halys deployed archers to ensure that anyone aboard *Arke* trying to pull them free or cut the lines found a hail of arrows pouring on them. Artemidorus watched, eyes narrow, face set like stone as the two ships were forced inexorably closer and closer together. And the first casualties aboard *Arke* fell back screaming with arrows sticking out of their chests, shoulders and faces.

As with Hunefer's rescue of Lucius from Cleopatra's dungeons, this part of the plan was costing a lot more lives than he had counted on.

But there was no going back now.

'Ramming speed!' ordered User, his voice coming from the convenient vantage point on top of the fighting tower. *Triton* surged forward more rapidly still, heading straight for *Arke*.

'He's not going to ram her, is he?' wondered Lucius, wide-eyed.

'He's trying to get us there as fast as possible,' Artemidorus assured him. But he found he was not so certain himself. Halys was clearly out of control – pursuing his own ends. Whose side was User really on? His mouth went dry and he wiped his palm down his thigh because it was suddenly a little moist. He looked around. The rest of the contubernium were there. It would soon be time to get up to the bow, ready to deploy the *corvus*.

A squad of sail-handlers dashed past, armed with bows, and vanished into the tower. Another squad came by, heading up the length of the deck. The *corvus* handlers, thought Artemidorus. 'Lets' go!' he called and led the way along the ship's length.

As they moved, the *contubernium* fell into their well-practiced fighting formation. Artemidorus in front, Quintus at his right shoulder, Puella at his left then Hercules towering behind him with Furius behind Quintus and Kyros behind Puella – both of them capable of using their left hands as well as their right. One-eyed Ferrata close behind, watching over Furius, and Notus watching over his forger colleague and friend Kyros. Lucius joined in at the back of the formidable wedge, as close as he could get to Puella. And Hunefer followed hard on the young patrician's heels. All in all, this steel-bound arrow-head formation would form the spear-point of the charge as soon as the *corvus* went down.

As they arrived in position, Artemidorus found that his vision was limited by the cheek-flaps and peak of his helmet. And by the fact that he was standing so close to the still upright *corvus*. But he could see around the wooden wall to where *Arke*'s side was slowly swinging into position. He understood what User was planning – to go alongside the smaller vessel opposite to *Glaros*. No sooner had the spy understood User's plan than *Triton*'s captain was putting it into action. 'Oars in!' came the bellowed order.

With a thunderous rumble the oarsmen obeyed.

'Hard over!'

Triton swung to her left, slammed into *Arke*, shuddered along her length, slowing as she did so. Grappling hooks flew. The bemused sailors in the trapped vessel didn't know which way to turn. Halys' men were pouring over *Glaros'* side and onto *Arke*'s deck. Howling like demons and swinging swords, clubs and axes. Artemidorus eased the shield on his left arm, pulled out his *gladius* and felt the others doing the same. 'Whatever happens,' he shouted, 'Don't fall overboard.'

Then he sent a swift, silent prayer to Achilleus. The noise of battle from *Arke* was almost overwhelming. Not to mention the earthquake rumbling as *Triton* ground to a stop along her length.

'*Corvus*!' came that enormous bellow from the fighting tower.

The boarding bridge slammed down. The huge spike at its far end stabbed right through Arke's decking, anchoring the two hulls together even more surely than the ropes and grappling irons. As the wooden wall transformed to a bridge between the vessels, so the melee on the messenger ship was revealed: legionaries in red; marines and oarsmen in blue, Cilician pirates in no sort of uniform at all, all hacking and stabbing, screaming, bleeding and dying. The Romans in helmets and mail shirts, with swords and shields vainly trying to fight in the Roman way – in regular lines and close-order units but having neither the chance nor the space to do so. Being broken up and forced into individual duels – often with two Cilician opponents at once. It was not going well. The whole deck seemed to be awash with Halys' pirates and the blood of *Arke*'s crew.

'Charge!' yelled Artemidorus, and he broke into a run.

iii

Artemidorus leapt onto the wide wooden bridge that the *corvus* had become and charged across it towards *Arke*. It was only a matter of a few steps, but the unco-ordinated movements of the two vessels made the boards heave and see-saw beneath him. The hob-nails on his *caligae* boots skidded, scoring the wood. He became intensely aware that there were no safety rails on either side of the restless bridge and the armour on his body was heavy, laced in place with leather and would be impossible to escape from if he went into the water. Being a skilful swimmer would be of no use whatsoever if he went into the sea.

He put all such thoughts out of his head as he leapt onto *Arke*'s deck, straight into a scrum of blue-dressed marines. 'It's all right, lads,' he yelled. 'We're here to help!' He gulped in a deep breath and bellowed the Spartan war-cry 'ALALA!'

Artemidorus and his *contubernium* simply cut across the narrow deck, pushing aside confused blue-dressed marines but meeting no real resistance until they faced Halys' Cilicians at the far side of the deck. This section of the ship was truly a battle-front. He had no time to be surprised by the revelation that Quintus' suspicions were so well-founded. Halys seemed to be intent on taking this ship and whatever she was carrying, because he had no sooner arrived at the point where *Glaros* was secured to *Arke* than he found himself face to face with a Cilician sailor.

With his face a mask of blood-lust, the Cilician swung a great curved sword at Artemidorus' head. The centurion ducked – but lost some of his gaudy horsehair crest. He raised his shield with all his might so that the metal rim at the top smashed into the pirate's elbow. The man gave a howl of pain but kept hold of his sword. Artemidorus stabbed, sliding his *gladius* blade past the side of his shield only to find the pirate was wearing a mail vest beneath his loose green tunic. The point of his sword scraped across it without doing any damage at all.

At the edge of his fiercely-focused vision, he saw the man on his opponent's left stagger back with his face cleft in two. Quintus had arrived. He pushed forward with his shield, using all his strength and body-weight enhanced by the weight of Quintus behind one shoulder and Puella behind the other. Trapped against *Arke*'s deck-rail, the pirate strove to swing his sword again only to discover there wasn't enough room to use such a large weapon effectively. This time, when Artemidorus stabbed, his *gladius* went low – under the bottom of the mail shirt and into the pirate's guts. The man howled, but refused to give up. Artemidorus jerked his blade fiercely from side to side and hot liquid cascaded over his knees, shins and feet. The spilt offal stench rose up, familiar from a hundred sacrifices where the *haruspex*' knife opened the belly of some animal, searching for its prophetic liver. Even with his life-blood pouring out of him, the pirate fought on. Taking the great sword in both hands and chopping down with what was left of his might. Artemidorus caught the blade on the top of his shield. The edge sliced a good hand's breadth into the armoured wood. Artemidorus twisted his whole torso, tearing the wedged sword out of the man's hands. As he did so, the man's face went blank. His eyes rolled up. His last breath released his spirit to puff into Artemidorus' face. But the corpse remained erect, wedged against the deck-rails by the weight of Artemidorus and his legionaries. Then, abruptly, the rail behind the dead man broke – and it was not the only section to do so, Artemidorus reckoned grimly. The power of *Glaros*' movements transmitted through the grappling hooks and taut ropes was fatally enhanced by the weight of men pushing against it. The ships stirred again. The corpse slipped into the gap and vanished, along with a section of the rail. The space closed again at once, trapping the dead Cilician. There was a sound like a sack of dry twigs being crushed.

The centurion stepped back from the gap as what was left of *Arke*'s deck-rail moved hard up against *Glaros*' slightly higher one, still bound together by many of the grappling hooks that *Glaros*' archers had protected so efficiently. Archers who might well be taking aim at his *contubernium* now.

That chilling thought had hardly occurred to Artemidorus when a flight of arrows passed low over his head to thump into *Glaros*' deck. And he remembered the archers User had sent up to the fighting tower. Now it was the pirate bowmen's turn to scream and seek shelter from the steel-tipped storm. The pressure behind him eased and he was able to step back. There was a heartbeat of calm.

'What are they waiting for? Why don't they retreat?' gasped Quintus. 'They must be outnumbered two-to one!'

'There's something else going on,' said Artemidorus. 'There must be!'

*

Artemidorus sheathed his sword for a moment, turned his shield side-on and wrestled the pirate's huge blade free. It was almost as big as Hunefer's. The thought of the massive Egyptian prompted him to glance around. Lucius, Hunefer and the *contubernium* all seemed safe for the time-being. The deck was littered with corpses. But small though she seemed compared with the ships on either side of her, *Arke* was still the better part of one hundred feet in length and it was impossible to take in her entire deck with one swift glance.

'I hope to Hades User's not involved in whatever it is or we're all dead men,' said Quintus, as Artemidorus' attention returned to him.

Then time for talking was over as another wave of pirates came screaming over *Glaros*' deck-rail, preceded by a shower of arrows. There was just enough warning to get their shields up, so the shafts thumped into these rather than into the legionaries' flesh. Artemidorus' focus closed down again as he faced a pair of pirates, his battle plan now complicated by the need to stay well clear of the deadly gap in *Arke*'s deck rail. As he prepared to fight, he realised he was still holding the dead Cilician's huge curved sword instead of his trusty *gladius*. The first pirate of the pair charged straight at him like a Germainan berserker, sword in one hand, dagger in the other. No shield. Armour – if he was wearing any – hidden by his yellow tunic. Artemidorus hurled the unwieldy sword into the man's face with all the strength he possessed. The pirate instinctively tried to knock it aside with his sword arm. The weighty blade lopped his hand off and buried itself in his forehead, splitting his helmet and the skull behind it. He went down flat on his back as though he had been hit in the face by a ballista bolt.

Artemidorus tore his *gladius* out of its sheath and turned to face his second opponent, swinging his shield to stand between them. The pirate crashed into the shield hard enough to drive one or two of the arrow-heads right through. The sharp edge of one of them opened Artemidorus' forearm. The wound stung like fire and began to bleed copiously, but was nowhere near enough to distract him – let alone stop him. He staggered under his assailant's weight but then drove forward with the pierced shield. The fact that his opponent had been able to drive the arrows through it warned Artemidorus that he was wearing armour beneath his tunic. So the battle-hardened centurion stooped slightly, slamming the lower edge of his shield down as hard as he could. The metal rim crushed the delicate bones of the pirate's feet. The man screamed. Artemidorus followed, repeating the move. The pirate's toes popped like grapes in a wine-press. He dropped his weapons at took hold of Artemidorus' shield, fists closing on either side of the wound left by the first man's sword. Vainly, he tried to lift the shield, to stop it crippling him entirely. Artemidorus straightened, still pushing down with his wounded forearm and stabbed over the top straight into the pirate's throat. A huge gout of blood burst out of the man, filling Artemidorus face and eyes, blinding him completely for a moment. He staggered back, disorientated, praying that he was not he was not heading for the gap in the deck-rail. Felt two huge bodies close on his right shoulder and his left. Praying that these were friends not foes, he wiped his face with the back of his sword-hand, blinking until he could see again. Hercules on one side. Hunefer on the other.

Puella and Quintus were gone.

iv

Suddenly terrified, he looked around. But breathed an immediate sigh of relief – his usual guardians were still close at hand, both engaged in brutal battles of their own. For a heartbeat he scanned the deck, searching for the rest of the *contubernium*. But there was no time for a proper roll-call. The pirates were falling back now. Retreating onto their own ship but a fighting retreat rather than a rout. Leaving *Arke*'s deck littered with their dead and dying but taking as many wounded with them as they safely could. As soon as they reached *Glaros*' deck they started to chop their vessel free. As the ships' sides began to move apart, more sections of *Arke*'s deck-rail fell away. There were screams, howls and splashes as combatants tumbled into the water between the hulls.

Artemidorus looked around the vessel he and his command had just rescued. And he saw that the hatch leading down into the lower decks was open. That surprised him. The hatches would have been opened to allow the armed and armoured oarsmen up onto the deck, but they would have been closed again once everyone was up. An open hatch in a battle was an invitation to disaster. And, now that he thought about it, he noticed that the square of darkness had the largest number of dead pirates piled around it. And pirates rarely if ever, in his experience, were willing to die in vain.

Collecting Puella and Quintus, Ferrata and Lucius as he went, Artemidorus crossed to the gaping hatchway. Another swift check to make sure that the deck nearby was clear of living pirates, he handed his shield to Hunefer who had disdained to use one so far, stepped over the corpses, ducked his head and ran below.

The rowing benches were empty. The oars neatly stowed. Light filtered in through the oar-holes revealing nothing apparently amiss. As he looked, so the last of the stamping footfalls of battle on the deck above him quietened. He glanced up. There was blood running through the spaces between some of the deck-boards. And the great spike of the *corvus* stabbed down nearby like the dagger of some Titan. *Arke* gave a lurch and the brightness intensified. *Glaros* was moving away.

Artemidorus noticed a lamp burning at the top of another companionway leading deeper into the hold. Taking this up, he went on, slowly, sword first. So he came to the vessel's accommodation areas. He had assumed – without giving the matter any thought – that all the fighting would have been on deck, but apparently not. The central passageway down here contained two dead pirates and, by the look of things one dead Roman. The Roman was lying face-down in a doorway that he had obviously died trying to defend. He had no helmet. The back of his head was a mass of blood-matted hair. Artemidorus stepped over him and entered a surprisingly spacious cabin.

He paused, raising the lamp and looking around in its flickering light. On a bunk – made up with military precision – lay a jumble of papers and documents beside a leather courier's satchel. Suddenly short of breath, he crossed to these and breathed a sigh of relief as he found a message case with Brutus' seal and Cassius' name on it. This was the treasure that his entire plan had sought to bring into his possession – or rather into the possession of his forgers. In the meantime he packed it all into the satchel and left it on the bed.

Then, his interest piqued, he looked further. At the end of the bunk was a large, iron-bound chest. Lock smashed. Open and rifled. Whatever it had contained was gone. He lowered the lamp for a closer look. Something gleamed at the bottom. He laid his sword on the bunk and reached in o find a gold coin. On one side was Brutus' face in profile and on the other two daggers. He straightened, looking closely at it as everything fell into place with the elegant precision of a Pythagorean theorem. User had been right. *Arke* was not just bringing Brutus' message. She had also been bringing Brutus' gold to pay Cassius' troops – quite a lot, judging by the size of the empty box. Halys had guessed it would be there as accurately as User. And, Cilician pirate that he was, he had been unable to resist the temptation.

Artemidorus' thoughts were interrupted by a groan. He returned to the doorway. The Roman wasn't dead after all. Artemidorus crouched, lowering the lamp to the deck and heaving the unconscious soldier onto his back as gently as possible, the wound on his left arm adding yet more blood to the Roman's legionary tunic. Then he froze.

For Brutus' courier was Marcus Valerius Messala.

*

'Messala!' said Lucius. 'Did you say he was dead?'

'Still alive,' answered Artemidorus, 'but only just by the look of things. We need to get him to Crinas as soon as possible. Puella, you and Kyros do what you can for him then see about moving him. Ferrata and Hercules, you help. Notus, you collect everything off his bed and bring it with him. Get Furius to help you when he gets here. Hunefer, Quintus, you two and I are going to talk to the captain and whoever is in charge of the marines.'

Artemidorus paused on the deck. *Glaros* was heading north – slowly, with about half her oars deployed, heading past Cyprus and then home to Cilicia no doubt. The surviving pirates rich beyond their dreams. His gaze came back aboard. Those pirates who had not survived were being stripped, their weapons and armour in one pile, and valuables in another. Then their bodies were being heaved overboard. A task made easier by the state of *Arke*'s broken deck-rail. Their disposal attracting the local sharks to a noisy, gruesome, frenzied feast.

The three men walked towards the stern, where a small knot of sailors and soldiers were deep in conversation. They stopped and turned as Artemidorus and his blood-soaked companions approached.

One of them stepped forward. 'I am Valerius Potitus, captain of this vessel,' he said, cordially. 'Thank you for saving her.'

Artemidorus introduced himself and his companions. Then he continued, 'We were happy to be of service, Captain Potitus. I wish we could have done more. Your vessel is damaged and I would guess you will need to re-organise your oarsmen. I see several dead and wounded. It will therefore take you some time to get into Ashkelon. However, speed is of the essence. Tribune Messala seems to have been seriously wounded trying to defend General Brutus' messages and the gold Brutus was sending to General Cassius. Unsuccessfully, as it turns out. The gold is gone. However, my vessel is not damaged. I have lost no oarsmen, as far as I know. And I have an Athenian physician aboard who will tend Tribune Messala and help him to recover if the gods will it. I therefore suggest we take the Tribune, his messages and his personal effects aboard *Triton* and get into port.'

He had just finished speaking when Ferrata arrived. 'We have Messala ready to move as soon as we have permission to do so,' he said. 'But I am sorry to say that we can't find Furius anywhere. He must have been one of the poor bastards who went overboard when the deck-rails started breaking.'

V

They had all been there when Mercury died, remembered Artemidorus. The messenger had been shot in an ambush. He lay choking to death with his head in Puella's lap. Arrows piercing his face from cheek to cheek through his teeth, gums and tongue; and through his throat from side to side. The experience had been horrible. But Furius' death seemed somehow worse – simply to vanish like that. His death unobserved. Unsuspected until Ferrata did a headcount. To die in such a terrible way, plunging below the surface, trapped in heavy armour, uselessly worrying at the knots in the leather securing it in place. Tearing nails to the quick on unyielding laces. Knowing it was hopeless. Knowing it was all over – that none of your friends and tent companions even realised. The death he had feared for himself.

'Well?' he said, pulling himself back to the present, the syllable seeming to fill the tiny room that Kyros and Notus were working in. He shivered, having sluiced himself in cold sea-water and changed his clothes. The wound on his arm stung from the salt and refused to stop oozing.

'It's in Greek and in code,' answered Notus. 'But my first thought is that it's Caesar's code, a simple transposition. Caesar favoured three places to the right, counting the first letter as all Romans do, so that Alpha became Gamma and so-on. If that proves to be the case then it shouldn't be too difficult to crack.'

'All you have to do, Septem, is to keep Messala away from us while we work,' added Kyros. 'If and when he comes round.'

'And I need to make sure User comes up with a plausible reason for taking his time coming into port,' said Artemidorus, nodding. 'Once we get on dry land, Messala is likely to want to deliver Brutus' message as soon as possible, whether he's fit to go or not. And we know Lucius is keen to go with anyone heading for Cassius' camp.'

He ran up onto *Triton*'s main deck and strode across to User.

'We need to make time before we land,' he said. 'I can keep control over things while we're at sea. But once we dock, Messala will want to get on. If I try to stop him then, he'll know something's up.'

'Tell him we came west in our attempt to help *Arke*,' User suggested. 'That took us away from Ashkelon. It has taken some time to move Messala safely, then free the *corvus*, doing as little damage to Captain Potitus' deck as possible, and raising it into position. It is true that my oar team are largely unwounded, but they have been through a nasty skirmish and are exhausted. We will proceed at a gentle pace until sunset, therefore. Then we will anchor, sacrifice the last of the livestock in thanks to the gods who held their hands over us today and feast to our victory. Then the men will rest. And we will reach Ashkelon tomorrow. Will that do?'

'Admirably,' said Artemidorus. 'I'll go through it if he asks.'

'And you could point out,' User added, 'that if it wasn't for us he would be dead or on his way to the pirates' favourite slave market by now. Where would his urgent message be then?'

Artemidorus turned away. User's argument was unanswerable, his logic unquestionable. They had the rest of the day and tonight to complete their work, and once the ship was at anchor she should ride easily enough for his forgers to do their work perfectly. At long last, having seen to everyone else, the centurion thought it was time to see about himself. The wound on his arm was still seeping, the edges of the cut gaping open. It wasn't deep enough to touch the bone and the arrowhead didn't seem to have severed any arteries. But his arm was stiff and sore.

*

Artemidorus went below, past the rowers, moving to the *pausarius*' easiest drumbeat, too tired to give much life to the song that kept them in rhythm. On down, past the area where Kyros and Notus were working on Brutus' message – ensuring there was no way they could be observed by a casual passer-by. And so he entered Crinas' area. The space was crowded. Two oarsmen had sustained slight wounds – no worse than Artemidorus'. Crinas was patching them up, preparing to send them back on duty. Lucius was there. Not because he was wounded but because his friend was. He knelt beside Messala's still body with a worried look on his face. Crinas glanced up as the centurion entered. 'Head wound,' he said, motioning across at Messala. 'Bathed and cleaned. I have no idea when he'll wake up. There is swelling but no softness. No evidence of a broken skull. That in itself is hopeful.'

Artemidorus nodded wearily, suddenly overcome by fatigue.

'That's a nasty-looking gash on your arm,' continued the physician gently. 'Better let me have a look at it.'

Artemidorus crossed to him with a little difficulty. Sat when the oarsmen left the crowded room. Held out his oozing arm. 'Do you think that drowning is a bad way to die?' he asked.

'I can think of worse,' said Crinas, picking up a jar of unguent that smelt strongly of sage. 'I'd guess the quicker you give into the inevitable the less painful it would be.'

'Look on the bright side,' added Lucius in an apparently genuine attempt to help. 'At least if you sink quickly the sharks won't get you before you die.'

After that, there was silence.

Crinas had spread the salve over Artemidorus' arm and was tying the bandage in place when Lucius spoke again, 'Crinas!'

They both looked over at the young man and saw at once why he had called out.

Messala's eyes were open.

vi

'They took the gold, but General Brutus' dispatches are safe,' said Artemidorus gently. 'We have them secure.'

'Where?' asked Messala, his voice faint 'Where are General Brutus' messages?'

'Just a moment…' Artemidorus went to the area assigned to

Messala and picked up the satchel. Thank the gods he had thought to put the empty tube and seal back in there after they had removed the vital scroll, prompted by Kyros' concerns. Only the closest examination would prove it to be empty. And Messala was in no condition to do more than glance at it, which was all he did before sagging back, exhausted by the effort. 'I'll keep it safe,' promised Artemidorus.

'Where am I?' asked the wounded Tribune.

Artemidorus drew breath to answer. But Kyros interrupted, pushing his head and shoulders into the little room. 'Septem, there is something you should see.'

'You explain, Lucius,' he said as he turned to follow his forger out.

Artemidorus followed Kyros out of Crinas' makeshift hospital, put the satchel with Messala's kit in case he asked for it again, then followed Kyros, his mouth dry and his heart pounding as though he was about to join another battle. There was a thunderous rumbling from the deck above him. The ship's motion changed. The oars were in and the anchor no doubt about to go down for the night.

Notus started speaking quietly as soon as Artemidorus entered the little cabin. 'It was Caesar's code,' he said, 'easy enough to break. Do you want it word for word – it's a bit long-winded – or shall I give you the important bits?'

'The important bits to begin with. We have all night so there isn't too much time pressure as long as we can all stay awake and focused, but I'll be happier when it's all done.'

'Right.' Notus cleared his throat. 'General Brutus says he has sent some of the gold General Cassius requested. Not all of it but enough for Cassius to get his legions across the border. Once in Egypt, they will be able to acquire as much gold as they could ever want, he says. Then Cassius can come back north – either over land or by sea from Alexandria. Bringing Egypt's gold with him. Brutus suggests that the generals can get together at Sardis. It is inland from Smyrna, which has a good port but is also easily accessible from further inland, so it doesn't matter which way he comes. Brutus' latest intelligence suggests Antony is stuck in Brundisium and Octavianus is in Sicily trying to destroy Sextus Pompey's fleet so they have plenty of time to get together and discuss their next move. If Cassius can get the Egyptian gold and put Cleopatra's sister Arsinoe on the throne, so they can be certain that they have a firm friend in Alexandria, then they can combine their armies, dig in at the strongest position they can find – preferably within easy reach of the sea to keep their armies well supplied – and wait for Antony, certain that he will have trouble with supply lines and communications as he moves further and further away from his base in Italy. Especially as Brutus and Cassius will rule the waves with three navies – Ahenobarbus', Murcus' and the Egyptian navy which the grateful Arsinoe will be happy to put under their command.'

'A disturbingly well conceived stratagem,' said Artemidorus. 'And one which, if Cassius moves swiftly enough, will almost certainly succeed. If Cassius acts on these suggestions both Cleopatra and Antony are doomed. Is there anything else?'

'Nothing of the same importance. Brutus passes on the news of his wife Porcia's death in case Cassius hasn't heard. He gives some idea of friends and associates killed or ruined in Antony's proscriptions, as well as listing those, like Messala, who have managed to escape and are coming east to join them. Then there's a list of the towns and cities from whom he has exacted tax revenues, with details of how he did so and how much he managed to get.' Notus looked at his translation of Brutus' dispatch, frowning. Then he asked, 'Captain User had family in Xanthus did he not?'

'He did. They all died when the city was destroyed. All the citizens were either killed by friends and families or committed suicide. No-one survived.'

'Not according to Brutus. He says here that he took a few prisoners in Xanthus, mostly women and children trying to escape the slaughter. He has sent them all to the slave market in Delos together with the captives from the other towns he has sacked. He estimates that their sale will add considerably to the war-chest he is getting together.'

*

'You know User best, Puella,' said Artemidorus moments later. They were standing in the shadow of the tower on *Triton*'s after deck. Near the main mast, the crew were gathered while a goat was sacrificed in thanks to the gods for their victory. The Spartan spy should have been sacrificing to Achilleus, but Olympus, the gods and demi-gods would have to wait. 'I've come to you because neither Ferrata nor Quintus likes or trusts him – even after today. When do you think we should tell him?'

'We must tell him soon!' Her voice was almost lost beneath the merriment down the deck. There was just enough light to see the shock in her face.

'Yes, we must,' he agreed. 'But when? If we tell him now, he's quite capable of turning *Triton* around and heading for Delos at once with all of us still aboard. I know his family is important and the least chance they are still alive needs to be followed up as swiftly as possible – before they are split up and sold on. But the fate of the Republic hangs on us getting our message to Cassius. The fate of Egypt too.'

'Tell him as soon as we dock, then. If you don't trust him to keep his word to you before he goes off to try and save them.'

'That's wise advice...'

'As long as you don't mind making an enemy of him. An enemy for life if he gets to Delos too late.'

Artemidorus nodded. 'That's true,' he said heavily. 'But I have many enemies, Puella, almost all of them more powerful and ruthless than User.'

She gave a sad smile. 'That's true enough,' she agreed.

'So. The moment we dock and get ashore with Messala and the dispatches. I will try and avoid him in the mean-time.'

'And I will tell him in the morning. Stay aboard for a while longer than the rest of you if I have to. It will be better coming from me.'

'Good,' he said. But he knew in his bones that it wasn't good at all.

Puella went forward onto the centre of the main deck where the fire tray blazed and the victory feast was beginning. Artemidorus looked around, glad to find User didn't seem to be present; immediately struck by the sad fact that Furius was not there either. His belly growled at the scent of roasting goat but at the same time he felt sick to his stomach. His body ached with fatigue and his head throbbed almost as painfully as his arm. But his work for the night was only just beginning.

He turned, bone-weary, and went back down to the cramped cabin where Kyros and Notus were waiting to hear what he wanted them to put in the forged dispatch to Cassius, to be delivered to the General and *Libertore* some time tomorrow. On the way, he visited Crinas' area. Messala seemed to be improving, which was a bad thing, though he was still complaining of a serious headache. 'I need my dispatch case,' he said, his voice a little slurred still. 'I don't want it disappearing like the gold.'

When Artemidorus returned with it, he met the physician's gaze. 'Perhaps a medicinal draught would ease the Tribune's pain,' he said. 'And help him sleep'

Crinas nodded once.

When he returned a little later, Messala was in a deep sleep. He eased the leather dispatch case out from his grasp and carried it to the door. 'I'll be sure to put it back before he wakes,' he said as he left.

XVI: Cassius

i

'Ride?' snarled Messala. 'Of course I can ride. It was my head that was wounded not my fornicating legs!'

In the pale light of an overcast morning, it was all too obvious his head was wounded. Crinas' thickly cushioned, carefully applied bandage largely lay on the dockside at the irate Tribune's feet so that he could jam his helmet in place. He had laboriously put on his best tunic, full armour and *specualtore*'s shoulder-bag before staggering ashore. He was standing firmly now, though he checked in the leather satchel every few moments to make sure that Brutus' crucial dispatch was still there.

Messala had walked down the gangplank and made it here from the securely-docked ship with only an occasional a stagger. But his face was pale, almost the colour of lead.

'We'll probably need to get a tumbrel for your baggage and effects,' persisted Artemidorus. 'If you feel dizzy – as Crinas warns you will – you can always sit in that.'

'No! I will ride. I will carry General Brutus' dispatches and hand them to General Cassius in person, as General Brutus ordered.' He checked in the satchel yet again.

'Very well, Tribune…' Artemidorus was about to add *on your own head be it* but thought better of that at the last moment.

He looked at Ashkelon's dockside. *Triton* was moored amongst half a dozen similar vessels, though she was the only one with a fighting tower and a *corvus*. User's crew were bringing the last of Lucius' and Messala's effects ashore. It was time to get going, he thought. The best thing to do with fear is to face it.

Quintus and Ferrata came down the gang-plank, side by side. As they approached, Artemidorus said, 'We'll need five horses and a tumbrel.' He unhooked his purse from his belt and tossed it to Quintus. 'I'll want you two to accompany me. The others can wait aboard until we return.'

'If we do,' said Ferrata, *sotto voce*.

The two legionaries vanished up the hill towards the centre of town. Messala abruptly collapsed onto a pile of boxes and travelling chests that made a convenient seat. The leather case jammed uncomfortably under his arm. He checked in it once again.

Artemidorus crossed the quay to the foot of *Triton*'s gangplank and looked up it. Kyros and Notus would be sound asleep after their long night of forgery. Hunefer was up and about, his massive form unmistakable on top of the fighting tower, with Hercules only slightly smaller by his side. Messala had left Crinas tidying his makeshift hospital in a huff, the Tribune having told him that the bandages would come off as soon as he reached dry land and put his helmet on. Furius was lying at the bottom of the sea out there beyond the harbour, his spirit, hopefully, running through the Elysian Fields.

And, somewhere deep in the heart of the ship, Puella was explaining to User what Brutus' message had revealed about his plans for the captives from Xanthus. And what he, Artemidorus, had chosen to do with that vital information.

'Here we are, Septem,' called Ferrata. 'Five fine horses and a lad with a tumbrel pulled by a mule. And you even have some change.'

*

They rode in two lines, Messala in front with Lucius on one side and Artemidorus on the other, as close as they dared – risking their knees in case Messala toppled sideways. Behind them, Quintus and Ferrata, side by side. The spy felt almost as faint as the courier. He had been up all night after the stress of yesterday's battle and the shock of losing Furius; the strain of undertaking the riskiest part of the most dangerous mission of his life. As he rode in brooding silence, he mentally rehearsed the conversations he would have with Cassius if things went wrong.

The General was no fool. Even if Kyros' and Notus' work was as perfect as it seemed, there might be some element of the carefully crafted message that would give the game away. And even if Cassius took the message and its contents at face value, he might still recognize Artemidorus as Antony's man. During the terrible days immediately after the Ides of March two years ago, Artemidorus had been the vital link between Antony, Cassius, Brutus and Cicero. Disguised of course, but Cassius wasn't blind – he could see through disguises…

But wait. Although he wasn't actually blind, Cassius did have notoriously bad eyesight. Bad and getting worse as he aged. Perhaps he wouldn't recognise Artemidorus after all.

But, even if Cassius accepted the story that Artemidorus had become involved simply because he had rescued first Lucius from Cleopatra and then Messala from pirates, wouldn't the unrivalled ruler of this part of the Roman Republic simply assign such a useful soldier to some duties in his own command? What if, instead of handing him over to his torturers for questioning and crucifixion, Cassius simply appointed Artemidorus to his staff?

Either way, Artemidorus, Quintus and Ferrata, it seemed, would be extremely lucky to get out of Cassius' camp – alive or dead.

Perhaps he had made a fatal mistake in coming.

And yet he simply had to see that the message was handed over in person. To support – physically if necessary – the wounded messenger and ensure he got to Cassius safely. Then he had to judge its effect on the general, his thinking and his actions. Both of which he had to report to Cleopatra and Antony. With the certainty of someone who had seen it for himself. The fate of the Republic hung on that careful forgery and Cassius' reaction to it. Even at the risk of his life – leaving aside how he was likely to die – he had to be there to witness it himself.

ii

The gate into Cassius' camp, the towers on either side and the wall it pierced were all much taller than Artemidorus remembered, which struck him as odd, for he had last seen them from the bottom of the ditch. The sound of the horses' hooves rang hollow as they trotted over the bridge and into the camp. The guards in the towers and on the ground looked at them, but Messala held up his courier's satchel which worked as a very efficient pass. The little group kicked their horses from their trot up to a canter.

'Rushing towards our *fatum* doom,' said Ferrata.

'You're a bundle of laughs this morning,' said Quintus. 'Our own little Plautus!'

Ferrata merely grunted in reply and looked apprehensively around, his one eye narrow with suspicion. But all there was to see were several thousand legionaries having breakfast of which bread and vinegar water.

All too quickly, they reached the camp's forum, the open space in front of the big command tent that was backed by the General's more modest private quarters and abutted by the two secure tents containing the legions' eagles and whatever gold Cassius still had left. The westerly wind made the legionary banners standing proudly around it flap and crack. The tent-flaps stirred over the entrance, between two guards, fully armoured, hands on *gladii* grips and fists clutching *pilae*. They were almost as big as Hunefer and Hercules.

The five men and the boy on the tumbrel reined to a stand-still. 'I bring dispatches from General Brutus under his seal to General Cassius,' said Messala, his voice carrying over the soft bluster of the wind and the more distant noise of the camp itself.

There was the briefest of silences, then the tent flap was pushed back. Cassius himself stepped out into the forum. He glanced up at Messala, nodded and clapped his hands. At once legionary slaves and grooms appeared. The horses' heads were held. Mounting stools placed. Messala and his companions climbed down, then Quintus and Ferrata. 'Come in,' said General Cassius.

As soon as Artemidorus got into the tent, concern set in. Gathered round a briefing table were five more of *Divus Julius'* murderers. Men to whom he had carried Antony's messages while *Divus Julius'* corpse was still warm in the Curia of Pompey's Theatre. Men whom he had seen – and who had seen him – in the Temple of Jupiter Optimus Maximus on top of the Capitoline in Rome when he accompanied Cicero.

Had the secret agent been less preoccupied, he would have already worked out that Cassius' brother Lucius Longinus would be there. But besides him there were the brothers Caecilius and Bucolianus. Gaius Cassius Parmensis was there too, as well as Decimus Turullius. Any or all of whom might recognise him.

As well as the Romans there were other men obviously from other countries judging by their costume, rich and powerful judging by their dress: Parthian, perhaps; and Judean? Two older, lean Parthians in rich but travel-stained clothing and a striking young man in the robes of a Judean prince. Artemidorus could guess their standing and origins but he had no idea who they were. Any more than they knew who he was, unlike the rest of the men at Cassius' table. He stood to attention at Messala's right shoulder as Lucius was standing at his left. Not quite holding him up, praying to Achilleus for a little good fortune here.

But then the prayers and the concern became irrelevant. 'I know you, Messala, and you Lucius,' said Cassius. 'And at least one of your companions is familiar, but I cannot call his name to mind…'

'That is Iacomus Graecas Artemidorus,' volunteered Lucius without a second thought. '*Primus Pilus* senior centurion of the old VIIth. He was Mark Antony's messenger to Cleopatra. The other two are his companions.'

'Really?' Cassius' hooded brown eyes rested on Artemidorus like the touch of death. 'Antony's man – and yet he dares to come here?'

*

'Well, it's a bit more complicated than that,' blabbered Lucius as Messala swayed gently, silently, fighting to stay erect. 'You see, General, I was General Brutus' courier to Queen Cleopatra, and when she read the letter he had sent her she was so enraged by it that she had me arrested, beaten and thrown in the dungeon. Artemidorus rescued me and helped me escape from Alexandria by hiring a boat and crew – and a second vessel to protect us from pursuit. But when we came across the ship bringing your message from Brutus, as carried by the Tribune Messala here, the second ship turned pirate, attacked the messenger ship, stole the gold aboard and would have slaughtered everybody except that Artemidorus managed to fight them off, rescuing Messala into the bargain!'

'Really!' purred Cassius. The purr of a hungry tiger. 'And why would he do all this?

'He had already helped Messala and me escape proscription then smuggled us out of Rome and across to Dyrrhachium!'

'Remarkable. Centurion Artemidorus, you do seem to be particularly well-disposed to the friends and relatives of your commander's mortal enemies!'

Artemidorus drew himself up. He felt Quintus and Ferrata doing the same. 'I was given direct orders in the matter by Caesar Octavianus himself, General. All I have done is to apply those orders consistently to a series of rapidly-changing situations.'

'Most impressive! Heroism almost worthy of Horatius Cocles himself. Who, I note, so famously kept the bridge with two like-minded companions just like the two you have brought with you today! Guards! Take these three men to the secure tent. Put them in chains. I will tell you how to deal with them later.'

iii

'That went well,' said Ferrata, rattling his chains. 'That bastard Cassius will have the torturers go to work on us next.'

'Maybe,' Artemidorus shrugged, before continuing in a hushed voice. 'Even so, it will have been worth it if he believes what we put in the dispatch has come directly from Brutus.'

'It certainly looked real enough. It fooled Messala with no trouble,' said Quintus.

'Well, let's hope it fools Cassius as well. Then our job is done.'

'How's that, lad?' asked Quintus.

'The new message contains two crucial sections that are almost true – but not quite, changed just enough to make all the difference, if the gods smile on us.'

'For instance?' demanded Ferrata grumpily.

'Take Egypt. The original suggested the gold Messala was bringing would finance an expedition over the border to invade the country and replace Cleopatra with her sister Arsinoe. Plunder Cleopatra's gold and commandeer her navy. This new one suggests the gold might be enough to get him over the border but the situation in Egypt is very risky and the whole adventure might turn out to be a dangerous distraction. He'd be better coming back for a conference as soon as he can. Brutus had already suggested Sardis as a good place to meet so we left that in.'

'A suggestion likely to be strengthened by the fact that there isn't any gold any more,' said Ferrata approvingly.

Quintus nodded. 'And Sardis is far away from here. Marching there will keep Cassius occupied for months.'

'That's the plan,' said Artemidorus.

'Good. So with any luck Egypt and Cleopatra are safe for the time-being,' said Quintus. 'Safe from Cassius at least. What else?'

'Antony and the reason for the meeting in Sardis. Brutus' original message letter says Antony's stuck. The same as we were in Brundisium. He's hardly bringing any troops over to Dyrrhachium. The new one says he's already sent two armies, one with General Norbanus and the other with General Saxa. Which is true – but neither Brutus nor Cassius can do anything about it at present. Then it says that Antony's ready to send more legions to guard the Via Egnatia and strengthen the route for his invasion with his full army and Octavianus' army as well – the better part of twenty legions in all. The invasion will happen as soon as Octavianus has defeated Sextus Pompey – which rumour suggests will be soon. Brutus and Cassius need to get together at Sardis as soon as possible to plan how to meet this imminent threat. And Cassius needs to send word to his Admirals Ahenobarbus and Murcus to get up to Brundisium and blockade the port at once.'

'Clearing the way for Cleopatra to move her fleet out in time to help Antony when he does, in fact, want to move,' said Ferrata. 'That's very neat.'

'And with a little smile from Fortuna it will all work whether we're alive to see it or not,' said Artemidorus.

*

He had no sooner stopped speaking than there was a bustle of movement outside the prison tent. 'I have the general's permission to speak to the prisoners,' said Lucius, his tone one of arrogant command.

A moment later, the flap opened and the young Tribune ducked into the tent. He was not alone. The young stranger in the robes of a Judean prince was with him. 'This is Herod Prince of Galilee, son of Antipater the Idumaean,' said Lucius.

Artemidorus looked at Herod unquestioningly, too exhausted to wonder why Lucius had brought him; or, indeed, why either man was here. The Prince of Galilee was a strikingly good-looking man. He was maybe thirty years old but he looked younger. He had wide brown eyes that seemed to flash. His beard and moustache were jet-black, oiled and curling, matching precisely the curls escaping from his headdress. No sooner had he entered than the tent filled with the scents of myrrh and sandalwood, reminding Artemidorus most forcibly of Cleopatra.

'I feel a little guilty,' said Lucius. 'You're really here because of me.'

'That's bloody true,' mumbled Ferrata, then disguised his words with a cough.

'No, Tribune,' answered Artemidorus. 'We are here through my fault and no-one else's.'

'Oh,' said the young man, clearly glad to shuffle responsibility. 'Right. General Cassius has sent me to tell you he plans to question you further, once he has read General Brutus' letters and discussed them with his senior staff.'

'Oh we'll look forward to that,' said Ferrata. 'Will there be wine and dancing girls?'

Artemidorus transferred his gaze to Herod. Raised an interrogative eyebrow which was about as close as he could get to asking why the prince was here.

But then Herod started to speak in beautifully modulated, accented and extremely formal Greek. 'If you were released from here,' he asked, 'whither would you go?'

Artemidorus saw no point in lying. 'To Alexandria, Highness,' he said. 'And then to Rome.'

'To see whom?'

'Queen Cleopatra and then Mark Antony.'

'You have the ears of the Queen and the Triumvir?'

'I have done some service to both in the past. Which, in all honesty, *dominus*, makes it highly unlikely that General Cassius will release us. Not alive at any rate.'

'Stranger things have been known,' said Herod. 'Stranger things.' He paused. 'Perhaps the One True God will smile upon you, unbeliever.'

The two men backed out of the tent.

'That was uplifting,' said Ferrata. 'It would have been even better if they'd brought something to eat.'

'Strange,' said Quintus. 'What was that all about?'

'Herod,' said Artemidorus. 'Prince Herod wanted to see us for some reason.'

'Perhaps to assure us that the One True God of the Judeans was going to look after us,' said Ferrata. 'As well as Achilleus, Jupiter and Venus Victrix.'

They fell silent. Time passed. The bustle of the camp around them seemed to intensify. Artemidorus strained to hear any individual sounds which might explain what was going on. Shouted orders. The sound of tents being pulled down. The creak of wagons being loaded. Legionaries gathering their equipment together and loading up for the march.

'You think they're breaking camp?' said Ferrata.

'They were always going to break camp,' answered Artemidorus. 'The question is, which way they'll go when they've done it: west into Egypt or north towards Sardis.'

No sooner had he finished speaking than the tent-flap was pulled back again and the two enormous legionaries who had been guarding the entrance to Cassius' command tent squeezed in. 'Right,' said the largest. 'On your feet and come with us. The General wants a word with you three. While you're still in a fit state to talk'

iv

This time Cassius was alone in the command tent. The three spies were bundled in all together, each individually chained, wrist to ankle, ankle to ankle. They couldn't straighten. They could only hobble, which, on the way here, had given them ample opportunity to look around. Artemidorus was right – Cassius was breaking camp. He just hoped he wasn't also right about the torturers and the crucifixion.

'My natural inclination,' said Cassius, 'is to have the three of you skinned alive, then crucified, a favourite punishment of my old commander Gaius Licinius Crassus. Remember the crosses all along the Appian Way after he defeated Spartacus? *Mile* after *mile*; both sides of the *via*.'

There was a brief silence, under which the bustle of the breaking camp continued.

'But, much against my better nature, I have been talked out of it. The collective wisdom of my senior commanders – and of the Prince of Galilee as a matter of fact – is that you represent a useful asset. I am assured that if you are released, you will return to Alexandria at once, and then to Rome.'

'Yes, General,' said Artemidorus.

'And that you have the ear of Queen Cleopatra herself. That the Divine Isis deigns to talk to a mere mortal Centurion such as yourself.'

'True, General.'

'That you can talk to Antony man-to-man almost as equals, I already know. And I have been convinced that someone who is capable of such things is too valuable simply to discard. I propose to give you two messages, therefore, one to be delivered into the hands of Queen Cleopatra and the other into the hands of Antony. In person. The one to Cleopatra warns her that any support she gives to Antony – in whatever way, shape or form – will bring about the certain destruction of her kingdom and her dynasty. Herself, I would like to emphasise, and her bastard son they call Ptolemy Caesarion. The one to Antony warns him that my navies are on the way to blockade Brundisium and he would be best advised to stay at home in Italy and give up all pretentions towards conquering the east. If he comes against us, we will cut his supply lines and his communications and we will annihilate him. He had much better stay where he is and spend the rest of his life in his favourite pursuits – fornication, gluttony and drunkenness.' Cassius leaned forward, elbow on the table, finger pointing at Artemidorus. 'I'm telling you the contents of the messages to save you the trouble of opening them and reading them before you deliver them. I am only grateful that General Brutus' message stayed with Tribune Messala at all times, well away from your prying eyes. Though, daring to open their messages, of course, is very likely to ruin your unusual relationships both with the queen and the general. Guards!'

The two huge guards appeared.

'Take their chains off. Let them use the latrines and eat. Stay with them at all times. I will send a message when I want them returned.'

'Fuck,' said Ferrata feelingly a few moments later as the guards led them through the camp towards the latrines. 'I think I'll consider turning Jewish like young Herod. Their One True God seems to have got us out of a really nasty scrape there!'

*

'I asked the general if I could call you to his tent,' said Herod, leading them slowly from the Centurions' refectory where they had just eaten, towards Cassius' command tent which were almost the last two tents still standing. 'He is suspicious of my motives – as he is of yours – but nevertheless he allowed me to come. I think he is simply too busy to deal with all of us in the way that he would like.'

'He learned not to be swayed by others the hard way on the Ides,' said Artemidorus. 'If he hadn't listened to Brutus none of us would be here. Both Fortuna and Achilleus have held their hands over us today.'

'The Lord moves in mysterious ways,' said Herod, with a nod of his head.

'Why did you want to talk to us? Indeed, Highness, why did you involve yourself in our case at all?'

'Septem! They do call you Septem do they not?'

'Among other things, *dominus*.'

'Surely a man of your reputation can work out at least a part of my situation.'

'I would guess that you have found some way to profit from Cassius' presence here...'

'Judea is my land after all. Galilee in the north is my princedom and my brother Phasel is prince of Jerusalem.'

'So I would assume that General Cassius paid you a certain amount on his march southward. To recompense any costs or damages caused by his troops. He would not want disgruntled princes waiting at his back and plotting revenge.'

'Indeed. Just so.'

'And I assume that he had promised considerable payment, should he march north and cross your princedoms once again. But he has little ready money left and the loss of Brutus' gold means that your promised income is unlikely to appear. Particularly unfortunate, as you will once again be forced to bear the great expense of having his legions marching across your land.'

'Your reputation does you less than justice, it appears. Right in every regard.'

'So far. But I think there may be more. I saw Parthians in Cassius' tent. Parthians are no friends of Rome's, especially after Carrhae and indeed particularly no friends of Cassius who was lucky to escape them after the battle. So these Parthians were unlikely to be diplomats. Traders, therefore. Offering something Cassius thinks he might need. And what does Parthia have that everyone wants at the moment? Grain. Had Cassius been serious about invading Egypt, he would have needed a good supply of grain because there is almost none left there. And, of course, to get grain shipments from Parthia to Egypt easily and swiftly – avoiding the long route via the mountainous deserts of the Sinai and the Land of Punt – the shipments might well come through Judea, across your lands. At a price.'

'You see the situation so clearly.'

'But as Cassius is turning north – and is lacking gold in any case – you and your Parthian partners must seek another market. And there is one place tantalisingly nearby where there are mountains of gold and hardly any grain at all. You wish me to be your ambassador to Queen Cleopatra as well as General Cassius' courier.'

'The fact that you have understood the situation with so much insight, Septem, means that you are uniquely qualified for the task.

V

Artemidorus found it disturbingly ironic that he was wearing Messala's dispatch case as he and his companions rode out of Cassius' camp, followed by the boy driving the donkey-powered tumbrel with Lucius and Messala's horses tied behind it. The two tribunes would be moving with Cassius and his legions. The spy was tempted to do what the Tribune had done and check every mile or so to make sure Cassius' two lean dispatches, and Herod's rather fatter one, were still safely there. Normally, he would have summoned a wry smile at such foolishness. But not now. His whole body ached for sleep. The physical, mental and emotional fatigue of battle, loss, sleeplessness and almost fatal risk of life was beginning to take its toll. Having survived it all seemed utterly exhausting.

'Sit up, lad, it won't be long 'til we're back,' said Quintus from close to his right shoulder. 'We'll be at Ashkelon soon enough. Then you can sleep all you want.'

'With Puella to keep you warm,' added Ferrata, close to his left.

Artemidorus realised that they were riding so close to him in case it was his turn to topple from his mount. He urged his horse into a trot and then into a canter, burning to get back to *Triton* and a warm bed – whether Puella was in it or not.

Then he realised that underneath his weariness, a kind of elation was building. He had pulled off something amazing. Cassius was on the point of marching north to meet Brutus at Sardis. Egypt had been saved from invasion. In spite of the dire warning from Cassius he carried in his dispatch pouch, Cleopatra was safe for the time-being, at least. Safe with time – and room – to build the navy Antony was asking for – to build it and send it to guard his supply lines. So Antony's plans would be furthered as well. With Cleopatra's navy to protect him he could move from Brundisium to Dyrrhachium whenever the winds permitted. And, if Cleopatra's Egyptian admiral could overcome Cassius' admirals, then she could reverse the situation and blockade any ports Brutus and Cassius were hoping to ship supplies through. Not only that, but if Herod was as good as his word and his Parthian merchants came through with the promised grain, Egypt's famine would soon be at an end. Then it only needed the Nile to inundate and all would be well again. Better than that – Brutus' and Cassius' abrupt and arrogant communications would ensure that Cleopatra would support Antony at whatever cost.

'That's better, lad,' said Quintus approvingly and Artemidorus realised he was sitting straight in the saddle, buoyed up by elation. And, to be fair, by the amazing fact that he had come safely through a situation that he had thought more than once would end in a protracted and agonising death.

Sitting tall in the saddle, therefore, with his companions on either side, Artemidorus rode into Ashkelon and down to the docks where *Triton* and a good sleep awaited.

Except that she didn't.

The three legionaries reined to a stop on the quayside. All the ships from this morning were still in place, but *Triton* was gone. Artemidorus looked around in simple disbelief. Three familiar figures detached themselves from the bustle of the dockside. Kyros, Notus and Crinas came towards them. Artemidorus swung himself round and slid off his horse. 'What's going on?' he demanded. 'Where's *Triton*?'

'Gone,' said Crinas gently. 'When Puella told User about Brutus selling survivors from Xanthus at the slave market in Delos, he put us all ashore...'

'With all our possessions and yours as well,' added Kyros. 'Everything we brought from Rome and still had with us it's all here at the *taberna* we found.'

'Right...' Artemidorus' mind was trying to weigh the alternatives presented by this unexpected news, which, he realised, he should have expected in any case, like the presence of Cassius' brother in his camp. But it was like trying to run through deep water. His mind just would not work fast enough. 'So we're all here,' he said. 'With all of our *impedimenta* kit. And User has gone with *Triton*. To look for his family in Delos.'

Notus and Kyros exchanged a glance. 'Well, not all of us,' said Crinas. 'We're not *all* here.'

'Not Furius. Yes I know. But do we have his stuff? Did User send it off as well? I'll return it to his family if I can...'

'We didn't mean Furius,' said Kyros.

'We meant Puella,' said Crinas. 'Puella stayed on *Triton* with User. She's gone with him.'

*

Artemidorus was drunk. He was by no means alone in this. The remainder of his *contubernium* were gathered around him in various states of inebriation. Only Crinas was sober. They were packed round a table in the rearmost corner of Ashkelon's foremost *taberna*, where they planned to spend the night. Everything unloaded from *Triton* was in various rooms upstairs – including what was left of Antony's gold, easily enough to pay for their accommodation tonight and passage to Alexandria tomorrow.

In the mean-time, the spy was receiving a range of sympathy and advice, most of which was utterly useless.

'Fair enough you've lost her,' said Quintus. 'But the point is you had her to lose in the first place. One of the most beautiful women in the Republic and she was yours.'

'Like that bitch Cyanea,' added Kyros, 'stunningly beautiful, madly in love with you, but treacherous in the end. Giving all our secrets to Minucius Basilus and the conspirators; if she hadn't betrayed us *Divus Julius* would still be alive.'

'Mind you,' added Hercules, who was growing maudlin, 'throwing her naked to a rioting mob was maybe taking revenge a little far. Especially as she escaped.'

'And she's still out there somewhere,' added Kyros shivering, 'with the money she stole from Basilus and Trebonius – both of whom met the most horrific ends I can imagine – plotting her revenge on you...' he shivered again and glanced around as though Cyanea, the human Fury, was somewhere close behind him.

'Fuck,' said Ferrata. 'All this looking back and weeping over spilt wine is a waste of time. You just have to get Puella out of your system. What you need to do is this. When we get to Alexandria and after we've reported to Cleopatra, go down to the slave market there. Find a girl who reminds you of Puella. Buy her. Screw her brains out then beat the shit out of her. Beat her to death if you like – she's only a possession after all. It would be as if you smashed this cup in your rage. Then you'll be over her, back on form and ready to move on. None of this Achilleus shit, though. No sulking in your tent because your girl's gone off with someone else.'

'And anyway, just think,' said Crinas reasonably. 'What if User finds his family on Delos? What's he going to do? Take two wives? A wife and a mistress? I don't know her as well as the rest of you, but it seems to me that Puella would never put up with a situation like that. If User finds his family, Puella will probably come looking for you.'

'I'd never take her back, though!' snarled Artemidorus. 'Never!'

'Decide that at the time, Septem,' suggested the physician gently.

'Besides, how in Jupiter's name would she find me?'

'That's the easy part,' said Crinas. 'All she has to do is find Mark Antony, and that's the simplest thing in the world. Everyone always seems to know where Antony is. And even if you're not there with him, Antony will know where you are.'

'That's true,' said Quintus. 'Wherever the hell you are, the chances are Antony or Tribune Enobarbus will have sent you there in the first place.'

XVII: Hecate

i

Artemidorus looked at the woman with utter astonishment. A wave of almost uncontrollable anger swept over him. He had supposed Ferrata to have forgotten his plan to remove Puella from his thoughts long ago. But apparently not. He had bought and brought a slave to be raped and beaten to death – but at the moment it was Ferrata he wished to beat rather than the woman.

She stood inside the door of his private chamber in Cleopatra's island palace, and the one-eyed legionary stood close behind her. Artemidorus slowly rose from his seat at the work desk, which was piled with papyrus scrolls on which he had been recording the numbers and types of vessels in Cleopatra's burgeoning navy. He turned, to get a better look at his two unexpected visitors, shaking with rage.

Ferrata wore an expression of pride. The woman stood with downcast eyes clothed in little more than a rough woven sack. Artemidorus fought to calm himself, aware the gesture was meant in friendship and arose out of concern for his short temper and dark mood, both of which had worsened during the weeks since their return. He was self-aware enough to see that he felt betrayed, alone, trapped by Cleopatra's decision that he should wait until her fleet was ready before returning to Rome and Antony. A decision rendered unanswerable by the information brought in by her spy ships.

'Yes, Admiral Ahenobarbus has moved northward with the majority of Cassius' navy,' she explained softly, feeling his frustration and speaking a friend rather than queen or goddess. 'But Cassius is no fool. He has ordered Admiral Murcus to wait with a fleet of more than fifty triremes and quadriremes. There seems to be an entire legion aboard. And they are all waiting to face us when we sail north and slow us if he cannot stop us. I am informed they are anchored off Cape Taenarum the southernmost point of Greece, waiting for anyone heading into the waters separating Italy and Macedonia.'

At least he won't have stopped User and Puella getting to Delos, he thought, as Cleopatra continued with her briefing. He's too far west and north. Halys will have escaped with Brutus' gold as well. Neither thought gave him any pleasure or relief from his sense of anger and betrayal. Nothing did, in fact.

*

'She's nothing like Puella, Ferrata.' For a start, he thought bitterly, her skin was far darker – darker even than User's. The only slaves he had seen as dark-skinned as this were those he had glimpsed following the camel trains of the traders who crossed the Great Sand Sea and brought goods from afar.

'Beautiful ones are expensive,' Ferrata was in no way abashed. 'Especially the black-skinned ones.'

'So you got this woman at reduced price?' the outrage surged again, bringing beads of perspiration to his upper lip.

Ferrata's expression became sheepish. 'Well if you were going to do what we discussed it seemed pointless buying an expensive one.'

'What is your name?' he asked the slave in Greek. When there was no reply he tried again in Latin. She remained silent, apparently not understanding either language, or, perhaps, frightened by the snarl beneath his words.

'In the market they called her *Magissa*, *Striga*, Witch,' said Ferrata helpfully.

Artemidorus smothered a sigh of frustration. 'Is that why she was cheap? Because she's a witch? Did anyone at the Agora explain?'

'She may have murdered her last master.' Ferrata shrugged as though the accusation meant nothing.

'Really! And she's still alive?' The rage and frustration eased under the weight of surprise.

Artemidorus studied her face, looking for signs of murderous evil. Her hair was short and tightly curled. Her forehead broad, her brows delicate. Her eyes, currently downcast, were slightly protuberant but large and fringed with extravagant lashes. Her cheekbones were sharp, leading back to neat ears that sat tight to her head. Her nose was straight, her nostrils broad. Her lips were full but defined and pushed forward in a way that made him think that her teeth would be large and angled slightly outward. Her chin was determined. Dimpled. Her neck long, making the spy think of the herons that flocked to the delta.

'And the dead master?' he enquired more calmly.

'Some Roman patrician,' answered Ferrata dismissively. 'Set up home here because of the fleshpots and gambling dens out in Canopus City apparently. Wanted more excitement than even Rome could offer...'

'Did *he* at least have a name?'

'Titus Volumnius Elva by all accounts.'

'I see. But the woman appears not to have a name.'

'Like I told you, Septem, *Striga*. Or *Magissa* if you want to stick with Greek.'

'*Striga*,' he said quietly in Latin, fixing the woman with an intense stare as he addressed her. The snarl of anger was gone from his tone now, but it was still abrupt. 'I cannot call you Witch, even if others do. Shall we settle for the meantime on the Goddess of magic? Would you prefer *Trivia* or *Hecate*?' She glanced up, with no sign of understanding on her face and met his gaze. Her dark brown eyes were flecked with gold, like those of a hawk. She hooded them again.

'She was spared execution and sold on the insistence of her dead owner's widow and his son – who inherit everything, apparently, and that adds to a considerable fortune even after all Titus Elva senior's years of gambling and whoring,' Ferrata was explaining. 'Anyway, it's only a rumour – nothing certain. And she's not so bad to look at either.' Ferrata unloosened the knots at the shoulders of the shapeless bag of material the woman was wearing, and it slid to the ground.

ii

She had been depilated and oiled ready for sale, the shine on her skin helping to define her body, which was in some ways the opposite of Puella's. Where his lost lover had been lithe, with the powerful muscularity of a black panther, this woman was square and solid, more like a bear from the Germanian forests in the far north. Broad shoulders led to strong, sinewy arms that ended in big square hands. The long neck led to a flat chest – her breasts mere extensions of her pectoral muscles. The aureolae large and dark, the nipples pointed. Her stomach was flat with not a sign of fat between skin and muscle. The nakedness of her belly showed that she had been circumcised, which the Greek spy found disturbingly shocking. He knew that Egyptian and Jewish boys were circumcised – and had heard rumours of the practice being inflicted on some Egyptian girls. But he had never come across a woman who had been maimed in this way before. Below the mutilated genitals were solid, muscular legs that would have done credit to a gladiator; a *cestus*-armed *pugil* boxer perhaps. Broad feet planted solidly, a little apart, as though she was about to start a fight to the death.

Seeing where his friend's gaze was directed, Ferrata span the silent woman round. Artemidorus clenched his teeth. The skin of her back was in many ways also a terrible counterpart for her wounded genitalia. It was ridged with the scars of whip-lashes that reached from the nape of her neck down past the dimples above her buttocks, many of them old but some new. And there was the mark of a recent brand, which suggested that the woman had been subject to something like the Roman legal system looking into the death of her late master – where slaves had to be tortured before they gave evidence. But that did not explain the older whip-marks.

Either this woman was dreadfully disobedient, self-destructively prone to running away, or her master Titus Volumnius Elva derived gratification from inflicting pain on others. He had known several men like this. Notably, the utterly depraved Minucius Basilus who had finally gone too far with his mutilations and been chopped to pieces by his slaves. But not before he had made Artemidorus' previous lover Cyanea reveal the details of their plot to counter the plans of Brutus and Cassius and to keep *Divus Julius* alive on the Ides. All in all, she aroused neither desire nor thirst for revenge in him. And yet, courtesy of Ferrata, she was his. Body and spirit.

'You may dress,' he said in Latin. She stooped to obey then froze. Her hawk's eyes flashed again. She was angry at herself for showing that she understood him. Interesting, he thought. In the absence of anything sexual, there might still be something here after all – a game of wits, the taming of a wild and abused creature – like Alexander with his great steed Bucephalus.

*

So Ferrata's gesture had an immediate effect – but not in the way the legionary had intended. For the last few weeks Artemidorus had divided his time between his chamber where his scrolls were and the Royal Dockyards where the subjects of his lists were being assembled, adapted or built from the keel up. Not that many of the great ships had a keel at all.

Having delivered Cassius' and Herod's messages to Cleopatra, and received her orders in turn, he avoided the court – as far as was possible in a palace. The only time he went into the city was to visit User's brother and tell him what had happened in Ashkelon. Hardly surprisingly, there was no word of or from User or Puella. But User's brother promised to pass on any news he got as soon as he could. Artemidorus returned to his bitter isolation in the island palace.

Cleopatra made it easier for him to avoid the distracting bustle of the court by moving back to her palace on the mainland – where she had easy access to the academics in the Musaeum and the Library, who were put to work designing the great vessels that the shipwrights ended up building. The island palace was more convenient to the docks so that was where Artemidorus and his *contubernium* remained. The centurion more and more isolated and bitter as time passed, the *contubernium* bored, inactive, waiting only for orders.

But the arrival of the woman began a series of changes. Like a new parent with a baby, Artemidorus found she filled his time – and thoughts – more than he could have expected. Right from the start, he tried to think of a name for her. Though *Striga* lingered in his memory he settled on Hecate, the goddess of witchcraft.

He was lucky in that Cleopatra often sent him messages or demanded updates and her messengers tended to be either Hunefer or Charmian. Hunefer had been reinstated, promoted, and rewarded for his services with a new suit of parade armour made from the toughened hide of a black Nile crocodile, which not only looked spectacular but was surprisingly robust. Even Quintus was a little jealous.

The day Ferrata gave him Hecate, however, the messenger was Charmian, and after they had looked over his records and decided which should be taken to the Queen, he also handed over his taciturn slave, asking that she be fed, bathed and clothed. And so he learned that even here the slave who – rumour had it – murdered the abusive Titus Elva with untraceable poisons at the request of his brutalised wife and bullied son, had something of a reputation.

'You should lock her up at night,' said Charmian as she returned the silent woman washed, fed and dressed – uneasily, almost uncomfortably – in a range of sensuous cloths and colours that would have eclipsed a peacock's tail. 'The gods know what she might do to you as you sleep.'

'We'll see,' he said.

iii

He kept her with him from that moment on. Although the attire of one of Cleopatra's handmaidens did nothing to disguise the muscularity of her square body, it seemed to gain her automatic acceptance wherever she went – as Artemidorus discovered at once. They went down the palace steps to the island's quayside together. She seemed to lose nothing of her firm stance even when she stepped into the skiff that would take them through the Royal Harbour to the Dockyards. The warm breeze of an Alexandrian spring day moulded the diaphanous silks and cottons she was wearing to her, leaving almost nothing to the imagination. Even so, none of the oarsmen gave her a second glance.

She went ashore with him and watched as Cleopatra's shipwrights continued building her ships. It was something she seemed to find fascinating. Like a parent amusing a recalcitrant child, he took her to see the largest hull of all. The flagship, a *deceres,* was designed to have ten banks of 100 rowers wielding six banks of oars on each side. 'The Queen has decreed that she will be called *Alexandros,*' he explained, following the Cilician tradition of giving ships feminine characteristics. 'Not only because she has been built in Alexander's city but because the name "Alexandros" means defender of the people. And that is what she is designed to do. Though I think her prime function will be to defend Antony's supply-lines rather than the people of Alexandria.'

The silent woman's falcon eyes widened at the spectacle of the great ship taking shape and she began to show signs of listening to Artemidorus, as he explained. His first move in this game of trust seemed to be working.

Keelan, the chief shipwright, came over – as he usually did when Artemidorus visited. He was a tall, austere man who habitually wore an expression of superior disdain, like many of his colleagues who divided their time between the Musaeum and the real world. But, the Roman soldier was the divine queen's representative after all. He treated the man and his companion with courtly courtesy, therefore.

'How much longer until *Alexandros* is ready?' Artemidorus asked.

'Perhaps by the celebration of *Pachons*, the first month of low water,' said Keelan. 'Though all months have been months of low water recently. Such is the will of Osiris and of Hapi the Nile God.'

Artemidorus did a rapid mental calculation. The feast of the month named *Pachons* – were there to be one – would be celebrated in the early days of the next month, *Payni.* That would be in mid-June according to *Divus Julius'* new Roman calendar. Previous experience, however, had taught him to take such confident predictions with a pinch of salt. Besides, even when *Alexandros* was ready to be launched, rigged and begin her sea-trials, there was still the matter of training 2,000 oarsmen. Not to mention the crew and sail-handlers – the better part of 200 of them, all needing to be schooled in the individual ways of this particular naval behemoth.

Divus Julius' month – the recently named July – looked more likely.

'But then again,' he said aloud to his silent companion, '*Alexandros* is likely to be the last ship ready. Divine Cleopatra is planning a fleet of one hundred and fifty large vessels, though no other *tens* like *Alexandros,* with another fifty smaller ships – supply ships and so-forth. A lot of the fleet is ready, but the modern battle ships are taking longer to prepare.'

*

This speech was sufficient to take them back out of the dockyard and onto the quay looking out across the Royal Harbour. They arrived just in time to see half a dozen huge *oneraria* transport ships, their square sails stowed, teams of skiffs at their bows, tugging them through the narrow harbour entrance. And, ahead of them, a neat, sleek trireme slid into a nearby berth.

'Take us to that trireme,' he ordered the oarsmen in is personal skiff. And it seemed that it was only a matter of heartbeats before he and Hecate were running up the water-steps onto the quay. Just as Herod, Prince of Galilee, came down the gangplank to greet them.

'I have brought Queen Cleopatra's Parthian grain as you see,' he called cheerfully. 'Now kindly conduct me to wherever she keeps her gold.'

Cleopatra welcomed the Judean prince and the grain he brought with a series of formal receptions – to which Artemidorus was invited as friend to both chief guest and divine hostess. Even when the formalities eased back, Herod's extravagant lifestyle did not. Officially housed in the main palace and made free of the Musaeum, Library and Menagerie, the young prince nevertheless came and went as his own desires dictated. Artemidorus allowed himself to be swept along by the energetic, sybaritic prince. He found this a more effective way to distract himself from Puella than Hecate and Ferrata's suggestions. Other members of the *contubernium*, notably Ferrata, Notus and the love-struck Kyros also came along – for as long as they could afford it. Quintus was always there, watching his back. And, increasingly often, Artemidorus took Hecate, though nothing seemed to fascinate her as much as the great ships did. However, actual communication between them remained minimal. Surprisingly swiftly, given the circumstances, Quintus seemed to be at ease with her and she with him – though they never talked. And, in spite of Ferrata's not-too gentle nudging, Artemidorus neither screwed her brains out nor beat the crap out of her. He was playing a deeper, more satisfying game than that.

iv

Early on, they took the road through the Canopic Gate to the Hippodrome to see the chariot races. 'I dislike wagering, though the One True God is not definitive in forbidding it entirely,' Herod announced one evening. 'Gambling is not mentioned in the Commandments He passed down to the prophet Moshe. Therefore I find some enjoyment from wagering on the races a little strange. Though I know I must show more interest when I finally go to Rome. I like ones that end in *naufragia* shipwrecks like this one.' Four chariots had collided coming too tightly round the final bend, loudly and bloodily destroying sixteen horses, four wicker chariots and the four drivers with the reins wrapped tightly round their bodies. Two of whom had been dragged to death by crippled horses stampeding towards the finish line. Long smears of blood marked the sand of the arena. There was some lively debate as to whether the man who left the longest smear should be declared the winner – and wagers settled accordingly.

The incident began another strand of change, allowing Artemidorus another set of moves in his secret game, in which Hecate's trust was his prize because she spoke publicly for the first time in answer to the Prince. She looked coldly on the bloody wreckage with its dying men and screaming horses. 'It is *impius* wicked,' she said in strangely accented but serviceable Latin. 'A waste of so much life. Even Ogun, god of war, fire and iron would not approve.'

Herod looked at her, stunned that she should hold such an opinion and that she should dare to voice it. A whisper of outrage went through the entourage that always followed him – as the *contubernium* followed Artemidorus.

Ferrata came to the rescue. 'So says the witch and murderess!' he jeered.

'Then I suppose she knows what she is talking about when she starts on about wickedness and waste of life eh?' Herod chuckled, allowing himself to be mollified.

After that, Artemidorus was more careful about bringing her on Herod's adventures – but the game went on as he took her to more and more places, talking inconsequentially to her, as though he expected answers – which he rarely got; or conversations – which never came.

At least she hadn't poisoned him or stabbed him in his sleep.

So far.

*

The river docks were ablaze. Great flaming torches lit the quays and jetties. Lanterns lit the boats as they arrived and departed, packed with revellers. Herod led them to the nearest jetty where the vessel he had hired for the night sat waiting. The bridge that bore the *via* between the Lake Docks and the Sun Gate arched high above them, its length lit by yet more blazing torches. 'It is as though we have come at noon, not at night,' said the prince, awed by the spectacle.

'Canopus is always as brightly lit, Majesty,' called one of the boat crew. 'It is never dark in Canopus!'

Artemidorus followed Herod down into the gilded vessel which was far too big for the prince, his entourage, Artemidorus and his *contubernium*, in which Hecate replaced Crinas for tonight at least.

As soon as they were all aboard, the boat pulled away, the oarsmen needing neither *pausator* nor rowing song to co-ordinate their rhythm, which was fortunate because everyone was deep in excited conversation except for Artemidorus and his taciturn slave – who seemed more interested in their vessel than in their destination. However, thought Artemidorus, if Canopus lived up to its reputation, it offered a range of pleasures and experiences unrivalled anywhere in the world. 'Certainly,' observed Herod – who was already a little less than sober, 'it does so now that Sodom and Gomorrah have been closed for business.'

The city of pleasure certainly lived up to its reputation at first sight, for just as the lights of the River Docks and Alexandria dimmed behind them and the vast star-spangled darkness of the desert closed over them, so Canopus seemed to rise like a new sun dead ahead. The attendant city's river docks were as busy as Alexandria's had been, but Herod's group all managed to stay together as they climbed from the canal and onto dry land, pushing through the crowds into the city itself. Canopus had no walls. Or, if it had in the past, they were invisible now. Away to their left, the old port lay open to the sea – a dark, quiet area stretching into a still, black north and an invisible cape reaching further northward still with only the light of the Pharos away to the west like a rising star. To their right – and soon enough dead ahead – the seething snake-pit of winding roads, bright-lit shops and taverns, brothels and gambling dens.

V

After the rigid geometric layout of Alexandria, Canopus' confusion of wandering streets came as a relief – almost an escape. Certainly the twisting alleyways and unexpected open spaces gave off an air of freedom which was almost dangerous. 'Anything goes in Canopus,' enthused Herod. 'If you have a vice you have never tried, then here is your chance!'

Artemidorus watched warily as the over-enthusiastic youngsters pushed forward. The brightness of the lights seemed to him to conceal the darkest of shadows. Beneath the heady scents of frankincense and myrrh, sandalwood and cedar, it seemed to him there lurked the stench of putrefaction. He was not surprised to find that Hecate was walking much closer to him than usual.

Happily unaware of all this, Herod plunged on into the heart of the place. And, in spite of what he had said at the Hippodrome, he ended up leading them into a gambling den.

Artemidorus looked around the place, fighting to take it all in and make some kind of sense of it. The place was enormous. One gigantic atrium open to all and packed with people, thunderous with the sound of conversation, shouted advice or recrimination, cheering and lamentation. To one side a massive open fire produced roast meat as well as stultifying heat. In spite of which, patrons were crowded round it, grabbing a bite to eat between bouts of wagering. Opposite was the largest and busiest bar the widely-travelled centurion had ever seen. It too was thronged with men taking a drink as they stood – briefly – back from the action. All surrounded by men and women of all ages, make-ups, colours and costumes who established at once that there was a good deal more on offer here than food, drink and the whims of Fortuna.

There was no doubting the main focus of the place. In one corner was a square area where two *pugils* were currently beating each-other to a bloody pulp while spectators bet on who would fall first or stay standing longest. Beside that, almost concealed by the crowds gathered round them, were a cock-pit and two dog-rings. The first occupied by a pair of fighting cocks whose spurs had been lengthened with metal spikes. The next contained two half-wild desert jackals currently tearing each-other to shreds with teeth that needed no enhancement. The third contained two cats currently clawing the life out of each-other, spitting and screaming like souls in Tartarus as they did so. A little way along, a pit with higher sides contained a small *tessem* hunting dog and a seething mess of rats which the dog was killing at lightning speed and tossing into the air as it did so. There was even, right at the back of the place, a huge bed where two naked men with set and stoical expressions were being attended by two naked women, each obviously racing to bring their companion to the peak of pleasure first.

Nearer at hand there were half a dozen gaming tables where dice and knucklebone games were in loud and excited motion. At least two tables where the more gullible were happy to bet on which of three upturned cups a dried pea could be found under. But, thought the secret agent, narrow-eyed, there were some games that demanded skill as well as luck. That were less easy to fix with loaded dice and sleight of hand. *Rota* and *Termi Lapili* were being played at the next two tables. Both games required opponents to move counters on simple boards in attempts to achieve straight rows of three. Both were similar to Greek games mentioned by Plato but had fewer variables, yet still demanding some skill.

These proper board games were more tempting to the centurion, especially the last one he saw. This was the famous Egyptian game which had come to Greece as *Petteia*, and which the Romans knew as *Latrunculi* or Little Soldiers. *Petteia* was a game which he liked because it required tactical skill to move the pebbles from one square to another and outmanoeuvre your adversary as though you were opponents in a battle. Artemidorus counted himself quite good at it. *Petteia* was supposed to be the game that Achilleus played while sulking in his tent outside the besieged walls of Troy, so it was above all the game Artemidorus had studied during the few moments of idleness he had enjoyed in his life so far. It was, in the form of a board-game, the very campaign he had been secretly waging against the walls of Hecate's silence and reserve.

*

Herod's group broke up at once; even the *contubernium* seemed to split into its constituent parts. Some went off to try their luck with the dice, led by Herod and Ferrata; others to watch the four-section reduction of an afternoon's games in the arena – one bout with gladiators, and three different animal-contests. None seemed to be tempted by the race towards climax on the bed. Or, for the moment at least, by the over-made-up creatures available for hire at the bar. Artemidorus chose to take his time. Glancing over his shoulder at Quintus and the silent Hecate, he said, 'Drink? Or food first.'

'Drink,' said Quintus.

Hecate said nothing but followed the men as they shouldered their way through the prostitutes heading for the bar. 'Any preference?' asked Artemidorus.

'They'll probably only have Mareotic. Local stuff but acceptable,' answered Quintus.

But when he got to the bar, Artemidorus paused. 'They have Shedeh,' he said, surprised. 'It's red. Local. I thought that was only used for ceremonial. It's the most expensive you can buy. And they have Roman Caecubum. That's outstanding. Also extremely expensive. Some say it's the best in Italy – makes Falernian taste like horse-piss in comparison.'

'And I crossed the Alps with Antony, so I should know,' said Quintus. 'It was all we had to drink,' he explained to Hecate who showed no sign of interest or understanding. 'Horse piss to drink and tree bark to eat.'

'Why not eat the horses?' Hecate asked unexpectedly.

'They were carrying stuff like tents that stopped us freezing to death. But the idea's put me off white wine for the moment. Let's try this Shedeh.'

Artemidorus bought three ruinously expensive cups of wine, then the three of them drifted over to the gaming tables. Artemidorus came to a halt at the *Petteia* table and stood, sipping the rich, blood-red liquid as he watched what was going on. A plump young man in expensive clothes was locked in combat with a wizened skeleton, more mummy than man, with wild hair and a straggly beard. He seemed out of place here – he should have been sitting in the Musaeum rather than in an atrium full of inveterate gamblers. Not that the two were mutually exclusive, thought Artemidorus. The old man reminded him a little of Keelan the shipwright – though the gambler was much more untidy and unkempt. On the table in front of each player sat a pile of gold. The wager seemed to be on the outcome of the game and appeared to work on three levels. Each of the two opponents bet against the other; spectators also bet against each-other. Or, he noted, they bet against a sly-looking man who probably represented the house. Friends and strangers simply held up their purses as proof that they could pay. The sly-looking man seemed to be offering lines of credit which he recorded in a double sided tablet bound like a book. And with very few credit limits. He scanned the crowd. There, behind the sly man –not close enough to be obviously with him – were two huge Macedonians. Palace guards, no doubt, earning a little extra on the side. Like everyone else they wore no armour, but whereas most people carried daggers, they carried nasty-looking clubs.

After a few minutes, the young man lost. Artemidorus smiled. The old man was a fox – cunningly concealing his winning move until his young victim was committed, unaware that he was falling into a trap. Dazed, he looked uncomprehendingly at the board, then pushed his pile of gold over to the old man and rose. All around him, wagers were being settled and several men, who had made arrangements with the book-keeper, tried to slink away. The Macedonian guards followed them, easing their shoulders and swinging their clubs. As everything settled, Artemidorus slid into the vacant chair opposite the ancient victor and put his purse on the table beside the board.

vi

'I'm wagering on the Roman,' said Quintus. 'Anyone care to take my money?'

There was no shortage of replies.

'And you, girl,' said Quintus still treating the silent woman much as he would have treated Puella. 'Would you like to wager?'

'I have no money,' she said. 'I have nothing. I *am* nothing. I am a slave.'

'Let's imagine you have an indulgent owner, then, who treats you as though you were a person rather than a thing. What would you like to wager?'

'The same as you.'

'Lucky I only wagered half of my money then,' said Quintus cheerfully.

'I'd be happy to offer credit,' said the book-keeper.

'I'm sure you would,' said Quintus. 'Like Marcus Licinius Crassus come back from the dead.'

Artemidorus shut everything out of his consciousness and leaned forward. 'Who goes first?'

The old man brought up two clenched fists. 'I hold a pebble,' he said. 'Right or left?'

'Left,' said Artemidorus.

The hand opened. It was empty.

'And the other one?' he demanded, keen to make sure all was honest – at this stage at least.

The old man opened it to reveal a pebble.

'Fair so far,' said Artemidorus. 'You go first then.'

The old man was an excellent opponent, devious, practised in concealing attacks behind apparently irrelevant or mistaken moves, yet bringing his little soldiers forward with the relentless precision of *Divus Julius* himself. But, while his opponent had no doubt been studying mathematics at the Musaeum, Artemidorus had actually been serving with *Divus Julius*. And that made the difference in the end. He erected *castra* that his opponent's troops could not break into. And when they tried, he launched counter-strikes of his own, just as *Divus Julius* had done at Alesia, Pharsalus and Munda. So at last the old man was forced to yield like Vercingetorix and Pompey.

*

Artemidorus handed his winnings up to Quintus, who went off to collect his own and Hecate's as Artemidorus pulled himself to his feet. How much time had passed since he sat and went to war? He had no idea. Glancing around the room he saw new *pugils* beating the blood out of each-other, replacement cocks, cats, dogs and rats. Two of Herod's entourage were trying to resist the naked girls' techniques on the big bed. But Herod himself was still caught up in dicing egged on by the rest of his companions, Ferrata, and the remainder of Artemidorus' *contubernium*.

'I need a breath of air,' he said to Hecate. 'Wait here for Quintus then bring him to me; I'll be just outside the door.'

Hecate nodded.

The street outside was busy. The air was scented and sultry – but still refreshing after the heat and humidity of the gambling den. Artemidorus hesitated. He turned, tempted to go back and invest some of his winnings in another glass full of that amazing Shedeh wine. Besides, he realised, he was very hungry indeed. What he saw when he turned put food and drink to the back of his mind. The two massive Macedonians were coming out of the main door and their eyes were fixed on him. He understood their mission in a heartbeat. 'So, boys,' he said, strolling back towards them, wishing he was armed with more than his *pugio*, 'the house never loses, is that it?'

They looked a little confused, as though this had never happened to them before. They lifted the clubs they carried with just a hint of uncertainty.

'The money you won from the old man,' rumbled one. 'He owed it to Spurius Arunculus.'

'The oily one with the book, no doubt,' nodded Artemidorus cheerfully. 'If he owed it to Spurius Arunculus then he shouldn't have gambled with it. And he certainly shouldn't have lost. But he did. Fortuna pissed on him tonight.'

'Spurius Arunculus wants it back. And he wants the money you wagered as well. The old man's debt was very large. He sent us to collect payment.'

'Well, Fortuna's pissing on you too, boys. I gave it all to my friend for safe-keeping. I haven't a sestertius on me.'

Just at that moment Quintus and Hecate came out. The legionary assessed the situation in the blink of an eye and stepped forward. 'Everything all right Septem?'

The Macedonians swung round to face him, raising their clubs.

'Fine thanks, Quintus. The boys and I were discussing the house rules.'

Hecate took one look at the situation and vanished.

'Ah. The one where they want their money back,' nodded Quintus knowledgeably. 'I've come across that one.'

'Spurius Arunculus is the man, apparently, the sly-looking oily bastard with the book full of lost wagers. And a purse full of gold almost as big as his belly.'

'I noticed him. Shall we deal with him after we've seen to his gorillas?'

'I think so. I think he owes us recompense for all the trouble we're going to have to go to.'

vii

The Macedonians were slow, but not stupid. They understood the byplay was a calculated waste of time, so they leapt into action. In spite of the idle weeks in Cleopatra's palace, both Artemidorus and Quintus were battle-fit. They had fought naked wild men in the black forests of Germania and knew that their lack of armour could be an advantage if they stayed quick enough to keep dodging the blows from those great clubs. 'D'you think we should kill them?' asked Quintus leaning sideways so that the first blow whispered harmlessly past his shoulder.

'Not unless we have to.' Artemidorus ducked as the club went a hairsbreadth above his head.

'Cripple them?' Quintus opponent's club was really too big for him. He swung again but signalled the move so clearly that Quintus once again was no longer there when the club arrived.

'May have to.' Artemidorus' opponent was a little better at this. He changed course mid-blow, stabbing the head of his club into the centurion's belly. Artemidorus leapt back, lessening the impact of the blow.

'Right!' Quintus' *pugio* was in his right fist, its long blade gleaming in the torchlight. At the sight of the dagger, his opponent hesitated. The legionary moved forward, waving the wicked blade in his face. Taking his cue from his companion, the Macedonian stabbed with his weapon, its head thumping into Quintus' shoulder. The legionary twisted and danced.

Artemidorus also slid his *pugio* out, leaping towards his opponent, ducking beneath another side-swipe as he did. His shoulder smashed into the Macedonian's chest as though into a brick wall. The Macedonian brought the club down vertically onto the spy's back. Any harder and the blow would have damaged his spine. Disregarding the pain, he drove his dagger into the Macedonian's thigh, twisted the blade, withdrew and danced back.

There was a crowd circling the combatants now. As Artemidorus came free, so the wall of bodies nearest to the door parted. Ferrata appeared with Hercules towering behind him. Then came Kyros and Notus. Artemidorus glanced back at his opponent, who had been slowed by the wound bleeding down his leg, but by no means stopped. With his *contubernium* behind him, however, Artemidorus felt more confident. He prepared to throw himself forward once again.

It looked as though he was going to have to kill his opponent after all.

'STOP!'

The *contubernium* parted in turn to reveal Spurius Arunculus with Herod immediately behind him, dagger at his throat. Behind Herod came Hecate and then the Prince's companions – even the two from the bed at the back, dressed and without their seductive companions.

'Centurion,' said the Prince of Galilee, 'Your slave-woman and I have talked things over with this person and he wishes to announce a decision we helped him reach.'

'Keep it!' screeched Spurius Arunculus. 'Keep the fornicating money!'

'*And...*' prompted Herod. His hand shook slightly. A fat worm of blood began to ooze down the book-keeper's throat.

'Take my purse as well. In recompense for any annoyance my over-zealous guards may inadvertently have caused you. Take all of it.'

*

'That was a good evening's work,' decided Herod. 'But there is still plenty of the night left. We can't go back in there, but I'm hungry. We need to find somewhere convenient to...'

His words were cut off by a sneering voice. 'Well *salve Canicula*! hello Bitch! I see your new owner has a sense of humour. To dress an ugly animal like you as though you were handmaiden to Cleopatra herself!'

Hecate seemed to turn into a statue. That one voice seemingly undoing the weeks of careful work Artemidorus had invested in her. He swung round, searching for the man who had just spoken. And there he was. In his mid-twenties, with a woman on his arm whose wig and make-up could not conceal the fact that she was old enough to be his mother. *Was* his mother, calculated Artemidorus, recognising family resemblance in the narrow little eyes, bulbous nose and fat, flaccid lips. And she had given birth to him very late in life.

'Still dumb as the dog I named you after, Bitch?' continued the young man, whose every word made Artemidorus more certain that this was Titus Volumnius Elva junior, recipient, with the hag beside him, of his poisoned father's fortune.

'I own this woman,' he said. Although he spoke quietly, his words carried across the entire forum. 'But Queen Cleopatra's handmaidens did indeed dress her. I am Centurion Iacomus Artemidorus, Primus Pilus of the VIIth legion, seconded to the staff of Triumvir and General Mark Antony. And I knew Marcus Tullius Cicero well.'

'Cicero! You knew Cicero! Well done! What has that to do with anything?' he jeered.

'You may regret that he is not here to defend you, if I take the trouble to bring you to justice.'

'Cicero! Why would I need Cicero even if you did?'

'Because it was Cicero who defended Sextus Roscius in the year 673 when young Roscius was also charged with *arranging his father's murder.*'

'That was good,' said Herod later as, replete and exhausted, they sat in his barge being rowed back to Alexandria. 'We won a fortune, won a fight, scared the life out of a murderous bully and his hag–mother – well Artemidorus did all of these things – and enjoyed one of the most satisfying dinners I can recall. The honeyed heron stuffed with perch and dates was unforgettable.'

Everyone fell silent after this summation of their evening, which in its precision was worthy of Cicero himself, thought Artemidorus.

He turned to the silent woman sitting close beside him and dropped his voice to little more than a whisper. 'That was the name they gave you?' he asked. '*Bitch*?'

'It was. Because I come from lands far beyond the Great Sand Sea, and looked almost nothing like other women they knew. They called me Bitch and beat me like a dog.'

'But what were you called in the lands beyond the Great sand Sea?' asked Artemidorus. 'What is your real name?'

She hesitated. 'I am content to be Hecate,' she answered. 'To give you my real name is to give you great power over me and my *ori inu* spirit. Such power should be given carefully and rarely.'

'Very well then, you are called Hecate, goddess of magic.'

She hesitated for a moment then whispered so quietly that he strained to hear, 'Lolade. My true name is Lolade.'

XVIII: Alexandros

i

Alexandros was ready for sea-trials by the feast of *Pachons*, just as Keelan the chief shipwright promised. She was painted, gilded, and rigged. Her sail was made of double-woven flax, oiled, edged with the leather of chamois goats from Macedonia and decorated with a portrait of Isis in her form as Goddess of Kingship and the Protection of the Kingdom. Her figurehead was the face of Alexander himself, cast in gold, and her massive ram had been covered in bronze which had been gilded. Her oarsmen were trained and ready. Her *navarchus* commander and senior officers appointed. Her *gubernator* helmsman and sailhands were in place. All that was left were her sea-trials.

'She is very beautiful,' observed Hecate who had watched the great ship come into being as she herself had moved from her defensive silence towards a lively intelligence, no longer afraid to speak her mind. Unaware she had been the subject of a carefully-planned strategy, like Gaul or Britannia being invaded by *Divus Julius*. With much less rape and slaughter, thought Artemidorus. Though, to be fair, Herod's visit had resulted in them missing the finishing touches – the laying of the deck, the stepping of the mast, the rigging of the sails and the turning of the oars. 'In my country we have war canoes that can carry a hundred warriors up the Great River or out into the sea,' she had announced unexpectedly. 'But we have nothing like this,' she continued, 'nothing with masts and sails.' She was standing at his shoulder on the quayside of the Royal Docks with the rest of his men behind them now. All watching as the great vessel rode the incoming rollers like a swan made of gold.

'We have been invited aboard,' Artemidorus said to her. 'So you will get a chance to see how everything works.' He turned to the others, raising his voice, 'Her commander, Admiral Minnakht has apparently heard that we've been watching her being built. Prompted, by Cleopatra who I know is getting worried that we are all bored now that Herod has gone home to Galilee.'

'Five minutes with Alexander's corpse is enough for anyone,' said Ferrata. 'And you can only go round the Menagerie so many times. Though some of us, I know, are trying to talk with every person in the Musaeum and read every book in the Library…'

'The admiral wonders whether we would like to be there for her first sea-trial,' continued Artemidorus. 'It will be a short voyage, designed to test the oars, the sails, the rigging. Everything is of the latest design, incorporating ideas from thinkers and designers such as Archimedes and Philo. The underside of her hull is sheathed in lead. There is even, I understand, a pair of devices like water-wheels at sea-level either side of her stern to measure her speed, designed by the engineers in the Musaeum.' He could scarcely keep the excitement from his voice.

His enthusiasm was contagious. Hecate was keen, fascinated by the masts, spars, sails and rigging as were the rest of the *contubernium*, including Crinas for once and, remarkably, Quintus. Perhaps Cleopatra and Ferrata were right about the boredom.

'Before you ask,' said Quintus truculently, 'I reckon something that big will be as solid as dry land in any case. No more upsetting than standing on this jetty.'

But he had forgotten the fact that they would need to go out to her in a skiff.

*

Alexandros' deck did indeed seem as solid and still as dry land when they came aboard, climbing a ladder hanging from the bow, well to the fore of the first rowing box, stepping through a gap in the deck-rail into an area that was still being worked on. 'It looks like they're putting a companionway here which can be raised or lowered – for people too important to shin up a role ladder,' said Ferrata.

Quintus' queasiness in the skiff passed off almost at once as they walked admiringly down the length of the vessel. She was not yet fully fitted. The deck was bare – no fighting towers or other battle-ready equipment was yet in place. Nor was her company of marines. But some modern touches were: winches for raising and lowering the anchors, for instance, pulley blocks, invented by Archimedes, for tightening the rigging and, no doubt, for raising and lowering the companionway when it was finished. Artemidorus scanned the rigging as the little group waited for Admiral Minnakht to arrive and call for the vessel to get under way.

'These are the ropes that will control the raising and lowering of the sails,' he explained to Hecate. 'And these pulley blocks control their tension.' He patted the nearest one as he spoke. The simple grooved wheel that captured and guided the line to the sail was set in a cradle of wood held together by tightly woven rope. The line running through it was lashed to wooden pins in the deck rail. The wooden sections of the simple device were made of ebony. They looked functional but also decorative.

'Even watching *Alexandros* being built did not prepare me for how complicated such things can become now she is afloat,' she said.

'It has taken centuries to work out, I think. Minoans, Phonecians, we Greeks, the Carthaginians, the Cilicians, the Romans, and the Egyptians. *Alexandros* is the result of all that history – with all the wisdom of the Musaeum added to it.'

'But how do you know so much about such things?' she asked.

He looked down at her, raking through memories. 'I have sailed with Cilicians and against Cilicains; with Pompey the Great and against Pompey the Great; with *Divus Julius*, but never against him. You might be surprised how many legions get put aboard ships,' he said.

No sooner had Artemidorus finished speaking than Admiral Minnakht came aboard. He had been rowed out from Cleopatra's main palace, following a formal briefing from her. Artemidorus watched as the Egyptian commander briefed his officers beneath the incurving sternpost. There was a moment of stasis, then they all hurried to their stations. One team ran to the bow to winch in the anchor. As soon as it was clear of the water, the officer in charge waved a flag. The Admiral gave an order. With a thunderous rumble two thousand oarsmen ran out twelve hundred oars, six hundred in three ranks a side, the topmost – longest – controlled by two oarsmen – sometimes more. The rowers pushed them past the leather flaps designed to keep the water from flooding the vessel in battle or foul weather. Seated at the stern, facing them, the *pausator* began to beat out a steady rhythm. The Egyptian version of Artemidorus' rowing song rang out and the great ship was in motion.

'Not long now,' said Ferrata.

'Not long 'til what?' asked Quintus.

'Not long 'til we're heading home,' answered the legionary. 'It's all well marching across the world, even as far as Alexandria. But there's no place like Rome.'

ii

Alexandros swiftly gathered way as the oars fell, pulled, and rose in unison. Almost as though the vessel were like the mechanical wonder Antony had sent to Cleopatra all those months ago. The admiral stood with his officers, the captain and the pilot cum helmsman at the rear of the ship, watching as she followed the course he dictated, out through the narrow entrance to the Royal Harbour then into the Great Harbour beyond. Artemidorus, Hecate and the rest stood entranced as the huge vessel surged onwards, gathering pace ever more swiftly as the *pausator* raised the rhythm and the rowing song grew faster.

The Island Palace fell swiftly astern. Wise seamen that they were, the admiral and the captain took the eastern course through the entrance to the Great Harbour, staying well clear of the rocks and reefs that ringed Pharos Island at the foot of the lighthouse and lay dangerously downwind. Then they were out into the sea proper.

Here the waves were taller and the wind seemed stronger out of Cape Lochias' shadow. But still *Alexandros* ran straight and true, heading northwards across the set of the sea.

Admiral Minnakht joined them. He was tall – but nowhere near Hercules height. He wore a full beard that flowed down his breast which was encased in a golden breast-plate. He wore the head-dress favoured by User and Hunefer, with a gold band denoting his rank. A long red cloak hung from broad shoulders and he held it in place with big, square hands at thigh level, to stop it flapping in the wind. His skin tone was lighter than User's and Puella's, with a decided golden undertone. He was unarmed. He had quick brown eyes that measured them all in a blink. 'Centurion,' he said courteously in heavily accented Greek. 'Divine Isis commanded that I invite you aboard, though of course I was happy to do as she ordered. Indeed, I planned to do so, having talked to the master shipwright and learned of your interest. Queen Cleopatra wishes that you and I both report to her at the conclusion of the voyage, so that we can each give her our observations.' He looked around them all, then his gaze flicked away to his massive vessel.

'So that you can be more confident about what is going on,' he continued, 'allow me to give you an outline of our planned voyage. We will soon be turning *anatoli* east – once we are clear of the notoriously shifting shoreline of the delta. We will then go at best speed under oars for ten Roman *miles* until we sight Cape Canopus. We have water-clocks aboard similar to those used in your Senate, I believe, as well as devices designed to measure our speed. It should take us little more than an hour to reach the cape. Then we will turn back, lower the sails, and proceed at best speed under sail westwards to the Pharos. The speed we reach will depend on the strength of the wind of course and cannot be predicted with such accuracy. When we reach the Pharos, we will put away the sails and enter the Great

Harbour under oars, go onto the Royal Harbour and report to Divine Isis as ordered.'

'Thank you, Admiral. We will be most interested to see what such a fine vessel can achieve,' said Artemidorus, matching the Egyptian's formality.

Ferrata sniggered but covered it with a cough.

As soon as he had gone, Artemidorus said, 'Right. We'll treat this seriously. There's not much to observe while she's under oars except for her speed. Ten *miles* in an hour sounds impossible to me. She's powerful and she's new, so her hull will be clean, but I've only ever heard of triremes and liburnians approaching anything like that speed. The real test will come when the sails go down. Quintus and Ferrata you go to the bows, keep an eye on the rigging of the foremast and the main mast. Hercules and Notus you go to the stern. Try not to get too close to the officers and sail handlers up there but keep an eye on the ropes to the mast as well. Crinas, you go below and find out whether that new device for measuring speed is working and if so, what speed we're doing when we turn east. Check it again when we run back west under sail. Kyros, you go with him. Memorise any numbers. Hecate, you stay with me. We're watching how the sails and the rigging that controls them works. Everyone clear?'

*

Alexandros swung eastwards. The *pausator* raised the speed and the oarsmen responded, their song and their oar-strokes quickening. The ship's sleek lead-sheathed hull cut through the water, her ram destroying the oncoming waves one after another. The head wind made her speed seem greater than it was, but Artemidorus began to wonder whether she really could go as fast as the admiral claimed. He and Hecate went to the bow, side by side, looking into the water as the ship raced on. There were dolphins playing in the bow-wave – surely a sign that Poseidon was holding his hands over them, thought Artemidorus. But then he was struck by a disturbing realisation. The admiral had made no sacrifice to any god or goddess before getting under way. That suddenly seemed to be a dangerous omission, even on a short testing voyage such as this one.

Despite this, he found himself catching his breath with every plunge and heave as they smashed their way eastwards. Hecate shared his exhilaration. Even the spume flying in over the bow to soak them was part of the excitement. Fortunately, both the wind and the water were warm, for it didn't take long for both his tunic and her cotton robes to become molded to their bodies. All at once he found her curiously distracting. Droplets hung like diamonds from her eyelashes and in the wildness of her curls. He found himself wondering whether what he felt for her was friendly affection or burgeoning lust. If the latter, did it arise from growing attraction – or simply from the fact that he hadn't slept with a woman since Puella vanished with User?

Fortunately, his thoughts were interrupted by Crinas who came hurrying forward. 'The machine suggests we will cover the distance to Cape Canopus in an hour, just as the admiral predicted. We seem to be moving at almost one and a half *stadia* every minute.'

'That's extraordinary. He can't possibly keep that up!' Even as Artemidorus spoke, the rhythm of the drumbeat, the song and the oar stokes slowed. *Alexandros*' speed eased. 'Now we'll get a better idea of her normal speed,' said Artemidorus. 'Go and see what this wonderful device says now.'

Crinas came puffing back ten minutes later as measured by the admiral's water clock. 'Just under a *stadion* a minute, say 500 *podes* feet.'

'Still impressive. Especially as the wind is freshening, which will be a handicap until we reach Cape Canopus, then it will be a big help on the homeward run, of course.'

Crinas nodded distractedly, his eyes on Hecate. 'And I hope the wind stays warm as well as strong. To help your clothes to dry if for no other reason. They are neither healthy nor decent as they are.'

iii

They reached Cape Canopus in a little over an hour according to the admiral's water clocks. Then they turned north, still under oars, and finally swung west. The oars rumbled back aboard. *Alexandros* sat slightly uneasily with the waves thundering against her stern as the dolphins swam away northward looking for another playmate. Even though the rear of the great vessel was almost as sharp as her prow, the configuration was very different. There were steering oars instead of that great bronze-bound ram. The slope of the stern sat high, allowing the restless, wind-driven sea to run beneath it, pitching the hull forward uneasily. The Admiral hesitated, feeling the new movement of his command, liking it less than the way she sailed under oars into wind and weather. But after a few moments, as the water clocks were re-set, he called for full sail.

The foresail blossomed and the hull steadied at once, her bow facing more purposefully westward. Then the mainsail came down, flapped twice with a rumbling like that made by the oars coming back inboard. Then the wind caught it and it bellied out, snapping taut in a heartbeat. The sail-handlers tied it off, checked the pulley and went to report to the captain and the admiral leaving Artemidorus and Hecate alone once more.

All around Artemidorus and Hecate a dizzying range of sounds rang out. Seagulls skimmed low, screaming. The mainsail continued to make muted thunder. The ropes holding it in place groaned with tension, as they tightened like the strings on a lyre. The ebony pulley blocks screamed with the strain. The masts themselves groaned under the stress of moving the great hull forwards as fast as the wind dictated.

Hecate put her hand on the greatest of the rigging ropes. 'It is alive!' she whispered, awed. 'I can feel its *ori inu* spirit stirring.' She moved her hand onto the deck-rail beside it. 'The whole ship has a spirit,' she said, hawk's eyes wide with disbelief. 'It has been awoken by the wind. I can feel it. I can hear it!'

Artemidorus smiled. How simple she seemed. Like a superstitious country girl. 'Is it a good spirit?' he asked.

Her eyes seemed to cloud over. Her face folded into a frown. Abruptly he remembered what they had called her in the slave market: *striga* witch. He found himself wondering who had supplied the secret poison with which Titus Elva's wife had murdered him. 'I do not think so,' she answered. 'Her spirit is at war with Oya goddess of the wind.'

'Here the god of the west wind is Zephyrus,' he said. 'He and *Alexandros* must be friends or there will be trouble.'

'Then there will be trouble,' said Hecate.

She touched the wooden pulley block holding the rigging line to the main sail again and jumped back as though it had burned her. Artemidorus stepped forward, reaching for her protectively – but with no idea what he was protecting her from.

The wooden block shattered, utterly destroyed by the strain of controlling the main sail. A sizeable piece smacked Artemidorus squarely between the shoulder blades, propelling him forward. He crashed into Hecate, automatically wrapping his arms around her as they both tumbled to the wet, slippery deck. The rope released by the failure of the block lashed free, tearing off a section of the deck-rail and cracking like a whip just above them, spreading splinters and chunks of wood far and wide. The deafening *snap* was followed at once by a sound like nothing Artemidorus had ever heard before: a ripping, tearing roar. He rolled over, dazed and in a good deal of pain, taking his weight off Hecate and looking upwards.

The mainsail was torn from top to bottom. One-half of it flew forward like a legionary *vexillum*. The other strained to remain in place. The whole deck seemed to heave beneath him as he looked up, dazed. It was probably his imagination, he thought, but the mast appeared to be twisting. Sail-handlers were running all over the deck like a nest of ants disturbed by a burning stick, slipping and sliding on the damp planks.

But then his thoughts were jerked away from what he could see to what he could feel. *Alexandros* heeled over, still beneath the dictates of the wind in the uneven sail. Artemidorus felt himself sliding towards the gaping hole in the rail. Visions of Furius' terrible death flashed once again. But then a strong black hand caught him. Steadied him. Hecate was firmly on her wide-spread knees. He reached and grabbed her sinewy wrist. His slide towards the edge stopped abruptly and he lay still gasping in shock and agony, looking up at the sail.

The figure of Isis, Goddess of Kingship, and the Protection of the Kingdom, had been utterly destroyed.

*

'This is a nasty bruise,' said Crinas. 'But you were lucky. The piece of wood that made it has done no more damage than the blow you got from the Macedonian's club outside the gambling den in Canopus. However, if it had hit Hecate in the face instead of you in the back it would have killed her.'

'I think we'd probably both be dead if she hadn't felt what was going to happen just before it did. Her head would have been smashed in by the wood from the pulley block and mine would have been removed by the rope it released and the section of deck-rail it took with it.'

'Do you think they were right in the slave-market?' asked Crinas, his voice just above a whisper. He was a follower of Hippocrates and was not usually superstitious. '*Is* she a witch?'

'Who can tell? It could be coincidence as much as magic.'

'Ah. More of a Cynic than a Stoic today?'

'Still a Stoic to put up with this pain. What is that stuff you're rubbing on my back?'

'An unguent that will make it feel better. Eventually.'

The conversation was brought to an abrupt end by the arrival of

Admiral Minnakht who stooped under the low lintel of the little cabin Crinas was using as a treatment room. 'How are you?' he asked as he straightened.

'I am well, thank you, Admiral. Please don't concern yourself. My physician assures me the bruise is not serious.'

'And the slave woman?'

'Hecate had the breath knocked out of her but that is all. And only because I fell on her.'

'We will have to report this to Divine Isis.' Minnakht looked worried. He stroked his beard like the pirate Halys, deep in thought.

'We will,' nodded Artemidorus, pulling his tunic into place. 'And I will tell her how lucky we were that this occurred now. The loss of the sail is unfortunate, but it is nothing compared with what we have learned. Imagine if this had happened in the middle of a battle or at the height of a storm. It would have been a disaster. All the pulley blocks need to be redesigned or re-made with tougher stuff than the ebony wood that failed. What is the hardest wood available? Can you substitute it somehow with metal? If so, would copper, bronze or iron be the best given that it must resist sea-water to be of any long-term use. Queen Cleopatra has the entire Musaeum at her disposal. They will surely come up with an answer in the shortest possible time.'

The admiral looked down at his guest. His worried expression faded. 'You're right,' he said. 'I suggest we report to Divine Isis together.'

'And then we should talk to Keelan the shipwright,' added Artemidorus.

iv

'We will test coconut wood pulleys,' said Keelan. 'It is the only wood I can think of that is tougher than ebony. And there is plenty to hand. But the mast has survived you say?'

Artemidorus remembered the strange twisting motion but before he could say anything Admiral Minnakht answered, 'Yes, it flexed at the moment the accident happened. But it is undamaged. I have looked at it myself, but you will no doubt wish to examine it too.'

'I will, of course. I was only concerned because, unlike coconut wood, pine trees of the height and quality needed for *Alexandros*' masts are not so easy to come by. Her current main mast came from Beoria in Assyria and it would take weeks to replace it. And Divine Isis has ordered that we proceed according to her schedule. She wishes to be at sea with her complete navy, heading northward within the next seven days.'

'*She* wishes to be at sea?' said Artemidorus. 'Is Cleopatra planning to come herself? In person?'

'Naturally,' answered Minnakht. 'She is Pharaoh of the Two Lands. She has always led her forces into battle. She will do so now.'

'But a week,' said Artemidorus. 'How will you repair *Alexandros* and still prepare her to accommodate Cleopatra – even if she is travelling with a much reduced entourage?'

Keelan shrugged with a hint of weariness. 'We will work much,' he said. 'And sleep little.'

'Almost all of the work will be completed within four days,' said Minnakht. 'I would invite you and your witch to come aboard again as we test the improvements. And any others of your *contubernium* who wish to join us.'

*

Things were different four days later. The first change, which was obvious from the jetty, was that *Alexandros*' fighting towers were in place, one on the deck in front of the forward mast and the other, larger, on the deck behind the main mast. There had, it seemed to Artemidorus, been some minor adjustment of the rigging to allow for their presence. The next change was the hinged stair that could be let down at the side, leading from water-level to deck-level between the cutwater and the first rowing box. They had scrambled aboard up a rope ladder last time. But Cleopatra, of course, would do no such thing. Artemidorus ran up the movable companionway with Hecate and the others close behind. The whole deck was now covered in a sheet of lead. The malleable metal had been beaten into every curve and corner. The point of the lead covering was so that the wooden planks did not burn, because fire was one of the most potent weapons in sea-battles. A fact attested by the presence of four large *onager* catapults among the scorpions and ballista bolt-throwers that now clustered around the castle on the after deck. *Onagers* with metal baskets instead of leather slings – designed to fire blazing projectiles as well as massive rocks at enemy vessels.

Beneath the hatches, steps led down past the rowing benches to the next hatch which led in turn down into the accommodation areas. There was no knowing where the oarsmen and sail-handlers were expected to sleep, for much lower deck was furnished fit for a queen and her attendants. No, it was fit for a goddess. But the luxurious apartments were not what he had come aboard to see. He left Hecate exploring wide-eyed and went back on deck to join the others who had been prowling around.

'Look at this,' said Quintus, leading him up to the forepeak. Leaning against the stempost, the pair of them looked down. The whole front of the vessel was now covered in metal plates of bronze to match the massive ram. And, above the primary ram, a smaller ram had been added. A modern vessel such as this one was not designed to need a *corvus*. She would ram her opponents, the double rams holding her steady as her marines streamed into the attack, protected by flights of arrows and hails of slingshot from the castle on the foredeck. As well as the extra armour, a great beam had been added hard against the foremost rowing box – designed to protect the rowers as *Alexandros* crashed into her enemies. But there had been a price to pay. The primary ram which had smashed through the waves last time he had been aboard now sat below the surface. He frowned, trying to work out whether having so much more of the hull submerged would add to the strain on the mast and sails as they tried to move her. Certainly, he thought, the oarsmen were going to have trouble getting this much heavier vessel up to the sort of speeds that managed on her first test run.

V

'We have re-rigged the entire ship, of course,' said Minnakht. The admiral was in full battle dress now. Formally accompanied by a pair of shaven-headed priests and a young man dressed in the pinnacle of Alexandrian fashion to whom everyone nearby seemed to defer. A court official he had never met before, Artemidorus supposed, and thought no more of the matter.

'And replaced the pulley blocks with stronger ones,' added Keelan, who was to accompany them this time. Better late than never, thought Artemidorus.

'Good,' he said. 'Because I'm sure that the changes and additions will alter the way she handles considerably. The steps you lowered to us, for instance, must affect her angle in the water, the same as the *corvus* did on *Triton*, so that side will sit lower than the other.'

'We have balanced the steps,' said Keelan, 'to ensure that *Alexandros* still sits level.'

'Level but lower, yes I noticed. Have you assessed the difference that will make on her speed?' Hecate reappeared, still seemingly dazzled by what she had seen in Cleopatra's quarters. So, he persisted for her benefit as much as his own, 'the difference it will make on the strain the sails and rigging will undergo when she's under sail rather than oars?'

Keelan drew himself up and looked down his nose with a haughty frown at the importunate soldier. 'We have had the best mathematicians in the Musaeum working on the calculations for us. We have replaced the original rigging with rope made of papyrus, leather and animal hair woven in the traditional manner. Such ropes raised the great statues that stand in the Valley of the Kings. Such ropes moved the great blocks that fashioned the death houses of the Pharaohs back at the dawn of time. And in all the pulley blocks which control them, we have replaced ebony with the toughest coconut wood. We have mended the sail – our only compromise because there was no time to weave another.'

'Could you not borrow from the other ships in the fleet?'

'We thought of that. None fit properly. *Alexandros* is the largest vessel in the fleet. Her masts, spars, rigging, and sails are unique. Besides, none of the others have Isis Goddess of Kingship and the Protection of the Kingdom woven into them.'

This conversation was sufficient to cover the preparations for departure. Minnakht went back to his command post with his captain and steersman at the stern, followed by the young courtier and the priests. After a moment, Keelan followed him, leaving Artemidorus and Hecate alone as the anchor was weighed. This time a man had been posted in the aft castle which obscured his view of proceedings in the bow. So, when the officer in charge of the winch waved his flag to signal that the anchor was up, another flag had to be waved before the *pausator* beat out his rhythm and the rowing song began.

Artemidorus went to the deck rail above the raised companionway, leaned against it and tried to put his thoughts in order. After a few moments Hecate came to stand beside him. The difference was apparent at once. Last week the *Alexandros* had sat high in the water. Now she sat lower. Almost all the added weight had been put on at deck level or only a little below. Unless the preparations for Cleopatra's arrival had added much more further below still, which he doubted. 'What was there in the Queen's quarters, Hecate?' he asked, idly watching the Pharos loom as they headed for the entrance to the Great Harbour. 'Anything of any weight?'

*

Hecate thought for a moment. 'A golden throne. The rest is light, cushions, cloths, sheets. Her bath I suppose. And whatever she has to fill it. There is a table and some chairs as well as formal dining couches like the ones from my old master Titus Elva's *triclinium*.'

'I cannot imagine how they've got half of that down there. The throne must at least be much smaller than the ones in her palaces. They would not fit it through the hatches.'

'Why? Is weight important?'

'That's what we're about to find out,' he said.

The others all began to gather round then. 'Right,' he said briskly. 'I want you all in the same places as you were last time, doing the same tasks. And let's hope things go better this time,' he said, looking up, struck by something strange. The anchor was up. The oars were out. Yet *Alexandros* was not moving. She sat motionless, as though waiting for something else to happen.

Artemidorus walked back towards the main mast, feeling Hecate at his shoulder. They looked at the stern where the senior officers and priests were gathered.

A kind of altar had appeared there, and as they watched, the young man he had assumed to be a courtier was stripped of his stylish clothes and laid naked upon it.

The priests began to sing.

Artemidorus realised what was going on with a shock that hit him like a blow to his belly. Hecate called something wordless as she understood as well. Before they could move, one of the chanting priests cut the young man's throat while the other held a bowl to catch his blood – as though he were a bullock being offered to Jupiter in Rome.

So, the sacrifice to Sekhmet, protector of the Pharaoh was made.

The *pausator* beat his drum and the oarsmen began their song.

XIX: Cleopatra

i

'Him,' said Hecate. 'It will be him.'

During the last three days, as *Alexandros*' sea-trials had been completed, there had been more sacrifices to Sekhmet on the temporary altar beneath the incurving sternpost, every morning before the great vessel set sail. These were apparently effective. The lion-faced goddess held her hands over them all. Although top heavy and hard to handle, *Alexandros* behaved well, even under sail. 'It's always a young man,' Hecate continued, 'with pale skin and features that the Romans would consider handsome….'

'I'd better watch out, then,' said Ferrata.

Hecate pretended not to have heard him. 'Always well-dressed and treated with respect…'

'That's you ruled out after all, Ferrata' said Quintus quietly, earning a glare from his one-eyed friend and a frown from Hecate.

'Still,' added Kyros with a glance across to Notus, 'It's a terrible waste of a beautiful boy.'

Despite everything, Hecate continued, 'until they strip him and slit his throat. In my country when such a sacrifice is to be made, the warrior who volunteers to intercede with the great god Olodumare is also treated with great respect. He is never stripped. And he passes to the higher realms through a blow to the forehead with a ritual club.'

Puella's departure had left a gap in the *contubernium* as well as in Artemidorus' heart. Neither of which Hecate could ever hope to fill. But she was beginning to fit into the group at least, if not into their centurion's bed. And with that acceptance, her confidence grew.

'The animal sacrifices in the Roman rituals are also that way,' added Kyros, who had been slave to the soothsayer Spurinna before he joined the *contubernium*. 'But then their throats are slit, so are their bellies. Then their livers are removed to be read for messages from the gods.'

'That's disgusting,' said Hecate outraged.

As Artemidorus, Hecate and the others made these observations, the group of courtiers they were watching hurried across the deck. They became part of a cluster which had arrived moments earlier – comprised mostly of guards led by Hunefer.

The *contubernium* had come aboard before dawn and watched the Macedonian and Judean legionaries seconded to the Egyptian navy come up the companionway and go down into the bowels of the ship with their armour and weapons ready for battle. As the sun rose they felt the long hull settle beneath the added weight of the troops and their supplies. But *Alexandros* remained badly balanced.

The rising sun also illuminated the Royal Docks and the Eastern Harbour beyond them. Both seemed surprisingly empty in the calm brightness of the early Summer's morning – until Artemidorus realised that Cleopatra's great fleet was anchored out on the Roman Sea itself, waiting for the arrival of their Queen and Commander in her flagship to lead them northward into battle.

No sooner had the courtiers joined Hunefer and the latest arrivals than an air of expectation settled on the whole ship. Behind them, Goddess, Queen and Pharaoh Cleopatra was carried up the companionway in her silk-walled golden litter. Admiral Minnakht strode forward to greet his commander. Cleopatra's handmaidens Charmian and Iras followed immediately behind the litter, and ran to open the curtain as Minnakht came to attention then went down on one knee beside it. Cleopatra stepped out and stood erect. Over her usual white clothing, she wore a golden breastplate and backplate. There was a wide gold belt around her waist. Charmian reached into the litter, brought out a *gladius* in a golden sheath which she hung from Cleopatra's belt. Meanwhile Iras pulled out a golden helmet which to Artemidorus' wise eyes seemed to owe more to Alexander's Greek design than *Divus Julius'* Roman one – though he knew the *gladius* was a present from her murdered lover. The sandals she usually wore had been replaced by Roman *caligae*. Above which were golden greaves that matched the glittering *bracer* arm-protectors, covering her from elbow to wrist.

Led by Minnakht, everyone nearby prostrated themselves on the cold grey lead except for Hunefer and his squad. The gigantic soldier stood resplendent in his crocodile-skin armour, his eyes raking the deck for any sign of trouble. Outside the safety of her palaces' walls, Cleopatra was still at risk. And Artemidorus' presence was simply a further reminder that she could all too easily go the way of her murdered lover *Divus Julius*.

Cleopatra surveyed the deck. The only people not prostrate apart from the guards were Artemidorus and his *contubernium*, and, at the far end of the vessel beside the altar, the captain and deck crew who were in charge of the ship. Cleopatra stepped forward, gesturing. Her litter was carried clear and Ptolemy Caesarion's replaced it. Her handmaidens opened the silken hangings and the boy also stepped out, his armour a small-scale copy of hers. When mother and son were standing side by side, Cleopatra said something so quietly that Artemidorus couldn't hear it. But it was obviously the order to rise, because first Minnakht and then everyone else pulled themselves to their feet. The Queen and her admiral walked down the length of the deck, followed by Caesarion. Behind them, handmaidens, slaves, and servants led by Charmian and Iras streamed below to make sure the Queen's apartments were ready at her convenience.

*

But the procession boarding *Alexandros* had not yet stopped. Behind Cleopatra came a surprisingly submissive white stallion, led by several young men just as handsome as the potential sacrifice Hecate had identified. Then a white bull, its horns garlanded, led by an equal number of beautiful young women. It was as docile as the stallion. Both had obviously been drugged. The horse and the bull were led along the length of the deck to the sacrificial altar where the three young men had met their ends. The sacrificial animals were followed by a group of priests and acolytes dressed in Egyptian, Greek, and Roman ceremonial garments.

The familiar rituals were swiftly and efficiently completed. Artemidorus had been to sea often enough to recognise the implacable imperatives of wind and tide. Both of which were favourable now – neither of which would be so for long. The horse died first, his liver, according to the Greek priest from the nearby Temple of Poseidon, prophesying a calm voyage and successful outcome. Then the bull conveyed a message from the founder of *Divus Julius'* family Venus Victrix – that the coming battle was assured of victory with glory for all. Having passed down the gods' reassurances, the beasts were carried below to be butchered and prepared for some future dinner. Then, the young man the Hecate had identified stepped forward onto the bloody deck, shrugged off his finery and offered his throat in turn to the shaven-headed priests of Sekmet. At least, it seemed, she was content to accept his sacrifice in silence and forgo the necessity of a reply. There was no need to disembowel him and read messages in his entrails.

'That leaves one set of priests,' whispered Ferrata. 'Nasty-looking bastards. What are they waiting for? Any idea, Kyros?'

His question was answered at once as the leader of the maidens who had conducted the bull aboard stepped forward. She sat on the altar that was still running with steaming blood. She retained her pure white clothing – which began to redden at once. The strongest-looking of the remaining priests stepped forward and slid a length of twine around the delicate, pale column of her neck. Then he tightened it with practiced efficiency and strangled her within a matter of moments.

'I've heard of this during my studies in the Musaeum,' said Crinas quietly. 'But never thought to see it. She is the Virgin of the Nile, sacrificed to the God Hapi, Lord of the River, and his consort Anuket. Her sacrifice can also be offered to Wadj-wer, God of the Deep Sea.'

'That's the one,' said Ferrata feelingly as the priests and their acolytes left carrying the human sacrifices. The companionway was lifted into place. The *pausator* began to beat his drum and the voyage got under way. 'It's the Gods of the Deep Sea we need on our side.'

'Hmmm' grunted Crinas. 'And maybe Set, the God of Chaos and Storms.'

ii

Alexandros powered out past the Pharos and into the Roman Sea, the rhythm of her oar-strokes at battle speed, the *pausator* pounding his drum and the oarsmen singing lustily. At first, Artemidorus remained at the bow, opposite the removable section of rail at the top of the raised companionway, pondering on how the ship builders had managed to balance its weight with some sort of ballast on the opposite side. But as the battle ship swept through the harbour entrance, he turned, strode across the deck, and climbed to the top of the forward fighting tower. He arrived in good time to appreciate the awe-inspiring sight of Cleopatra's battle-ready navy spread out over what looked like a couple of Roman *miles* to east and west, all facing northward, waiting for their Queen and Commander.

'How many are there?' asked Hecate, arriving, breathlessly at his side as the rest pounded up behind her.

There were too many of them to count at a glance, their numbers fading into distance and invisibility. 'Well over two hundred,' he answered. 'One hundred and forty battle ships ready to destroy Murcus and then Ahenobarbus with their fleets. More than fifty supply vessels ready to back us up. And Poseidon alone knows how many triremes and liburnians, spies and messengers.'

The pair of them looked from the eastern horizon to the western one as *Alexandros* punched her way through the rollers, powering out past the forward line to take her place at the head of the Egyptian navy. No sooner had she done so, than the beat of drums echoed away into the distance on either hand and the raucous rhythmic singing of the oarsmen followed. The entire navy began to surge forward, northwards away from the Egyptian coast and a little westward with the late-morning sun behind their right shoulders. 'Like a legion marching onto the battlefield,' said Ferrata. 'All that's missing is the *barritus* war cry to terrify the enemy.'

'I don't know,' said Quintus. 'The way they sing their rowing song would probably do just as well…'

*

'Queen Cleopatra wishes to see you,' said Charmian as the Egyptian navy continued to surge north-westward towards Greece and Murcus' sixty-ship squadron. He followed Cleopatra's handmaiden down to the Royal apartments where Cleopatra and her admiral were looking over a chart of the great eastern section of the Roman Sea.

Cleopatra glanced up and acknowledged him with a nod then she turned back to the matter in hand. Artemidorus had a moment's leisure to admire the silken, gilded, magnificence of his admittedly cramped surroundings. As though the tail-feathers of a peacock had been made cloth and hung on the walls, laid on the deck and stretched over the furniture.

'If we proceed at the speed we maintained during our test runs and allowing for rest periods at night,' Minnakht was saying, 'we will sight Murcus and his squadron in five days' time. By our best estimate, his ships are more than four hundred Roman *miles* away. But as Your Majesty will observe, the island of Krete is a convenient stopping point along the way. It is three days distant, less if the south-easterly wind strengthens sufficiently to let us use our sails.'

'And what is the purpose of waiting at Krete?' asked the queen.

'So that we can reform, re-supply if necessary, bring the captains aboard while safe at anchor for a final tactical briefing and then proceed across the last hundred *miles* or so in tight formation to face Murcus. If he is still where we believe him to be.'

'And if he is not?' she probed.

'Then we head straight for Brundisium and Ahenobarbus himself.'

Cleopatra was still staring thoughtfully at the map when another messenger arrived, crashed to his knees, and pressed his forehead to the exquisitely carpeted floor. 'I have a message for the admiral,

Majesty,' he said.

'Stand and give it to him,' said Cleopatra.

But Artemidorus already knew what it was – the stirring of the ship's long hull warned him.

'Admiral, the captain says to tell you that the wind is strengthening from the south-east. He wishes to ship the oars and deploy the sails.'

Minnakht paused for an instant, then he answered. 'Tell the captain I will be on deck at once.' He turned to Cleopatra. 'With your permission, Majesty.'

'I think, Admiral, that we had better come to an understanding. I may be your queen and commander of the navy – in name at least – but I do not know the sea or your ship as well as you do. You may act on your own initiative then inform me what is going on at your earliest convenience. And remind your men that this is a warship, not a floating palace. There is no need for them to prostrate themselves. They just need to follow their orders quickly, efficiently and remaining erect at all times.'

iii

'Have you read the message you are taking from Cassius to Antony, Septem?' enquired Cleopatra as Minnakht headed towards the captain and the weather deck.

'No, Majesty. There seemed little point. If I opened it I would probably anger Antony, no matter how carefully I resealed it. He has a nose for that sort of thing. In any case, it is not hard to guess the contents – threats against himself, the Triumvirs and possibly yourself. Perhaps a request for negotiation, no doubt stating terms the General would find impossible to consider let alone to meet. And in any case, I am likely to be there when he reads it – then he will tell me anything he thinks important and relevant to me.'

'You have thought this through, Septem.'

'Of course, Majesty.'

'Good. I will be writing to Antony myself and giving you the letter to take to him along with Cassius' scroll of threats and impossible demands.'

'Of course, Majesty.'

'I propose to write it while we are at anchor off Krete. The motion of the ship under oars or sail will make it difficult for my secretaries to achieve the level of penmanship I require. And in any case, there is no hurry because you cannot go until we have seen off Murcus at the very least; perhaps Ahenobarbus too. Unless we do that, any vessel I send you home in is likely to be stopped and boarded long before it reaches safe haven in Italy.'

'That is true, Majesty, but if you are worried about your secretaries' penmanship, I can lend you Kyros and his friend Notus. They are more than mere forgers and code-breakers.'

'That will not be necessary. In the mean-time, we will have a meeting like this every morning so we can discuss what I wish to put in my letters to Antony, beyond explaining to your General what you have managed to achieve in terms of saving my two kingdoms from invasion by Cassius, and from starvation by getting Herod to bring me corn from Parthia. Informing him of what you told me about Cassius' and Brutus' past and future activities. Balancing what you know of Antony and his plans with what I know of my own plans in the immediate future and in the longer term, now that, thanks to you, I have room and opportunity to make them.'

'As you wish, Majesty.'

'Of course, it is as I wish, Septem,' answered Cleopatra with a smile. 'Everything always is. That is what *majesty* means.'

*

Three days later an unseasonably hot afternoon found them anchored in a wide bay off the south coast of Krete, that lay between two tiny fishing villages called Gailos and Palaiochora, each built on a promontory.

It was just over two days since they had seen the first sail appearing briefly over the northern horizon, then turning away and running back towards Greece. It had been a liburnian by the look of things; and was obviously one of Murcus' spy ships. Minnakht sent his own triremes hurrying north to seek out his enemy. Of five sent out, two came back this morning. They reported that Murcus and his sixty-ship squadron were still waiting off Cape Tenaro, the southernmost cape of Greece.

A humid, breathless calm settled on the bay as the afternoon passed. It was as though the south-easterly breeze had been enough to blow the furnace-hot air from above the great deserts of the Sinai and those to the east of Egypt ruled by the Sassanid Kings, westwards towards Greece and then to leave it hanging over Krete in a dead calm. The oarsmen bringing the war ships to anchor, tugging the supply ships, and rowing the hundred and fifty captains to the admiral's briefing aboard *Alexandros,* sweating and complaining. The fire-trays cooking the crews' *cena* – their first hot meal since putting to sea – simply seemed to make matters worse. Their smoke rose straight up on the afternoon air, more than two-hundred vertical columns, tying the individual ships to the realms of the gods above. Artemidorus and his *contubernium* stood to the rear of the crowd of captains, sweating like the rest. Artemidorus had never experienced anything quite like this weather.

The briefing given by Minnakht and Cleopatra was to the point. 'Once we have rounded the western cape of Krete, we need to go at once onto a war-footing,' ordered the admiral. 'We will be within easy reach of Murcus and his fleet if they are still where they were last reported to be. If they have come south, we will be at war tomorrow. If they have stayed close to the Greek coast it may take two days to bring them to battle. But we must be ready at once.'

'It is impossible to overstate the importance of this battle,' emphasised Cleopatra. 'If we lose, then Antony loses. If Antony loses, then Egypt loses. With Antony gone, Brutus and Cassius will rip the Two Kingdoms apart like jackals tearing a wounded lion. I, your queen, will either die or be taken, chained, in triumph to Rome. Alexandria will go the way of Carthage, burned to the ground and then that very ground salted and made barren. Every man here who has stood with me will lose everything he possesses, loves, or worships.

'However, if we win then Antony wins. Egypt will be placed in a position of power beside Rome itself. We will rule the east of the Roman Sea as Rome rules the west. Our future will be assured, and our fortunes made. And, beyond that and the promise it brings, I will personally reward each of you with gold, property and honour. This is what I want you to remember above everything when you confront Murcus and his war-ships and call for *ramming speed*!'

iv

The night was as airless and sultry as the day. Sleep would have been impossible, had they even wished for it. But most of the men and women in Cleopatra's navy treated this as though it was the eve of battle. Swapping stories designed to build their courage, praying to their various gods, polishing their armour and sharpening their weapons.

'You remember Alesia?' said Quintus. 'Hades, I thought we were done for there, with one army of Gauls in a fort up on the hill above us and then another even bigger army sneaking up behind us, trapping us like bones between the jaws of hungry dogs…'

'I heard about Pharsalus too,' said Kyros.

'How Antony led the legions for once instead of the cavalry…' added Notus, wide-eyed.

'True enough, boys,' agreed Quintus. 'And he did it well.'

'And Alexandria,' added Artemidorus, 'when the riots started and that snake Pothinus joined with General Achillas in their attempt to kill *Divus Julius* and Queen Cleopatra, slaughter the lot of us and put Ptolemy XIII and his sister Arsinoe on the throne of the Two Kingdoms. Hot work! Even before the fleet, the Royal Harbour and that part of the library went up in flames. Hot work but worth it.'

'Oh yes!' said Ferrata. 'And look where your *hot work* has got us in the end. Out of the cooking pot and into the fire!'

'Oh, stop complaining!' said Kyros, 'and pass Notus your sword while we have the whetstones.'

'I always sharpen my own sword!' spat Ferrata.

'Yes,' chuckled Quintus. 'That's what we've heard. Here, lad, take mine. And a good edge, mind – I might need to use the blade as well as the point. You can never be sure in a sea-battle…' He handed the sword to Kyros.

'Then my *pugio*,' said Artemidorus. 'But be careful with it – it's almost magically sharp. It used to belong to Brutus himself.' He handed it to Notus.

'Is it the one Brutus used to stab *Divus Julius*?' asked the young forger.

'As a matter of fact, it is.'

'Oh! Tell me how you got your hands on it,' demanded Hecate.

'Well…' Artemidorus leaned forward to begin the story that was familiar to the rest of them but popular enough to warrant re-telling as it involved a detailed description of *Divus Julius'* death.

So the night passed.

At first light, even before the sun crept over the horizon, the first signals were run up. The *pausators* began to beat their rhythms and the Egyptian navy started to move. Admiral Minnakht led them due west, with the rising sun behind him, until the shadowy hulk of the land on his right ended abruptly in a wall of hillsides and bays running away to the east of north. Then, giving his squadrons sea-room to form up on either flank astern, he turned north and began to pound across the hundred miles that separated him from the first of Cleopatra's enemies.

Artemidorus took his accustomed place at the top of the forward castle, directly in front of the foremast, straining to see ahead, eyes narrowed and shaded in the molten-gold light of the morning. But the only ships immediately visible were Minnakht's liburnians, skimming ahead at battle speed as they hunted the enemy. He turned and leaned back against the castle's low wall. The sun on his left struck across the distant hills of Krete to make the masts of the ships in *Alexandros*' wake gleam like a forest of golden trees. The sea behind them should have made the day feel cool. But the great blue-green surface shone like soiled silk, stirring sluggishly, only breaking into ripples where oars in their thousands dipped, pulled, and rose.

Shading his eyes again, Artemidorus looked away to the east and frowned. There on the farthest horizon, sitting well below the rising sun, was a line of pitch-black cloud. The sight of it somehow seemed to chill him, even as he felt the first zephyr of breeze stirring against his cheek.

*

When it steadied, the wind came from the south east once again. Even though the Egyptian navy was sailing due north, they were able to deploy their sails and give the sweating oarsmen a chance to rest. Artemidorus didn't like it, though. 'It's too hot,' he said to Hecate and Quintus as they stood on either side of him. 'And there's that bank of cloud astern that seems to be following closer and closer behind. Like a pack of black wolves hunting us.'

'Hunting the sun,' said Hecate.

'If it is,' said Quintus, 'then it'll catch up soon enough. Apollo had better whip the horses of his fiery chariot pretty smartly, because it looks like Tempestes, goddess of storms, is hard on his heels.'

Quintus' prediction proved as accurate as any of Hecate's. As the Egyptian fleet surged north with a strengthening south-easterly behind them, the sun was gulped down by the wall of black clouds. The heat was oppressive. The clouds seemed so low overhead that they appeared to attain weight, pressing down on the fleet like the roof of some unimaginable underworld cave. As the light faded and the clouds writhed, the sea began to grow more restless and the wind grew stronger, carrying with it a distant roaring as though the greatest cavalry charge ever to thunder into battle was bearing relentlessly down on them.

'I'll go down and see what the admiral thinks of this,' said Artemidorus. 'Because it doesn't look good to me.' He turned and was about to climb onto the main deck when Hecate's hand fell on his shoulder. He stopped. Turned. Looked. She was pointing silently dead ahead, her eyes wide.

And there, right on the edge of the northern horizon, revealed by the last gleam of that strange, fading light, was a line of battle ships coming towards them. 'Murcus' fleet!' he said.

But his voice was lost under the cacophony of orders, drumbeats, and scurrying feet as *Alexandros* went to battle stations.

V

Artemidorus arrived at the command area at *Alexandros*' stern part-way through a conversation. 'We have the wind, Majesty!' Minnakht was saying urgently to Cleopatra. 'Yes, there is a storm gathering but even that gives us an advantage because it is coming in behind us, putting wind and waves under our stern and in our sails. All that power will push our fleet forward while Murcus has to fight against it just to come at us! It is as though we are attacking him by charging downhill!'

'As long as the storm doesn't overwhelm us all, Admiral!' Cleopatra sounded – and looked – unaccustomedly uncertain. Artemidorus had seen her in the midst of battle and she had never looked as nervous as she did now.

'If it gets too serious, we can always turn and run for Krete.' Minnakht explained, his voice calm, as though soothing a startled horse. 'As the wind is from the south, the island will protect us as soon as we approach the north coast. We can get there in a matter of hours if we must. Especially as our oarsmen will be rested.'

'And you see this as a risk worth taking?' Cleopatra was wavering. The promise of victory overcoming her nervousness.

'It is a gift from the gods, Majesty. We will never get an opportunity as good as this again. Although the sky is overcast, it is still mid-afternoon. We can dispense with Murcus and his fleet by nightfall. Then we can deal with the storm and run for shelter if we have to!'

Cleopatra nodded her acquiescence. Not too happy but convinced by his argument.

Artemidorus looked around, testing his own belief in the admiral's confident words. The sky was completely covered now. But, there was a strange, leaden light which made everything clear and visible: the line of ships sitting on the northern horizon, for example. Even while the two fleets were beginning to close with each other, the existence of a second battle-line behind Murcus' first.

Cleopatra, in full armour, labored up into her favourite position in the after castle, with Hunefer towering beside her on one side and

Caesarion on the other. Admiral Minnakht turned to his captain and helmsman. 'We will use the wind for as long as we can,' he said. 'We will sail to within attacking distance, deploy the *onagers* with incendiary ammunition while the scorpions and ballistas fire their bolts through sails, masts, towers and castles. Then we get rid of the sails, run out the oars and proceed at ramming speed. Our oarsmen will be fresh. Murcus' will be at least tired – perhaps exhausted – rowing against the wind and waves like they are doing.'

'And the rest of the fleet?'

'Will take their lead from us as ordered. *Alexandros* is the tip of an arrow-head. We will attack the centre of Murcus' line and ram straight through. Then our battle ships will peel off to right and left, taking on his ships individually, ram against ram. While the triremes and liburnians attack from the sides, spreading fear and confusion. The tactics were successful when Rome fought Carthage at Ecnomus. Let us hope they will be equally successful for us now.'

*

The *contubernium* were among the last to strap on their armour. When Artemidorus arrived at the top of the stern castle, he was glad he was wearing his steel band cuirass at least, because Cleopatra was of course already fully armed. As was everyone with her except for her messenger Charmian and her other handmaiden Iras who was standing at her side. He had left his helmet and gladius with the others. Only Brutus' deadly sharp *pugio* hung from his belt. And, in a haze, he had left off his greaves and arm guards. When he knew where he was to be deployed, he would know where to hang his shield on the deck-rail, ready to hand.

'You sent for me, Majesty?'

'I did. My message to Antony is now complete – has been substantially finished since we left the anchorage in the bay south of Krete. But now is the time to give it to you, I think.'

'As you wish, Majesty.'

She turned to Iras who handed him a leather case bound in gold, sealed in wax, containing Cleopatra's message. 'And therefore, as my messenger,' the queen continued, 'I forbid you or your companions to take any part in the battle when it begins. I see you are armed, and I know you will find this order hard to follow. But you are worth more to me as Antony's secret agent and trusted courier than you are as a centurion. Even as an outstanding, battle-hardened centurion. The mission I give you is to stay alive. Get ready to go aboard one of the fast triremes Admiral Minnakht has ready for the purpose, and head for Italy the moment we have destroyed Murcus and his fleet. Before word of our victory reaches Ahenobarbus off Brundisum and he thinks to send patrols south to cover the gaps in the blockade left by Murcus' destruction. Do I make myself clear?'

'You have clearly thought this through very carefully, Majesty.'

'I have.'

There was the briefest of silences. The wind howled in the rigging. Surf thundered against *Alexandros*' side. The tower rocked as the hull heaved.

'Septem?' she prompted.

'It will be as you order, Majesty.'

'Of course, it will,' she said.

vi

'What do you mean we stay clear of the fighting?' demanded Quintus outraged. 'We're all in battle-dress. Even Hecate and Crinas have armour on; so do Kyros and Notus!'

'There was never any question of Hecate joining the fight,' snapped Artemidorus. 'She is not a trained soldier. At least Kyros and Notus have some experience. And Crinas will be needed to tend the wounded. Well, now none of us will get in the fight either. Our mission is more important.'

They were standing beside the fore castle shouting at each-other. This was not because of anger or frustration, but because the weather had worsened while Artemidorus was with Cleopatra. The wind was now blustering towards a full tempest, tearing the tops of the grey seas following them northward and screaming in the rigging. The belly of the sail was taut. Glancing at it, Artemidorus found himself praying that whoever had sewn it back together had done a good job. And, now he thought of it, that the coconut-wood blocks and tackles were a good deal stronger than the ebony ones had been.

'We go back to the stern,' he said. 'Join Hunefer and his squad keeping an eye on the queen and the admiral. That's the closest we come to battle. Understand?'

No sooner had he asked the question than the importance of his instructions was emphasised by the arrival of the Macedonian and Judean legionaries, who ran up the deck and crowded into the bows, obviously ready to leap aboard whichever of Murcus' ships *Alexandros* rammed and start their slaughter there. Bowmen and slingers pushed past them, mounting the fore-castle, ready to rain death down on Murcus' men. As the *contubernium* reluctantly worked their way back down the deck, so the fire-trays that had cooked *cena* in the anchorage were re-ignited and the great flammable bundles to be fired from the *onagers* were prepared.

Halfway down the deck, the secret agents shouldered past the sail-handlers who were beginning to exchange anxious looks interspersed with glances up at the sloping mast and straining sail. Then, as though a waterfall had been unleashed in the clouds low above them, the rain came.

One moment the opposing vessel was clearly visible more than a *mile* ahead, the next they had vanished behind a grey wall of water. Artemidorus and his companions sloshed through the downpour as it thundered off the leaden deck, and arrived at the stern castle, the admiral, his captain and the helmsman. Artemidorus went on past them to the sternpost, looking behind *Alexandros* at the fleet. At least it was still visible. Indeed, it made a stirring sight, stretching away into grey invisibility on either hand, square sails full of the wind, prows and rams smashing through the foaming white horses which were Poseidon's creatures. All in battle order, each great vessel holding its line. Looking at it, he could easily understand Minnakht's confidence. If Murcus hoped to stand against this great wave of armoured wood and bronze rams then he was clearly making a fatal miscalculation.

He turned, just in time to see more of Cleopatra's guards go into the after castle and climb to stand beside their queen at her favourite vantage point. Admiral Minnakht exchanged a further word or two with his captain and then went up to join her. Artemidorus strode forward just in time to hear the captain say to his *gubernator*, 'The Admiral wants us to wait until we catch our first sight of Murcus' ships then we run up the signal to drop sails, run out oars and proceed immediately to battle speed.'

'Better send the man with the sharpest eyes up to the forward castle, then,' advised the *gubernator*. 'The more warning we get the better. And I hope we spot them soon, the conditions are fast going from difficult to impossible.'

'For them as well as for us, old friend.'

'Unless they used the cover of the rain to turn and run for safe haven,' said the captain, 'which is what I'd have done if I was Murcus.'

*

As they waited moment after breathless moment for the signal from the forward tower that told of *enemy in sight*, the weather only worsened. The wind continued to strengthen. The waves pounding their stern became larger and more widely-spaced. Even *Alexandros'* massive hull began to pitch and heave, her masts and rigging howling and screaming. Suddenly, the foresail carried away with a report that was clearly audible above the other pandemonium of sounds. No sooner had it done so than a signal came from, the forecastle. 'What is that?' demanded the captain. 'That's not *enemy in sight…*'

But the next wild heave answered his question. The entire tower tilted over and crashed onto the deck, crushing many of the soldiers waiting there and throwing the signaler and his companions overboard.

Half a dozen heartbeats later Minnakht arrived back down at the command post. 'That's it!' he said. 'The Queen says we must turn and run for safe haven.'

'Turn?' repeated the captain, aghast. 'In *this*?'

'Her direct orders,' gasped the admiral. 'Do it now.'

'We need to lose the sails then,' decided the captain with a speaking glance to his *gubernator*. 'Only the oars will get us round. And the rest of the fleet…'

'Will see what we are doing and copy us,' snapped the admiral. 'Septem! You and your men make yourselves useful. Go and tell the sail-handlers to loosen the sails!'

'But they need to do it gently and under absolute control!' added the captain anxiously.

Artemidorus led his companions along the deck at a run. As they passed the stern castle, they split into two teams, Quintus heading for the right side with Kyros, Notus and Crinas; Artemidorus for the left. He arrived at the anxious deck-team with Hercules, Hecate and Ferrata at his back. 'The captain says you must slacken the sail,' he bellowed. 'But do it slowly and carefully.'

The leader of the sail-handlers nodded. He and his men ran to the point where the rigging was secured after it had been run through the wooden blocks. They loosened the knots carefully, five of them in a line together taking the strain like children playing tug-rope. But no sooner had they taken their first step forward, feeding the line through the block to the bottom of the sail than the coconut-wood block shattered. The line snagged. The sail was stuck. Without a word, Artemidorus pounded over to the far side – only to discover that Quintus' team was in the same predicament. Below the raving of the storm, he heard the rumble of the oars being run out. *Alexandros*' head swooped down the back of a storm wave. The secret agent turned, ready to run back and warn the admiral and the captain what was going on. He had an instantaneous vision of the after castle with Cleopatra standing on the top of it, her armour gleaming like a candle-flame with the dark hulk of Hunefer beside her. Beside the castle stood the admiral, almost as gaudily armed, with the captain beside him, calling to the *gubernator* – no doubt demanding that he bring the ship hard round.

But then, in a heartbeat, everything changed once more. With a great, tearing bellow, the mainsail burst. Not just half of it. As Artemidorus swung back he realised it had all failed; burst like an over-filled bladder. The whole sail reduced to rags flapping madly in the wind. The mast, which had been straining forward under the enormous pressure of the tempest, lashed back. Its movement was so fearsome that the standing rigging securing it to the bows snapped. The mast itself, the unblemished heart of a pine tree one hundred cubits high and two cubits wide, snapped like a twig. With the yards still attached and the remnants of the sail flapping wildly, it crashed back onto the sternpost as the admiral, captain, *gubernator,* and crew dived for safety. Then it slid down towards the deck in a tangle of oiled linen and rigging, the spars destroying the deck-rails on either side.

And even as they did so the weight of the toppling mast itself smashed the stern castle to pieces.

vii

Artemidorus glanced over his shoulder as he ran towards the wreckage and saw with horror that Cleopatra's decision had destroyed her fleet. As *Alexandros* was turning, so were the others, following their leader, precisely as ordered. Even those whose sails were safely down, were tossing helplessly in the cross-swell that was now smashing into their sides instead of their sterns as the wild wind tore the spray across their decks. While there had been sea-room for them all to sail northward side by side – room even for their oars to be run out clear of each-other – as they turned, they were moving too close to one-another. And the instant before he looked away, he saw the first two collide.

But then all his concentration was focused on the ruin of the stern castle and Cleopatra trapped somewhere beneath it. The wind-driven rain and spray beat against his back. The deck heaved. The great column of the mast stirred uneasily across the castle. It had fallen to the left, upwind, side of the stern post and it was clear to the secret agent that it would need to be moved somehow to allow access to anyone trapped beneath it. By the grace of the gods, it had not fallen flat onto the deck. It was being supported on the stout aft rail behind the stern-post itself, even though the rails immediately forward of the section still standing had been destroyed by the spars. He pulled out his dagger, certain that no matter what else might be involved, he was going to have to cut his way in through the Gordian knot of cordage and get access to the area beneath the mast before the last of the rail yielded and the whole thing was crushed flat against the deck. Vaguely aware of the others gathering around him, he crashed to his knees beside the wreckage. 'Majesty?' he bellowed. 'Queen Cleopatra?'

There was no reply.

As he sucked in breath to try again, Minnakht arrived beside him. 'We need to get the mast free and pushed overboard,' he bellowed up at the stricken admiral, 'before it crushes everything beneath it. And everyone!'

Minnakht turned, looking at the captain and the helmsman as they picked themselves up. He ran back towards them, repeating Artemidorus' words at full bellow. The secret agent turned back to the job in hand. He thrust himself forward over the icily cold and slippery lead, snaking beneath the mast as he tried to get through into the wreckage. Pressed against the deck, with the weight of the mast restlessly above him, his whole body seemed to feel the new movement of the ship as she rolled from side to side at the behest of wind and waves; distractingly so. His mind raced, with the mast and both castles gone by the board, she was riding higher and much less steadily. There was even a chance that the unbalanced hull might roll right over. He pushed himself forward once again until he was confronted by a wall of shattered wood. There were arms and legs sticking out of it and he began to pray they didn't belong to anyone he was here to rescue. Because the state they were in made it clear that their owners were well beyond help.

The mast moved, rolling slightly, and settling. As fast as he could, he reversed and pulled himself free. Clearly it would be hopeless to approach things from this direction. He pushed himself upright and ran a little way down the deck, then he vaulted over the mast and ran back to the opposite side. He paused, looking around. This part of the castle was less damaged. What looked like most of the side-wall lay sticking out in a kind of ledge at waist height, supported by some debris beneath it. The edge was straight and the structure still looked strong. This was a better way in than trying to worm beneath the mast, he thought. But he would need a little help to get any distance into the wreckage.

Activity had begun all around him. The admiral and the captain were summoning teams of soldiers and sailors to get the mast loose of the rigging and push it over the side. The *gubernator* and his team had regained control of the tiller-oar. And, most importantly, his *contubernium* had all come running to his side. 'Hercules, Quintus, Ferrata, I want the three of you to lift this section while I go under it,' he ordered. 'Do it carefully, though. I don't want anything disturbed if we can help it. I certainly don't want anything collapsing on top of me.' He paused to draw breath. The thought of being crushed was followed by the instant decision to keep his own armour on – but some of the others would need to reduce their bulk if they were going to go deeper. 'Kyros, Notus, you are slimmer and slighter than I am. Get your armour off and get ready to follow me in.'

He turned and squatted, utterly focused. Beside him, the three men took hold of the section and began to heave it upwards. Everything Artemidorus could see beneath it remained apparently solidly in place, despite the rolling of the deck and the battering of spray, wind, and rain. He rocked forward onto his knees, went flat on his belly and slithered in.

There was definitely more cordage here. It was as though he was crawling into a tangle of wild vine stems. He began cutting it free with his keen-edged dagger, passing lengths of it back to Kyros and Notus as soon as they got close enough behind. After the rigging, he came to more wood. He could make out little in the drizzling gloom, but it looked like a solid wall of the stuff to him. No way round it or through it, which left only one alternative that he could think of. 'Can they lift higher?' he called over his shoulder. As soon as the message was passed on back, the ruined roof of the flattened wall began to move upward inch by inch. He slid his fingers into the gap and felt vacancy beyond. 'Higher!' he bellowed. The section above his head stirred, lifted. He pushed his hands and forearms into the gap. '*If they drop it now…* he thought.

But suddenly, unexpectedly, someone on the far side of the wooden wall clasped his hands. Artemidorus was so surprised that it required all his self-control not to jerk his arms back. Instead, he called, 'who's there?'

'Septem?' came the reply. 'Septem is that you?'

'Hunefer!' he called. 'Are you all right? Where is Queen Cleopatra?'

'Her Majesty is beside me. Unconscious. I cannot tell how she is.'

'And Caesarion?'

'Beside the queen. He is hurt, but not badly, I think.'

'Very well. We are going to try and lift this section higher so you have a chance to move yourself, the queen and the boy out to safety. Is there anyone else there?'

'No. Give me a moment. I believe I can get in a position to help.'

There was the sound of movement. 'I am on my knees,' gasped the captain of Cleopatra's guard. 'Lift the section higher so that I can wedge my shoulders…'

'Lift,' called Artemidorus, automatically glancing back as he did so, just in time to see Hecate stoop under the crazily-angled roof, also stripped of her useless armour, carrying a brightly-burning lamp. As the broken planks eased higher still, she passed the lamp forward so that Artemidorus was able to take it and hold it up. Shading the flame with his hand, he looked over the wooden barrier into the chamber occupied by Hunefer, Cleopatra and Caesarion. He gasped. The space was so tiny! It seemed to him to be hardly any larger than one of the ornate sarcophagi he had seen in the Valley of the Kings. Hunefer was crouching nearby feet flat on the deck, knees almost touching his shoulders which were wedged beneath the boards that Hercules, Quintus and Ferrata were holding and fighting to raise higher. Immediately beyond him, Cleopatra lay curled, her golden armour battered and dusty, her golden helmet gone, her face pallid even in the golden lamplight. Beyond her lay Caesarion, his face also pale, his eyes huge and terrified but his jaw set with brave determination. Very much his father's boy, though the centurion proudly.

'Now!' grated Hunefer.

'Heave!' bellowed Artemidorus. He handed the lamp back to Hecate positioned himself in a low crouch bending his body just like the captain of the guard and joined Hunefer with his back and shoulders against the makeshift ceiling. Then like the others he was pushing upwards with all his might, straining his back, belly, calves and – most especially – his thighs. The top of Cleopatra's premature sarcophagus groaned upwards by a cubit, then by another. All at once there was an unexpected movement beside the secret agent. Hecate handed the lamp back to Notus and slid her slim, muscular frame through the narrow gap the heaving men had opened. There was hardly room for three people in there, let alone four, but somehow she managed to move with swift and effective economy. A moment after she clambered in, she was guiding Caesarion out onto the deck.

'Can you move the queen?' asked Artemidorus breathlessly. His whole torso and straining legs seemed to be burning. A sensation intensified by each roll of the ship, each blast of storm wind.

'Be quick,' grated Hunefer.

'She's tangled in the rigging,' answered Hecate. 'I need to cut her free.'

'Notus,' hasped Artemidorus. 'Take my dagger. I put it back in my sheath. Pass it through to her – quickly!'

Notus obeyed. Hecate took the lethally sharp blade and went to work.

'Quick!' gasped Hunefer again. 'We can't hold it for much longer.'

The guard captain's warning was given added weight, suddenly, by a movement from the far side of the wreckage. 'What's going on?' gasped Artemidorus.

'They're trying to move the mast,' bellowed Hercules in answer. 'They want to roll it away from us over the side. But they're pushing it this way towards us first to get it free of the rigging.

'Quickly, Hecate,' called Artemidorus, aware that if the weight of the mast was added to the boards they were supporting, it would simply crush them all. Sweat was running down his face and neck. Beneath his tunic underneath the armour protecting his back and shoulders.

'Got it!' called Hecate. 'She's free.' Holding the dagger between her teeth, she took the unconscious queen and heaved her head and shoulders over to the makeshift wall immediately in front of Hunefer. She lifted the comatose woman into a sitting position with her back to the wooden partition, then hoisted her over the wall. In spite of his twisted position and his acute pain, Artemidorus was just able to reach through the gap and grasp the queen's shoulders. As Hecate pushed, he pulled and Cleopatra slowly slid out to safety. As soon as her torso was clear, Notus placed the lamp on the heaving deck, then he and Kyros took her and slid her out onto the streaming lead outside beside her son.

Hecate followed close behind, the dagger still clenched in her teeth. She slid through the gap above the wooden wall, wormed past

Artemidorus, picked up the lamp and replaced Notus at his side.

'Now you, Hunefer,' wheezed Artemidorus. But his mind, racing ahead, saw how impossible it would be for Hunefer to get out without a lot more help. And all the help available now appeared to be aiding the admiral and the captain in their attempt to get rid of the mast. 'Hercules,' he called. 'Can we raise this any higher and hold it?'

'Not without more help Septem. And… NO!'

Artemidorus never discovered precisely what the final shout meant. But events made him pretty certain. Minnakht and his captain had clearly freed the mast. They rolled it inboard, then pushed it fiercely out praying that it would simply roll over the left side, the oars no doubt retracted to preserve them from damage.

But rolling it inboard to the right destroyed the fragile balance between the straining men and the heavy board they were holding up. The wooden edge tore out of Hercules', Quintus' and Ferrata's grip. Artemidorus felt it closing down and threw himself out with Hecate at his side. The last thing he saw in the flickering lamplight was the whole thing shutting down like an enormous trapdoor on Hunefer's crouching figure. It hesitated momentarily on the top of the frail wooden wall that had preserved them all so far, then it slammed hard against the deck. Whatever sound was made by Hunefer's bones as they were crushed was lost in the raving of the wind. Whatever surge of blood exploded from him as his massive body burst was washed away invisibly by the rain and the spray.

By that time, Artemidorus was out onto the icy lead of the weather deck, Hecate at his side. Kyros and Notus kneeling beside the queen and her son. Hercules, Quintus and Ferrata staggering away from the flattened ruin of the tower. Artemidorus tried to straighten but the torn muscles of his shoulders and chest would not allow him. His thighs cramped, and he staggered like a drunkard, shocked and disorientated. The wind clawed at him, nearly pushing him over as *Alexandros*, unbalanced by the weight of the mast rolling across the deck reared back, plunging her right side down.

A huge sea grasped her at that moment. It tore the heavy boarding platform clean off. The counterweight on the left side, unbalanced, instantly pulled the ship over almost onto her opposite quarter. The mast slid down the sloping deck to tumble free on the far side of the ruined after castle. Relieved of the weight, *Alexandros* rolled wildly back, given extra power by the storm wind and the huge seas beating against her from the south. Artemidorus staggered first one way and then the other on legs that felt like wood. Forward towards the wreckage, then backwards towards the edge of the deck. Forward again, then back once more, ever closer to the deck-rail which was no longer there because the spars had smashed it out of existence.

He only realised at the last moment he was going over the side. It was far too late to call for help. There was no-one near enough to reach him. The closest person to him was Hecate and she was far off as she stood there, pulling the dagger from between her teeth. He threw himself forward, seeking some kind of purchase on the deck. Measured his length, face down on the unforgiving surface. But there was only the lead which was as slick as ice, rising like a hillside in front of him as he continued to slide powerlessly backward, arms and legs spread uselessly; polished iron armour sliding smoothly across the dull grey metal almost as if it had been oiled.

Hecate saw what was happening. Understood the dreadful inevitability and how there was so little she could do.

But there was something.

As Artemidorus went over the side, she threw him his dagger.

XX: Murcus

Admiral Lucius Statius Murcus surveyed his sixty-ship squadron as it rode safely in the lee of Cape Tenaro, one of the southernmost capes in Greece. Mentally, he thanked the gods that he had had the foresight to turn and run for shelter when the rain-storm hid him from Cleopatra's fleet. He would have to sacrifice a good fat bull to Jupiter Optimus Maximus as soon as he returned to Rome. He had called on the greatest of the gods and promised the sacrifice as he realised how powerful the approaching storm would be. An effective prayer and promise – not one of his ships had been lost. True enough there was some mending to be done. Sails, spars and rigging to be repaired or replaced. One or two men lost overboard, the odd accident – broken limbs and skulls as might be expected under such circumstances. But if Cleopatra did still appear now that the tempest was past, the sky clear, the sea calm and the wind firmly southerly, he would have no real trouble in turning to face her.

As he considered his options if the Egyptian fleet did appear, there was a distant shout.

A few moments later, his captain came hurrying up. 'Sail sighted, Admiral.'

'Egyptian?' he asked, his heartbeat quickening.

'Hard to tell. A fast trireme, coming east of south, and heading west towards us. She's sitting just south enough to get a good breeze into her sails. That's all we know at the moment. They're all alike, triremes.'

'Keep me informed.' Murcus ordered.

'Of course, Admiral,' answered the captain.

The captain hurried back to his post. Murcus went back to his assessment of the current situation. His flagship had not been badly treated by the storm – but there were still repairs to be completed. And if the trireme turned out to be one of Cleopatra's, the whole Egyptian fleet could be down on them in no time.'

Murcus pursed his lips, clasped his hands behind his back and strode to the deck-rail, looking east. Yes. There it was. A white speck on the blue-grey line where the sky and the sea met. Still coming onwards. On the one hand, anyone coming from that direction was likely to be from the Egyptian fleet, he thought. On the other, an Egyptian spy ship would have turned as soon as they sighted the squadron and be hurrying back to Cleopatra with news of their location.

But it looked like this trireme was coming straight on, which almost certainly made it one of their own – with a message from General Brutus, perhaps. The thought of it quickened Murcus' heart still further. Like his friend and co-admiral Gnaeus Domitius Ahenobarbus, Murcus was a man of action and a bit of a pirate at heart. Patrol duty did not really suit him. He would have been far happier to take his fifty ships and go raiding along the Ionian coast. But if he did that there would be trouble. And one way or another, whether or not the Egyptian fleet turned up, he was in the middle of a war zone here.

*

It took another couple of hours for the trireme to come alongside. Then it dropped a skiff and a team of oarsmen held it in place while a young man in a red legionary tunic climbed down a rope ladder into it. When he was safely aboard, a bag was lowered to him.

The skiff brought him over and he climbed aboard the admiral's ship, opened the bag and pulled out the badges of rank the proclaimed him to be a tribune. He attached these to his tunic and presented himself to Murcus, who was at once amazed and amused by the performance.

'Too sensible to wear full armour in a skiff rowing between warships, eh?' he said.

'I don't believe it's worth the risk, Admiral. One might fall into the water after all. And if one was wearing armour, that would be the end of everything. Even in the unlikely event that one had learned the rather plebeian pastime of swimming.'

'Very true. And very wise. So, you have avoided drowning like a true patrician. But I don't believe we've met. You are...?'

The young man drew himself up and threw out his chest. 'Marcus Valerius Messala Corvinus, Admiral.'

'Ah yes, I knew your wife's grandfather Marcus Porcius Cato. I was sorry to hear about the death of your wife's mother, General Brutus' wife Porcia. Eating hot coals, I hear. Dreadful. But what brings you hurrying to me?'

'I am currently acting tribune to General Marcus Junius Brutus. Carrying messages from the General...' Messala held out the sealed leather message-tube he had also taken from the bag containing his badges of rank. He held it out.

Murcus took it, continuing to speak, 'And lucky to get here to deliver them, young man. Don't you know there's a huge Egyptian fleet out in these waters?'

Messala gave an irritatingly superior grin. 'Yes, Admiral. I have seen Queen Cleopatra's navy.'

'Have you indeed?' Murcus' normally open face folded into a worried frown. '*When*. May I ask?'

'On my way here, Admiral.'

Murcus sucked in a breath, tiring of this pompous young tribune and his games. 'And *where* did you see them?'

'On most of the beaches we passed, Admiral. What remains of Queen Cleopatra's ships at least. Nothing more than wreckage washing ashore with the tide...'

THE END

Historical Characters

Porcia Porcia Catonis, widow of Marcus Calpurnius Bibulus, mother of Lucius Calpurnius Bibulus and Calpurnia Calpurnius Bibulus. After the death of her first husband, scandalously married her cousin Marcus Junius Brutus. May have committed suicide (42BCE/712AUC?) by eating live coals.

Calpurnia, daughter to Porcia Catonis, married to Marcus Velarius Messala Corvinus

Lucius Lucius Calpurnius Bibulus, proscribed but escaped Rome and joined Brutus.

Messala Marcus Velarius Messala Corvinus, proscribed, escaped, became one of Brutus' most outstanding lieutenants.

Octavianus Gaius Julius Caesar Octavianus *Divus Fili* – usually referred to as Octavian but later became Augustus. Triumvir. History presents him in two main lights – the cold, calculating but effective politician and the womanising occasionally sadistic manipulator. In early 42BCE/712AUC his main preoccupation was dealing with Sextus Pompey. I have not seen this proposition examined at any depth anywhere – but the symptoms of his life-long illness seem to fit with those of malaria.

Sextus Pompey the only surviving son of Pompey the Great, established with a large fleet in Sicily. Accepting escapees from the proscriptions, posing a threat to Rome's grain supplies, but not really taking sides.

Murcus Lucius Statius Murcus, general with *imperium* for one of the *Libertore* fleets (The word 'Admiral' is a recent coinage (C12th Arabic origin) but I have used it to discriminate from Generals with *imperium* over land forces). It was Murcus who is said to have observed Cleopatra's fleet as wreckage on the beaches of southern Greece.

Ahenobarbus Gnaeus Domitius Ahenobarbus, general with *imperium* over the largest of the *Libertore* fleets. Turned pirate later & joined first Antony and then Octavian. The basis for Shakespeare's ultimately treacherous Enobarbus in *Antony and Cleopatra*.

Artemidorus a Greek man about whom only one thing is known for certain – it was Artemidorus who gave Julius Caesar a list containing the names of the men planning to murder him just before they did so. Caesar never read it and died in consequence. In these books he is reimagined as a secret agent currently working for Antony.

Antony Marcus Antonius. Triumvir. History presents him as a headstrong, womanising soldier of relatively limited experience but outstanding leadership qualities and occasional flashes of military genius. Octavian may have used the proscriptions to get women to sleep with him; Appian says Antony certainly did so – and names some. Southern suggests persuasively that he underwent a character change when crossing the Alps after losing the Battle of Mutina – he became much more calculating and ruthless *vide* his vendetta with Cicero. He may also have been an alcoholic – something life with Cleopatra exacerbated.

Fulvia One of the most powerful women of the late Republic (and there were several) First married to Clodius Pulcher the notorious gang leader & political fixer. Started a riot that nearly destroyed the city when he was murdered by rival gangleader Milo on the Appian Way. Then married another politician Scribonius Curio – who died in battle. Then she married Antony and was a very active part of his rise to power especially after Caesar's assassination. She seems to have accepted his constant womanising and even stood by him raising armies to fight Octavian in Italy while Octavian was attacking Antony and Cleopatra in the east. She is reputed to have stuck pins and a stylus through Cicero's tongue when Laenas brought his severed head to Antony.

Saxa & Norbanus Lucius Decidius Saxa & Gaius Norbanus Flaccus were the two generals Antony sent ahead of his invasion of Macedonia with several legions each and orders to secure his army's approach routes, which they did until they were forced back by Cassius and Brutus soon before the final battles at Philippi.

Popilius Laenas a Tribune who asked special permission to be the man who executed Cicero. Took his head and hands to Antony and Fulvia. Used some of his reward to have a gold statue made of himself standing with one foot on Cicero's severed head. In these books, a brutal villain working for Octavian.

Herrenius Popilius Laenas' Centurion and accomplice.

Brutus Marcus Junius Brutus Husband and first cousin to Porcia Catonis. The 'heart' of the plot to assassinate Caesar; traditionally presented as the one who insisted that only Caesar should die – a decision later presented by Cassius and Cicero as a major error. A

better administrator than general, however noted as a ruthlessly efficient tax-gatherer (vide Xanthus below).
(**Xanthus**) A city not a person. Committed corporate suicide rather than pay Brutus' tax demands (42BCE/712AUC). Before/during his siege, the entire population is recorded as having killed each-other with the last survivors setting fire to the city before killing themselves.
Quintus Dellius Although in this story an alias used by Artemidorus without much thought, this is me setting things up for later. Dellius was a real person – sent to Cleopatra by Antony after Philippi to ask why she failed to support the Triumvirs. Dellius apparently fell under her spell. It was he who arranged the meeting at Tarsus on the River Cydnus that famously swept Antony off his feet.
Cassius Gaius Cassius Longinus the 'head' of the plot to assassinate Caesar. Brutus' brother-in-law. A ruthless politician and an able soldier (on land and sea), he was forgiven by Caesar for his part in the Civil War when he fought on Pompey's side. He was famous in the East for leading 10,000 survivors out of Parthia after the defeat of Crassus at Carrhae. He had no trouble raising troops therefore and was (briefly) appointed Governor by the Senate. He advanced on Egypt and may just have been about to invade when he was recalled by Brutus to a meeting in Sardis – where they planned their final campaign against the Triumvirs. He is reputed to have had problems with his eyesight.
Herod Herod (Later Herod the Great) Prince of Galilee at this time, later King of Judea. (Senate approved him King of the Jews in 40/39BCE). There is some question as to what extent he followed the Jewish faith. His relationship with the Parthians was more usually negative than positive, especially later; but his positive relations with Rome allowed him to rule for 33 years. He died in 4 BCE and is therefore not the Herod referred to as being visited by the Magi in Matthew's Gospel (it was Herod Antipas)
Cleopatra Cleopatra VIIth Philopator perhaps the most enigmatic figure in history. Modern scholarship emphasises that her reputation far outstrips her actual importance. She was a client ruler of an admittedly significant country in Rome's sphere of influence. The last one, as Augustus replaced the Ptolemies with personally-appointed governors after her death. In 42BCE/712AUC she was in considerable danger. The Nile had not inundated for 2 successive years & the grain harvest had failed. Vermin (esp rats) from the fields invaded villages & towns bringing Plague. A sizeable

proportion of the population of Egypt died. Even though she opened all the grain stores (Pharonic and Religious) her starving people were on the verge of open revolt – especially in the always fractious Alexandria. Cassius and his 12 legions (4 of which were the turncoat Egyptian legions) was at her borders considering invasion. Providentially Brutus called him North to Sardis and Cleopatra found a way to buy grain from Parthia. She did in fact take sides with Antony and built a fleet to help him – but it was destroyed in a storm. An angry Antony was later to send Quintus Dellius to find out why she had let him down so badly at such a crucial time. But as recorded above, Dellius simply engineered the meeting in the city of Tarsus which she famously approached in her golden barge down the Cydnus River. And the rest really is history.

Bibliography

Major source in each category:

Ancient:
Appian *The Civil Wars*
Modern (General)
Life of Caesar podcast by Cameron Reilly and Ray Harris
Ronald Syme *The Roman Revolution*
Mediterranean:
Ernle Bradford *Mediterranean Portrait of a Sea*
Via Egnatia:
Firmin O'Sullivan *The Egnatian Way*
Alexandria:
Harold T Davis *Alexandria The Golden City (2 vols)*
Legions:
Lawrence Keppie *The Making of the Roman Army*
Pollard & Berry *The Complete Roman Legions*
Secret Service:
Rose Mary Sheldon *Trust in the Gods but Verify: Intelligence activities in Ancient Rome*
Ships:
Rafaele D'Amato *Republican Roman Warships 509 – 27 BC*
Philippi:
Si Sheppard *Philippi 42 BC The death of the Roman Republic*
Augustus:
Adrian Goldsworthy *Augustus from Revolutionary to Emperor*
Antony:
Patricia Southern *Mark Antony A Life*
Cleopatra:
Stacy Schiff *Cleopatra A Life*

*

Printed in Great Britain
by Amazon

50325995R00192